Jo Leonard is the pseudonym for the writing partnership of Joan and Mike Hudson, who live in Suffolk. They have spent their working lives teaching in secondary schools and now support trainee teachers. The couple are married, have collaborated professionally for many years and have each published a PhD thesis on education. *Who Cares?* is their debut novel.

In memory of Elsie, Bill, Lillie and Les.

Jo Leonard

WHO CARES?

A story of love, loss and the
power of caring

AUSTIN MACAULEY PUBLISHERS™
LONDON * CAMBRIDGE * NEW YORK * SHARJAH

A CIP catalogue record for this title is available from the British Library.

ISBN 9781528963688 (Paperback)
ISBN 9781528971478 (ePub e-book)

www.austinmacauley.com

First Published 2022
Austin Macauley Publishers Ltd®
1 Canada Square
Canary Wharf
London
E14 5AA

Huge thanks to all those who care for others. You are our modern-day heroes.

Chapter 1

The door slammed. Jake slumped into a chair by the window and watched the last glimmers of light fading. His thoughts wandered back to the beginning of the day when dawn was breaking through the black sky as he was disappearing through the factory door. His life must be no different from that of the rats scurrying about in the sewers beneath him at that very moment. He longed for the lighter days of spring when he would be able to spend a couple of hours in the evening tending his allotment. There he was his own boss. He could hide away from the unpleasant realities of his existence. At present, the only escape was the local pub where the beer's main purpose was to act as an anaesthetic for his all too keen senses. His life seemed empty, just like the house. His wife Connie had just gone out to work for the evening, a willing partner in their battle to make ends meet.

Jake struggled to his feet, seemingly every limb of his body aching, and switched on the local radio station. It was not a case of wanting to listen to a specific programme; he was simply responding to a subconscious need for background noise, for a presence other than his own. Through the typically thin walls of his terraced house, he could make out the sound of the twins next door arguing above the sound of his radio. Nevertheless, even this negative sign of family life filled Jake with envy. At that moment, the parents would probably have traded their warring offspring for five minutes of peace but to Jake they seemed to emphasise the nothingness of his own life.

A glance through the keyhole of Jake's living room would have revealed a man approaching his fortieth birthday. His thinning dark brown hair hung in lifeless strands over his lined forehead, his ears and the polo neck of his baggy jumper. He was slightly overweight, more as a result of consuming too much beer than overeating. His waist bulged over crumpled brown cotton corduroy trousers and his size nine feet were hidden inside mud-bespattered size ten shoes. The light brown stain on the fingers of his left hand indicated the twenty cigarettes he smoked each day. The room was permeated by the smell of stale tobacco which would have been overwhelming to any non-smoker but to which Jake had become accustomed and to which he was therefore oblivious.

As Jake inhaled the smoke of yet another cigarette, he reflected on his situation. It was usually something he tried to avoid but he sensed the time had come for him to face up to the problems caused by thirty-nine years of drifting. His existence was empty and meaningless, whereas the lives of other people appeared to be so interesting and above all fulfilling. Not for him the richly rewarding career in one of the professions, the successful business or even the humdrum but well-paid jobs enjoyed by friends. Yes, agreed, he was at least in employment, unlike many of his contemporaries. What must life be like for them, he wondered, stubbing out his cigarette and immediately reaching for another?

As far as he was concerned, working at the factory reduced any notion of the dignity of human labour to a sick joke. Nor was he the least fortunate of the people who attempted to make a living there, for he had risen to the heady heights of Production Manager. This meant that he was responsible for all the staff and machinery involved in bottling the many flavours of lemonade mixed elsewhere in the factory. The scene which confronted him every day was like something out of the Charlie Chaplin film, *Modern Times*. The factory floor was dominated by endless lines of bottles in perpetual motion along a conveyor belt serviced at intervals by stainless steel robots which successively added syrup and carbonated mineral water, sealed the bottles and shook them up, before they were disgorged at the other end of the line.

The dehumanising and soul-destroying tasks performed by his workmates was what filled Jake with despair. At the rear of the machine, people spent eight hours a day emptying crates and placing the empty bottles into an ever-greedy washing machine. Conversation was made almost impossible by the din, so what did they think about? At the front of the machine two other people had to remove the cleaned articles and make sure that they safely progressed on to the production line, under pressure to avoid the bottles piling up and shattering on the floor. Somebody spent all day topping up the contents of the bottles where there was a deficiency. Finally, every one of the thousands of these glass vessels had to be packed into crates or cartons.

The machines dominated the whole process and the human beings worked desperately to keep pace with them. Jake looked forward to the day when the plant became fully automated, in spite of the possible job repercussions. Surely there were more worthwhile jobs that these people could do. If not, jobs should be created for them, because it was obvious to him as soon as he stepped outside the door that much could be done to improve the environment. His street was strewn with litter, the road was pockmarked with holes dating from the harsh winter two years previously, and most of the council-owned houses required a coat of paint. These were tasks to restore pride to people like his fellow workers rather than being subjected to daily degradation. They were jobs in which the worthwhile end product was clearly visible.

Jake had never been involved or interested in politics of any kind, but he had enough of a social conscience to realise that something ought to be done about it. Not for one minute did he envisage himself, or anybody like himself, taking action to try to change the situation. That sort of thing was no part of his world: it was the prerogative of the anonymous people at the council and those who lived in a different area of the town to himself. Jake would sometimes read about their exploits in the local paper, but only rarely did it seem to concern him in any way.

Jake snapped out of his reverie as the ash of his fourth consecutive cigarette burned through to his fingers. He crushed the life out of it in the ashtray and got to his feet. It was time to think about something to eat. He had become quite adept in the kitchen, thanks to the fact that his wife was rarely in the house at the same time as himself. She worked for an agency of office cleaners who operated like a flying squad, travelling from office block to office block throughout the evening into the early hours of the morning. Therefore, Jake and Connie's lonely lives only coincided at weekends.

The next morning, Jake prepared his usual breakfast and was just about to start on his bowl of cornflakes when he heard the sound of a letter dropping on to the floor in the hallway. The new postman was much more efficient and reliable than the last one who might arrive at any time of day to deliver his pile of letters and parcels. Jake opened the kitchen door and spied a brown envelope on the carpet. His mood darkened even more. Another bill to be paid. Oh joy. He was finding it all a bit of a struggle and the bills were an endless reminder of how hard he and Connie had to work just to make ends meet.

He moved down the hallway and picked up the envelope and turned it over to see his name, Mr Jacob Wilkins, typed out neatly under a stamp which bore the names of Grey, Brown and Girling Solicitors. His heart missed a beat. What on earth was a firm of solicitors doing writing to him? Was he in some sort of trouble? He thought back over the last few weeks and was sure he hadn't violated any law or upset anyone. He stared at the envelope for a few moments and then returned to the kitchen, squeezed himself back on to his chair. With difficulty, he opened the envelope with his left hand whilst directing his spoon of cornflakes into his mouth with his other hand.

He read the opening lines of the letter which was typed on high quality paper. 'My late client, Mrs Agnes Cartwright, has instructed me to contact you as the sole inheritor of her estate immediately after her demise. Please would you kindly contact my secretary at your earliest convenience to arrange an appointment to meet with me at my office.' The short letter was signed by Jonathan Grey.

Immediately, Jake pictured him as a young, privileged, besuited man who would never have had dealings with anyone like him. What on earth did this all mean? Who on earth was Agnes Cartwright? Was this letter a hoax? Did he have time to get in touch with this office before he was due to set off for work? Would the office actually be open at this hour? His curiosity and strange anxiety got the better of him. He certainly couldn't let this linger all day whilst he was in the factory or he wouldn't be able to concentrate. The only way to find out the answer to his questions was to phone the London office of Grey, Brown and Girling and then all his questions could be answered in one go.

He pushed aside his cereal bowl, lifted down from the wall the corded telephone receiver that Connie had insisted on and dialled the number which was on the letter. He was surprised when the phone was answered immediately by a woman who sounded business-like and efficient. Jake introduced himself and after several minutes conversation he was told that Mrs Agnes Cartwright had been his great aunt. Could he attend an appointment that very afternoon as Mr Grey was going away on holiday early the next morning and would be away for the next three weeks.

Without further ado, Jake agreed to the 3.45 appointment and when he put the phone down, he suddenly became aware of the enormity of the undertaking. He now had several new phone calls to make, first to Charlie, his firm's General Manager, to explain why he wasn't able to come into work today. He then had to phone his hairdresser to cancel his late afternoon appointment. His hair would just have to wait. He thought the occasion of going to London deserved the wearing of a smarter outfit.

After all, it was only the third time he had been to the big city and he didn't want to look like a country bumpkin. He hoped the new shirt that had hung in his wardrobe since his mother's funeral still fitted him. He searched through his drawers and eventually found his only tie, a dark grey tweed, also bought especially for the funeral. Today was only the third time he had worn it in the last ten years. The first time was for his dad's funeral, followed five years later by his Mum's, and now he was wearing it for this trip into London to find out what fate awaited him.

He left a note on the kitchen surface for Connie to read when she returned from work. She had had a very tiring week. Her evening shifts had been unusually changed for this week. She had been asked to work from 5am until 7pm as there had been a number of absences by other cleaners who had caught the sickness bug and they needed someone who could check on the new agency staff brought in to cover for the absentees. The company wanted to make sure that both the day and night staff were pulling their weight. Connie had therefore been asked to monitor the early morning cleaning work and then do extra duties for the rest of the day. She had been promised a £20 bonus, a windfall by her standards, so she had agreed to work these particularly unsociable hours just for one week until the other cleaners returned to work.

What it actually meant was that even though Jake saw Connie at 8pm when she eventually got home, she was far too tired to talk. As soon as she had eaten her meal she went off to bed before 9 pm so she could rise at 3.30 the following morning. He had better make sure she knew where he was, just in case he got home late. Jake was unused to small talk and conversational niceties as the loud factory environment meant that the workers bellowed at each other in short bursts of conversation. Most of the men barely talked all day and Jake had gotten used to this lack of communication. His note, like his conversation, was to the point. 'Had a letter about an inheritance. Gone to London to find out more. See you tonight. X'

Chapter 2

On the train, Jake took out the letter and reread the four lines over and over again. He could just about remember his Mum talking about her Aunty Agnes. She must have been ancient even then. If he was right in his thinking, she had been married to Uncle Tom. Agnes had been his grandmother's sister and she had married Thomas Cartwright and Jake vaguely remembered meeting them both when he was very young. They had had no children and he could remember his Mum receiving a letter from Agnes many years before saying that Tom had died.

Now that both his parents were dead, frustratingly he had no way of checking the facts. He had no siblings or cousins and his only one aunt and uncle had died long ago. He was left with nothing but his imperfect memory to try to piece together bits of the family history. All he knew was that she was his great aunt and he was her only living relative. The more he thought about it, the more he was convinced that she would only be leaving a small amount of money. He couldn't imagine that any relative would be more financially adept than him and so his expectations were not high.

Mr Jonathan Grey was actually much older than Jake had imagined. He was a tall, thin and bespectacled man in his early sixties. He shook Jake's hand and ushered him into his office, a handsome room lined with leather bound books. The leaded window looked out on to Duke Street, not far from Liverpool Street station, and the muffled sounds of city life could be heard as background to the loud ticking of the grandfather clock which stood at the other end of this capacious room.

Crikey, Jake thought, *my whole house could fit into this room*. The whole ambience was designed to intimidate, and Jake certainly was affected by the splendour of what he saw. His own shabbiness, even in his best clothes, seemed to be highlighted by the grandeur of the room. There was a cup of tea set out for Jake, already poured and ready for drinking. He nervously took a quick gulp and immediately had a coughing fit as the liquid went down the wrong way. Tea dribbled from his mouth as he fought to clear his airways and he reached for a tissue to wipe away the offending liquid.

After calm had been restored, Jonathan Grey opened a large file on his desk. He began by saying that he had acted as solicitor for Agnes over the previous thirty-five years. He had got to know her well and she had asked him from the start of her enterprises to manage the legal side of her business affairs. He tapped the file to indicate that everything that Jake needed to know was housed inside the buff covers. Agnes had lived in London for most of the last forty years and, after Tom had died, she had found herself in need of distraction from her grief. With the small amount of savings that she and Tom had accumulated, she had nearly everything that she needed, but she made a decision, unfashionable at that time, to speculate in property, buying cheaply old houses in run down areas, updating them and then selling them for a substantial profit.

She had, over the years of her widowhood, amassed a considerable portfolio and not only did she still own eight large properties of significant value, in what had become fashionable and eye-wateringly expensive parts of London, she also had a bank balance of over 15 million pounds. Jonathan Grey explained how he had recently completed the sale of two of Agnes's houses only a few months before she died, and because she hadn't had the strength to consider how to invest the money from the sale, these funds were still lying dormant in another account. The money and investments were now Jake's responsibility.

Mr Grey took out Agnes's will and read the contents to a startled Jake, not least because she called him Jacob, a name that he had not used since he was a small child. She stipulated that Jacob, her great-nephew, should be the sole inheritor of all her properties, their contents and any other possessions. In her will she added that she wished she had gotten to know him better, but even though their lives never touched, she believed in the importance of family and wanted to support succeeding generations. She had been very fond of her niece, Clara, Jake's mother, who had apparently written a letter to Aunt Agnes every year, along with her Christmas card, sending news of her only son.

Goodness, Jake thought, *I bet that made dreadful reading*. He wondered whether she had given a graphic account of his life in the soft-drinks factory, as that, until this moment, was all that his life had consisted of.

"Mr Wilkin," concluded Mr Grey, "you are now a person of considerable wealth. I wish you luck in your new enterprises."

These were the words which echoed in Jake's brain all the way home. He couldn't wait to tell Connie. If she had gone to bed, he would get her up and insist that they open the bottle of red wine which had been won in the factory raffle last Christmas. One unexpected letter had changed their lives and they must drink to Great Aunt Agnes and celebrate whatever was to come in the future. After all, how many people, without prospects and almost as poor as church mice, could toast a future of new-found security and wealth? He closed his eyes and smiled throughout the remainder of the train journey home.

As Jake walked down his street, taking care to avoid the dog mess and remnants of food that had been discarded by late-night revellers, he tried to think of what he would say to Connie. In the event, matters were taken out of his hands:

"Where the hell have you been? I've been worried sick thinking you had been mugged or had an accident. Couldn't you have sent me a text or phoned even? The meal is ruined. It's been in the oven for hours."

"Hello darling. Nice to see you too. What a welcome!" said Jake with an air of resignation. "And no, I haven't eaten, though judging by the smell coming from the oven, I'm not sure I want to eat whatever is in there. I suppose you've already had something to eat."

"Well, how long did you expect me to wait? I've had a really tough day and then I arrive home with you nowhere to be seen. What was I supposed to do?" asked Connie in exasperation.

"I can see that you've looked after yourself. I've had a hard day too and I'm starving. I've had enough of this. I'm going to grab something from the burger bar." With that he stormed out of the house, slamming the door behind him. In the distance, he could hear Connie shouting at the top of her voice, "Don't think I haven't had enough too. Take your time and don't rush back because I'm going to bed."

Jake changed his mind about the burger bar, heading instead for the Dun Cow where he ordered a pint of bitter and some fish and chips. He quickly polished off the pint and, still waiting for the food order, ordered another one. I'm going to enjoy myself from now on, he reflected, and if Connie wants to have fun too, that's great; but if not that's just too bad. He sat alone in the corner watching the football match on the TV for want of anything better to do, eating his fish and chips and working his way through more pints than he could remember.

Normally, he was quite restrained in his consumption of alcohol, but money was now not a problem and the more he drank the better his mood became.

Connie and he loved each other really and by tomorrow she would have calmed down and they could start to plan a new life together. As he made his way home, unsteady on his feet, a golden haze was starting to blot out both the argument and the despair he had been feeling about his life up to that point. Already he was feeling more positive than he'd felt for years.

The following morning, in spite of his tiredness after the heavy drinking of the previous evening, he was still feeling relatively upbeat, an unusual state of mind for him. He went downstairs to find Connie halfway through eating a bowl of cereal.

"Morning darling, sorry I was a bit late getting home yesterday but I thought you would understand."

"What do you mean? I'm not a mind reader, you know." Connie's tone was less aggressive than the previous evening so she must have slept well in spite of the row.

"I left you a note…" Jake noticed Connie's look of confusion. "It was by the front door where we normally leave reminders. Did you not notice it?"

"No, there was a pile of junk mail and as usual I put it straight in the recycling bin."

"You must have mixed my message up with the junk mail. I'm really sorry. I should have tried to phone or text, but the mobile signal is non-existent where you work. In any case, I was going to explain last night but things did not go to plan."

"So, what's the news?"

"You're never going to believe this…" Jake proceeded to explain the inheritance of several London properties and a stack of cash from his now deceased Great Aunt Agnes. "So, what do you make of that, Connie?"

"I've got to leave for work within the next 15 minutes. I'm struggling to work out what it all means." She looked perplexed and then an avalanche of questions poured out.

"How much money are we inheriting exactly? How soon can we have it or is it locked away in investments that we can't touch? What about the houses? Are they being rented out and, if so, how much income are they earning? Could we sell them if we wanted?" She paused and smiled at Jake who had looked startled at all her questions. "Whilst I'm out at work, why don't you research all these details and then we can discuss things this evening when I return? You won't walk out on me again, will you?" she said with a wry smile.

"Let's have a hug before you dash off. All I will say is that this inheritance looks as if it could be life-changing. We'll have the scope to do things that we could only dream about until this happened."

After Connie's rushed departure, Jake made himself a pot of tea, a bowl of cereal and some well-buttered toast and settled down to consider the answers to Connie's questions. He had been warned by the solicitor that there would be a considerable amount of inheritance tax to be paid so the first thing he did was to google how much that was likely to be. "Blimey, 40%. I've worked all my life, paid my taxes in full and now the government wants to take away 40% of my gift. How can that be right, especially when Agnes will have paid taxes on her income already?" Setting aside his indignation with some difficulty, Jake methodically worked through all the details. "£25 million in cash. I'm allowed a little bit tax free, so that leaves a large amount on which I've got to pay 40%. Wow, that's literally millions!"

A couple of days earlier, Jake and Connie had precisely £75.84 in their current account, the sum total of a life's work for two struggling earners. Now he was failing to see the irony that he was moaning about the fact that he was inheriting millions! More shocks were in store. Jake discovered that each of the eight London properties was being rented and that the income from even the smallest was several thousand pounds a month. Suddenly, he had rocketed into the top income tax bracket. By this time, Jake had worked himself into a mixture of fury, at the greed of the Government, and depression that he would be losing so much of his new-found wealth so quickly.

Only when Connie arrived home later that evening was a sense of proportion restored.

"Jake, what on earth are you thinking? How can we possibly be downhearted? Millions in the bank, to say nothing of thousands a month in income, and that's after tax. You've become a wealthy man. Why are you moaning? You can stop working at that dreadful factory. You can stop working altogether if you want. What's not to like? I'm wondering where I fit in with all this. I suppose you'll now want to find yourself a young attractive model girlfriend to go with your fancy sports car, your yacht in Cannes and your flat in Monte Carlo?"

"Mm, you've given me some good ideas there," he said, dodging the cushion she threw at him with a smile. "Look, to be serious," he continued, "there's a lot of thinking to be done about how to move forward and we need time away from all this."

"All this?"

"The work, this house, the area. Everything really."

"What about me? Are we talking about planning this exciting future together?"

"Why not?" he asked, adding unwisely, "I haven't got anybody else lined up. Not yet anyway."

"I'll take that as a joke but it's in very bad taste. I do have my admirers, you know."

"Really? Tell me more."

Before the conversation descended into a full-scale row like the previous evening, Connie interjected: "Look, one thing I've always wanted to do is to go on a cruise. If we got away and spent some time together, we could work out what to do next. What do you think?"

"That's a brilliant idea. Why didn't I think of that? Nothing is going to happen till the probate has been completed, meaning that we won't have any money for a while. I'll go to the bank and ask for a loan whilst you do some research on cruises. Let's get away as soon as we can."

Chapter 3

The following morning, Jake phoned the factory to say he was not well and would not be in work for the rest of the week. He was probably not going to return but he did not feel ready to make a final decision. He set off on foot in the direction of his bank before remembering that his local branch had closed the previous year. An hour later, he arrived at a shiny new building that catered for the customers of half a dozen branches that had closed and was welcomed inside the doorway by a youngster who looked like a schoolgirl despite the thick layer of make-up. With a broad smile, she asked how she could help. When he told her that he wanted to enquire about a loan, she said that she would see if an adviser was available.

"Actually, I don't need any advice. I've been a customer with this bank for 20 years and I just want to borrow some money. Can't you help me?" Jake asked.

"I'm afraid not. I'm not qualified to deal with loans, but somebody should be with you soon. Please take a seat over there. Would you like a coffee?"

Jake refused the coffee, inwardly fuming at the delay and wondering why he couldn't have gone to the counter like previously. Even the factory, not the most efficient of enterprises, would not have been able to afford to have a person at the front door basically directing customers from one part of the premises to another. Maybe that was why his bank charges kept rising. Eventually, he was ushered into a glass-enclosed space with a desk and 3 chairs, where he could talk privately whilst being watched by customers waiting in the queue outside. The bank clerk was a smart young man, wearing a suit and a tie decorated with the bank's logo.

"How may I help you sir?" he asked.

Jake patiently explained that he was about to inherit a large amount of money but needed in the short term to take out a loan to cover some expenses until his Great Aunt's probate was finalised.

"I need to go through some security checks first of all sir," said the young man as he desperately tried to open up the appropriate screen on his computer. "It's running slowly today sir, I'm afraid."

"Look, I'm in a bit of a hurry. Is all this really necessary? I've been a customer of this bank for 20 years and all I want is to borrow £5,000."

"Yes, but I need to know who you are first of all. What is your name?"

"Jacob Wilkins. W-I-L-K-I-N-S."

"And your date of birth?"

Despite Jake's obvious irritation, there was no hurrying the bank clerk who was reading his question-and-answer script in the most robotic fashion.

"And how much did you want to borrow sir?"

Jake took a deep breath and repeated £5,000 as calmly as he could, noticing as he did so the clerk's sharp intake of breath and the deepening furrow of his brow.

"I'm afraid the bank cannot sanction the loan. There appears to be a problem with your credit worthiness."

"But I've never had a loan in my life."

"That may be the problem, sir. If you've never had a loan, we have no evidence that you can handle the repayments."

"But I need a loan so that I can prove that I can."

"That's not the point, sir. Not to worry though, I can see that you have one of our credit cards attached to your current account and the credit limit is currently £5,000. Is that enough or would you like me to raise it to a higher amount, £10,000 maybe? Especially as you are about to inherit some money."

Jake finally saw some light at the end of this frustrating tunnel and agreed to the raising of his credit limit. As he left the building, he made a mental note never to ask the bank for anything ever again. If they were in financial need, he would have to look for another solution.

Connie had also been busy whilst Jake had been at the bank. She had called into the cleaning agency and handed in her notice with immediate effect. For the first time in her life, she had felt powerful and in control of her own fate. It had taken many hours for the reality of their situation to sink in and now that she had adjusted to her new status as a person of means, she was certainly not going to waste anymore of her time being a drudge and at the beck and call of others. She left the agency and almost skipped down the high street and headed towards the parade of shops. She wanted to window shop at this stage. After all, this would be part of the reward. She could look at the clothes and shoes on sale and know that she could buy whatever she wanted. She had always watched every penny and now she almost felt drunk with elation.

After half an hour of browsing and fingering the various items for sale, Connie started to lose interest. She had spotted one dress which she quite liked and thought would do nicely for their trip to London to sign the probate papers, but the thought of having to buy a whole new set of clothes for a cruise daunted her. What on earth did people wear on those ships? She had heard about dinners with the captain and the wearing of formal clothes. Could she be really bothered with it all? Would that lifestyle suit her?

She realised that her energy levels were low because she had missed both breakfast and lunch. They had been talking into the early hours of the morning, voicing their dreams, and her excitement had curbed her morning appetite. Now, she realised, she was in need of a sandwich and a pot of tea and, above all, she wanted the sanctuary of her own home where she could continue thinking about how their future could—no, she must start to think in more positive language—would unfold. The inheritance had changed her expectations and suddenly she realised that she was almost a different person to the Connie of a few days before. She was a person of substance. They had inherited money and she was now going to become ambitious. She could go anywhere she chose. She could stay in expensive hotels and, goodness me, travel first class if she wanted. This new-found personal agency was both frightening and exhilarating.

Jake was already home when she opened the front door. He had heard her key in the lock and rushed down the hallway to greet her. Connie immediately noticed the physical change in him. He was looking younger than he had for a long time. He had had his hair cut after he had been to the bank and also shaved properly. Jake was talking before she could close the door:

"So, he said we could spend up to £10,000 which is the limit of our credit card. We can easily pay the interest on what we spend and when we get the inheritance money in our bank account, any amount we have spent over the next few days will seem of no consequence…"

He trailed off and looked at her. She started to smile at what he was saying, and the smile then quickly turned into a laugh. Jake too laughed at the absurdity of their situation and suddenly, quite out of character, he picked Connie up and twirled her around, taking care not to bang her into the walls of the narrow hallway.

Another phone call with Mr Grey's secretary confirmed that the probate papers would be ready for signing as soon as Mr Grey returned from holiday. A date was agreed and Connie marked the day and time on the calendar which was hanging on the kitchen wall. There were only a few other markings on the calendar, dental and hair appointments, and these seemed to sum up the paucity of their life experiences so far. Money and property were now the new order of the day. They had decided they would spend the following day in London visiting the houses that they now owned.

Charlotte Jenks, Jonathan Grey's secretary, had given Jake a list of addresses of the properties owned by Agnes. The solicitor agreed that they could know the location of these houses, but until the probate had been signed, they were not allowed inside them. Jake had already made a start on the map, indicating where each house could be found. He also google-earthed the roads and was even more startled when he realised that six out of the eight were immensely large Victorian or Edwardian three or more storey houses in leafy and select parts of London.

He could imagine what these houses had been like when Agnes first saw them. They would have been nasty rundown hovels containing numerous flats, but after extensive renovation, they had been restored to their original purpose, family homes for the prosperous middle classes. Jake marvelled at Agnes's foresight and ability to see beyond the decay. Would he ever have had the courage or imagination to buy local houses and transform them? He certainly doubted whether this would have been the case.

Jake and Connie travelled first class on the train for the first time in their lives. They enjoyed the calmer atmosphere of the first-class carriage and giggled when they were served with newspapers, snacks and drinks by a uniformed attendant. They whispered to each other, sharing their wonderment and guilt at having paid so much extra for this luxury. At Liverpool Street station, Jake unfolded the single sheet map marked where all the properties were to be found, and they set off to the first of the houses, stopping off for a coffee and a toilet break at Prêt à Manger.

The first house was in a fine street. It was one of several imposing houses, slightly secluded from the pavement by a trimmed hedge. They stood at the end of the short drive and looked at the building in front of them. "Gosh," was all that Connie could say. Jake remained silent and Connie noticed that he looked slightly intimidated. By the end of the day, they had followed the plan and visited all the other seven houses, having covered endless miles across different parts of affluent London. They were both exhausted and bewildered by what fate had thrust upon them.

Jake spent the day trying to recall more about Aunt Agnes, but his memory offered no more than his original recollections. How he wished his mother were here so he could find out more about his remarkable relative. Perhaps Jonathan Grey would be able to tell them more when they were to meet up in a couple of weeks. He said he had known her for over thirty years, so Jake was determined to ask about this amazing woman so that he could properly appreciate what she had achieved in the last four decades. His own world had stretched from home to the soft drinks factory and he couldn't imagine another life beyond these two places. She, on the other hand, had become a shrewd businesswoman, searching out run down properties to renovate, at an age when other people were giving up work and thinking about taking it easy. And she had done it alone.

Jake suddenly felt a failure and was ashamed. He had starved himself of ambition, making excuses that he was overworked, underpaid, underqualified and justified it all with the excuse that someone from his background couldn't expect to achieve anything in life. But here, in front of him, was a hugely expensive property, renovated and improved by his only relative when she would have been in her sixties. He was determined that he would, from now on, become more capable, creative and ambitious for the two of them. He glanced at Connie beside him and made a silent vow that he would work hard to change their lives for the better.

Chapter 4

Two weeks passed and the meeting with Jonathan Grey was pleasant. Connie, just like Jake, had been impressed with the office. She had had years of experience cleaning other offices but this one was more like a gentleman's study in a grand manor house and it seemed to reflect the taste and character of the tanned solicitor sitting on the other side of the desk. Jonathan had enjoyed his holiday in Provence and getting back to work to enable this engaging couple to change their lives gave him great pleasure.

Jake signed the papers and then was given a folder containing the details of the properties and the exact sum which had been transferred into his bank account now that the solicitor's fees had been deducted from it. Jake stared at the contents of the estate and he let out a deep sigh of relief and incredulity. He had almost convinced himself that none of this was actually happening, but the hard evidence of the papers in the file confirmed that this was his new reality.

Jake settled the file on his lap and asked Jonathan about Aunt Agnes. He explained that she was really a stranger to him and that he would be glad to know any details about her life. Fortunately, Jake and Connie were Jonathan's only appointment that day and he had time to spend talking about Agnes whom he had admired ever since he first met her.

"She was a remarkable woman. I often thought of her as my own aunt, which sounds silly, but she was always so interested in my life whenever we met. I got to know her well. She worked in the Civil Service with her husband Tom for many years. She was a clerk and dealt with the pensions of people who were physically or mentally incapacitated and unable to work. Agnes always said that there would be days when she went home in tears after reading particularly traumatic case histories of people who were hoping to gain a small pension to help them cope with their condition. She often felt powerless, as though the state was making it harder for these people rather than giving them the help that they really needed.

"When Tom died," he paused, "she found him dead in his chair, you know. She had left him watching the cricket on television and went to make them both a cup of tea. When she came back into the room he looked as if he had fallen asleep, but in fact he had suddenly died. She said that he would have been amused that such a dramatic event had taken place during a cricket match. But what it meant was that Agnes had to make a choice. She could continue in the Civil Service for a few more years living alone or do something completely different. She had always wondered whether she had the nerve to be enterprising and this choice to leave a safe, steady job was her grand adventure.

"She had read an article in The Times apparently about some people who were improving properties for healthy profits. She wasn't interested in making money, well not at first anyway. She wanted a distraction from the loneliness which came after Tom's death. What better way than to have an army of builders, plasterers, electricians and gardeners that she had to communicate with every day as they transformed her first property." Jonathan pointed to the file in Jake's hands.

"She soon realised that she had a talent for choosing the right property and her team of workmen got to know her well. They admired the fact that she wanted the best quality workmanship carried out on every house. They didn't cut corners with their work as Agnes was there every day checking on what they had done and made them redo anything that was shoddy. So began the long relationship with this set of builders. It was mainly a family firm. They were called Burtons, if I remember rightly. She actually went through two generations of the Burtons, as once old Jim retired, Owen, his son, took over and he worked closely with Agnes.

"As it was, Agnes project managed the team well and got involved in ordering the supplies which gave the workmen more time to do work rather than spending hours sourcing the materials. She loved her involvement and she also gave me lots of advice about work done at my home by the Burtons actually, and also here in this room. Agnes had quite an eye for style, you know. You could say that you are actually sitting with Agnes in this room, Jake, as she chose everything here. If you want to know more about your Great Aunt, all you have to do is look around you. She applied the same standards in preparing all her houses and as her reputation grew people became very keen to buy one of her properties. That is why they rose in value in such a short time.

"She seemed to be the one who put some of the fashionable areas on the map and the yuppies wanted to be associated with her by purchasing her houses. She bought and sold a great many over the years and reinvested the profit in buying up new places to improve. I am sure you have been impressed by the exterior of the houses. Then get ready for even more delight when you go inside the eight houses which you now own."

Jake felt proud of his aunt, but also cheated that he had never got to know her. Why hadn't his mother told him any of this?

"What did she look like?" Connie asked. Jonathan reached for his laptop and typed in her name and a series of articles appeared on the screen. He pulled up a photograph of Agnes on her 90th birthday, just 4 years earlier. Jake noticed that Agnes bore quite a resemblance to his mother who had died in her 60s, but he was sure that if she had survived another 20 years then she would have looked very much like Agnes. The article in The Evening Standard was about those who had made a creative impact in the last fifty years. Agnes beamed out of the photograph as she received a bouquet of flowers. Once again, the same tagline was used "A remarkable lady" and her creative career was discussed at length acknowledging the part she had played in transforming tired areas of London.

"There is plenty to read when you have time, Jake. Just google Agnes Cartwright and you will learn quite a bit about her."

Jake and Connie left the office and walked back to the station chatting about the remarkable day. Little did they know that their lives were about to take another dramatic turn.

Chapter 5

The station concourse was packed with commuters desperate to return home after a long day in the office. As they made their way to platform 10 for the Norwich train, Jake and Connie shared a knowing smile: the daily grind for them was about to become a thing of the past. They checked the departure board and decided to wait a little longer for the train that left on the hour because it tended to be faster and have more comfortable seating. Although the busyness of the station was normal at this hour, there was a slightly threatening atmosphere that was difficult to define. Had there been some cancellations leading to more people hanging around, tired and frustrated, or was there another reason? Jake noticed that there was a large group of people wearing white football shirts, with a tick above the right breast publicising the Nike sports brand, a cockerel above the left breast and the letters "A I A" in large red block capitals dominating the front of the shirt.

"They're Tottenham Hotspur fans," he said to Connie, pointing to the swell of people heading to platform 10. "I've just remembered that Spurs are playing against Ipswich this evening. It could be quite rowdy on the train but at least they will be getting off before our stop at Diss."

Many of the football-shirted contingent boarded the earlier train, unaware or unbothered that the later one would be a better option, but by the time of Jake and Connie's train a further large group had arrived, chanting their eternal support for their favourite team, carrying cans and bottles. The couple were reasonably well insulated in their first-class section from the commotion elsewhere. As the train pulled out of the station, they noticed the steward being jostled as he squeezed through the carriage to bring Jake and Connie their complimentary coffee.

"Why doesn't the train company ban alcoholic drinks on the train altogether?" asked Connie.

"I agree that groups like this would behave better if they weren't fuelled on alcohol but just imagine if it were my job to enforce such a rule. It would probably lead to more trouble. In any case, we need all the passengers we can get. Have you seen the press coverage of our punctuality record? I don't want to end up losing my job," replied the steward. "Anyway, don't worry; they're in a good mood at the moment and I'll be off duty before they return after the match. It's usually worse when they lose."

Jake and Connie settled to enjoy their coffee and chatting about their future plans took their minds off the noise from the next carriage that was starting to get louder as they whistled at speed through Shenfield and Ingatestone before the first stop at Chelmsford where more people joined the train. Apart from in the small first-class compartment all the seats now seemed to be full and Jake noticed a couple of young lads, early 20s, both wearing exactly the same outfit, white T-shirts, blue jeans, brown leather jackets and blue and white scarves standing next to their doorway.

"Look, Connie, they're brave, those two Ipswich-supporting lads sharing the carriage with Spurs fans."

As he spoke, he noticed that they were holding hands, laughing and giggling, and as they kissed each other, a group of about 6 Spurs fans erupted with a roar of anger, fingers pointing, eyes wild with fury, obviously disapproving of this display of affection. One of the Ipswich boys must have then said something which enraged the Spurs fans even more because now a much larger group was looking, pointing and shouting in their direction.

"I don't like the look of this, Jake. Can we move to somewhere else on the train?"

"What, and push our way through that mob? You can't be serious."

"I'm sorry, I can't stand to see this kind of aggression, and it looks as if it could develop into a dangerous situation. Let's move."

Without further discussion, Connie opened the compartment door, slipped past the two young Ipswich men and started to squeeze through the rest of the carriage.

"You ought to be ashamed of yourselves, using that sort of language," said Connie to nobody in particular.

"Are you defending those two queers? Why don't you mind your own business, you silly bitch!" shouted a grey-bearded, bald-headed chap whose football shirt was a couple of sizes too small and whose belly spilled over the top of his trousers.

"Don't you speak to my wife like that," yelled Jake.

In the circumstances, this response demonstrated Jake's courage but was perhaps ill-advised as the man lumbered to his feet and hit Jake full in the face. If there had been enough space Jake would have collapsed on to the floor because it had been a fearsome blow. The fact that he was surrounded by people meant that, as his legs buckled, he swayed but was supported from falling by those standing near him. Blood was gushing from his nose, his eyes were closed and he had lost consciousness.

"Oh, my God, what have you done to him? Jake, Jake…" Connie cradled his face in his hands. "Please help me somebody."

The two Ipswich boys and a couple of the Spurs fans helped Connie carry Jake back to the first-class compartment, where they laid him flat across the seats and splashed water across his face. One of them held his wrist: "His pulse is fine, so I think he'll be alright."

Already an angry dark reddish blue swelling was appearing on Jake's left cheekbone and suddenly his eyes flickered and gradually he regained consciousness.

"I don't feel well," he moaned.

"Should we pull the emergency cord and call for an ambulance?" asked Connie.

"No, don't do that, I'll probably be alright."

Connie tended Jake's bruises and the two Ipswich fans decided that they were safer staying where they were.

"We're always attracting this sort of trouble when we leave London. Thanks for standing up for us."

"Maybe if you were more discreet in your behaviour, you would not provoke people and my husband would not have been attacked," replied Connie.

"We're really sorry about what's happened but, on the other hand, why should we have to change behaviour that seems normal to us?" said one of the boys.

Jake lay there for the rest of the journey, occasionally yelping in discomfort as the train lurched violently on the rails. By the time the train reached Ipswich, the venue for the football match, the pains in his head were worsening rather than easing.

"I'm worried about you, Jake. I think you need to see a doctor. The GP practice in Diss will be closed by now so I think our best option is to leave the train now and go straight to Ipswich hospital."

Connie was already on the move, grabbing her bag and helping Jake to his feet. Jake did not want to go to the hospital but did not have the energy to argue, so intense was the pain in his head. Connie supported him on to the platform and as they made their way across the footbridge towards the exit, she noticed the two young Ipswich supporters hanging back to speak to them.

"We spotted you were having difficulties. The least we can do is try to help."

At this point, Jake's legs gave way. He would have collapsed on to the ground if Connie had not been holding him on one side and one of the Ipswich boys had not rushed to support him on the other side. Jake was moaning, incoherently, his lips were blue, and he was struggling to breathe.

"I need to get him to the hospital. This is an emergency. It will take too long to call an ambulance. Do you have a car by any chance?" asked Connie, trying to control her rising sense of panic and aware that she needed to act quickly.

"No, but there's a taxi rank outside. Let's carry him."

One of the boys took Jake by the legs and Connie and the other boy carried him by the shoulders, down the footbridge stairs, along the platform, through the exit gate which a ticket collector had kindly unlocked. They deposited Jake along the back seat of the first cab. Connie thanked the two boys for their help and instructed the driver to head for the hospital as fast as possible. The driver nodded and set off, just managing to exit through the green traffic lights as it was turning to red.

"I'm going to go down Wherstead Road and over the Orwell Bridge because it will be quickest at this time with all the traffic."

Fortunately, there was little delay making their way out of town and within 5 minutes they were crossing the River Orwell. By now Jake had lost consciousness and Connie knew that any delay would be significant. His pulse rate was high. She slopped some water from her bottle over his face in an attempt to rouse him and his eyes flickered open briefly before closing again. He tried to say something, his face screwed up with the effort and concentration, but no words came out of his mouth and he lost consciousness again.

"Only two more minutes and we'll be there," mumbled the taxi driver, casting anxious glances through his rear-view mirror. He started to give a running commentary of where they were and how near they were to the hospital.

"Don't worry, we're now on Heath Road...and turning into the car park...there's the main entrance. You stay here. I'll rush in to get some assistance."

There was an ambulance next to them and the crew were about to leave to tackle their next emergency. The taxi driver persuaded them to lift Jake out of his taxi and take him into the hospital. By now Jake was completely lifeless but Connie felt a strange sense of relief that she no longer had sole responsibility for him. Even in her panicked state, she took a few seconds to thrust a couple of twenty-pound notes into the taxi driver's hands and dashed off to follow Jake as he disappeared on a stretcher with the ambulance crew into the hospital.

"Thanks, and good luck, madam," shouted the taxi driver as she rushed into the building.

We're going to need it, she thought.

"We are moving him into the Intensive Care unit. His scans show that he has had a massive bleed of the brain from the blow. We have done all we can here at the moment, but we need him to be closely observed over the next few days to watch what is happening in his brain. We suggest you go and have a drink in the café which is next to the main entrance and by then Jake should be installed in the unit and you will be able to sit with him there. You are in shock at the moment, and as you haven't eaten since lunchtime, I suggest you try a small piece of cake and ask for a weak tea but put a couple of spoons of sugar in to avoid your blood sugar level falling. You must pay attention to yourself as well as your husband as you were involved in the incident too. I believe there will be a police officer wanting to speak with you shortly too, so go straight away and get the food before you get side-tracked."

With that the doctor moved away to another curtained section of the Emergency Ward and Connie looked across at the unconscious body of her husband. Jake had tubes attached to him and his clothes had been replaced with a thin checked hospital gown. She stroked his hair away from his forehead and kissed his cheek lightly. The bruising and swelling of his face made him almost unrecognisable. A young nurse with a purple fringe bustled in and led Connie out of the cubicle, leaving another nurse to tend to Jake. She repeated what the doctor had just said and ushered her to the swing doors which opened on to a corridor. She pointed to where Connie would find the café and then turned back to greet two auxiliaries who had arrived to transfer Jake to the ICU.

Connie wiped her tears from her cheek and slowly moved down the corridor to the café. She joined the short queue and repeated the instructions she had been given by the doctor.

"A weak tea, please, and a piece of plain sponge."

Connie loaded a spoon with sugar and stirred it into her tea. Even that action was alien to her. She must have been about twelve years old when she last put sugar in a drink. She sipped the tea and shuddered as she swallowed the sweet liquid. She broke off a small portion of the sponge, but merely crumbled it between her fingers. She relived the train journey in her mind and stirred the crumbs around the plate with her finger as she tried to get the events clear in her brain so that when she was questioned, she would make some sense of what had happened not more than four hours previously. There would be very little chance of catching the thug who had attacked Jake. Why, oh why, did this all have to happen? Today was supposed to be a turning point in their lives and little did she expect this type of change when they set off from Mr Grey's offices discussing how their lives, with the security of money and property, could now alter forever.

Connie looked at her watch. She had been in the café for twenty minutes. She had given them enough time to get Jake into the ICU, surely? She wouldn't be in the way. She would just sit with him quietly whilst they did their work. It was far too upsetting sitting here in the café with people holding conversations. She wanted to be near Jake and so she drank the last mouthful of tea, removed her tray from the table and set off to find the ICU. Notices were displayed on the walls, pointing in all directions for hospital wards, day units and such like.

Eventually, she found the directions to Intensive Care and followed the long corridors and climbed the flight of stairs to the ward. She introduced herself at the reception desk and a nurse pointed out which part of the unit Jake was in. She also mentioned that a police officer was already waiting for her to arrive to give a statement. The nurse smiled kindly at her. Connie thanked her and set off to find Jake.

Jake's motionless body was tethered to the bed by a tangle of tubes all attached to monitors, constantly recalculating body temperature, blood pressure, pulse, and respiration. She gasped when she moved nearer to his bed. The ward was an efficient, quiet, busy environment with teams of nurses working with each patient and checking the monitors and attending their needs. Connie introduced herself to the male and female nurses who were adjusting one of Jake's tubes. They smiled at her and the female nurse suggested Connie sit alongside Jake whilst they completed their checks, but warned her that as Jake was unconscious, she should just sit quietly. She could ask the doctors for more information when they did their rounds shortly.

She observed two young doctors further along from Jake discussing an X-ray of one of the patients. The X-ray monitor was on the wall and she could make out shadows on what appeared to be a lung. They looked serious as they regarded the image. Bad news for other people too. I am not alone in my grief, she thought, as she surveyed the occupants of all the other beds. They were a mixture of ages and one or two seemed younger than Jake. Connie sat on the chair next to Jake's bed and suddenly noticed that the skin on her thumb was bleeding. She had been tearing at it in her distress and now her thumb throbbed which directed her attention away from Jake. She sucked at her wound and wrapped the torn bleeding skin in a crumpled tissue that she found in her pocket. She looked up from tending her wound to find a policeman standing at the foot of the bed.

"Mrs Wilkins? I am PC Johnson from Ipswich Constabulary. Could I have a word with you about the incident on the train, please? Perhaps we could go into the visitors' lounge along the corridor to have a talk?"

Connie got up and followed the policeman to the lounge, a room filled with wingback seats set out in a row like a dentist's waiting room. Thankfully the room was empty. The two of them sat down and the policeman made notes as Connie recalled as much as she could of the journey home from London. Her description of the attacker might have matched almost any one of the hundreds of supporters on the train. The men had looked as though they were clones of each other.

Thankfully, said PC Johnson, the two young lads who had helped lift Jake into the taxi had contacted the police as soon as they had watched Connie and Jake drive off. One of them had miraculously taken a photograph on his mobile phone of the group who had surrounded Jake on the train as they left the station singing and thrusting their arms in the air, but they had been unable to state definitely which one had struck the blow to Jake's head. Connie muttered that was good of them. She finished her story and answered the policeman's questions. Suddenly she slumped forward, the policeman nimbly catching her before she fell to the floor. When she came out of her faint, she found herself on the floor in recovery position. Kneeling beside her was a plump nurse, old enough to be her mother. She was taking Connie's pulse and talking to the policeman.

"I will get you something to eat, dear. You look as white as a sheet and the shock of the day has made you faint. Stay on the floor until I get back. I don't want you fainting again, particularly when I am not around. I won't be a minute."

She smiled at Connie, winked at the policeman who found himself in charge of her and bustled out of the room.

After eating a couple of digestive biscuits and drinking a glass of milk, Connie began to feel much better. She returned to Jake's bedside and once more took her place next to him. The two doctors were by now at the bedside of Jake's neighbour and within minutes they had turned their attention to the charts at the foot of Jake's bed. They introduced themselves as Dr Wilton and Dr Greenwich. Jake had had a severe traumatic injury resulting from the blow which had caused the brain to collide at high velocity with the inside of his skull. There had been bruising of the brain tissue and damage to blood vessels.

They used terms unfamiliar to Connie, and she merely nodded as she listened to their diagnosis of her husband. He was unconscious and they wanted him to remain in this state to help with the healing process. He would have an MRI scan to check for further damage, but they warned Connie that she would have to be patient, as this was the start of a long journey ahead for them both. When the two doctors left, Connie looked across at Jake, tears once more rolling down her cheeks.

Chapter 6

Over the next few days, Connie gradually acclimatised to this new rhythm of her life. Her heart beat in unison with the gentle bleep of the monitor at the head of Jake's bed. Her eyes blinked in relation to the changing fluorescent green numbers of his vital signs. She read his monitor without really understanding what the changing numbers represented. Her only conversations now centred around Jake's progress with Sean and Jennie, the nurses, and Drs Wilton and Greenwich. How long would Jake remain in a coma? Would he ever regain consciousness? Would he ever be able to lead a normal life?

Connie, at first, slept in the family room down the corridor instead of going home. She had bought soap, a toothbrush, toothpaste and a comb from the hospital shop to tide her over but after three nights she decided she needed to return home to shower and change her clothes. She was still wearing her new and expensive dress that she had bought to wear for the signing of the probate and other legal papers. Jake's clothes, jacket, new shirt, best trousers and his dark grey tie, were folded and stuffed into a plastic bag. She took them home with her to wash and bring back a pair of pyjamas which he could wear instead of the hospital gown.

Their house was no longer the sanctuary it once was. She had always scurried home after a shift at work, glad to be returning to Jake and everything that was familiar to her. However, as she sat at the kitchen table opening the mail which had piled up by the front door, she longed to get back to the ICU. She opened a card which was amongst the pile of letters. 'Good luck with all your future endeavours. Lovely to meet you both. Best wishes, Jonathan Grey.'

Mr Grey had suggested to them at their first meeting that, as they had gained a substantial inheritance, they should immediately make a will and also set up a power of attorney so that each could take over the other's affairs if either of them became ill or died. He had advised them to leave the money to each other in the will. Fortunately, in the light of recent events, the power of attorney would now help Connie to manage Jake's financial affairs, including the inheritance, if he did not recover. Connie remembered how they had laughed at the absurdity of all this legal protection, frightened at the prospect of their potential fragility, but they had been convinced by Mr Grey's sober arguments.

It occurred to Connie that she would have to start informing people about what had happened to Jake. Her family was small, just one sister who lived in Australia with her husband. Jake was now without relatives and the number of friends was painfully limited. What a dreadful situation to be in. She hadn't realised that their social circle was so narrow. When she had been working, she had little energy to socialise, but now that she was in the throes of trauma, who did she really have to help her through?

She picked up the phone and left a message on the answer machine at Grey, Brown and Girling. She briefly explained what had happened to them the day they left the office and thanked Mr Grey for his card. She mentioned that she might need to activate the power of attorney if Jake did not recover. Connie flicked through the buff file that they had been given by the solicitor. She pushed it aside and turned back to the rest of the post.

How strange life is, she thought. *I have a husband in a coma, our lives are turned upside down, he may never return home again and yet the bills still keep coming through the letterbox.* She made a pile of the electricity, gas and water bills, which, although now on standing order, needed to be checked through.

Life for Connie took on a new routine. She slept at home each night, got up early, breakfasted then drove to the station to catch the train to Ipswich. She indulged herself by taking a taxi from the station to the hospital and spent all day next to Jake reading and doing crosswords. She even took knitting with her, creating a long scarf which required no pattern. The simple act of knitting repetitive rows occupied her hands whilst she sat quietly.

Jake had started to stir slightly, but doctors warned her not to expect too much as a result of these movements. The scans had revealed extensive damage to the brain. They explained to Connie that once Jake regained consciousness, he could be different from the person she used to know. His movements might be affected, his speech might be impaired, his memory might be faulty. All these 'mights' testified to the fact that there was no certainty in their lives anymore and they would just have to wait and see what the long-term effects would be.

After a long day of vigilance, which she now viewed as giving Jake company, she embarked on her journey home by taxi, train and car. When she settled down in front of the television, not really watching what was on, she pondered over how they would cope with their future. Dr Greenwich suggested a nursing home for Jake after he had spent some time in a general ward. The home must have a good standard of nursing to cope with Jake's specific needs. He suggested she started to research which ones were rated excellent and to visit them so that she would be prepared for the time when Jake was to leave hospital.

That night, Connie did not sleep very well. Within days, her expectations had gone from hope that Jake could make a full recovery to expectation that it would be a partial recovery and now the doctors were talking about the need for a care home, implying that recovery would be very limited indeed. As she lay in bed, she wrestled with her despair, made worse by all the uncertainties before her. How long would he be in hospital? Were the doctors more concerned about freeing up a bed than ensuring that Jake was given every chance to make progress? Before eventually falling asleep, Connie decided that she needed a proper conversation with a specialist, one to one in a private room, not a couple of minutes in public as part of the doctor's ward round.

The following morning, not feeling very rested but clear about what she needed to do, she phoned the hospital to check the identity of the most senior doctor dealing with Jake. To her surprise she found it was Mr Westwood rather than Dr Westwood, that is the same doctor she had met several times without realising his seniority as the consultant in charge of Jake's care. When told that it would not be possible to phone him directly, she asked for the number of his secretary who turned out to be Jo Strachan, a lady with a strong Scottish accent.

"Jo Strachan here, can I help?"

"Hello, I'm Connie Wilkins. My husband Jake is one of Mr Westwood's patients."

"Aye, I recognise the name."

"I wonder if I could arrange to have a private meeting with Mr Westwood?"

"He's a very busy man. Can I help in any way?"

"I really would appreciate speaking to Mr Westwood directly so that I can understand how Jake is likely to progress and the implications for the future."

"I'll see what I can do," said Jo, fairly brusquely. "I'll try to catch him when he calls into the office."

"Do you have any idea how long that will take?" asked Connie.

"No, but I'll phone you when I've had his reply. I can tell you're worried, but Mr Westwood does have a lot of other patients too."

Connie remained polite in thanking the secretary, whilst inwardly seething with frustration. Jake was the most important person in the world as far as she was concerned and, surely, she was entitled to a proper conversation with his consultant. However, she had misjudged Jo's manner because 5 minutes later the phone rang, and Jo was telling her that Mr Westwood had just finished his round and could see her within the next hour but otherwise not for another couple of days. 50 minutes later, having neither showered nor eaten breakfast, Connie was sitting in a barely furnished side room not far from Jake's ward, nervous with consternation at the news that Mr Westwood might be conveying to her.

"Hello, Mrs Wilkins," said Mr Westwood, bustling into the room looking flustered, "I can see you're very anxious about your husband, and that's very understandable, so let me update you with what we know so far. The good news is that Mr Wilkins' vital signs are all very positive, so I don't think there is any danger of damage from a further stroke. The swelling of his brain is gradually reducing, helped by the fact that he is still in a coma. It's always difficult to know how long the coma will last but I expect him to show signs of consciousness within the next few days.'

"That's very encouraging," interjected Connie.

"Yes, but only when he regains consciousness will we be able to assess the extent of the damage."

"You are an expert in these matters though, Mr Westwood, so can you give me an idea of what to expect? Will he be able to walk? What about his sight and his speech?"

"It would be wrong of me to go beyond what we know for sure. I'm confident that he will survive, and I'm very hopeful that he will regain consciousness soon. Beyond that, you know as much as I do. I've had patients with similar injuries who have made a full recovery but on the other hand I've known them to be extremely disabled with a much-reduced quality of life."

"Oh goodness, I was hoping you were not going to say that," said Connie with a gulp.

"Let's just wait and see. We are keeping a very close eye on him and my staff are very good at their job. Mr Wilkins is in very capable hands."

"What is your best estimate for how long he will be in the hospital?"

"If he regains consciousness in the next week, we will need to monitor him for at least a couple more weeks, identifying the support he needs when he moves on to the next stage of his recovery."

Mr Westwood chose his words carefully, to be encouraging but at the same time to avoid giving false hope.

"The recovery period is going to be long and hard. Hospitals are very good for emergencies but not great for convalescence. Our aim will be to ensure, therefore, that his stay in hospital is as short as possible. Mr Wilkins will, however, need extensive nursing care for quite a time after he leaves here."

"Is this beyond the level of care that I could offer at home?" asked Connie.

"The support of community practitioners is much better than it was, but essentially you would be isolated for much of the time if he were at home, and Mr Wilkins will need 24-hour care, at least initially. My advice to you is to investigate care homes in the area."

"I've already started thinking about that," said Connie. "I'm really grateful that you've explained things so clearly to me, as far as anything is clear at the moment."

"Every time you visit Jake, keep talking to him because patients always respond better when they feel supported. Before long, we should be seeing some responses from him. I hope our chat has helped in some way," said Mr Westwood, shaking Connie's hand, "but I'm afraid I now have a patient waiting on the operating table."

Mr Westwood left Connie with a clearer idea about the challenge ahead. She knew she would have to cope with the high degree of uncertainty about what the future held. At the same time, it was becoming evident that she needed to go back to work. Organising a care home for Jake was also essential for when he was ready to be discharged from hospital. As she made her way home, Connie phoned her manager Monika and told her that she wanted to return to work. Monika tried to dissuade her, but Connie was insistent because she knew that she needed to work in order to maintain some kind of normality in her daily life.

Fortunately, where many would have been overwhelmed by these challenges, Connie surprised herself by her stoicism. Somehow, maybe because there was no alternative, she knew she would find the strength to confront her difficulties. After all, she had not had the easiest upbringing. Her mother had died when she was 13, leaving her father alone with Connie and her two younger sisters. Her Dad did his best, but he had a demanding job, involving travel all over the country, and though he tried to be at home as much as possible, the reality was that Connie was forced to take on a lot of responsibility for her sisters and managing the household.

Although she generally enjoyed being at school, she often found concentration difficult, especially in the crucial GCSE years and she was so disappointed with her results, feeling that they did not do her justice, that she decided to leave school at 16. Shortly afterwards she had met Monika, the manager of a cleaning company, and had been persuaded to join her team of ladies who offered a 24 hour a day cleaning service for local businesses. Monika quickly became aware of Connie's highly professional approach, able to work well with colleagues and clients, and tried to persuade her to become a partner in her company.

"I just cannot take on any more responsibility at the moment," had been Connie's reply and by the time her father had remarried and her two sisters had grown up, the opportunity was no longer there. Jenny, the younger sister, much to Connie's horror, was killed in a car crash months after her father had remarried and Beth, her other sister, used her life's savings to buy a return ticket to Australia as soon as she had left school. She originally went on a backpacking adventure with the aim of working her way around Australia but soon formed a relationship with a young Australian, Pete Stokoe, and had never returned to England.

Monika's business had grown to the extent that she now employed an administrator to ensure that cleaners were available to service all the offices and premises at a time that suited the clients, a role for which Connie would have been well suited. By the time Connie's domestic commitments were waning, she had already met Jake, who had a similar family background except that he was the only child and that his father had left his mother when Jake was 5. The story was that Jake's father wanted to spend some time on his own, but they later discovered that he had moved in with the mother of one of Connie's school friends.

The fact that Jake and Connie had both had to cope with major changes during their younger years somehow helped to establish a strong emotional bond between them. Jake was not classically handsome, but he had a dry sense of humour, a winning smile and nothing seemed to trouble him. With Jake, Connie had always felt safe and secure and, given her childhood traumas, this was important to her. Throughout this period, Connie had been so busy concerning herself about her father, her sisters and later Jake and his parents, that she had given little attention to her own development. She knew she was capable, but her priority was not letting people down, whether Monika, clients, Jake, her father,

her sisters. Her life had continued in this way for over 20 years, doing the cleaning job and looking after others.

Suddenly, with Jake critically ill in hospital, everything had changed but also everything had stayed the same. The change was that she was potentially wealthier than she could ever have dreamed possible whilst her key priority remained the care of others, essentially Jake. In a strange way, Connie sensed that her whole life had prepared her for this challenge, and she felt sure that she would be able to cope. These reflections had been flashing through her mind on the way home and, as she walked through the door of her house, she muttered to herself, with grim determination, "What will be will be."

The next morning, just as Connie was about to go to work, there was an unexpected knock on the door. A policeman was standing on the threshold.

"Mrs Wilkins?" Connie nodded.

"Could I ask you to accompany me to the station, please. We have a line of suspects for you to inspect. We hope that one of them might be the person who attacked your husband."

"I don't think I can help you," stuttered Connie who had long since forgotten about the police investigation. "I don't think I paid enough attention to the thug who caused the injury. I was more concerned about Jake's welfare…" Her voice trailed off and within minutes she was sitting in the back of the police car on the way to Ipswich Police Headquarters.

"Oh, good morning, Mrs Wilkins."

Inside the building, Connie came face to face with PC Johnson who had been with her at the hospital weeks before.

"Now, don't worry about this. The men in the line-up have been videoed and we want you to look at them and see whether you recognise anyone. As you are only going to look at these nine videos in a room away from the men themselves you are quite safe."

He led Connie down the corridor to a small room which was bare of furniture except for a table, a chair and a computer. As she browsed through the images, she shook her head and repeated, "Sorry, I am not sure. It doesn't seem to be any of them."

Suddenly, at the seventh image, she gave out a little squeak. "Oh, that could be him. I suddenly remember the scar above his mouth. I remember seeing it and thinking he must have been in this sort of altercation before. My mind was whirling as he was hitting Jake, imagining the thug in a fight and being cut with a beer glass. Fancy having these thoughts when your husband is being beaten to pulp."

Connie was asked to look at the remaining two images to complete the line-up and when she had done so she was asked to scrutinise the images of number seven once more.

"Yes, yes, I am now sure that he was the one. He wore a skull ring on his left hand too. I can see the whole thing in my mind. I remember thinking that this was the reason Jake was so badly bruised. The guy was left-handed and hit Jake a massive blow with the ring. Why have I only just remembered these details now, PC Johnson? You asked me several times for details and at the time I couldn't remember clearly what had happened. I felt numb and I suppose I was in shock, but now I can remember the whole thing as if it were happening now."

"I will have to ask for another statement from you, Connie, if you don't mind. Then we will be able to proceed with the arrest."

Connie nodded at PC Johnson and she was led back down the corridor to another office where she gave a more detailed account of the incident. It was almost lunchtime by the time she arrived home, so she phoned Monika to apologise for letting her down. She told her why she had missed the morning shift and that she would be at the hospital that afternoon.

On arrival at the ward, she told the sleeping Jake what had happened.

"I had to live through the assault all over again, Jake. If only I could have stopped them then you wouldn't be here in bed like this. Sorry, I let you down."

At that moment she felt a slight movement of Jake's hand in hers. His fingers seemed to stretch out and then curl around her own hand.

"Oh, Jake. Are you waking up? Can you hear me?" Jake squeezed his fingers against her flesh and Connie cried out, "Nurse, come quickly."

The young nurse who was checking a monitor two beds away ran over and checked Jake's responses.

"Can you hear me, Jake?" she asked and gently shook his shoulders. Jake opened his eyes slowly but looked dazed and confused. The nurse shone a light into his eyes and took his temperature. She noted the time on Jake's progress sheet and said she would send a message to Mr Westwood who wanted to be informed when Jake showed signs of returning to consciousness.

"Jake, oh Jake, it's me, Connie. Can you hear me?"

Jake adjusted his gaze towards Connie and imperceptibly nodded but he looked weary and scared. He looked like a young lost boy. He glanced around him and seemed totally alarmed and confused by his surroundings.

"You are in hospital, Jake. You were beaten up and you have been here for quite some time. They are looking after you really well. Don't be scared. They are really good at their job and they are watching over you day and night. I am here most of the time too so don't worry about being alone."

With that, he closed his eyes and seemed to go back to sleep and his fingers released their grip of Connie's hand. She slumped back on to her chair and stared at the man she loved and wondered what long term effect there would be from the dreadful assault.

Mr Westwood arrived down the corridor, accompanied by a junior doctor struggling to keep up with him. He looked at Jake's chart and monitor and carried out several tests on him. He spoke his name and gingerly Jake opened one eye in response.

"Well, that's good," said the consultant. "If he can respond to his name then that is a hopeful sign. He will take some time to come out of his coma. He will be confused and dazed for quite a while and much of that is down to the drugs we have been giving him to let him sleep and keep him calm. He might get agitated over the next few days, but don't worry, that is just part of the healing process. We will take out his breathing tube soon and see how he responds on his own, but don't be alarmed if we have to replace it as Jake might need longer to recover considering the severity of his injury."

Connie stood at the end of Jake's bed and watched in silence as he underwent further tests and then his breathing tube was removed. Gradually, Jake's lungs adjusted to coping without external support and, before long, his breathing settled into a relaxed rhythm which encouraged Connie to think she could safely leave him to slumber alone for a few hours.

"Oh dear," she said to herself, "I was going to spend the day looking into nursing and care homes. I forgot all about it. What a day it has been." With that she collected her bags and gave the sleeping Jake a kiss on his cheek and she set off for home.

Chapter 7

Connie didn't arrive home because on leaving the hospital she changed her plans. She told the taxi driver to take her to the train station where she bought a return ticket to London. She was in an empty carriage and the peace and quiet allowed her to think through her actions. She had a burning need to retrace their steps on the day of the assault. She did not want to relive the assault, but she did want to look again at the houses which were part and parcel of Jake's inheritance.

She remembered most of the route they had taken and after looking at three of the houses, she fished out her diary which was always lurking at the bottom of her bag to confirm the addresses of the other properties. She had made a note of each one during the return journey from Jonathan Grey's office copying the details of them into her diary so that she had a record of where they were located. She was even more impressed on second viewing as she surveyed each house and calculated their actual worth.

We will need to keep the most expensive ones to have a regular income to pay for Jake's care, she told herself, *but the smaller ones could be sold off to give extra cash when and if we need it.* She made notes against each of the properties: leafy street, 4 storeys, impressive neighbourhood, at least 6 bedrooms; large Victorian house, parking for several cars, 3 storeys, possibly 4 or 5 bedrooms, at least two reception rooms, close to tube station.

On her journey home, she allowed herself a few minutes recalling the train attack and then focused her energy instead on their future plans. She scrutinised her notes and acknowledged that the properties were their security for an unpredictable future. What if we were to move into one of the houses and convert it with a lift and widen the doorways to allow Jake to move freely in a wheelchair, she wondered. They would be near the main hospitals that she had researched over the last few days, Kings College Hospital, University College Hospital, the list was quite impressive. Jake might have a chance of recovery if he got the right treatment by those who specialised in neurological complications. What was to

45

stop them changing their lives altogether considering fate had given them a mighty push? They could build a new life in London and enjoy what it had to offer when Jake got stronger.

She instinctively knew that his recovery would be difficult, and she foresaw that he might be in a wheelchair possibly for the rest of his life. That didn't mean that he had to be a prisoner in their small home or in a care home away from her. She decided she would do everything she could to care for him at home, but what she was sure about was that she would employ people to help with his care. She couldn't do it alone.

"The next stop is Ipswich," announced the train conductor.

Connie hailed another taxi to drive her home. It was pitch black and nearly ten o clock. Once again, she hadn't eaten much during the day, so she heated up some milk and took it to bed with her along with a box of biscuits. She couldn't face anything else and knew that she had to nourish herself or she would never sleep. After her trip she now had some kind of plan for the future and couldn't wait to share her ideas with Jake in the morning.

The ringing of the phone by her bed awakened her with a start. She reached for her mobile, sending the alarm clock clattering on to the floor:

"Connie, can you come to work today? One of my cleaners has just called in sick."

"Hello Monika," she said, fumbling for the alarm clock which said 4.38, "I'd love to help out but there are new developments with Jake's condition and I need to be at the hospital again today."

"Can't you at least spare me a few hours this morning? I wouldn't ask unless I was desperate."

"Would you prefer me to resign completely? I'm in a difficult situation too and although I like working for you, I'd rather give up the job than having to mess you around all the time. I really need a few days to work out how I am going to cope with Jake."

"I don't want to lose you, Connie. Don't worry, I'll manage. I've got a few people I can call, though they are not as good as you. Give my love to Jake. Speak to you soon."

Connie replaced the mobile on the bedside table with a sigh. She hated letting people down, but her priority had to be Jake. A few moments later, she picked up her mobile again and composed the following text: 'Sorry about today. Can't work at the moment. Will be in touch as soon as I can.' No sooner had she pressed

46

send when the phone rang again. Not recognising the number, she nearly switched off the call, but something made her pause and she pressed the green button:

"If you are trying to sell me something, I'm not interested. Besides it's ten to five in the morning. Goodbye."

"Connie, don't hang up. Are you still there? I'm really sorry, I'm always getting the time difference wrong. It's nearly midday here in Melbourne. How are you anyway?"

"Truthfully, things could be better, Beth."

"I'm sorry I've not been in touch for a while. I've just had a terrible shock. I receive the online version of the Ipswich Star, just to see if there's any news about old Ipswich friends, and I was browsing through last week's edition when I noticed a report about the attack on Jake. It sounds horrific. How is he?"

Connie had had no contact with Beth for a couple of years and, although it was good to hear the familiar voice of her sister, she could not help wondering whether Jake's welfare was the only reason she was calling.

"Jake has been in intensive care ever since the attack. He has been in a coma but just started to regain consciousness yesterday."

"Is he going to be alright?"

"We don't know, Beth. He is going to need a long time to recover and whether he fully regains his health we'll have to wait and see."

"That's terrible. I'd no idea it was so serious. How are you coping yourself, Connie?" Connie was suddenly conscious of Beth's Australian accent.

"I'm doing better than Jake but that's all I can say really. It is not the best of times. Hospitals are not my favourite places and I'm spending a lot of time by his bedside, hoping he'll wake up. Yesterday was a good day because he opened his eyes for a couple of minutes and squeezed my hand. It won't sound much to you, I'm sure, but it felt like a really big step forward for me."

"As soon as I saw the newspaper article, I just had to call you."

"How's Pete, by the way?"

"We're no longer together. That's not a problem though because we were arguing all the time and in the end we both decided that that we should go our separate ways. We still meet up for a drink occasionally with other friends. I think he's started seeing somebody but I'm past caring, to be honest."

"And how's the work going, Beth?"

47

"I'm not having a lot of luck there either, Connie. The company had to cut back staff, and as I was the last recruit, I was the first to be shown the door."

"What about money? How are you managing?"

"There's plenty of bar and restaurant work here in Melbourne and I've managed to get a couple of part-time jobs. The pay isn't great but I'm surviving, especially as I've moved into a small flat. A friend and I share the rent. It's only temporary until I get back on my feet. Listen, Connie, it's great to talk to you but I've got to go to work. Give my love to Jake. Speak soon."

With that she was gone. After two years of silence, why the sudden phone call? Was it really because of the article in The Ipswich Star? Connie and Beth had somehow drifted apart as they had struggled to cope in their different ways from their sister Jennie's death. Whereas Beth had accepted their father's new partner, Connie felt that starting a new relationship was disrespectful to their mother's memory and this created another barrier between them. By the time Beth decided to leave for Australia, both women were glad to be taking separate paths into the future. Both needed time apart.

It was still not yet 6 o'clock but Connie decided that there was no point trying to sleep again, especially with so much to do. She showered, had a quick breakfast of cereal, yoghurt and black coffee and set off for the hospital. Formal visiting hours were in the afternoon and evening, but normal rules tended to be relaxed in the intensive care ward. She had been told that she could visit at more or less any time, though whether the nurses would consider 6.45 am to be reasonable she did not know.

In any case, she was prepared to fight for her rights because she no longer had any provision for sleeping in the hospital. Initially, she had been given a bed in the family room, but once Jake was stable, the family of a more recently seriously injured young man was given priority. On the children's wards, parents were able to sleep next to their sick child, presumably to help speed their recovery, so why was Jake, an adult with no visitors other than Connie, deemed less important? After all, how much would a reclining chair next to each bed in the intensive care ward cost? Surely a trivial expenditure in the big scheme of things, thought Connie.

There were 8 beds on the ward and Jake was at the far end against the wall. Next to one bed a monitor was beeping, presumably to indicate to the staff that the patient's heartbeat was dangerously high. When Jake first arrived, his heartbeat had frequently risen above 200 beats per minute, much to Connie's alarm, but it had steadily fallen each day and had now settled into the mid-70s. Most of the patients were attached to drips, in order to be hydrated intravenously, and Jake was no exception. Some were also connected to a machine that helped them breathe but Jake's lungs had been functioning normally for a couple of days, though he had a clear tube clipped to his nose that provided a steady flow of oxygen into his airways.

Throughout the ward, at regular but disjointed intervals, there was the sound of air being gently pumped into the mattress of each patient, and then slowly expelled, in order to avoid the development of bedsores. Connie moved quietly along the ward towards Jake's bed, waving to the nurse in the little glass-fronted office as she passed, and sat down next to him. She took hold of his hand and squeezed gently, hoping that Jake would reciprocate, but nothing happened. His eyes remained closed, his breathing rhythmic and unaltered by her touch. She began to talk to him in a quiet whisper so as not to disturb the other patients, nevertheless hoping that her voice would permeate Jake's consciousness.

"I've told Monika I won't be working for a few days and if she gives me any grief, I'll pack in work altogether. By the way, Beth called. Would you believe it, after all this time? She says she saw the report in the Ipswich Star about your accident. As you know, Beth has not been in touch for months, even years. It is funny to think that Beth, Jennie and I used to be so close when we were younger. We had to stick together to survive but everything changed with Beth after Mum died, and even more so after Jennie died."

At each mention of the names of the family, Connie sensed a slight twitch in Jake's hand. Was she imagining it? "Beth, Jennie, Mum…" she repeated several times until Jake's hand was definitely squeezing hers, and his eyes started to open. She continued repeating the names until his eyes became focused on her eyes. Jake seemed to be struggling to say something, but no sound came out. Connie doused the lollipop sponge into the glass of water on the bedside cabinet and stroked it along his lips, which parted slightly to drink in the cool liquid. He tried to speak again, and after several attempts she could make out the word "Andy". Of course, he was asking after her father Andy.

"He's fine, as far as I know."

Jake whispered again, this time two words: "Andy, Beth." Connie now realised that Jake's brain was working well.

"Beth found out about your accident from a newspaper report, and then she's been talking to Andy."

She detected a faint smile from the slight crinkling of the skin around Jake's eyes and he continued to stare at her with a look full of meaning until she exclaimed:

"Wow, Andy's told her about Aunt Agnes. That's why she has been phoning me. She'll be hoping for some of the inheritance. You are clever, Jake."

The crinkling around Jake's eyes deepened and Connie started to laugh, much to the surprise of the nurse who had appeared unnoticed alongside her.

"Well, I'm glad to see you two are having a good time. What's so funny?"

"It's a long story," said Connie. "One thing is for certain: Jake's mental faculties are working well, no matter what the machines are telling you!"

The nurse went through her hourly checking ritual, noting the data on a chart for each measure: blood pressure, pulse rate, temperature, blood oxygen levels, liquid intake, urine levels. Connie scrutinised the nurse's face looking for evidence of Jake's progress, but the nurse remained impassive apart from a nod of encouragement before moving on to the next patient: "He's doing fine."

Connie returned her focus to Jake who seemed to have drifted off to sleep again. Undeterred, she soaked his lips with the sponge lollipop again, stroked his forehead and told him about her trip to London. As she spoke with enthusiasm about the houses in London and her plans for them, Jake's eyes opened again. Connie felt so much better now that she could see those lovely blue eyes, even if the pupils were like pinpricks, probably as a result of the drugs he was being given, and even if the whites were bloodshot and rather yellow.

However, there was a noticeable change in response when Connie started outlining her ideas for moving to London and using one of the houses as a base for managing Jake's recuperation. His eyelids fluttered frantically as if he was trying to clear some debris from his eyeball, his lips started to twitch as if he was trying to speak and his grip on Connie's hand tightened.

"What's the matter, Jake? Is what I am saying bothering you? These are just ideas. Nothing is decided. We'll discuss possibilities together when you are a little stronger."

Jake seemed reassured, his eyelids closing, his features relaxing almost into a smile. Once again, without a word being spoken, he had made his feelings crystal clear and Connie knew that she would need to use all her powers of persuasion to convince him that moving to London would be in both their interests.

Chapter 8

Jake's wheelchair was manoeuvred into the ambulance and he was driven the six miles from the hospital to the convalescence home where he was to spend the next two weeks, before being transferred to the nursing home. Connie was waiting outside the imposing main entrance of Seaview House as she watched the ambulance sweep up the drive and park feet away from where she was standing.

"Was it a comfortable journey, Jake?

He nodded as his chair was lowered by the ambulance ramp. It had been four months since the attack, and this was his first outing. Jake looked across at the distant sea before the ambulance crew turned his wheelchair and pushed him into the convalescent home. Connie carried his few personal possessions in two plastic bags and when they reached his new room, she tidied his clothes and shaving equipment away in the small bedside lockers.

"Oh, good, you have arrived and seem to be settling in."

Carol Jones was a friendly and efficient manager of the convalescent home and, without further ado, she quickly rattled off the visiting hours, meal and medicine times for all the patients. Connie had met Carol the day before and she had had to use all her powers of persuasion to get a private room for Jake. The other patients lay in regimented rows and had looked positively miserable with their situation. Connie was far from convinced that such an environment would be good for Jake and she had promised a new bedside chair for the room if Jake could be allowed some privacy.

"Well, I will leave you both in peace for the moment whilst you get used to your new surroundings."

Jake slowly looked around him and his face crumpled as if he were about to cry.

"Now don't get upset, love, it is only for a short time until we get you settled into the other place. They will give you the extra attention that you still need and it's important that you get stronger. When you have been here for a few days I will push you along the promenade and you will be able to watch what is going on out at sea. You used to love the seaside. Do you remember that, Jake?"

Jake slowly nodded his head. His voice was still barely audible, and it was a huge effort for him to say a few words. He seemed to prefer to communicate with his eyes and the nodding of his head. Connie had been advised by the consultant to let him take his own time. He would speak when he felt stronger and more mentally alert. For now, he was comfortable saying very little, but appeared to understand quite a lot of what was said to him.

If Connie turned away from him when she was talking, he seemed confused and upset, but if she stood next to him and talked slowly and in short sentences, he relaxed and followed what she was saying. They built a routine for themselves and each day Jake made small steps in his progress. His tiredness, however, never seemed to leave him. He slept many hours in the day and when Connie arrived to visit, she would gently waken him by shaking his shoulder and calling his name.

The door opened suddenly and in breezed a young nurse.

"Hello, I am Jenny. I will be looking after you whilst you are here, Mr Wilkins."

"Call him Jake, please, Jenny. I don't think he recognises himself as Mr Wilkins at the moment."

"Right you are," she replied and after giving Jake a warm smile, she busied herself with taking his temperature and checking his medicine which had been locked away in the small cupboard on the wall opposite his bed.

"You will be wanting a nice cup of tea after your journey. I'll get the kitchen to sort out a drink and a biscuit for you both. It is another couple of hours before Jake's teatime and you might be a bit peckish."

With that Jenny twirled out of the room and left Connie and Jake sharing a smile.

"Well, Jake, do you think you will settle in better now?"

She winked at her husband as she used to do when they were sharing a joke and Jake nodded, this time allowing his face to relax. He suddenly looked happier compared to only a few minutes before.

The two weeks passed quickly, and Connie managed to push Jake along the promenade during the second week. He had been weary and listless during the first few days at Seaview House, but he began to improve significantly as a result of Jenny's attention. She was very bubbly and positive in her manner and she changed the atmosphere of their lives giving them hope for the future. Jenny was only in her mid-twenties, but she seemed to have the wisdom of someone so much older. She told them stories about her own family and her father who had been wheelchair bound throughout the time she was growing up.

"Oh, he could do anything he set his mind on. He never thought of himself as disabled. He used his chair like it was an extension of his body. I would often have to run to catch up with him whenever we went outside. He got us all dancing around him, mind. He liked the attention and he was always saying, 'Jenny, just run upstairs and get me my reading glasses from the bedside table' and, you know, it was a pleasure to do it for him. He always had a tube of Smarties in his pocket and my reward was a sweet when I brought him what he wanted. He laughed so much that we forgot that he might be in pain. His wheelchair was just like yours, Jake, but his had a bell and a mirror on the handlebars. My Dad was great fun. He used to give us rides on his chair and his speciality was showing us how he could do a wheelie."

Connie had spent quite some time thinking through the logistics of Jake and his wheelchair. When Agnes's money was safely in their joint account, she decided she needed to buy a car. She had passed her test when she was eighteen but the only car she had ever owned was an ancient blue mini which needed a peg to hold out the choke when she started the engine.

She eventually sold the car after it had broken down for the eighth time and because their home was in walking distance of the town, she never felt the need to replace it. However, she soon realised that they would be stupid to rely on taxis for ever more so she set about researching cars suitable for wheelchair passengers. She visited a showroom and was shown around a Fiat which had got tremendous reviews and had been described as smart, sleek and perfect for wheelchair users. Much to her relief, the salesman had a wheelchair in the showroom. He demonstrated how the front seat could be easily removed and he talked her through the best possible way of loading the wheelchair with the passenger still sitting in it.

Connie was impressed and she enjoyed the experience of having a test drive. When the salesman and she returned to the showroom, she ordered a brand new white compact people carrier with a mobile ramp which would enable her to push Jake and the chair into place. She took possession of her new car a week later and only then did she tell Jake what she had done.

"Look through the window, Jake. Can you see that lovely shining white car down in the carpark? Well, it belongs to us and now we can go anywhere we want from now on."

Her surprise, which she had feared might have caused Jake to get cross and argumentative was greeted with a nod and a smile. At least their future wouldn't now be confined to one room and, under Jenny's influence, their mood became optimistic.

"You can do anything you want when you have a good set of wheels," she would say every day, and this became their mantra.

As the two-week period was drawing to a close, Connie went to see the manager, Carol, about the possibility of Jake remaining at Seaview House:

"I'm afraid our job is to smooth the transition from hospital to home, so we are not allowed to keep patients over the longer term," said Carol.

"Jake has made so much progress during his time here. Is there any way you could let him stay a little longer because I'm struggling to find a care home that will best meet his needs."

"The best I can do is give you 3 extra days. We're allowed to do that in an emergency only because there is a waiting list of people desperate to have a place here. Jake's room is particularly in demand; it's the only single room we have," replied Carol with a worried frown. Her job was to manage the home and sometimes that included telling people what they didn't want to hear.

"That's a help because I need to check whether my preferred care home can actually accommodate Jake. You and your staff have done a great job with him, but I can't understand why he can't stay with you indefinitely."

"As usual, the problem is funding. We have to be able to stick to our budget and the money we are given only provides care for a maximum 2 week stay. I can offer you an extra 3 days because one of our patients moved out earlier than expected and it will take 3 days to fill her place."

"I'm really grateful for all you've done for Jake. I'm visiting the care home later today and I will let you know how I got on."

Connie walked down the corridor to let Jake know that her visit today would be short and to explain why, though she wasn't sure whether the information would mean much to him. Jenny was in the room and whilst doing the usual checks she was singing "All you need is love."

"I thought you'd be too young to be a Beatles fan," said Connie.

"My parents loved the Beatles and we used to sing along to their songs, especially on long car journeys. Besides, when I came into the room, Jake had his eyes closed but I could hear him humming the tune so I thought it would help if we could actually get him to sing along. So far, I have not managed to get him to go beyond humming. The only words I can remember are the chorus in any case."

"Let's just do the chorus together and see if he will join in. Jake loves the Beatles and it's one of his favourite songs. He used to sing it to me whenever we had an argument."

Connie held one of Jake's hands and Jenny the other and together they sang the chorus repeatedly, whilst looking encouragingly at Jake whose eyes were now wide open, a smile on his face. To their amazement, Jake's mouth started to move and before long all three were singing in harmony. Connie's face was a picture of delight.

"Jenny, I don't know how we are going to survive without you. You have made such a positive impact on Jake. We have to leave in the next few days and we are going to miss you terribly."

Connie rushed out of the room, joyful at the sound of the two Beatles impersonators she could still hear as she went down the corridor, and yet sad at the enforced move which she now had to finalise. She had already visited several care homes and her final shortlist had been narrowed down to two. It was a difficult process because the manager of each home usually presented the place in a very positive light and Connie was keen to find out what the people who lived there thought. She had already looked at the website of each home, focusing on the reviews.

She found it strange that most of the online reviews were so positive. Where were the negative or even lukewarm comments? For example, one home with a very good reputation only had 3 reviews on the website, all full of praise. But why only such a small number? Had the negative reviews been deleted by the home? Another home had lots of reviews, again mainly positive, but Monika had been critical of the way this home had looked after her mother so who was she to believe? Many of the homes had been quite recently built, reflecting the explosion of people living in care homes, and modern facilities were an attraction but how could she find out about the people who worked there? Did they like looking after people? Were they well-trained? Was any form of entertainment provided?

In the end, Connie realised that she was going to have to speed up the decision-making process because time was now short. She couldn't interview the residents, even if the managers would allow it, so her judgement would have to be based on her reaction to the meeting with the manager, the quality of the building and the attractiveness of the rooms and the general atmosphere amongst the people she met, whether staff or residents. Several of the homes were immediately discounted because of the overpowering smell of urine and, in the end, it was a choice between two, Hilltop, just north of Ipswich, and Pleasant Valley, situated on the banks of the River Deben near Woodbridge.

Both had been built in the last ten years, had attractive décor and furnishings and their managers enthused about the quality of the service they offered. Both were eye-wateringly expensive at £1200 a week. Connie was hugely grateful that Aunt Agnes's bequest had removed any financial worries. Ultimately, the final decision was simplified by the fact that when Connie arrived at Pleasant Valley, she found that the manager had gone to a meeting at Head Office. If Head Office is more important than Jake, he's definitely not coming here, thought Connie, making her way back to her car and setting off for Hilltop.

The manager at Hilltop welcomed Connie into his large office and immediately offered her a coffee from the machine in the corner of the room. Connie gladly accepted, hoping that this would be the start of a positive relationship with the home. Peter Scott had recently taken up his post, having been promoted from his Assistant Managership of another home that belonged to the same company, Home from Home. He wore a white shirt and a blue patterned tie with a sober dark suit, though the jacket with his name card attached, was hanging from a hook on the back of the door.

Connie was impressed by Peter's business-like appearance and manner, guessing that he was in his late 30's though his dark-framed glasses, greying beard and receding hair hinted that he could be several years older. The thick pile of the beige carpet, the leather sofa near the door, the large oak desk and the prints of Van Gogh paintings on the walls all gave an air of solidity, even opulence, that Connie hoped were a reflection of high standards elsewhere in the home. She noted too that the computer on Peter's desk was the latest Apple model, around which were carefully arranged photographs of a youngish-looking woman that Connie took to be his wife and two boys and a girl she guessed were his primary age children. When Peter spoke, he made every effort to confirm an impression of professionalism and caring.

"At Hilltop, we want our residents to feel as if they are living in their own homes, Mrs Wilkins. Everybody has their own room of course and we freshly paint the walls to suit the taste of the new customer before moving in."

"Do you have a vacant room now, Mr Scott, because my husband Jake needs somewhere urgently?" asked Connie.

"You're in luck, Mrs Wilkins, as I have a couple of possibilities and you can choose the one you prefer."

"How many residents do you have?"

"We have the capacity for 50 altogether, with 15 places in our specialist dementia unit. I know that is not relevant to Jake," replied Peter.

"And how many staff do you have?"

"Well, there is one member of staff for every 4 residents on average," said Peter, frowning slightly as he realised that that Connie was asking the right questions from Jake's point of view, though not necessarily from his own.

"What does on average mean exactly?" said Connie, determined to dig beneath the rhetoric in order to gain a picture of how much support Jake would have in practice.

"Well, it's difficult to be precise. Having 50 residents gives us the funding for 15 care assistants working 24 hours a day but of course the staff work in shifts of between 8 and 12 hours and some are part-time, so I employ probably about 30 people in total."

"In the convalescent home, Jake had a dedicated member of staff looking after him."

"Yes, exactly the same will be the case at Hilltop. Your husband will be allocated a member of staff who will be overall responsible for his care."

"What if Jake needs help in the middle of the night?" asked Connie.

"There is a button next to the bed that sounds a buzzer. We closely monitor whether calls for help receive a rapid response and our latest figures show that, on average, we are acting within 5 minutes."

"Is that one of your buzzers that I can hear down the corridor?"

"Yes, I'm sure somebody will arrive shortly."

"Jake still needs assistance at mealtimes. Will that be a problem?"

"I'm sure somebody will be available to help him even if his named assistant is not on duty. Would you like to have a look at the two rooms, Mrs Wilkins, and we can continue our conversation as we walk."

"That's a good idea. I really want to have a look around."

As they walked down the corridor, Connie noted the fresh paintwork, the vague smell of disinfectant and the continuing sound of the buzzer, now surely reaching the 5-minute limit. They walked past a large lounge area with lots of armchairs and a large flat screen TV on the wall. The whole of one wall was made up of windows that looked out on to an attractive garden filled with young bushes and colourful flowers. What was striking was that she could only see two people.

In the garden, there was a small, wiry man with a few strands of white hair walking repeatedly up and down the same stretch of land, seemingly enthralled by the plants, occasionally removing dead flowers and throwing them into the bushes. The other person was a very old lady, seated in a large armchair and staring intently at the television, as if watching a fascinating programme being transmitted through a blank screen.

"Where is everybody?" asked Connie.

"This is the afternoon quiet period, so most people are in their rooms at the moment resting after their lunch."

Sure enough, most of the rooms that they passed had open doors. Where Connie spotted somebody, she gave a little wave and a friendly smile, but only occasionally did she receive a friendly greeting in return. With relief, she noted that the distant buzzer had now stopped, only to be replaced by another much closer one.

"We're looking into the buzzer system," said Peter, "I'm hoping to be able to upgrade to pagers for all the care assistants but I'm waiting for approval from head office. Here we are. This is the first room that you could have."

It was a pleasant enough room, quite large, with a bed, an armchair and an en-suite bathroom. The problem for Connie was that the view from the window was directly on to a brick wall, taking away the light and any possibility of outside visual stimulation. The second room was next door and had exactly the same layout but this time there was a glass door giving access to a small patio area and the view across the garden was impressive, with its well-tended lawn, a small pond and glorious rose bushes.

"This is much better," said Connie, "but I don't like these red walls. Jake would like something more soothing, a gentle beige colour perhaps with a white ceiling to reflect the light around the room."

"That would be no problem, Mrs Wilkins."

"How soon can I move Jake into the room then, Mr Scott?"

"We need a couple of days to do the decorating and to make sure everything is clean and tidy. How about Friday afternoon? I know I'm available then."

"That's great. Thank you so much. I'm so relieved to know that Jake now has somewhere to live."

"I'm delighted that he will be joining us and I look forward to seeing you on Friday."

For the second time in as many weeks, Jake's belongings were packed away in the same two plastic carrier bags. Connie loaded them into the car and returned to Jake's room where Jenny and Jake were singing their favourite song. Connie smiled at them both and joined in with the singing. She noticed how much clearer his words were compared to the first time he had sung them. His progress was quite staggering considering he had been unable to say a word when they first arrived at Seaview House. She knew how important a part Jenny had played in his recuperation. Her energy and relentless happy nature had been a tremendous tonic.

For the last two weeks, Jake had had no chance to feel depressed about his situation because, if she noticed his mood was beginning to change, Jenny loaded him straight into his wheelchair and pushed him up and down the promenade. He had little resistance against the east wind which blew in his face as they battled along the sea front and he enjoyed listening to Jenny's endless chatter. By the time they returned to Jake's room he was tired but quietly content. He had never had such devoted focus from one so young and he thrived on her attention.

"Oh, Jenny, we will miss you. You have been a godsend to us since Jake has been here. He has really enjoyed all your care and kindness. If only we could take you with us into his new home…"

"You will be OK, Jake, don't you worry. I'll keep in touch with Connie to see how you are getting on. Always remember my old dad. He never let anything get him down, so you have got to be the same. It is a real struggle at times, but if you are determined to recover then you will. I promise."

Jenny leant down and gave him a quick kiss on his cheek and then turned his wheelchair around and pushed him out of the room. The two women hugged and then loaded Jake into the car. Connie gave her an envelope which contained her contact details so that they could keep in touch with each other. Jenny had become important to Connie too and this made the departing that bit harder.

The journey went smoothly. When Connie glanced across, she noticed that Jake, once again, looked slightly apprehensive about moving to a new home.

When he saw the name of the company, Home from Home, he gave an ironic chuckle and moved his head from side to side. He rolled his eyes and sighed. Connie patted his knee.

"I know. It would be so much better if we were going home, Jake. Let us see how you get on here. You never know, there might be another Jenny waiting for you."

In fact, there was no one quite like Jenny waiting for him. He looked about his room and then his face lit up when he saw the small pond just outside his patio doors. A duck and three of her large offspring right on cue came waddling along the path making a bee line for the pond. She launched herself gracefully into the water and glided in to the middle and watched her brood as they stepped confidently into the water and moved into position like a shadow behind their mother.

"Well, you haven't got ducks at home, Jake. They should give you plenty of entertainment."

There was a forceful knock on the door and a tall, solid young woman wearing a maroon uniform entered.

"Hello. I am just coming to introduce myself. My name is Clare and I am your named carer. Have you settled in OK? I have to check your medicines, Jake, and then I will talk you both through the routines of each day."

With that she unpacked the separate bag of medicines that Jenny had brought and marked each one on the sheet. She locked them away in the small medicine cupboard which was fixed to the wall and returned the key to the fob she had attached to her waist. She sat herself down on Jake's bed and explained mealtimes and morning routines. Connie asked that Jake should be given a cup of tea when he first woke up in the morning as he had enjoyed this treat at Seaview, and it had helped him face the day.

"I'll see what I can do," was Clare's response but it wasn't said with conviction and Connie made a mental note that this was something else she had to keep an eye on. After all, she was paying a fortune for Jake's stay and she wanted him to be given whatever was reasonable to make him feel at home. He would have his breakfast in his room, informed Clare, but Connie wanted him to try having his lunch and evening meal in the dining room which was just down the corridor. She hoped this would encourage him to settle in and get to know some of the other residents. Jake pulled a face at this, but Connie said, "Just give it a go, Jake. You might like it and it will get you out of your room several times a day."

"Yes, well, regarding that," added Clare, "we have a number of clubs on each week. You could try painting, gardening, feeding the chickens which are in the little farm in the grounds. We also have quizzes and musical events each week which you might like to try."

Clare smiled triumphantly as if what was on offer would make Jake's life worthwhile. Connie and Jake looked at each other reading each other's mind. After Clare had left them alone and Connie had tidied Jake's clothes away in the few drawers on offer, she decided to take him for a tour of the care home. She pushed him up and down the carpeted corridors and they discovered separate drawing rooms where one or two residents were sitting with family visitors or reading books. The windows were large and looked out on gardens and inner courtyards.

Connie was suddenly conscious of how hot it was in the building. She took off her jacket and continued to explore the different wings with Jake. Eventually, they found themselves back at the main reception where they had entered only an hour or so earlier. There was a bright, garishly patterned bistro area opposite the reception and tables and chairs were set out to encourage conversation. At one end of the bistro was a bar on which several trays of freshly baked cakes and biscuits were on offer to all. There were drink making facilities behind the counter offering tea, coffee, hot chocolate and, just like in a licenced bar, on the wall were suspended several bottles of spirits.

Connie was impressed by this area because it offered residents a chance to entertain their family friends with food and drink just as they would have done in their own homes. Newspapers and magazines were scattered around on the tables and three older women were sitting separately reading the papers. They looked quite content, but Connie noticed that there was very little interaction between them.

As she pushed Jake past them, he said hello, but no one replied to him.

"They must be quite deaf, Jake. Never mind, no doubt you will get to know them sooner or later."

Jake's mood seemed to drop like a stone. During this day's move, he had worn a pleasant smile most of the time, curious to see what was on offer. Now, he was struck by the fact that he was no longer the independent person he once had been. Instead he had moved into the ranks of the helpless and dependent. He stirred restlessly in his wheelchair and Connie sensed the thoughts going through his mind. She decided to push him outside, following the manicured pathway, looking at the delightful planting outside every resident's room. The pocket handkerchief-sized patio allowed, in theory, the resident of the room to sit outside, but Connie had been told that the residents' doors were kept locked for security reasons and Jake would have to ask Clare to open the door if he wanted to sit outdoors.

Connie had suggested that she might be given a key to unlock the doors so that she and Jake could sit outside in the fresh air, but this was declined. Apparently, this was a health and safety issue and so Connie wasn't to be trusted with a key. It was all very official and rather too controlling for Connie's taste, but for the moment she kept her own counsel and didn't mention her irritation to Jake.

"I had better be going now, love. It will soon be time for your evening meal, and I need to get home to do a number of things before bedtime. Clare said one of the carers will come and push you to the dining room. I hope you will be alright and try your best to start a conversation with someone at your table so that you get to know them. I will be back in the morning and, regardless of the weather, I think we will have short drive out into the countryside."

She gave him a lingering kiss on his cheek and set off home. She hadn't realised how upset she would be about leaving him there. She sat in her car for a few minutes before starting the engine, trying to reassure herself that Jake would start to see this place as his home. She would visit him every day and try to build a routine so that they would both feel that life was going on as normal. She couldn't help making comparisons though. When he was in the nursing home, Jenny had made it easy for them both. Her warm nature had won them over and she had treated Jake as if he were a favourite uncle.

Now he was at Hilltop, Connie couldn't identify anyone like Jenny. The carers she had met seemed friendly and smiled a great deal, but they lacked Jenny's warmth and the way she had made Jake seem special. Connie knew that his recovery depended on his mental as well as physical wellbeing. If he were left alone in his room for too long, there was the chance that he would become depressed and that his recovery would stall.

Meanwhile, Jake was left alone in his room looking out of the closed patio doors. He watched the pond hoping that the duck and her offspring would reappear. Instead, one or two elderly residents ambled past his window, negotiating their walking frames along the winding pathway. He closed his eyes and tried to block out the scene in front of him. The size of the challenge before him was daunting but he did not want to sink into despair. Were there any positive elements to his situation?

His thought processes were unimpaired. He knew where he was and what had happened to him. He understood what people said when they spoke to him. Although his ability to form words was slow and unclear, he was starting to build sentences. Upper body movement was sluggish, but he was able to move his arms and manipulate cutlery with his hands. Maybe eventually he would be able to operate a wheelchair without any assistance. The biggest surprise to him was the support he was receiving from Connie.

After all, it would have been so much easier for her to gradually drift away from him now that he was such a burden but, on the contrary, she was more attentive than ever before and was doing whatever she could to help him recover. As he opened his eyes, shafts of sunlight reflected on the pond outside his window, a robin darted in and out of the bushes and Jake felt a surge of optimism well up inside him.

At 40, he was still a relatively young man, so his body's ability to repair was still strong and there was hope that his communication and mobility would improve. His mindset had to be one of determination to help himself rather than simply to rely on others. If he was going to become more independent, he needed a speech coach to develop his communication skills and a physiotherapist to improve his mobility. Connie would surely be able to organise this so he would have to try very hard to ensure she understood what he wanted.

Chapter 9

Early the next morning, Connie was having breakfast when the front doorbell rang. A familiar shape stood outlined on the other side of the frosted glass and she tried desperately to recall who it might be before deciding that it would be easier to simply open the door.

"Hello Connie," said a tall, slim, red-haired lady, with a tinge of an Australian accent. "How are you?"

"Beth, what on earth are you doing here?" said Connie, clearly taken aback. "I thought you were in Melbourne."

"Well, that's a fine welcome." The two women hugged each other, smiling broadly, clearly delighted to see each other. "It's lovely to see you, Connie."

"You too, Beth. You might have given me some warning though. I promised Jake that I would see him at about 10 o'clock."

"Can I come with you? I'd love to see Jake too."

"Of course, that's a great idea. It will do him good to see somebody other than me and a lot of very old people. Be prepared though. The Jake you will see is not the same Jake. He struggles to speak and is wheelchair-bound at the moment."

Driving to the care home, Beth told Connie that life in Melbourne had become difficult after she had lost her job, that she was becoming tired of the temporary bar work and that she had been feeling homesick.

"I'm not sure I know what I want to do. I could stay on in Australia and try to gain full citizenship but is that what I really want to do? I've missed seeing Dad and you and Jake too."

"Where are you staying? asked Connie.

"I'm with Dad and his girlfriend, Maria, for a few days. I get on quite well with Maria now although she and Dad seem to argue every time they are together, but I want to travel up to Scotland for a few days before flying back to Australia."

They drove on in silence, each wondering what the other was thinking.

"You're lucky that you have so many choices before you, Beth. My life changed forever the day that football hooligan smashed Jake in the face. It's a struggle for me to come to terms with what has happened and obviously it's very difficult for Jake too, as you will see in a few minutes."

"You've definitely had a tough time. You seem to be coping well though."

"Appearances can be deceptive. I lie awake at night fretting about the future. The uncertainty is the worst thing. I don't know how far Jake will progress, if at all. How can I ensure he has a good quality of life when he is so disabled? So many questions whirl around my head. Then I start worrying about the properties Jake has inherited from Aunt Agnes."

"Is that not a good thing? I mean, presumably at least you won't have any financial worries?"

Connie squeezed into the last parking space at the care home and they made their way through the flower-bedecked entrance area past the office of Mr Scott, the manager, who was engrossed in his computer screen. He looked up and waved but Connie approached him:

"How is Jake today?" she asked.

"I've only just come on duty, but Clare is in the building somewhere so do have a chat with her. As far as I know, he is doing well." He nodded towards Beth: "Pleased to meet you. Are you Connie's sister by any chance?"

"Is it that obvious? At least you're not guessing I'm her mother," said Beth with a grin.

As they headed down the corridor towards Jake's room, Connie grumbled: "You'd think that as the boss, he would spend a bit more time talking to his customers and less time looking at his spreadsheets."

"I'm sure he's a very busy man," said Beth. "Everything is so nice and modern. This is much better than I expected."

"Yes, maybe, but everybody here is so frail and ill. How can that help Jake recover?"

Jake was sitting in his armchair by the window and as they entered the room his face lit up with a big smile, followed by a look of surprise and then, recognition when he saw Beth.

"Hello. So…you've…come… to visit…the Poms," said Jake, halting after almost every word, his face screwed up with concentration.

"Hi Jake, good to see you haven't lost your sense of humour. I like your room. You are lucky to have such a nice view of the garden."

Jake winced: "Luck?" he said.

"Not sure about the word 'luck', are we Jake?" said Connie with a rueful smile, "Your speech is improving already though."

Jake frowned. "N…n…no. Not…good…enough. Need…practice."

"I hadn't thought about that, Jake. You're right, you need lots of practice. It's the only way you'll improve."

"I could help with that," interjected Beth, "Don't you remember me telling you that I did a speech therapy course during the day whilst doing evening bar work in Melbourne. I need to build a new career for myself and I thought there might be opportunities at the hospital there. I'd love to spend time trying to help Jake whilst I'm staying with Dad. It will be good experience for me."

"What do you think, Jake?"

Jake nodded as enthusiastically as he was able. Just then, Clare bustled in with the drugs trolley which she unlocked to reveal an array of labelled packets. Placing a small blue container on Jake's bedside table, she carefully dropped into it a dozen tablets of various colours before handing Jake a glass of water so that he could swallow each in turn.

"You're very popular today, Jake."

"This is my sister Beth visiting from Australia. She has very kindly offered to work with Jake on improving his speech," said Connie.

"Oh, I'll have to check that with Mr Scott. You see, I requested an appointment with a speech therapist last week.

"It surely won't do any harm," said Connie sharply. "Look, Beth is only going to talk to him. The only reason I mentioned it to you is so that you are aware that Beth will be visiting as well as me. Please pursue the appointment with the speech therapist as well though."

Clare looked disconcerted. She was not used to her authority being questioned but before she had time to think of a response, Jake grabbed her arm and stammered: "Fizz…Fizzi…Physio…?"

"Oh yes, that's another thing," said Connie. "Jake needs physiotherapy as well to improve his mobility. I've mentioned this to Mr Scott and to you a few times."

A look of panic came over Clare's face. "Oh, my goodness, I'd forgotten all about that."

Connie struggled to control her mounting anger: "You promised you'd organise physiotherapy. It's absolutely vital that Jake has all the support he needs as he rebuilds his life. I'm really disappointed…"

Beth could see her sister's temper was about to explode: "Look, I've done keep-fit classes for years and I'm sure that I can adapt some of the exercises to suit Jake, at least until a proper physiotherapist is available. Why don't I come for a couple of hours each day, with one hour focused on speech and the other on exercise?"

Clare was about to say that she needed to check with Mr Scott but thought better of it when she saw the look on Connie's face and, having locked up the drugs trolley, she hurried to the door, doing her best to avoid Connie's glare.

"Nice to see you all," she said, disappearing down the corridor and into the next room.

"That woman is really starting to irritate me. Thanks for your kind offer, Beth. Are you sure you want to spend time with Jake every day? It would certainly be a big help to me too. What do you think about all that Jake?"

Jake smiled and gave an enthusiastic thumbs-up signal. This was exactly what he needed: practical help to enable him to return to some form of normality. He'd always liked Beth and he was sure that they would work well together.

"How is Dad these days?" asked Connie, "I haven't seen him for months, even though he must know I've been struggling. He has been nowhere near us since the attack. You would have thought that he could have made some sort of effort to see how we are getting on."

"He's fine, though he has his problems too," replied Beth.

"Really?"

"Yes, he and Maria have had a few arguments which have resulted in Maria walking out and leaving him on a couple of occasions. I don't think the relationship can last. They are back together at the moment, but the atmosphere is tense. That's one of the reasons I want to keep out of the house as much as possible…apart from wanting to help you, Jake."

"What are they rowing about?" asked Connie.

"It's difficult to know for sure. They are always arguing about money. Maria moans about Dad spending time in the pub and Dad complains that Maria won't come to the pub with him. Dad likes to be out of the house a lot whereas Maria always wants to stay at home. I think she resents the fact that Jake has had an inheritance and she seems to think that Dad should be asking for a share of it.

Dad is a very proud man, though, and he wouldn't dream of asking you for money."

"Well, he will have to ask if he really needs help, but I've spent my life supporting him and my priority is now Jake. In any case, why does he not come and see Jake? It's the least he can do."

"Would that be OK?"

"Of course, it would," said Connie, looking at Jake for approval. "Can you cope with all this attention, Jake?"

Jake looked the happiest she had seen for a long time. "That's agreed then," said Beth, "I'll bring him with me tomorrow."

When Connie and Beth were driving home, Connie began to confide in her sister.

"I am actually very glad that you and Dad will be visiting tomorrow. It will give me a chance to go to London again to see our solicitor." Connie looked across at Beth to gauge her reaction.

"Really, have you got another problem?"

"No, it's nothing like that. I have to see him about our financial situation and talk about the houses we now own."

"Right, I will tell Dad when I get back, but could you pick us up in the morning and drop us off at Hilltop and then we will get a taxi home. Hilltop seems difficult to find and I don't expect there will be any buses going past the drive."

"Yes, OK. I will be outside the house at 8.30. Make sure Dad is ready though. I don't want to miss my train as I have quite a hike across London from Liverpool Street."

"OK. I will tell him you are arriving at 8.00 so that will hurry him up."

The two sisters smiled conspiratorially at the ruse to sharpen their father's actions. They used to think of ways to manipulate him when they were younger and they both realised that, even with advancing years, he still needed to be handled carefully.

Connie continued telling Beth her story. "Mr Grey was Aunt Agnes's solicitor and financial adviser and I saw him a couple of weeks ago and he agreed that he would offer the same service for us too. The inheritances are so complicated. I think I understand everything when I read the documents and then after an hour or so things become a blur. I need to discuss certain ideas with him and get up to date regarding the financing of Jake's care."

Beth noticed her sister's forehead beginning to frown, a sure sign that she was anxious and uncertain. "I haven't mentioned this to Jake yet." Connie paused, "No, that's a lie. I did mention my idea to him whilst he was in a coma." She smiled at the memory. "I used to tell him everything. I thought if I carried on talking then he wouldn't feel so alone and scared. I tried to sound as normal as possible even when tears were streaming down my face." Connie peeped her horn at a driver who pulled out straight in front of them without even looking to his left.

"You idiot," she shouted, but as the windows were closed only Beth got the full force of Connie's irritation.

"Anyway," continued Connie, as if nothing had happened, "the doctors told me that I must avoid upsetting him as there's research which shows how much coma patients can hear and understand, even though they look almost dead." Connie's face crumpled at the memory of Jake. "I used to chat away and sound happy and excited about our future so that he had some hope that he would soon be better." Connie paused and looked at her sister's reactions.

Beth was listening and seemed interested in what was being said. "So then, what can this solicitor do for you? I thought they just did legal form-filling rather than sorting out people's finances. Don't you need a separate financial adviser for that side of things?"

"Yes," replied Connie, "normally, that is what you would do, but Mr Grey is different. He knows our property business inside out. He has been involved in it for over thirty years and he has a much better knowledge of London prices and rents than I do." She pulled down the sun visor to shade her eyes from the unaccustomed sunshine. "He had initially decided not to take on any new clients, but after much persuasion, and you know I can be persuasive when I put my mind to it," she smiled across at Beth, "he agreed to work with us for the next three years before he retires so that I can learn the ropes. I think he used to have a soft spot for Agnes, and because Jake is her only living relative, he is really doing Jake a favour."

Beth fiddled with her bag as Connie spoke. She had something on her mind, and Connie recognised the old familiar tell-tale signs that all was not well with her sister. She could see that Beth was bursting to say something, but Connie wasn't giving her space to discuss her problems. Connie knew that whenever Beth or her dad were on the scene it usually meant trouble and she didn't have the emotional capacity to deal with any more problems.

Connie's tone of voice changed, becoming more serious. "I actually haven't mentioned my last visit to Mr Grey as I don't want to confuse Jake with the money side of things. I can't make any mistakes with this money or fritter it away. I will be needing every penny for Jake's care, which could last many years. Hilltop costs a fortune, so I am employing Mr Grey to act as my financial guru. He will watch what I am spending and warn me about making any mistakes.

She glanced across at Beth as she drew up outside her father's house. Connie was coming to the end of what she wanted to say to Beth. Her message was quite clear and a warning to her sister. "Jake can't cope at the moment with extra anxiety. I need him to concentrate on getting stronger. I will only tell him what has been agreed with Mr Grey when I know he is able to process my ideas. Hopefully, he will think I have been sensible and realise I am doing it all for him, which I am," Connie added with conviction.

Beth undid her seatbelt and opened the car door. "Well, at least you have two things in your favour, Connie. One is that you have the love of your life and he adores you; secondly, you now have the money to get him really good care. That is more than most people have," she said knowingly, "so even though he has had this terrible attack and your lives have been turned upside down, you can count yourselves lucky for those two very good reasons." Beth patted Connie's knee just as she had done to Jake a few days before. Connie smiled at the memory as she drove away leaving Beth standing outside the house watching her car disappear down the road.

The next morning Connie dropped Beth and her dad outside Hilltop and reminded them to tell Jake she would visit later that evening. She made them promise not to mention her trip to London. When Connie saw her father, she gave him a quick peck on the cheek, saying "Alright, Dad," and left it at that. She knew he wouldn't need any further encouragement to start moaning. Beth rolled her eyes as he started on his tirade. She had heard it several times in graphic detail since she had arrived from Australia.

Her Dad carried on as if he had seen Connie only yesterday, spending the whole journey moaning about Maria and what an unhappy life he was leading. By the time they arrived at Hilltop, both sisters had switched off. Connie made the occasional "Oh dear" remark to keep him happy and then returned to her own thoughts of planning the day in London. She gave a huge sigh of relief when she drove away from Hilltop, hoping Jake would be able to cope with the two of them. She had instructed her dad not to stay too long and certainly not to give

Jake any worries about his life with Maria. Her Dad had shrugged, turned away and walked up to the main reception. Beth waved her off and followed her father into the care home.

Connie's first-class journey on the train lived up to her expectations for once. There were only a handful of passengers travelling mid-morning now that the mad frenzy of computers had arrived at their work destination. The train attendant served her a mug of tea and a croissant. She flicked through the morning newspaper that she had been handed when she sat down in her comfortable window seat. She tried hard to clear her mind of Jake and his visitors and concentrate instead on the purpose of her visit to see Mr Grey. She made some notes in her diary and checked one or two legal areas on her phone so that she would appear more business-like, even though she felt impossibly naïve and inexperienced in financial decision making.

"Oh, welcome, Mrs Wilkins. Mr Grey is expecting you and he told me to show you straight in."

Charlotte Jenks moved swiftly across the room and Connie was shown into Mr Grey's office. He stood up, shook her hand and gestured for her to sit in the chair opposite him. He had her file in front of him and he had clearly been rereading it just before she entered the room. I'm not the only one swotting up, she thought.

"Right, Connie, have you given our last conversation much thought?"

There were no pleasantries, no small talk, no asking about her journey or Jake's progress. He was a businessman focusing on the job in hand. She supposed that, as a solicitor, time was money and that many of his clients would be looking at their watches wondering how long the meeting would last and what the hourly charge was. In short, he had learned, over the years, to get straight to the point.

"Yes, and I think I have come to a decision. I really need help with the sorting out of the money and revenue from the houses. I have never had any savings to talk of. Our house is small and, up to now, we just about managed to pay the mortgage with nothing left over for anything else, so I really have no experience of dealing with these huge sums of money."

She found herself blushing, embarrassed at her ignorance, but Mr Grey tried to alleviate her discomfort:

"Well, my job is to help you become the successful businesswoman that Agnes learned to be. She started off in a very humble way, but soon understood how to become very successful." He moved a spreadsheet in front of Connie.

"These are the eight properties. As you can see, seven are rented leaving the eighth one, which is the largest property, empty. I suggest in a few minutes that we go and look at this house which is only a ten-minute walk away from here. Once inside, you might be able to decide what you want to do with it. It is all very well looking at these figures, but what you really need to do is look around your property and get the feel of the place. That is what Agnes used to do. She would stroll from room to room, looking out of the windows, checking for signs of damp or wet rot.

Connie looked alarmed and was about to say something, but Mr Grey was too quick for her. "Don't worry. You will soon recognise these problems, especially when you begin working with the Burton brothers who have agreed to maintain your houses and remodel or renovate this one. You will find them very personable, honest and extremely helpful."

Connie nodded, thinking that she didn't care how much he charged her for his services, he was worth every penny, she concluded. As they approached the empty house she gasped. The house was not large. It was huge. Connie was amazed at the proportions of the rooms. On the fourth floor the rooms shrank in dimension as they had been the servants' quarters. Their footsteps rang out as they moved from floor to floor.

"Oh, my goodness," Connie squeaked, "it is like a mansion. I had no idea any of the houses could be this large."

"Three of the other seven are almost as big and that is why you are receiving a very healthy annual income from them. I have prepared a dossier for you to take home. It contains the square footage of each house. You will also see information about who is renting each one."

Connie smiled as she opened the door of a first-floor reception room. It was flooded with light and the bay windows gave a perfect view across the park.

"Oh, it is beautiful."

"Just from the three largest rented houses alone, you will receive enough annual income to pay Jake's care home fees. These houses are highly sought after and Miss Jenks has a list of clients hoping to be able to move in to any one of them over the next few years. Rich clients are always keen to show off their wealth with enviable addresses and, you, my dear, own several of these." Mr

Grey smiled at Connie as she struggled to grasp the extent of their good fortune. She had concentrated so much on Jake up to this point that she had had little time to speculate on the London houses.

"Jake has to know about this. I wanted to keep it all from him until he was stronger. I have even made my sister promise not to say a word, but I have to tell him. If I don't, I will explode!"

By the time she was back on the train heading for Ipswich she was overwhelmed by what she had seen and heard. She replayed the visit to London in her mind a thousand times during the journey. She finally decided what she would tell Jake when she got to his room in less than an hour, traffic permitting. She looked at the photos she had taken on her phone to show him and she read the files she had been given by Mr Grey. It was exciting and daunting in equal measure. She now felt optimistic that they would be able to overcome their difficulties and cope with whatever the future had in store for them.

In fact, the visit to Jake did not take place until the following morning. Just after pulling out of Manningtree station, the train came to a halt. The muffled voice of the conductor could be heard offering an apology for what he hoped would be a short delay. Fifteen minutes later came the announcement that there had been an incident on the line. Connie immediately began to worry about Jake, having promised to visit him that evening and aware that sometimes an "incident on the line" could lead to a long wait.

An hour later, her fellow passengers seemed outwardly unperturbed. They continued to read books or newspapers, tapped away on phones, tablets or laptops or chatted to fellow passengers. After 90 minutes, and several further apologies from the conductor, a sense of frustration in the carriage became evident. Connie could hear people phoning to let family and friends know that they were going to arrive home much later than planned.

"It's been on the news that there has been an accident on the level crossing just ahead of us," said a young man sitting just in front of Connie.

"Just my luck, but what's taking so long. Surely it's easy enough to clear the line and then we can all go home," grumbled Connie.

"As far as I can make out a car entered the level crossing too quickly and somehow the rails have been damaged. I'm guessing that the car's suspension has collapsed. Apparently, the firemen have removed the car, but a rail engineer has declared the line closed."

The voice of the conductor again apologised for the delay but gave no further details even though the story of the train standstill was now the number one news item on local radio. Twitter users were having a field day moaning about the quality of the service offered by Greater Anglia. By now Connie was convinced that she would be too late to visit Jake, so she phoned Beth.

"Hi Beth. Have you heard? I'm stuck on the train just outside Manningtree."

"I've seen the news and I wondered if you'd be on that train. Don't worry, I'll pop in to let Jake know you can't make it this evening."

"I'm so grateful, Beth. Thank you so much. Please let him know that I'll be there in the morning. By the way, how did your visit go today?"

"Well, what a surprise: I've never seen Dad so animated. He was telling Jake about his arguments with Maria, but he was doing it in such an amusing way that Jake was laughing to the point that tears were rolling down his cheeks. Just as I thought he was going to revert to the character we normally see, he would say '…and another thing' and launch into a story that Jake found equally amusing."

"That's wonderful. I'm amazed because the drive to Hilltop this morning with him was quite depressing."

"He and Jake got on like a house on fire. When the entertaining stories eventually ran out, Dad concentrated on asking him questions and was extremely patient in waiting for Jake to string a sentence together."

"This is a side of Dad that I've not seen for a long time. Maybe spending time with Jake will be as good for him as it clearly is for Jake."

"By the end of the visit, Jake's speaking was definitely improving."

"That's good because I need to have an important conversation with him tomorrow."

"That sounds intriguing. Look, I have to go. I'm cooking for Dad tonight. Speak to you later."

"Thanks for everything, Beth. Where would I be without you?"

Connie noticed that people were starting to pack away their possessions.

"What's happening?" she asked the young man in front of her.

"From what I could hear on the tannoy, which is not very much, I gather that the track will not be cleared before morning, so we are being asked to leave the train."

The passengers moved towards the exit doors and Connie could see yellow-coated officials helping people leave the train. The lack of a platform meant that descending from the carriage was no easy task, even though a temporary wooden step had reduced the drop. An elderly couple had to be lifted to the ground, no doubt in contravention of all health and safety regulations, she thought wryly. The passengers were led along the track to the road just beyond the level crossing where a line of coaches was waiting to ferry people to their destinations. By the time she arrived home exhausted, after an hour on the bus to Diss and 15 minutes by taxi from the station, the whole journey from Liverpool Street had taken 6 hours.

The next morning Connie was telling Jake about her travails coming home from London.

"It's…a…good…job…you…don't…have…to…do…that…journey…ever y…day," said Jake, squeezing her hand in consolation.

After Jake had told Connie how much he had enjoyed seeing Beth and her dad, she told him all about her visit to see Mr Grey and the tour of the large house. She talked excitedly about the possibilities of converting the house to make it wheelchair-friendly for Jake and of creating other rooms where other disabled, bed-bound or wheelchair-dependent individuals could be accommodated in their own private space, with en-suite bathrooms.

"I'm thinking of starting small, Jake, of creating a luxury version of a care home where we can enable people to live as independently as possible. You could help me with the design of the building and, later on as you recover, with the running of the home. I think this is a great opportunity," she said excitedly, "to cater for your needs and also to create a new version of a care home in which we all help each other. I know it's going to be costly, especially at the beginning with all the renovations. We have the big advantage, thanks to Aunt Agnes, of having lots of money but I think we can keep running costs low by doing a lot of the work ourselves. I'm going to ask Beth and Dad if they would like to be part of this exciting new venture as well."

Jake sat thoughtfully in his chair, looking out on to the patio, the pond and the little robin that had become a daily companion.

"Like…the…idea…but…London?"

"I know it would mean uprooting our lives, but don't you think we are ready for a change?"

"Not sure."

Rather than insisting, Connie decided that it would be good for both of them to take time to reflect rather than rushing such a major decision. She changed the subject to the robin, the weather, the unreliability of Greater Anglia trains, the food at Hilltop, Carol and Mr Scott. Jake seemed unwilling to fully engage in any of these topics, whether it was because he was tired after all the chatting with Dad the day before or because he was distracted at the thought of moving to London, she was unsure. Whatever the reason, Connie could see that he was struggling to stay awake so she kissed him gently on the cheek, saying she would see him later in the day, and wandered off down the corridor.

"Hello Connie," said Clare, "how is Jake today?"

"He's fine, just a bit sleepy. That's why I'm leaving him alone for a while, so that he can sleep."

"That's a shame because I need to wake him so that he can take his tablets."

"Can't you leave him till he wakes up?"

"Afraid not. I have so many people to see and I don't want him to miss out."

"But can't you change the order so that you see Jake at the end of the round when he's a had a good rest?"

"It's easy for you to say that but it's more than my job's worth to make that sort of change. Sorry but I'll just have to rouse him."

Connie walked away seething, thinking that this was exactly why she wanted to move Jake to where she could care for him. Not only that, she wanted to be able to offer a better quality of service for others as well. For £1,200 a week, she was convinced that she could provide a better service than Mr Scott and his care staff, and more cheerfully too. Her next task was to chat with Beth and Dad. If they weren't interested in being part of this new venture, maybe she would have to think of another way forward.

Connie could see that Dad and Beth were intrigued with her proposal to set up a Care Home, but she sensed reservations too.

"OK, what's the problem? Don't you want to be involved?"

"I'm really interested and I'd like to help you, but I can't see how it's going to work for me. Travelling to London every day is not exactly convenient," said Dad.

"But you could live in the home."

"What about Maria though? I've lost one life partner and, though we are always arguing, I don't want to lose another. I really need to stay in this area with Maria because all her friends and relatives live locally and I'm pretty certain that she would not want to move to London."

"What do you think, Beth? I'd love you to be involved," said Connie, who was starting to think that her idea might need some adjustment, especially as Jake had not been madly enthusiastic about London either.

"I think your idea is superb. The idea of enabling old, infirm and disabled people to support themselves and live a fulfilling life instead of being hidden away from society and forgotten really appeals to me. What's less attractive is living in London. I've had a couple of years living in Melbourne and although I enjoyed my time there, apart from my failing relationships with boyfriends, I really do prefer being in the countryside. I like the big open skies, the clean air and the peacefulness."

"So, what you are both saying is that you are prepared to work with me on this but that you are not prepared to live in London. Is that it?"

"Yes, that's it," they said in unison.

"Ok, back to the drawing board. Let me have a think. Surely, if you are keen to help, we can find a solution though it might not be straightforward."

Over the following weeks, Connie found herself getting more irritated with the staff at Hilltop. She saw a difference in Jake too. He had become quieter when she visited him each day. He would spend a portion of her visit either asleep in his chair or looking out of the window not making any attempt to converse with her.

"What is wrong, Jake? You must tell me what is on your mind," she asked him on numerous occasions. Jake would shrug his shoulders in reply to her question leaving Connie more baffled.

She had noticed that the routine during the week went fairly smoothly most of the time and Jake seemed to enjoy seeing Kate and Mary, carers who regularly called in to his room when Connie was there. They fussed around him and made sure that his room was neat and tidy, putting away his clothes in his tiny wardrobe and clearing the surfaces of combs and toiletries that had been left out after Jake had been washed and shaved by other members of the care team. They would often bring him a mug of tea and a freshly baked biscuit from the bistro. She liked the fact that they chatted with Jake and called him 'love' and 'our young handsome hero'. She also was heartened by Jake's smile when they gave him a departing kiss on his cheek.

However, Connie's heart sank when weekends came around, particularly in the autumn months. The regular carers suddenly seemed to have a change of contract. There had been a notice pinned up on the reception welcome board about this several weeks earlier. Permanent carers would be working five days a week, Monday to Friday and were to be replaced with agency carers at weekends. Connie noticed straightaway that the agency staff who breezed in on Saturday and Sunday to tend the residents were never the same ones.

Each week there was a new team of carers. Connie was sure she had never seen the same group twice and they moved from room to room at lightning speed rousing the residents, bathing them, making beds and delivering their breakfast. There seemed to be little or no conversation with the residents whilst these tasks were performed and there were a number of agency staff who seemed to have very little English. Connie found that she too became slightly intimidated by their presence. They were strangers performing intimate tasks on confused and anxious residents who had become hostages to this new regime.

Connie noticed that Jake was troubled and watchful whenever the agency staff entered his room even when she was with him. She decided that she needed to arrive at unexpected times so that she could monitor what was going on, starting with weekends and then extending her varied visiting times during the week too. One Sunday, she was appalled to find Jake slumped in his wing chair in complete darkness. The curtains were still drawn, even though it was ten o clock, and the sun was shining brightly.

Jake was in his nightwear and his room was chaotic. His bedclothes and most of his belongings were strewn around him. Connie immediately drew back the curtains and picked up his duvet and pillows off the floor and started to make his bed. An agency carer was passing the open door and Connie called her into the room.

"What on earth has been happening in my husband's room, please?"

The carer shrugged and replied, "This isn't my floor. I work upstairs. I have no idea," and with that she turned and left the room, leaving Connie dumbfounded and immensely cross.

"This is awful, Jake. This should never happen to you. Don't worry, love, I will get you washed instead. Can you help me by standing and holding your walking frame whilst I clear a passage for you through to your bathroom?"

Jake stood up shakily, but the walking frame supported him so that Connie was able to move his large, heavy, winged chair from the centre of the floor to clear a passage for him to walk to the bathroom. She quickly gathered up his clothes and books which had been thrown down by some unknown person. In the bathroom, Connie started to give Jake a gentle body wash with a soapy facecloth. She noticed a set of bruises up his right arm. They looked as though they were a few days old.

"How on earth did you get these marks, Jake? Has someone been rough with you?"

Jake nodded and, at that moment, he started to lose his balance. Connie quickly gave him support to stop him falling over and managed to move him across to sit on the toilet whilst she dragged his wheelchair into his small bathroom space.

"Sit down, Jake," she gasped as she manoeuvred him on to his wheelchair, "now don't worry, I will sort this out. You don't have to get upset. Is this why you have seemed unhappy and quiet recently?"

Once again, Jake nodded. He took a deep breath and replied, "I...didn't want...to...worry you."

"Oh, Jake, my love, this is appalling." She pushed his chair in front of the window. "I am not going to let this continue. Let me just finish off here so you can be dressed and ready for the day. Then I am going to complain to Mr Scott as soon as you are settled."

Once he was dressed, Connie left Jake in his room eating a bowl of cereal which she had collected from the dining room and she went storming down the corridor to the main reception area. The administration offices were nicely tucked away behind the front reception. Connie knocked on Mr Scott's door.

"Come in," he called. She marched in and stood in front of his desk, even though he had asked her to take a seat. She began her attack of the state of the care Jake was now receiving. "I suppose it means that the honeymoon period is now over for Jake?"

"I am not sure what you mean by that Mrs Wilkins. Can you give me detailed examples of why you are so upset?"

Connie began her account, not pausing for ten minutes.

"On every occasion recently at weekends, I have found Jake sitting in his wheelchair wearing his pyjamas at ten o clock. His breakfast bowl and mug are left on his side table not having been cleared away. Today, however, I think your agency staff have surpassed themselves, Mr Scott."

She went through the turmoil in Jake's room, his bruises and the off-hand manner of the passing agency carer. As frustration burst through her lips, she continued her list of irritations and concerns.

"On at least three occasions, when I have arrived to visit my husband, I have found Jake wearing someone else's jumper or tee-shirt. A new fleece top which I bought him only two weeks ago has been returned from the laundry several sizes too small for him. Clearly, whoever has been doing the residents' laundry has been washing the clothes at the wrong temperature."

"You can claim for the cost of the article, Mrs Wilkins. If you fill in one of our forms and supply us with the shop receipt, we will be happy to reimburse you."

Connie's face grew more strained. "And what happens if I haven't kept the receipt, please, Mr Scott?"

"Well, we would have to agree on some figure that would buy a replacement article of clothing…"

"Oh, for goodness' sake. This is so annoying." Connie's voice got louder. "Even though all his clothes have been marked with his name, several items have recently gone astray. I have started a new routine going down to the basement and rifling through the drying garments to find his clothing. This shouldn't be the case, Mr Scott. You have to improve your system, or the men will soon be wearing the women's clothes and vice versa."

Mr Scott took off his glasses, smiled at the last image and began to clean his lenses as Connie got even more annoyed.

"The other day, I noticed Tom, who lives four doors from my husband, sporting Jake's jumper that Beth, my sister, had bought him for his birthday. He had only worn it once and it was immediately collected by one of the carers to be washed. Obviously, hygiene is important, I can see that, but you have to have some respect for the belongings of the residents. After all, this is their home and they are paying a fortune for this service."

"Have you spoken to any of the carers about all these concerns, Mrs Wilkins?"

"Obviously I have." Connie recalled how she complained to Clare and anyone who would stop and listen to her for more than five minutes. The tacit message was 'Don't disturb us, we are far too busy. What do you expect with communal living?'

"It's just not good enough, Mr Scott. When you showed me around Hilltop you assured me that no agency staff were employed here. That was one of the main reasons for selecting this care home for my husband. It is important for residents to know who is caring for them. I am complaining on behalf of my husband, but you have quite a number of residents who don't have anyone to fight on their behalf." She paused whilst she got her breath back. "I think it would be a useful exercise for you to leave this office and walk around the corridors so you can see for yourself how your residents are being treated by the agency staff and also by some of your own permanent carers."

"Yes, well, now that your complaints have come to my notice, I will have a walk around as you say." He remained seated and rifled for a form for Connie to fill in. Connie snatched the form which was proffered. She was exhausted by her own tirade.

"Now would be a good time, Mr Scott."

Connie turned away and stormed out of the office, heading back towards Jake's room. She heard footsteps behind her and somebody tugged at the sleeve of her jacket. She turned to see Kate, a carer liked by Jake and now seen as a friend to both of them, beckoning her into an empty room, holding a finger up to her lips to encourage her not to speak. Kate closed the door and whispered:

"Sorry to startle you but I wanted a word with you in private. We need to speak quietly because these walls are not very thick, and I don't want to be overheard. Please don't tell anybody that I've spoken to you because I don't want to lose my job."

"Don't worry, Kate, I certainly won't be speaking to that boss of yours in a hurry. When I first met him, I thought he was impressive but I'm beginning to realise how incompetent he is."

"At least you don't have to work for him! He's always asking me to do extra hours at the last minute because somebody hasn't turned up for work. I don't feel I can refuse because I need the job and the money and also because I can't bear the thought of there not being enough staff on duty, particularly overnight and at weekends to look after the residents. I am very fond of Jake, and I love the way that you, Beth and your dad are doing all you can to support him."

"And we very much appreciate the help that you and Mary in particular give to Jake. However, after making very good progress in the first two or three weeks here, I feel Jake has declined: his speech is not improving, and he seems downcast a lot of the time."

"Because we don't have enough carers, he is not getting the attention he needs. I've noticed that whenever visitors arrive, Mr Scott checks who they are here to see and then instructs us to call in the room to clean the bathroom, sort out clothing, give medication and so on. In other words when you, Beth and your dad visit Jake an impression of constant support for him is created but as soon as you leave things go back to normal. We are supposed to answer the buzzer requesting attention within 3 minutes, but the reality is that it might be closer to 30 because there just are not enough of us."

"I'd suspected as much because some of his clothes have disappeared and yesterday it was obvious that he had not been shaved."

"I'm only saying this because I regard you as a friend, Connie, but it's risky for me because I could lose my job. One of my carer friends is no longer working here and the rumour is that Mr Scott sacked her for telling a family that their father was not receiving adequate support."

"Don't worry, Kate. I've just had a row with Mr Scott so he knows I'm not satisfied and that was before you spoke to me."

"The problem is worse overnight. As you know, many of the carers are young women with childcare responsibilities and they refuse, quite rightly in my view, to do the overnight shift. As a result, Mr Scott brings in temporary agency staff who, with the best will in the world, struggle to get to know the residents. This means that no sooner has Jake established a relationship with a carer than they leave. You may have noticed that Mary and I are the only ones who have worked here for more than a couple of years. People come and then before long they leave."

"Why is that, Kate? Is it because the pay is so poor?"

"Well, we are only paid the minimum wage."

"And it's such important work that you do."

"Yes, the money is terrible, but the atmosphere is not good which makes things even worse. Mr Scott never speaks to us and when he does, he very quickly becomes annoyed. And so we don't like to speak to him when we see issues that need sorting."

"I've already spotted that Mr Scott is part of the problem, Kate, and I'm thinking that we need to find a better solution for Jake."

Kate's pager buzzed: "I'll have to go, Connie, but there's one more thing I need to say. Have you noticed the bruising on Jake's arms?"

"Yes, I've mentioned that to Mr Scott already."

"I came to work a bit earlier than usual before the staff on the night shift had left. As I went past Jake's room, I could hear shouting, so I opened the door and found two staff that I've never met before, one man and one woman, tugging Jake by the wrist, trying to yank him out of bed. There had clearly been a struggle as the two carers were red-faced with their exertions and looked quite angry. Jake, on the other hand, looked distressed and his bedding was in complete disarray. 'He won't let us get him out of bed', said the man, with a foreign accent. Clearly, Jake had soiled the bed because the smell was overwhelming."

Connie's eyes filled with tears at the thought of Jake's situation: incontinent, unable to help himself and at the mercy of uncaring carers.

"I told the overnight staff to leave the room," continued Kate. "I helped Jake out of bed, showered him, dressed him and removed the soiled bedding and replaced it with fresh sheets. Then I made us both a cup of tea and sat down to talk to him. It took a while for his anger to subside. Apparently, he had needed to use the toilet so had pressed the buzzer to ask for help but nobody arrived, and he had been unable to prevent himself from soiling the bed. This was upsetting enough for him but when the two carers finally arrived, a few minutes before I appeared on the scene, they were furious, shouting at Jake, blaming him for the extra work he had created.

"When they tried to get him out of bed, Jake used all his strength, weak as he is, to resist them. He knew they would be rough with him in the shower and he wanted to wait for somebody else to help him. When I examined his arms, the imprints of their fingers were still visible. The skin was swollen and red and already starting to darken in colour."

"I noticed the bruising because it lasted for more than a week. Did you tell Mr Scott about this?"

"Yes, he said he would look into it. I wouldn't be surprised if nothing has happened." The pager on Kate's uniform bleeped again. "I really must go. I just needed to tell you."

"Thank you so much. I really appreciate your whistle-blowing on this. After all, how many other residents are being roughly handled too?"

Connie marched down the corridor in search of Mr Scott, only to see him disappearing through the front door, getting into his car and driving out of the carpark. "If he thinks, he's going to escape that easily, he has another thing coming," she muttered, deciding to check Kate's account with Jake himself. He was asleep when she arrived in his room, so she wheeled a trolley that had been left in the corridor into the room, loaded up all his belongings and transferred them into the boot of her car. She returned, roused Jake and helped him into his wheelchair.

"Where are we going?" he asked in bemusement.

"We're going home, Jake. I've had enough of this place."

"So have I, but I didn't like to say. I was afraid of causing even more bother for you." Jake had a look of relief on his face, and it remained there as Connie bundled him into the car, drove home and wheeled him through the front door of their house.

"It's great to be back home, it really is, but how are we going to cope?"

"As a temporary measure we can convert the sofa in the lounge into a bed, so you won't need to go upstairs to the bedroom. Thank goodness, we have a downstairs toilet as well. You can now wheel yourself into there and I'll help you whenever necessary. When I need to leave the house, I'll ask Beth to come round. I'm going to ask Dad to fit some grab-rails so that you can pull yourself out of the wheelchair too."

"My mobility is slowly improving but it's still going to be tough because I've become so used to Kate, Mary and the others helping me."

"You know what they say, Jake. When the going gets tough, the tough get going. We've all had a difficult time in the last few months, but we have survived and we are going to meet this new challenge in the same way. I'm going to phone Beth in a minute to see if she and Dad are still prepared to help us. After I've done that, I have a job for you. I want you to record on my mobile phone all the details of your mistreatment at Hilltop. You don't need to rush because there is plenty of battery life."

Whilst Jake slowly recounted episodes of mistreatment, particularly by temporary care workers, and the general incompetence of Mr Scott in managing the home and its staff, Connie rearranged the furniture in the lounge so that there was enough space for the wheelchair to park next to the sofa. She then brought some bedlinen from upstairs and made the sofa into a comfortable bed. By the time she had also made a pot of tea, Jake had finished his sad account.

"I'd no idea it was as bad as that, Jake. Once you've drunk this tea, I'll help you into bed because you look tired."

Connie was just sipping her tea when her mobile rang. "Hello Beth. You're the very person I want to talk to. Can you and Dad come round here tomorrow? I've brought Jake home and I need help because I want to go to Hilltop to speak to Mr Scott."

The following morning, Beth arrived early to check on the still sleeping Jake.

"He'll be fine for a while," said Connie. "He takes time to get going in the morning. You know where everything is in the kitchen for his breakfast and help yourself to whatever you fancy. What time is Dad arriving?"

"He said he would be here by 11 with his toolbox after he has collected some wood for the handrails that he is going to install. You don't need to worry about us. Enjoy your visit to Hilltop."

"I will. Thanks for helping out. I should be home by the afternoon."

Connie arrived at Hilltop just as Mr Scott was getting out of his car and she followed him into his office.

"Can I have a word, Mr Scott?"

"I'm really busy today but please have a seat. Would you like a coffee?"

"No thanks. I want to get straight down to business. From what I have seen, it's clear to me that you are struggling to run this home effectively. The care you are providing is in my view inadequate."

Mr Scott's brow furrowed. He spluttered: "We do our best. I'm sorry you take that view."

"Your best is not good enough and I want to do something about it. I want to buy this care home and run it myself."

"How do you think you can possibly do that?" Mr Scott was now smiling, thinking that this woman had taken leave of her senses.

"I want you to contact head office and tell them that I'm going to buy this place. I will pay a fair price and I'm sure they will sell because it's obvious that the company is in financial difficulty. Let's face it, you don't have the budget to hire enough staff. That's why you are recruiting untrained carers on hourly rates. That's why Jake has been mistreated by people who don't understand the job and care even less. That's why the food is poorly cooked and served cold. That's why residents are left to eat alone even when they don't have the strength to feed themselves. That's why the buzzer is unanswered for so long and why so many beds are soiled. And that's why residents are left unwashed, unshaven, unclothed for such long periods.

Connie was really warming to her theme now. "That's why, Mr Scott, you will approach your boss at Head Office and tell them that I will take this place off the company's hands. My research tells me that the firm is going bankrupt in any case. It will be no help to them if I tell my story to the press. Nor will it help them to fight an expensive legal case against me. It makes sense for the company to sell to me so please explain that clearly to your boss. If you want me to speak directly, feel free to arrange a meeting. Be in no doubt that I can afford to do what I say, Mr Scott, and that I mean to go to any lengths to ensure that Hilltop belongs to me and Jake."

Mr Scott was stunned and sat in silence throughout Connie's diatribe. He knew in his heart that most of what Connie was saying was true. The company for whom he worked was failing. His best chance of staying in work might well be to collaborate with this fearsome lady. "I'll do my best," was all he said, before she stormed out of his office.

"You'd better," she shouted as she headed out into the carpark.

Three weeks later, Connie and Jonathan Grey entered the offices of Home from Home. They were shown into the Managing Director's office and John Thompson shook both their hands and indicated where they were to sit for the meeting. Connie could see the transcript of Jake's taped experiences on his desk. She had sent him a copy of Jake's story accompanied by a detailed account of her own dealings with the staff at Hilltop and a letter indicating her intention to purchase the care home.

Jonathan Grey had also sent out a more official request and had indicated what they considered a fair price was for the premises and all the furnishings. He had also explained that if they purchased the business, they would be writing a new contract of employment for many of the existing staff with the exception of a small number who would be offered severance packages.

John Thompson was just about to launch into his prepared speech about the difficulties the owners of care homes face and how the money is quickly gobbled up with maintenance bills and such like, when Jonathan Grey briskly addressed him.

"You now have a record of our concerns so we presume you will be pleased to sell Hilltop to my client at the price we have offered. I have a detailed breakdown here," he indicated to the file on his knee, "of the financial difficulties that your company is currently facing. My client has serious grounds of concern and I have recommended that she should take your company to court for neglect and physical abuse of her husband whilst he has been in the care of your staff at Hilltop. We also have a key witness of the abuse he suffered at the hands of the agency staff who worked there whilst employed by your company and a photograph of his bruises.

"We are not using this as a threat, Mr Thompson, as we believe it would be in the best interests of yourself and your residents to avoid adverse publicity. It would not bode well for the future of the three other care homes that you own as, no doubt, your clients' relatives would soon be thinking of finding alternate accommodation for their loved ones if they read in the papers of the dreadful treatment that has been meted out in one of your homes. If it can happen at Hilltop, then surely it can happen at the homes that their relatives live in.

Jonathan Grey paused and checked the expression on John Thompson's face. He noticed a slight twitching at the corner of his mouth and then he was sure that they would be purchasing the care home.

"We are not going to haggle over the price, Mr Thompson. My client is a very fair person and she does not want your residents in the other homes having to face increased fees as a result of her bargaining. She does, however, want to take over the business at Hilltop in its entirety, which includes all your clients, the furnishings and everything which we have listed in the documents you have received from us. You will know, from your own research, that your business is not really worth what Mrs Wilkins is prepared to pay. She will take over the business forthwith once you have signed the documents we sent you and the money will be transferred into your account within the week. What do you say, Mr Thompson?"

There was a lengthy pause and Connie held her breath whilst she watched both men closely. John Thompson was about to launch his defence but thought better of it. He coughed, twisted his wedding ring three times, then turned his gaze towards Connie.

"I accept your offer, Mrs Wilkins. I am prepared to sell my business to you at the price stated in these documents. My solicitor will draw up the necessary transfer papers and he will send them to Mr Grey. I hope you will be able to make Hilltop work. It isn't as easy as it looks, Mrs Wilkins. You are dependent on the daily goodwill of your staff to ensure everything runs smoothly. Clearly, from the transcript of your husband's account, we have failed him and we are sorry that this is the case. We actually went into this business for the same reason as you, Mrs Wilkins.

"My wife and I wanted to make the lives of elderly and fragile people better. Unfortunately, soaring costs and the threat of Brexit which has affected the lives of many of our staff means that we have in the last couple of years got into difficulties. I am very saddened to think we have failed you and your husband. It isn't the type of feedback we had hoped for but nevertheless, we wish you luck and success for Hilltop's future."

He bent forward, took out an expensive fountain pen from his breast pocket and signed the documents which Jonathan Grey had laid out on the table. Connie was also asked to sign where he indicated. Once the documents were signed all three parties took it in turn to shake the other's hands. Mr Grey gathered the documents together and secreted them away inside his briefcase leaving a copy on the table for Mr Thompson.

"I really do wish you luck, Mrs Wilkins. I will be ploughing your money into my other care homes so that the lives of my residents can be more comfortable and secure. I don't suppose you will be employing Mr Scott as the manager of the home based on what both you and Mr Wilkin have said in your statements."

Connie just smiled at him and her silence was enough of an answer.

"Goodbye, Mr Thompson. I do hope in future you are more attentive towards your other residents than you were at Hilltop." With that, she turned and headed for the door closely followed by Mr Grey.

After the formalities were over, Connie accompanied Mr Grey to his office to finish talking through the arrangements. When they arrived, Jonathan nodded at Charlotte Jenks who scuttled into the side room and returned with a tray containing two flutes of champagne.

"This was always the tradition with Agnes," he explained. "Whenever a deal was completed successfully, we would toast the new property. She believed this ritual always seemed to bring her luck so she would never leave my office until we had had our drink. You don't mind, do you?"

"I don't think I could ever turn down champagne and, let's face it, I have only ever bought one property before now and I think Jake and I toasted that purchase over a cup of tea, so I am happy to continue Aunt Agnes's tradition. If it was lucky for her, then let us hope the same luck rubs off on Jake and me. Cheers," she exclaimed as they chinked glasses and had their first mouthful.

As the bubbles cascaded down her throat, Connie had to reassure herself that she wasn't dreaming. She had just become the owner of a large and attractive care home, was also the owner of several breathtakingly expensive London properties and still had a fortune in the bank and here she was drinking expensive champagne at 4 in the afternoon to celebrate her latest success. She was amazed at how, in such a short time, her life had been transformed. She again raised her glass.

"To Jake and his recovery."

"Now, Connie, have you given any thought to the house we visited a few months ago? I think you really should be thinking about what to do with it. It is not a good idea to leave it empty for long as squatters will soon know about it and then you will have a real headache trying to remove them from your property. Even though it is in a prime location, these streets are regularly scrutinised by gangs who want to move in or remove fittings and such like."

Connie looked troubled by what he had just said. She took another sip and explained how Jake and she had discussed what to do with the property.

"Jake was really unhappy about moving to London as he wants to have the comfort of familiar surroundings to help him get stronger." She explained her initial plans and what the responses were from her sister and father. "So, you see, no one wants to move to London, which is a pity, as I quite fancied a city life for a change. I really enjoy my trips to London to see you and discuss business, but I don't suppose living here is the same as visiting for the day. Anyway, we think that if we sell that enormous house then we could have ready cash to upgrade Hilltop and eventually buy a brand new flat that Jake and I could use in the future when he is stronger and less exhausted."

"Do you want me to put the property up for sale in that case?"

"Yes, and the sooner the better based on what you have just told me. I never thought that the house could be at risk and I have no idea what it is worth, so if we could leave this to you to fix the price, sort out the details and the advertising, then we would be really grateful."

"Charlotte," Jonathan called his secretary who emerged from her office, "please could you contact our property valuers and then start the process rolling of putting Lyndhurst on the market. If you could do some research today, then we could have the property on sale by the end of the week."

Charlotte Jenks cleared the glasses and returned to her office. Within minutes, they could hear her in the distance speaking with the valuer. The valuation would take place the next day. Connie was comforted by the swiftness of the actions. She mused on how long it would have taken her to trawl the Internet of similar properties, google the estate agents and eventually agree with some unknown agent the price the property would be sold for.

She looked across at Jonathan who was sorting through the file he had taken to John Thompson's office, checking on the papers from the earlier transaction. She could see why Agnes had had so much trust in him. He had an old-fashioned, but honest air about him. He was obviously being paid handsomely for his services, in fact her mind whirled when she considered his hourly rate, but he seemed a genuinely decent man and she was confident that she could leave the business in his competent hands.

Chapter 10

Three months later, Jake was reflecting on the rapid changes that had taken place since Connie had completed the purchase of Hilltop. Gradually his health was improving: his speech had more or less returned to normal apart from occasional difficulties when he couldn't remember a word; his mobility was still restricted in that he was spending most of his time in a wheelchair but, supported by Beth and the exercises she had devised to develop the muscles in his legs, he was walking a few extra paces each day. He was also able to contribute to the running of Hilltop for a couple of hours on most days and, in fact, his desire to be involved in their newly acquired care home business was one of the reasons that he and Connie had moved into Hilltop more or less full-time.

They had created a wheelchair-friendly flat at one end of the building so that they were always on-site to deal with emergencies and also to ensure that their staff maintained high standards of care at all times. Jake had emphasised to Connie from the outset that their care home would be only as good as the quality of people they recruited so they agreed that Jake would always be present at recruitment interviews. After several months of feeling cut off from the world, he was enjoying his involvement in the business and also in being surrounded by residents who did not view him simply as a dependent patient but as a co-owner of the home.

Jake and Connie had called a meeting to explain the change of ownership to the residents and their families, outlining their vision of high-quality care with no increase in fees. One very sick old lady died the day after the takeover, but the rest showed their faith in the new owners by deciding to stay at Hilltop, though Connie was under no illusion that they needed to back up their vision with actions in order to keep their rooms full. Even a small number of empty rooms would undermine the sustainability of the business.

Connie had taken over the general management of Hilltop from Peter Scott from the very first day. Mr Scott was contractually entitled to a month's notice, but Connie was keen to make a fresh start so paid him his salary and told him not to return. However, running a care home is a 24 hour a day commitment and it was vital to recruit somebody they could trust and who had the right approach towards the work. Connie thought back to Jake's time in Seaview convalescent home and the expert way that Jennie had helped him to start speaking again. Would Jennie be prepared to take a risk on leaving her secure job and manage Hilltop?

The timing was perfect because Jennie was ready for a new challenge. The discussion with Jennie helped Connie to realise that she needed to recruit another manager who, alongside herself, Jennie and Jake, could form a four-person management team who would work shifts so that one of them was always on duty. Once Jennie had agreed to join them at Hilltop, Connie discussed the need for another manager with Jake.

"Have you considered asking Beth? She has been a massive help to me. Would she be interested in building a career here rather than returning to Australia?"

"That's a great idea, Jake. I'll ask her."

Beth's enthusiasm for the role surprised Connie.

"I've done a lot of travelling over the last couple of years in Australia, but I now realise that I am ready to settle down and do something worthwhile. Working with Jake and seeing him improve has actually made me aware that helping others motivates me so I'd love to take on this challenge with you. Thank you so much for the offer. By the way, have you thought about offering a role to Dad? He has been a changed man since he's been helping with Jake's care."

"I would like Dad to be responsible for everything to do with the maintenance of the building. He has been such a help in so many practical ways in recent months. Would you mind mentioning that to him?"

It turned out that Andy was just as keen as Beth to play a part in the Hilltop adventure. The next task was to focus on the rest of the staff. Connie had decided with Jake, Beth and Jennie that the only way to build a new culture was to terminate all contracts and to ask everybody to apply for newly created posts. Connie had seen from her experiences with Jake the importance of carers who, as well as being responsible and hard-working, were cheerful and really enjoyed working with people.

Jake knew quite a lot about many of the individuals already employed but he was given the task of moving around Hilltop to observe each in action and to write a brief report on his findings. By the time the one-to-one interviews were held, Connie already knew which colleagues she wanted to remain at Hilltop and which ones she would be asking to leave. A complicating factor was that the government's plans to leave the European Union, so-called Brexit, meant that some of her Eastern European staff might not be allowed to remain in the country. She had also been told by the local employment agency that European nationals were now reluctant to move to the UK. In addition, people who already lived in the local area were often able to earn more money in supermarkets, so the pool of potential recruits was small.

Nevertheless, Connie was determined that only the best individuals would be appointed on permanent contracts. The rest would be offered temporary contracts and the opportunity to prove themselves until better replacements could be found.

Jake attended all the interviews and proved particularly adept at asking probing questions which illuminated the strengths and weaknesses of each applicant. The interview process was useful for uncovering the hidden skills and talents of their staff. They discovered that Jurgen, who had grown up in East Berlin before the collapse of the Berlin Wall in 1989, had managed to escape to the West by clambering over the wall in the middle of the night and was wounded by the gunfire of the sentries.

He eventually built a career as a music teacher in a German school. He met and married an English girl who was working as an assistant teacher of English in the same school. Jurgen's wife, Jackie, had been keen to return to her native Suffolk so they had set up home just outside Diss, close to Jackie's parents, and Jurgen worked at the local high school. Tragedy struck when Jackie was diagnosed with motor neurone disease at the age of 41. Gradually she lost the strength in her muscles and within a year became so weak that Jurgen had to give up his job to care for her full-time. He had to feed her, wash her, lift her in and out of bed but struggled alone, too proud to ask for help until finally a neighbour convinced him that he could not continue on his own and recommended Hilltop as a possible care home.

Jurgen was so desperate that he started to consider a possibility which twelve months previously he would have discounted without a second's thought. Mr Roberts had been on sick leave on the day of his visit, so he had been welcomed and shown round the home by Kate who had impressed him greatly. She was so understanding of his predicament, and he could see, as they walked round the home, how cheerfully and respectfully she engaged with all the residents. Jurgen said that he would only move Jackie into the home if he could work there as a carer too, so Jackie spent the last two years of her life at Hilltop, supported by Jurgen and the other carers who made her sad decline as dignified as possible.

Jurgen had always gained a lot of satisfaction from teaching his pupils, but enabling the residents to lead a happy life in their final years gave him a level of fulfilment he had never experienced before, so he continued to work at Hilltop after Jackie's death.

"What about your music teaching?" asked Jake when he and Connie were interviewing him.

"I don't work in school any longer. Obviously, my full-time work here takes priority, but I run a choir for adults every Tuesday evening and we give the occasional public concert to raise funds for the Motor Neurone Disease Association charity."

Jurgen spoke very clearly but with a still strong German accent which had perhaps discouraged Mr Roberts from exploiting his talents at Hilltop more fully.

"I've realised that the days in Hilltop are very long for our residents. Many, like me, have mobility issues and rarely leave the home and it's very easy to become isolated so I'd like to introduce more activities that bring people together and which are fun. Would you be prepared to set up a choir here?" asked Jake, looking at Connie for approval as this was an idea they had not discussed.

"What a great idea. Why did we not think of it before? What do you say, Jurgen?" said Connie.

"I'd love to, but do you think there would be enough interest?"

"As long as you use material that they remember from their younger days, I suspect you'll be able to recruit quite a few members. Let's agree anyway that we are offering you a full-time permanent contract as a member of staff. In addition, we'll pay you for your work with the choir," said Connie glancing at Jake to check he agreed. "I think you will inject much-needed energy into the home. I'm quite excited about it."

The interview with Jurgen led Jake and Connie to question the other members of staff very carefully about their previous experiences. One of the part-time staff, Andrea, a cheerful lady, always full of energy, explained her situation.

"I can only work part-time because my partner and I have separated and I have two young children who are just starting primary school. I'm also very worried about being allowed to stay in the UK after Brexit. Who knows? It's all so unsettling."

"We certainly want you to stay and we'll do all we can to help with that. You are just the sort of person we want at Hilltop," said Jake.

They were aware that Andrea had moved to the UK in the mid-2000s, in search of a better life, had been living with her English boyfriend, but that the relationship had broken down recently, leaving her to cope alone with their two children.

"Life is hard at the moment, but I love my children and my work here. I'm an optimist so maybe things will turn out OK. When the children are in bed, I amuse myself with my painting. When I was at school in Romania, I loved art lessons and wanted to study art at college but the opportunity to come to England arose when Romania joined the European Union and I forgot about going to college. Painting is still my hobby. It's so relaxing."

Without further ado, Jake and Connie offered Andrea a permanent part-time contract and asked whether she would consider setting up an Art Club for the residents.

"Now that your children are at primary school, could you spare one or two mornings a week to run a club for residents who want to do some painting?" asked Connie. "I've noticed one or two do quite a bit of sketching in their rooms. We'll provide whatever materials you need and of course we'll pay you too."

Andrea's eyes shone with excitement at the thought that she would finally be able to exploit her artistic skills.

"I'd love to create a group. I hope they'll get as much pleasure from painting as I do. Yes, I'm sure they will."

"We're starting to make progress, Jake," said Connie after Andrea left the room. "I want this home to be fun as well as caring. I wonder how many others have hidden talents that we can exploit?"

"Let's see," said Jake. "Of course, we need to keep an eye on the budget, but these activities are all pretty inexpensive. Maybe some of the residents themselves also have skills we know nothing about and could organise activities? A good morning's work though, Connie. Time for lunch?"

During their lunch break Sam, the head chef, joined them at their table to discuss the following week's menus. He had increased his range since Connie and Jake had taken over. He had added vegetarian choices and a buffet of desserts which the residents could help themselves to. All the original selections were still available as Sean didn't want to have a riot on his hands from the diehards who liked a simple uncomplicated diet. He thought of Alice who was now 93 years old. "It's Friday, Sam, I hope there is fish on the menu," she said each week and he knew that she wouldn't eat anything if her established way of dining was altered radically. However, his new selection, but especially the strawberry pavlovas, were becoming popular with the residents, and he was keen to broaden his range further. He found the new owners inspiring and his previous intention of leaving Hilltop was now replaced by a burning desire to build a 5-star eating reputation.

"I was thinking this morning that I could do some food demonstrations once a week if you like. I could clear an area in the meeting room just by the kitchen, set out a couple of rows of chairs and I could roll a range of equipment into the room on a trolley. I would then be able to cook a few dishes in front of the residents whilst talking through what I was doing, where the food had been sourced and how we could vary the dish I was demonstrating by adding other ingredients. We could then have a tasting session and they could grade what they had tasted. It would be a bit like the television programme with chefs being judged by the experts. Let's face it, most of our residents are experts on the type of menus enjoyed by older folk, even though they are fighting with false teeth or sore gums most of the time. It might even become a TV programme. The first broadcast from inside a care home!"

Sean was really warming to his subject. His passion was infectious and both Jake and Connie nodded at all of his suggestions. He seemed to grow in stature as he spoke and his face, which at one time rarely broke into a smile, lit up as he described his ideas.

"Andy, the young lad who makes the puddings, has also said he wouldn't mind having a baking club for the residents. He thought that he could have them making scones for the teatime slot initially, and then, they could learn to bake all the afternoon fancy cakes which we could take round to the residents in their rooms along with their afternoon cup of tea. We could also put them out for the visitors to eat when they are with their relatives in the bistro area. What do you think? We could even have our very own Bake Off challenge as the residents get more confident.

Sean chortled as his thoughts developed rapidly. "Gladys was telling me only the other day that she hadn't baked a thing for the last eight years and she missed it dreadfully as she had spent most of her life baking for her family. Apparently, for the last few years before she came to Hilltop when she was in her eighties, she had also baked cakes and biscuits for the church meetings she used to attend.

"You know, she even has her old recipe book in her room. It is a notebook full of handwritten recipes that she used for years. She showed it to me yesterday when I delivered her afternoon tea. If we could get these clubs going, we would help many of them to recover the part of themselves that has been lost or neglected. The old saying 'if you don't use it, you lose it' is especially relevant for our old people and surely that can't be right."

Sean paused and watched Connie scribbling down all his ideas in her notebook. When she had completed her notes, she looked up at him and then reached across and gave him a hug.

"Thanks ever so much, Sam. This is just what we need. We want to restore dignity and purpose to our clients, but also make it clear that life is still exciting. Oh, how I hate that word. We call them clients or residents. Just the words alone take away their dignity. These people live here, this is their home. They are family members who share the same roof and now these suggestions of yours and Andy are just the type of thing that will make them feel involved in the running of their home, in the same way they used to make decisions about their previous homes when they were younger.

"You know, it has just struck me that we now need to ask them all what they really want to have on offer here. Your ideas have made me realise that our residents—no, family members—are the ones who have to tell us what they miss about the lives they lived before they came to Hilltop and then we must try to meet those needs as best we can.

She looked across at Jake who was nodding vigorously.

"When you have a moment, could you and Andy write a list of all the equipment you will both need to get your demonstrations and clubs up and running. You could then start to calculate what ingredients you will need each week to ensure the clubs run efficiently. Jake and I will discuss what we are going to pay you both for these activities. I know you get a salary from us, but these ideas are certainly over and above your normal work and we will pay you both well for what you do. I actually now wonder whether you also need extra hands in your kitchen, Sam? Talk it through with Andy and let us know whether you need any more cooks or assistants. We will then do our best to swell your numbers."

Sean returned to the kitchen his enthusiasm and excitement reflected in his demeanour as he left the room. Connie and Jake looked across at each other and again smiled.

"Oh, Connie, love, it is starting to be the place we had hoped for and it makes me feel so proud of you as you have caused this change to take place."

As the days went on, they both felt that Hilltop was definitely changing for the better. There was suddenly new energy in the place. News got around fast and at the weekly staff meeting Connie shared their vision with everyone and told them about the activities that had been offered at this stage. Within hours, other staff were offering all sorts of hobbies and the range of ideas was mind-blowing to Connie.

Who would have thought that Stella, the cleaner, was an advanced bridge player? She wanted to offer a bridge school three times a week after her cleaning shift ended at 2.30. Janice, one of the administration staff, wanted to have a corner of the hairdressing salon to offer manicure and nail design. Phil, the head gardener, offered weekly talks about gardening and trips to local gardens. The list just kept growing and Connie now had the task of coordinating the schedule of these new clubs and activities.

However, the enthusiasm wasn't just felt by the staff. The care team couldn't help gossiping to the 'family members' about these changes and the older folk became excited about the changes that were taking place. As Christmas drew near, Sally from the laundry, was busy rehearsing the large number of residents who had volunteered to be in the pantomime. She had been involved in amateur dramatics for many years and so was able to provide a considerable wardrobe of outfits for these new Hilltop actors.

Sally, assisted by young Charlie who worked with Phil in the gardens, chose Cinderella for their first production based on the number of available costumes. They began their rehearsals and Gladys's great granddaughter was recruited to be Cinders and Phil's grandson was to be the prince. The script was written by John Richards, a Hilltop resident, who revealed that he had been a professional actor when he was younger. Not only that, he was a fine musician. He explained that at drama school he had been trained to play at least three musical instruments, as well as act, sing and dance.

Jurgen was particularly interested in John's past and spent time chatting with him and they soon developed a friendship based on their love for music. Even though John was twice Jurgen's age, the two of them sitting together in the lounge listening to all different genres of music, was a wonderful sight. Jurgen had gained a father figure in John and John, who had never married, had found a son to share his interests. They were seen on many occasions chatting in the corridors or in the dining room.

Jurgen started to take John out for drives into the countryside during his lunch break so that they could listen to 'The Lark Ascending' as they negotiated the narrow lanes. Elgar, William Walton and Vaughan Williams were listened to and discussed in detail, both men eager to explain their preferences and criticisms of whatever had just been playing.

"Now, listen to that violin, Jurgen. You can visualise the bird soaring almost into the sky. The note is as light as a feather and perfectly captures the manoeuvres of the little bird."

"Yes, and you would never have guessed that such a delicate and beautiful sound was produced on the cusp of the first world war in 1914. No wonder it became a favourite of generations because it allowed people to remember former times when the world was not struggling with war and terror."

And so, the hour's drive continued and by the time they returned to Hilltop the two music critics were either in total agreement or at odds with each other. "Well, let us just remember that music is an individual taste" was the parting comment when they had challenged each other's choice. Their music appreciation soon delved into modern music and they found themselves discussing the merits of Ed Sheeran as they passed through Framlingham.

The pantomime was well underway by late November and the lunchtime drives had to be put on the back burner whilst John immersed himself in his acting commitments. Jurgen was often in the rehearsal room watching John step out of the body of an old man and transformed into another character. With John in the role of Buttons, rehearsals often became hysterically funny. He had a range of voices which mimicked beautifully the prime minister, various celebrities and he even had a stab at being Connie, invariably beginning her sentences with 'Oh Jake…" Everyone laughed and Connie blushed as she watched the rehearsal. She hadn't been aware that she ever used this phrase but the laughter from everyone in the room confirmed John's keen observation.

Phil had managed to borrow a number of musical instruments from the local secondary school which his grandson attended and the pantomime changed shape, with a greater musical element, much to the delight of Jurgen and John. Jurgen found himself in charge of the practice sessions with a small group of aged musicians who, in their youth, could play the piano, trumpet, violin and saxophone.

"Why don't we call ourselves the Hilltop Players?" offered Cyril, who played the saxophone rather rustily.

"Brilliant idea," agreed Jurgen, "maybe we can do some concerts once we've finished working on the pantomime."

Every afternoon was marked by the gales of laughter coming from one of the residents' lounge where the rehearsals took place. As the weeks passed, more and more members of Hilltop either booked with their carers to roll them to the lounge to watch the rehearsals or they went under their own steam using walking sticks or frames to claim a seat to watch the pantomime develop. Sean had been thwarted on a number of occasions as he went from room to room to serve tea and cakes only to find that many rooms were vacant when he got to them. He thought that it was an ideal time for the players and observers to have afternoon tea together.

Many of those in the audience had, up to this point, stayed in their rooms and eaten their cakes and drunk their tea on their own. Now, however, because of the attraction of the pantomime rehearsals, suddenly they found themselves socialising over afternoon tea. They were getting to know each other and the 'family' that Connie had envisaged was becoming a reality.

Fifteen minutes before the rehearsal session ended, John led them in a singsong accompanied by the Hilltop Players. The swell of voices got stronger and more tuneful each week and the fifteen minutes eventually became an hour. Jenny had to intervene reluctantly at this stage to ensure everyone was ready for the evening meal. She couldn't bear the thought that all Sam's efforts would be spoilt by them being late to dinner.

Jake made a point of being in the corridor as they filed out at the end of the rehearsal and watched with delight the smiles on all their faces, both young carers and older residents alike. They were animated and excited by what they had seen and taken part in. He knew this must be more than just a once-a-year performance. He began to imagine murder mysteries, love stories, political satires but he knew he needed somebody to coordinate all these possibilities. The art club could devise advertisement flyers for the pantomime and help with scenery painting, the dressmaking group could make costumes. There were endless possibilities.

The look on everyone's face as they made their way back to their rooms made him realise that he had to make these plans a reality. He became totally convinced when Ethel, an 87-year-old, who had rarely left her room since she had arrived 3 years earlier, was given a small part in the production. She had been taken in a wheelchair to one of the rehearsals by Jennie who had made it her mission to socialise with the shy and reluctant residents. Ethel had initially refused to go but Jennie had promised that she wouldn't leave her side throughout the rehearsal session and this had worn down Ethel's resolve.

By the end of the 90-minute session, Ethel was singing away and chatting with Betty who had been parked next to her at the back of the room by the door. A friendship blossomed between them, so much so that they now met for lunch each day in the restaurant and then moved to the lounge to sit and read for the rest of the afternoon, both happy in each other's company. By the end of the fourth week, Ethel offered to take on the very small part as a friend of the wicked stepmother. She had only a very small cameo part but she loved every minute of her new pastime and even drew a picture of the type of costume she wanted the dressmakers to create for her.

The level of excitement over the last couple of months had exhausted Jake. He hadn't realised that he was getting more and more involved and he was missing out the afternoon naps that his consultant had recommended. Connie noticed he was looking grey-faced and his lips were pale most of the day, a sure sign that he was unwell. She booked an appointment to see the consultant and she drove Jake to the hospital to discuss his deterioration.

On the way, Jake's conditioned worsened to the extent that Connie wondered whether going directly to the Accident and Emergency Department rather than the Neurology Department where Jake had been supported in his rehabilitation would be more sensible. As she hurried across town, cursing every red light and pedestrian crossing, quick glances at Jake only increased her worries. His face was as white as a sheet, there were beads of sweat on his forehead, his breathing was shallow and laboured. He kept moaning every time the car was jolted by the unevenness of the road surface until, eventually, he became silent, slumped in his seat, held upright only by his seatbelt.

Connie's driving became even more frantic as she realised that Jake had lost consciousness but, finally, she pulled into a spare ambulance parking bay at the entrance to A and E.

"You can't park there," said a paramedic who was just about to set off in his ambulance. "Oh sorry, I didn't realise. Let me help."

He slid a stretcher from the back of his vehicle, opened out the trolley wheels and hurried over to help Connie lift the unconscious Jake from her car. They laid him on the trolley and wheeled him inside, past the reception area, directly along the emergency arrivals corridor where a nurse directed them into a holding bay and closed the curtains around them. She hooked him up to a machine which confirmed that his blood pressure was dangerously low and then pressed an alarm button to summon help.

"Stay with us, Jake," said Connie, holding his hand and trying to remain calm despite her inner turmoil at the prospect of losing the man who was the love of her life, her friend, her partner. By now, a couple of other nurses and a fresh-faced doctor, who hardly looked old enough to carry the responsibility of saving lives, arrived and immediately took control of the situation. Wires and tubes were attached, drugs were administered and the monitoring machine indicated that Jake's blood pressure was slowly returning to more normal levels.

"We need to do some tests, but my guess is that there has been some kind of incident which has affected the supply of blood to Jake's brain. Given his medical history, we know that there is a weakness in that area," said the doctor. "Let's keep him in hospital for a couple of days and we'll see how he progresses."

"Jake has been making such good progress, particularly in recent weeks. How much of a setback do you think this is for him, doctor?" asked Connie anxiously.

"Impossible to say at this stage but we will do our best. The nurses are searching for a bed and hopefully he will be moved on to a ward very shortly. Do you have any further questions?"

"I'm sure I will have as soon as you have gone, but I can't think of anything just now. Oh yes, can I just ask if I will be able to stay with Jake overnight?"

"That's not a question for me," said the doctor, "it will depend on the sister who is in charge of the ward. I will leave you in the capable hands of my colleagues for now. I'll look in on Jake later this afternoon." With that, the doctor hastened away, his pager flashing, in search of his next patient.

Connie spent the rest of the afternoon with Jake in the holding bay, surrounded by blue curtains, waiting for a bed to be found on one of the wards. Whilst Jake slept, she spent her time messaging Beth, her dad and Jennie to update them on Jake's latest mishap. She also pondered the future. How was she going to cope with running Hilltop and the property business in London whilst now having to care for Jake again? Would he return to the levels he'd previously achieved, or would he be more incapacitated? Would he recover at all even? She shuddered at the last thought.

Her life had been intertwined with Jake for so long that the very notion of losing him was horrifying. She had to acknowledge, however reluctantly, that Jake's health was more fragile than ever. It had been a real battle to recover from the terrible injuries he'd suffered during the unprovoked attack by the so-called football fan and now, even though she was still waiting for the outcome of the tests, she had a feeling that this was a major setback. Her reverie was interrupted by a nurse.

"Good news! We have found a bed for your husband. He'll be alongside a group of expectant mothers because it's the maternity ward. Not ideal, but it is literally the only spare bed in the hospital. We'll move him as soon as we can to another ward. We'll be able to keep him under observation perfectly well there. You'll be able to sit with him as long as you like. We always relax the rules in that ward," she said with a smile.

"Well, at least he'll be in a ward where the numbers are likely to rise rather than fall," said Connie with a smile.

The movement roused Jake from his slumber. "What's happening?" he asked.

"You're on the way to the maternity ward, Jake."

"You're joking."

"No, it's the only place where there's a spare bed for you. I must say you are looking a bit better than earlier. You gave me quite a fright. How are you feeling?"

"A bit groggy but not too bad otherwise. Can I go home?"

"They want to keep you here for a day or two to find out what the problem is."

"I'm not going to get much peace in a maternity ward though," moaned Jake.

"You're definitely improving if you're complaining. That's cheered me up enormously."

A couple of days later, during which time 4 babies had been born on the maternity ward, Jake was back home at Hilltop. The doctors had told him that there had been 'a minor incident' in his brain and that he would need to return for regular check-ups every three months. He should try to live as normal a life as possible, with plenty of rest and avoidance of stress. Life is nothing if unpredictable, however, and sure enough within a couple of hours of his return problems started to mount.

"I'm glad you two are back," said Jennie, looking flustered, "we have eighteen residents suffering from sickness and diarrhoea. It began yesterday after the midday meal when we started to receive calls for help. Buzzers were going off all over the building. I stayed on to help the overnight staff and I can tell you that it's all a bit of a nightmare. Soiled bedlinen, vomit everywhere, people collapsing in the bathroom. We phoned for the doctor who, when he finally arrived, has been a great help in giving medication to calm the sickness. Three patients were so ill that they have been sent to hospital but gradually order is being restored. We have had to inform Environmental Health about the outbreak and a team will be arriving shortly."

"OK, well done for what you've done so far. Make sure that everybody is cleaned up and as comfortable as possible. Could you ask Sean to come to my office and we'll try to find out how this has happened."

"There's one other thing I haven't told you," said Jennie, looking worried. "Once things had started to quieten down at about 4am, I decided I'd go around all the rooms of the residents who had not reported any illness, just to check that all was well." Jennie stopped, struggling to control her emotions as the tears started to roll down her cheeks. "You remember the very old Indian lady, Mrs Singh, who joined us only last week?"

"Yes, I do. She arrived with her large family who were very concerned that she was moving into a care home. A lovely lady who tries hard to be cheerful in spite of her many health problems. I remember her well," said Jake.

"Well, when I arrived at her room, which as you know is at the far end of the building, chosen by her family to give her as much privacy as possible," Jennie gulped, "she seemed to be in a deep sleep. I was about to leave her in peace but something about the eerie silence in the room made me pause. As I moved closer to her, I became more alarmed. She was so still, with no sound of breathing. Her eyes were closed, face upturned, a smile frozen on her lips. She looked totally lifeless. I felt for a pulse and… and my worst fears were confirmed."

"Oh dear," said Connie, "can things get any worse?"

"I'm afraid they can, because as I checked for a heartbeat her body was totally cold."

"You mean she had been dead for some time?" asked Jake.

"Exactly. I dragged the doctor away from the chaos elsewhere to confirm the death. He said there would need to be an investigation to find out when and how she died but his best guess was that she had been dead for at least 12 hours." Jennie was desperately trying, and failing, to stem the flow of tears with a bundle of tissues.

"The fact she has died is one thing, but the fact she has been lying there for twelve hours without anybody noticing, that's a much more serious matter. How can this have happened?" Connie looked across at Jake for support.

"Well, it has happened, so we need to keep calm, make some good decisions and face up to the problems," said Jake.

He tried his best to exude an air of confidence, though he knew that they were in the middle of a serious crisis which might threaten the very existence of Hilltop. His own illness, the sickness of the residents and the untimely and, more seriously, unsupervised death of Mrs Singh all conspired to create a perfect storm of events that threatened to sweep away all the good work of the last year.

"Everything happened at the same time whilst you two were at the hospital," said Jennie. "Obviously, the regular checks fell by the wayside as we coped with so many sick patients. Poor Mrs Singh was forgotten in the confusion. Mary, her carer, had gone home sick the day before yesterday. She was the first of the five staff to go home ill and with all the chaos we must have forgotten that there was no one monitoring Mary's corridor, especially as Mrs Singh's room is that one which is tucked out of sight around the corner from the main corridor."

"As Jake says, we now have to do whatever we can to rescue the situation," said Connie. She too could see that their care home project was under threat, but she was now used to life being difficult and she was not going to surrender without a fight. There was a knock on the door. Outside were a group of six people, dressed in blue overalls, wearing white hats, carrying clipboards.

"We are looking for Mrs Wilkins who I understand is the manager here," said a short, rotund lady in a business-like manner.

"That's me. Please call me Connie," said Connie defiantly, "this is my husband, Jake, and this is Jennie. We're all part of the Hilltop management team."

"Pleased to meet you all. I'm Asha Bitok. I'm the senior Environmental Health Officer for Suffolk and this is my team of officers. I understand you have a lot of residents and staff suffering from sickness and diarrhoea." They all nodded their heads in acknowledgement. "We are required by law to thoroughly investigate how this has happened. We will need access to all your premises: the kitchens, the laundry, the residents' rooms, in fact everywhere. I'm afraid we'll be here for at least a couple of days and I hope we can count on your full cooperation."

"Of course," said Connie, "anything we can do to help please let us know. I will sort out the meeting room for you to use as your base."

"Thank you," said Asha briskly, moving off down the corridor. "OK team, let's get to work."

Connie, Jake and Jennie looked at each other. "Are you both thinking what I'm thinking?" asked Connie.

"We need to speak to Sam," said Jake and Jennie in unison.

"Jennie, tell him to cancel the food demonstration he was organising for today and to join us here. Let's try to find out what has happened in the kitchen. When we've done that, we'll move on to the even more delicate matter of Mrs Singh, said Connie, grim-faced. "When the going gets tough, the tough get going, as my grandmother used to say."

"Has anyone informed Mrs Singh's family that she has died?" asked Jake.

"Yes, the doctor on duty here has been in touch and they are expected to arrive anytime soon. Apparently, they were at a family wedding in Birmingham, so they are now on their way back here. I think Doctor Pollock rang them about four hours ago so they should be here shortly."

"Oh, great," moaned Connie, "they will be tired and furious by the time they arrive. Jennie, can you go and find Doctor Pollock and ask him to be with us when the family arrives. I think he will be better placed to explain what has happened to their Mum and they might be less hostile towards him."

A quiet knock on the office door announced the arrival of a distraught Sam. He entered the office and looked at the three anxious faces before him.

"Oh, Sam, thanks for coming. First of all, let us just clear the air. Do you think this outbreak is food-related? Can you think that the hygiene levels in the kitchen have fallen and might be the cause of this disaster?" Connie tried to smile weakly, but her face twitched nervously. She was very fond of Sean and didn't want to lay the blame on his shoulders, but she felt that she had to be blunt.

"No," Sean replied defensively. "There is nothing wrong with the kitchens. Our hygiene standards are extremely high. We change the mops and cloths daily. Everything is scoured so that you can see your face in every surface. We never fail to wash our hands after each course is prepared. We are really strict in everything to do with food preparation, cooking and dishwashing. We have been using the new dishwasher for the last month now and it really boils and sterilises the pots and cutlery…" Sean looked crestfallen at having to defend his position as a manager and their high standards.

"That is fine, Sam," interrupted Jake. "We just wanted to check with you before the Environmental Health team move into your kitchen and start to take samples. Just get on with your work and answer any questions they ask you and, by the way, thanks for helping the care staff over the last couple of days. I hear you have stayed on until late at night helping Jennie out."

Another knock on the door interrupted them and Doctor Pollock entered. "Mrs Singh's family have just arrived. I have put them in the bistro area to get a drink of tea after their journey. They all look very distressed. I suggest you let me go through the cause of death as we know it so far and then see how they respond."

Jennie was sent to collect the group and eight members of the family squeezed into the office. They organised themselves in three rows as though they were about to have a group photograph. In the centre was the son who had caused considerable hassle when they first brought their mother to Hilltop. He was the one who had insisted that she should be given the room tucked away from the main corridor so that she wouldn't be disturbed. He was the one who had given a lengthy list of dos and don'ts regarding the welfare of their mother and now he stood ready for a fight with anyone who gave him a chance.

They listened to Doctor Pollock's quietly considered account and the condolences offered by Connie and Jake, then Mrs Singh's eldest son began to ask a series of questions. What had they found out about the sickness in the home? Why wasn't their mother found sooner? When had she been last checked? Who found the body? When was the doctor called? The questions were endless and Connie, Jennie and Doctor Pollock answered everything the best they could.

Jake looked on and tried to keep as calm as he possibly could, but the tension in the room was seeping into his body. He could feel his anxiety levels rising and had begun to feel faint. He excused himself from the room and went upstairs to their flat and lay down on his bed and closed his eyes. *What a mess*, he thought, *how are we ever going to recover from all this?*

Nearly an hour later, Connie joined him. Mrs Singh's family had now gone home and her body had been collected by the undertaker. She explained that

Doctor Pollock had managed to convince them that Mrs Singh had died of natural causes, not from the sickness illness. He was now calling it norovirus as he had received confirmation during the meeting that the virus had been formally identified. The Environmental team were still moving from room to room taking samples and the remaining residents were being kept in their rooms so that the virus would have a chance of being contained. The heavy cleaning unit had also arrived and they were starting to deep clean everywhere in the home.

"It is pure chaos, Jake. You have never seen so many people in white overalls and face masks moving around Hilltop. It would be best for you to stay up here away from the drama. I expect they will eventually want to inspect our flat but, in the meantime, hide away up here and Jennie and I will liaise with them all."

He closed his eyes and she was relieved to see that his face had gained a slight blush of colour. She kissed his cheek and quickly returned to the affray. Jennie meanwhile was trying to downplay the problem with a local journalist who had phoned through to discuss the disaster which had befallen Hilltop. The journalist insisted that the elderly residents were in danger of dying if they stayed in the home. Jennie made light of the problem and explained that a deep clean was taking place and everyone was being monitored. Fortunately, she hadn't yet heard about Mrs Singh, or the headline would be about neglect amidst chaos rather than just a bout of sickness and diarrhoea. As soon as she put down the phone, she called Connie over.

"We have got to get our stories right so that we don't cause alarm with the families of the residents. We had better ask Doctor Pollock what to say when we are asked by other journalists and families regarding the virus."

Jennie went in search of the doctor and she found him listening to Mary Towers' breathing. He tapped her hand when he had finished.

"That is fine, Mary. You can button up your blouse again. Your cough is settling nicely and I suggest you stay in the warmth of your room for the next few days and perhaps read or watch television rather than going along to the lounge. You will improve if you don't exert yourself and we don't want you picking up any germs when you are just getting over a heavy cold."

He looked over at Jennie and gave a knowing smile.

"Could we ask you to join us in the office when you have finished here, please, Doctor."

"By all means. I will be along in a minute after I have written out Mary's new prescription."

Ten minutes later, he joined Connie and Jennie and they settled down to discuss the course of action to fend off further trouble. They were soon joined by Asha Bitok who wanted to report the good news that so far all was well. Despite her formidable appearance she had a gentle side to her nature.

"I must congratulate you and your staff, Connie. I have spent years visiting many different residencies and hospitals and yours is one of the best I have seen. The level of cleanliness is exemplary. The deep cleaning should help to stop the virus in its tracks and then, after a couple of days, you could get Hilltop back to normal."

She had overheard some of the conversation between the three of them when she entered the room and she offered to supply a statement on behalf of the Environmental Agency if they wanted further support against the meddling media. Connie was relieved that the virus was almost defeated, but she had found the level of stress which had started with Jake, was intensified by the death of Mrs `Singh and the subsequent interview with her distressed family just too much to cope with. She suddenly burst into tears, excused herself and ran outside into the garden and found a quiet corner to howl away her distress.

"Connie, where are you?" Jennie's voice echoed around the buildings.

Connie quickly dried her eyes and pinched her cheeks.

"I am here, Jennie." She stepped out of the shadows of the building. "Sorry about that, I just had to get out of the room. Are they all still in the office?"

"No, everyone has gone back to what they were doing. Doctor Pollock has gone as he has a surgery starting shortly, but he said he would be back later and Asha has gone to check on her team. Come and have a drink and one of Sam's special cookies. He has just sent a plate of them to the office with a note which said they are not contaminated as they are freshly baked."

Connie smiled at Jennie and the two of them linked arms and returned to the office.

"I think he likes you, Jennie. I saw how you looked when you said he helped you out the last couple of evenings."

"Well," she replied coyly, "I do actually like him a lot. He is an incredibly kind man and he is just like me in many ways. We care for others and want to do our best for them. I feel that he is my soul mate if that doesn't sound too soppy."

"And do you know how he feels?"

"No, I haven't a clue. All I know about him really is that he is unmarried and has an elderly mother who lives close by. He tries to visit her most days after work but since the sickness bug he has stayed away so that he doesn't pass on any infection. I like that about him. He is sensitive to others and is very affectionate towards his Mum. I think that says a great deal about a person, don't you?"

"Yes, yes I do. I didn't have such a close family connection when I was growing up but since Dad has been helping out with the maintenance jobs, I have got to know him that bit more and I actually like what I see."

That evening, trying to wind down after a difficult day, Connie and Jake had just begun watching a reality TV programme when there was a knock on the door.

"Hello Connie," said her dad, "sorry to bother you, but Beth and I are very worried about you and Jake. In the last year, you've had to nurse Jake back to health, launch a new business, manage Hilltop 24 hours a day and now deal with this latest crisis. You must admit that, although Beth, Jennie and I are supposed to be part of your management team, the reality is that the biggest burden falls on your shoulders. We think it's time for a change so that you and the business can flourish over the long term."

"I agree that I've been struggling recently," said Connie, glancing at Jake.

"Your Dad is right, Connie, you need to share your responsibilities. I've noticed you have not been sleeping well and you're always tired."

"What do you suggest then, Dad?" asked Connie.

"We think you need a break. Take a couple of weeks off work and have a holiday. Fly out to the Bahamas for some sun and relaxation or, if you prefer, go up to the Lake District for some rain and walking. Money is no object to you these days. What are you waiting for?"

"Well, for a start, who's going to look after Hilltop?"

"That's exactly the point," said Andy, relishing the chance to give vent to his frustration, "it's our job to look after Hilltop as well. Are you saying you don't trust us?"

"Of course, I do. Maybe I hadn't realised what a control freak I've become."

"That's agreed then. From tomorrow morning for the next two weeks, Beth, Jennie and I will take over whilst you and Jake take a break. You both need it."

Chapter 11

Dad, known to all at Hilltop as Andy the handyman, had served his carpentry apprenticeship, after leaving school at 15, with a local building company that no longer existed. He had moved from one firm to another before eventually setting up his own small business. He prided himself on the quality of his workmanship, taking care to build a good reputation amongst his customers. In his keenness to please, he frequently undercharged for his labour, meaning that his income was steady rather than substantial. In order to maintain a flow of work, he had accepted commissions from all over the country, meaning he was often absent as the girls grew up.

By the time Connie and Jake took on the Hilltop business, Andy was ready for a change of direction. One reason was that he had discovered that he had the ability to build good relationships with people and enjoyed helping them. He also relished the thought of spending more time with his daughters, something he had found difficult when they were children because he had been so busy.

Life at home had been tough in those days because his wife had been so ill and then the trauma of losing her to cancer had hit them all very hard. None of them had coped well with the overwhelming sadness of losing a wife and mother and there had been lots of recriminations, with each blaming the others for not doing enough to support the dying person.

Time enabled them to gradually rebuild their relationships but there were further setbacks when Andy started a new relationship and then Connie and Beth's younger sister Jennie was killed in a car crash. Old wounds had been reopened by their mutual grief, anger and guilt. In a way, the Hilltop project was helping them to move forward through sharing a common purpose. They were learning to be kind not only to the residents but also to each other. They had started to enjoy each other's company.

Andy had been surprised that Connie had agreed to take a break and he had been cautious in passing on the news to Beth and Jennie.

"Connie has agreed to take a holiday but don't be surprised if she changes her mind," he said. "However, let's work on the basis that we are in charge for the next two weeks and hope that things will be back to normal by the time they return. I'm still worried about possible repercussions with regard to both Mrs Singh and the norovirus outbreak."

In truth, Connie was relieved that she now had a good excuse to escape. Her life had been a continuous struggle from the start and strangely the inheritance had created unexpected pressures in that she felt that Aunt Agnes' life's work should not be frittered away. There was so much to learn about managing wealth, property and above all Hilltop care home, not to mention the desperate struggle to keep Jake alive and then to restore him to a reasonable state of health. On top of all that she was now worried about the potential damage to the reputation of Hilltop resulting from the unsupervised death of Mrs Singh and the norovirus outbreak. She realised that, not only did she need to look after Jake, but she needed to protect herself from total physical and mental collapse.

As soon as her dad had left, she had needed no further encouragement to search the internet for a possible holiday. Not wanting hassle of any kind, she rejected air travel, keen to avoid long delays in airport lounges, and travel by ship because Jake had always suffered from seasickness. A car journey would be easiest for Jake, still not fully mobile, and would be less restrictive on luggage. Hotels were rejected too on the basis that that would be too similar to living at Hilltop and a complete change was what she needed.

In the end, the choice was between two places that were advertised on Airbnb. One was in the "charming" Cotswold village of Broadway and the other was a small modern hotel in Le Touquet on the northern French coast. By the time Connie had discussed things with Jake, the choice had been simplified because the Cotswold cottage was no longer available, having been reserved at the last minute by another customer.

"We're off to Le Touquet in the morning, Jake. We'll take the shuttle and then it's only a 45-minute journey down the French motorway. The sea air will do us both good and I'm looking forward to sampling some high-quality French cuisine and wine."

Connie's excitement was contagious and Jake too began to look forward to tomorrow's adventure. It was a while since he had seen her so cheerful.

Early the next morning, after Connie and Jake's departure, Andy, Beth and Jennie held a team briefing and agreed that their priority was to be extra vigilant that things were returning to normal. Above all, they were to watch out for any new norovirus cases and to listen for any rumours that might be spreading about Mrs Singh amongst residents and visitors. Everything seemed to be going well, to the extent that Jennie joked to Andy and Beth, as they shared a mid-morning coffee break, that things were running more smoothly without Connie and Jake.

Shortly afterwards, the early edition of the local evening paper was delivered. Andy grabbed a copy to check the previous evening's football results, but his attention was grabbed by the front-page banner headline: "HILLTOP DEATH MYSTERY". He did not even have chance to read the article before Jennie arrived to say that the local radio station wanted to speak to the "boss".

"That's Connie," stammered Andy.

"Not today," replied Jennie, "I'm afraid you're in charge."

"What do they want?"

"I think that's obvious," said Jennie, looking at the newspaper in his hand.

"What on earth am I going to tell them?"

"All you can say at the moment is that the matter is under investigation."

Andy spent five very uncomfortable minutes being interviewed live on the radio, emphasising that he was unable to share any details about the case. Legal and medical matters required total confidentiality, especially until the facts had been established. Although he tried to emphasise that Hilltop had built a very strong reputation since his daughter, currently unavailable, had been in charge, the interviewer seemed more interested in building a sensational story that would interest the listeners, to the potential detriment of the Hilltop residents and their families.

"That was tough," he said wearily to Beth and Jennie who had been listening in a nearby room. "I didn't realise that I needed media training to do this job."

Within minutes, Andy was outside in the carpark being interviewed by a local television news team who were asking him about the unexplained death of Mrs Singh and whether the norovirus outbreak was under control. Having learned from his hesitations and lack of fluency on the radio, he was determined to sound confident, trying very hard to give the impression that everything was under control. It was not easy because the interviewer continually rephrased his questions in an attempt to catch him out, but Andy stuck to his line that he could make no comment at this stage about Mrs Singh and that all the residents were recovering well from their illness.

"So, Andy, are you expecting any more deaths?" was the final question and the last straw for Andy whose patience was wearing thin.

"Thank you for your interest but I have nothing more to say." Andy turned on his heel and disappeared into the building. That evening, Hilltop was the main item on the local evening news. Andy's lengthy interview had been abbreviated and finished with his obvious annoyance, his "nothing more to say" comment and the image of him stalking away from the camera.

"Oh dear," said Beth, "that doesn't look good. People will think we've got something to hide."

"Maybe you should do the next interview then," said Andy angrily.

"You did as well as you could in the circumstances and I would not have coped any better," replied Beth, keen to restore an air of calm to this fraught situation.

All evening the phone kept ringing because relatives had heard or seen the interviews and wanted to know what was happening. Andy, Beth and Jennie managed to find a few minutes to sit down and discuss whether to contact Connie and Jake but decided there was no point in ruining a holiday that had only just begun. They agreed to write a press statement which they worked on together and then emailed to all local media outlets. It read as follows:

"As you will by now be aware, we have had an outbreak of norovirus at Hilltop over the last three days, affecting twenty-three residents, all of whom are now recovering. Environmental Health officers were unable to find the cause of the outbreak and have complimented us on the high standard of hygiene at Hilltop. Unfortunately, one of our residents passed away during the outbreak and we await the results of tests regarding cause of death. We ask for your understanding at this time, especially as Hilltop will be closed to visitors until we are certain that there is no further danger of contagion."

Keen to make the most of their short break, Connie and Jake got up at 4 am and had a hurried bite of toast before loading their weekend case into the car. The previous evening, they decided to drive from Calais to Le Touquet as Jake had heard that the route was quite spectacular along the coast. Connie had managed to book a place for 9.30 the next morning on the shuttle. They set off thinking they had given themselves plenty of time to get to the terminus near Dover. However, even at this early hour there was a continuous stream of traffic and roadworks slowed them down every 30 miles or so.

By the time they reached the terminus, they had exactly ten minutes to rush to the toilet, buy a hot drink and a croissant and then drive to the loading area to wait for their turn to embark. During the short train journey, they stretched their legs, ate their late breakfast and double-checked the route on the iPad.

Connie had never driven in France. She was quite cautious for the first few kilometres until she got used to driving on the right. She asked a fellow passenger who was in the car in front of them on the train whether she should use headlamp reflectors and was reassured that she wouldn't need them as long as she drove in daylight. She was relieved that the next stage of the journey was quiet and civilised. The roads were moderately busy, but the surfaces were smooth and pothole-free and Connie found herself enjoying travelling along the main roads which offered wide open vistas across the English Channel. Thankfully, throughout this last leg of the journey, the sun shone, and the sea shimmered in the distance.

"There must be nearly ten passenger boats out there," Jake observed.

"Yeah, I believe it is one of the busiest sea routes in the world. I am very glad we decided to drive though as this countryside is delightful and I feel that we are really on holiday now."

Jake was in charge of the music for the journey and he had made playlists of their old favourites, bringing back memories of their lives together. Connie could feel her stress lifting and when they pulled up outside the hotel she marvelled at its sleek modern lines and immense glass windows. A beautiful swimming pool was housed within the glass annexe, overlooking rows of pine trees and the sea beyond.

"Oh, this will do nicely," sighed Connie. "This place will chase away our worries, Jake."

After settling into their room, they decided they would have a swim before the evening meal. Jake was already in the water swimming lengths of the pool by the time Connie emerged. She joined him and they enjoyed having this magnificent pool to themselves. They had races up and down with Jake finishing marginally ahead of Connie. He had once been a member of the county squad when he was in his early teens, but his illness and injuries had slowed him down.

Jake insisted on swimming through Connie's legs and, as he did so, he made the menacing sound mimicking the music of *Jaws* and Connie squealed with delight as he swam between her legs and then tipped her beneath the surface of the water. They spent over 30 minutes enjoying their games and finally, tired and satisfied, they got dressed and returned to their bedroom to change and relax before the evening meal.

During the meal, Connie noticed a slight change in Jake. He sipped at his sparkling wine which they had ordered to celebrate their first holiday abroad together. He complained that he was feeling chilly and this was swiftly followed by a bout of sweating. Connie noticed that he had developed a cough after leaving the swimming pool and by the end of the meal, most of which he had hardly touched, he was experiencing some discomfort in his chest.

"Let's go straight back to the room and get you to bed, Jake. It might be the journey which has tired you out."

Connie supported Jake out of the restaurant and got him back to their room, undressed him with a struggle and he flopped into bed. He fell into a fitful asleep within minutes and Connie noticed that his breathing had become shallow and slightly rasping. She put an extra cover over him, as he periodically shook quite uncontrollably, even though he appeared to be sleeping. She sat alongside him and held his hand and, as she looked at his pale face, she decided that his condition was more serious than she first feared. She went down to reception to ask where she could find a doctor to take a look at him.

"I will phone for one, Madame. He is our local doctor and he is used to visiting guests when they need attention."

Connie hurried back to Jake. She was disconcerted by his noisy breathing. She made him a hot drink from the wide selection available in the room but struggled to get Jake to sit up to swallow his hot mug of tea. Jake was now feeling incredibly weak and he had difficulty talking. He sipped the drink but after two attempts he abandoned the effort and retreated under the duvet. Connie went down to reception and asked how long the doctor might be, but the receptionist was unmoved by her concern.

"He is on his way, Madame. He lives three kilometres from the hotel, so he won't be too long. I will bring him to your room as soon he arrives." She returned to her screen and effectively blanked Connie out.

"It won't be too long now before the doctor arrives, Jake. Try to sleep for a while and I will waken you when he appears." Jake's moaning sounds were muffled by the duvet and she bent over to feel his forehead which was hot and damp. Connie opened her tablet, googled Jake's symptoms and was horrified to discover that pneumonia was a likely possibility.

She became even more anxious that he had developed these symptoms immediately after his swim. She talked to him in the same way she had done when he had been unconscious in hospital after the attack, offering words of encouragement, desperately trying to conceal her anxiety. She jumped on hearing a knock on the door and was very relieved to see the doctor standing there with the young woman from reception.

"Entrez, s'il vous plait," she attempted, but her meagre French wouldn't stretch beyond these few simple phrases.

The doctor replied in almost flawless English. "So, tell me what has happened." As he talked, he took Jake's temperature by pointing a small innocuous instrument into his ear.

"Well, we arrived about three hours ago, went for a swim in the hotel pool and as soon as we came back to the room, my husband began to feel unwell. I put him to bed but he has just deteriorated."

"How was his health when you started your journey?"

"He was fine. He was lively, alert and very talkative."

The next few minutes were spent recounting the story of the previous couple of years and the doctor frowned whilst continuing to check Jake's responses.

"Considering his recent history, Madame, I think it is important for your husband to go into hospital. He has worrying signs which need to be monitored closely. I will send for an ambulance to take him to the main hospital in Le Touquet. Will you be able to follow in your car as he certainly will be there for a number of days and you won't want to be stranded without transport?"

Connie nodded and then she gathered together the few items that they had unpacked and sat beside Jake waiting for the ambulance to arrive. Within ten minutes of the doctor's phone call an ambulance squealed to a halt outside the main entrance. The doctor spoke for a few moments with the ambulance crew who then transferred Jake on to their gurney. He was whisked away to the hospital with Connie in close pursuit.

Meanwhile at Hilltop, the press release had provoked even more concerned phone calls from the families of residents, interview requests from local and national media and finally, a few days later, a visit from the police. Andy guided the two detectives into his office and offered them a cup of coffee, which was refused by the older of the two, a man that Andy presumed from his greying and thinning hair to be in his forties.

"I'm Detective Sergeant Milligan and this is my colleague, Detective Constable Mishra, and we are here to investigate what exactly happened around the time of Mrs Singh's death."

"Yes, that's right, Andy. Do you mind if we call you Andy?" said the younger, rather stern looking policewoman. Her piercing dark eyes stared at him, clearly not interested in Andy's reply because she continued without hesitation: "By the way, I understand that you have had an outbreak of norovirus here. Do we need to take any special precautions whilst we are in the building?"

"The premises have been professionally deep-cleaned, from top to bottom, from end to end," said Andy emphatically, "so you won't be at risk at all. With regard to Mrs Singh, she died of natural causes according to everything I've heard from the medical investigators so far and I'm expecting the pathologist's report to confirm that. Dealing with death is part of our job unfortunately, because obviously, we are looking after a lot of elderly people here. I hope you can understand that, Detective Mishra." Andy scanned the faces of the two detectives, looking for signs of support but found nothing but chilling impassivity.

"Mrs Singh's family have asked us to investigate the circumstances surrounding their mother's death. They are concerned that she had already been dead for some time when her body was found. Is that correct, Andy?" asked the gruff more senior Detective Sergeant Milligan. He was a well-built man, maybe a rugby player in his youth, but the passage of time had not been kind to him. There was more than a hint of excess flesh bulging around his midriff and his lined face pointed to a career dealing with the darker side of life.

"That is true—"

Before he could say any more, Constable Mishra interrupted: "Mrs Singh's death is recorded as approximately 7 pm but her body was not found until 7 am the following morning. What is your policy on the supervision of residents, Andy?"

The detective was poised with her notebook to record whatever he said. Andy decided that he would simply recount the facts of the story as far as he knew them and let events take their course. Once he had clarified his thinking, his anxiety at the passively aggressive body language of the detectives dissipated and he spoke confidently.

"As far as possible, apart from those who are completely bed-ridden, all the residents eat their three daily meals together in the dining room. Although Mrs

118

Singh needed a wheelchair because of her mobility problems, our records show that she joined the rest of the group for breakfast at about 8.30, for lunch at 12.30 and for dinner at 6 pm."

"So," said Detective Mishra, scribbling furiously whilst Detective Milligan stared at Andy, presumably striving to see whether he could trust Andy's story, "you would only know where Mrs Singh was at those 3 times?"

"No, please allow me to finish. Our policy is that when a resident has no family visitor during the day, the dedicated member of staff has to ensure that they call in the room to offer a hot drink mid-morning and mid-afternoon. Mrs Singh's dedicated carer, Mary, visited her in her room at 11.05 and again at 3.25. We know this because all carers record every visit in their logbooks. You are very welcome to check Mary's logbook because here it is." Andy picked up the document from his desk and handed it over to Detective Milligan whilst Detective Mishra continued writing and asking questions.

"So, she was seen 5 times during the day?"

"No. Mrs Singh needed quite a lot of medication for a range of medical issues. We have a senior carer, Wahida, who is also a qualified nurse and therefore the only person who is allowed to administer drugs. Everything that Wahida does is, as you would expect, carefully recorded, as you can see from this sheet," said Andy, handing it over to Milligan.

"What time did she visit Mrs Singh?" asked Mishra.

"According to this, 10.15 for an injection of insulin—"

"Yes, I forgot to mention that Mrs Singh had type 1 diabetes," interjected Andy.

"…and at 6 pm to administer various other tablets for blood pressure, blood thinning, digestion and depression," said Milligan, reading slowly aloud from the sheet Andy had given him.

"So that's 7 times in total that Mrs Singh was seen during the day?"

"That's not quite accurate. Her carer Mary was also with her in the room at various points during the day to make her bed, help her to wash and generally tidy her room. Because Mary focuses on only half a dozen residents, she is in and out of their rooms all the time. I'm sure you'll want to talk to her yourself. Mary has a lively outgoing personality and we appointed her to cheer people up as well as to look after them. I know that she was very upset when she heard that Mrs Singh had died."

"Given all this contact with Mrs Singh, were there any signs that she was ill?" asked Milligan.

"None at all. Everything was as normal with her, which was surprising because that day we had people falling ill all over the building. By the end of the day 21 of our residents were suffering with what turned out to be norovirus and, frankly, that was the start of a rather chaotic period which lasted for a few days. Mary accompanied Mrs Singh to the dining room at 6.30. After the meal she took her back to her room just before 7, helped her into bed for the night and then went home. Mary should have been on duty till 9 but we decided it was better for all concerned if she left the premises as she too had started to suffer from sickness and diarrhoea."

"So, who was looking after Mrs Singh during the night?" asked Mishra, glad to have a rest from all the note-taking.

"At night-time, there are fewer staff on duty but, although I managed to bring in a couple of agency staff, because of the sickness we were 5 short of our normal numbers, even though my daughter Beth, also part of the management team, and I stayed here the whole time. It was a very difficult night because 21 residents had to be helped into and out of the bathroom. There was lots of clearing of soiled bedding and cleaning up of patients. With the best will in the world, we were unable to maintain our normal standards of supervision.

"As a routine, somebody would check each room every two hours during the night. Maybe this happened with Mrs Singh and maybe not. I could not be sure of that because we were rushed off our feet. All I can say is that at 7 am the following morning, Jennie found Mrs Singh in her bed and, unfortunately, it was obvious that she had been dead for some time."

Andy sighed. The memory of that night was distressing but he found no comfort in the faces of the two detectives who were busy processing the information he had given them.

"Well," said Milligan slowly, "we need to consider all the information you have given us very carefully. If the pathologist confirms that Mrs Singh died of natural causes, it's most unfortunate from your point of view that it occurred at the same time as the norovirus outbreak. We owe it to the Singh family to be as thorough as we can in our investigation. Of course, the press will be keen to run either a 'police incompetence' or 'failing care home' story so that should keep all of us on our toes."

"We have nothing to hide, I can assure you, Sergeant. My daughter, Connie, who is on holiday with her husband, has transformed this care home for the better in the short time she has been in charge. She had been at her very sick husband's bedside in hospital for several days when all this happened. They were in desperate need of a break after they returned from hospital and dealt with the consequences of the illness and Mrs Singh's death, so we persuaded them to have a holiday. They have gone to France. I will be phoning her shortly to let her know about your involvement."

That's a good idea," said Mishra, "because we'll probably need to interview her at some point. We would like to talk to Mary though as she was the last person to see Mrs Singh alive. Is she here today?"

"No, we've asked her to stay at home until there is no chance of her spreading the infection. I'll give you her address if you like," said Andy, jotting down the information on a post-it. "You'll find her keen to help all she can. Is there anything else you need from me?"

"We'd like to wander around the home and in particular look at Mrs Singh's room."

"I'll ask Beth to show you the way," said Andy, pressing his pager to alert his younger daughter.

The two detectives shook Andy's hand, a little more warmly than when they arrived, but without giving any indication of what might happen next. Beth had by now arrived to escort them on a tour of the building, leaving Andy to make the call to Connie that he was dreading. He knew that this was the last thing Connie needed but it had to be done. He managed to delay the phone call by convincing himself that he needed a coffee to recover from being interrogated by the police. The coffee machine had just finished filling his cup when his mobile rang, the flashing screen indicating an incoming call from Connie.

"Hello darling, how are you?"

"Dad, I'm afraid I've got some very bad news. Jake has just died."

Andy was both shocked by the news but at the same time amazed at the calm and matter-of-fact way in which Connie conveyed the information. She had realised that Jake would always be vulnerable to further illness, given the way that his immune system had been so damaged following the violent attack and during his slow recovery. She was devastated that he had simply slipped away from life, despite the efforts of the emergency care staff in the hospital to revive him.

Tears were rolling down Andy's face as she spoke; it broke his heart that his daughter was suffering in this way, even more so because she was being so stoic. Having ascertained that Connie would be travelling back to Hilltop shortly with Jake's body, provided all the formalities had been completed, Andy broke the news of the swirl of events that had taken place in Connie's absence.

"Don't worry, Dad. You've done your best." There was a long pause as Connie processed what he had said. "We'll be able to work on things together when I get back. These are problems that we can solve. In a strange way, Jake's death puts everything into perspective. His life is over, our lives are changed, but we carry on," said Connie defiantly.

Chapter 12

Andy, Beth and Jennie were standing at the doorway to Hilltop watching the two vehicles advance up the driveway. The first, a taxi, housed the small slumped figure of Connie and the following transit van with blackened windows contained Jake's body. The insurance company had arranged a flight home and Connie's car, which she had left at the hotel, was due to be returned to her the next day. Andy rushed forward and opened Connie's door and helped his daughter out of her seat. He folded her in his arms. She felt like a tiny fragile doll and Connie instinctively returned his hug and buried her face into his neck. Andy's cheek became wet from the silent tears that cascaded down his daughter's face. These were the first tears she had cried since Jake's death.

She had needed to be strong in order to focus on the arrangements to ensure Jake's body returned home as soon as possible. One of the first things she had done back at the hotel was to make a phone call to Jonathan Grey. "I have some terrible news and I need your help," was all she could say for the moment. Her voice had dried and become hoarse. She blinked hard to stop any tears from escaping. Now wasn't the time to cry, that could come later. Her life had become unreal and she was unable to process the enormity of what had just happened.

"Tell me what the problem is, Connie."

"Jake is dead…and I am here in France and I don't know what to do…" Her voice trailed away.

"Right, now first of all, where are you?"

"I am at this hotel in Le Touquet." Her news poured out of her like an avalanche. "I have just got back from the hospital where Jake died this morning. I wanted to stay with him, but they sent me back to the hotel. I haven't slept for two days as I have been at his bedside. The doctors said he suffered complications from pneumonia. It has all been such a shock because everything happened so quickly.

"He seemed to be in such good health when we drove out here for a holiday. He was happy and excited about being in France. The doctors said his weakened immune system was unable to fight off the infection which he picked up from the swimming pool here in this hotel." The effort of the explanation exhausted her and the memory of what had happened shocked her. The reality of her situation was suddenly clear.

"Oh, my dear, I am so sorry. Right, first things first. Let us think how we are going to get you both home. Do you have insurance for this trip?"

"Yes, I took it out with the company you recommended to us. Holiday cover was part of the overall package, if I remember correctly. I can't think straight, Jonathan.

"Yes, you're right," replied Jonathan. "I will get right on to this and tell them what you have told me, but we will need all the documentation from the hospital before Jake is allowed out of the country. Do they have to do an autopsy, do you know?"

"No, I don't think so. One of the doctors who spoke English said Jake's body was just too weak to fight off such a virulent infection. They emailed the English hospital where Jake stayed after the attack and also when he became ill the second time. They had his records sent across to them. The French staff were very kind, but by the time Jake was put on a life support machine, it soon became obvious that he would not recover. They asked me whether they could turn off the machine. Jake's brain injury was so severe that to all intents and purposes, he was already dead but I wanted some more time with him. After I had had a chance to say goodbye, they came into his room and turned off the apparatus. Jake died less than an hour later." Connie went silent, remembering the horror of the last few days.

"Have a quick rest, Connie, then I need you to go back to the hospital and ask for the forms that we require. I will email you a list so that we have everything we need. As I said, have a quick sleep then phone when you have got all the necessary forms."

Jonathan was business-like and forceful. He realised he had to direct her actions and his manner was almost brusque. Whilst Connie relayed the sad news to Andy and Beth, Jonathan set the wheels in motion to bring them both back to England. The hospital had to first inform the police. It was obligatory to have a police tag for the body and they also had to inform the local mayor. Another requirement before travel was Jake's body had to be embalmed. He was then housed in a wooden coffin ready for transportation. The hospital at Le Touquet had fortunately been unusually quiet over the previous three days which enabled the medical staff to process Jake's return home as swiftly as possible. After all the paperwork was completed, the doctors gave Connie permission to arrange for Jake's return to England.

Connie's journey back home was a nightmare. She waited on the tarmac by the side of the plane watching her husband's coffin being loaded into the hold of the aircraft and then she began her lonely flight in a first-class seat away from the curious gaze of fellow passengers. On the tarmac at Stansted, Jake's transport, a transit van with blackened windows, waited for his coffin to be unloaded. Connie was ushered into an awaiting taxi which led the small procession back to Hilltop. The driver of the taxi tried to make small talk for the first mile, but he was soon silenced by Connie's reflection in his mirror. She seemed like a wounded bird, squeezed into the corner of the rear seat, a lost and tragic soul.

"Let's get you inside," said Jennie to Connie, taking the small amount of luggage passed to her by the taxi driver. Jennie steered Connie straight into the office and closed the door making sure the Engaged sign was evident. Andy excused himself from the group and went back outside again to attend to the driver of the transit van. He had a few words, then watched as the van continued its journey to the Cooperative Funeral parlour in the centre of town, where Jake was to rest before his funeral.

Andy stood in the cool evening light watching the headlamps disappearing down the road and quietly sighed. "Cheerio, son, see you later." He went back to the office and sat beside his distraught daughter. He picked up her hand and caressed it, exactly as he used to do when she was an unhappy three-year-old needing some comfort. Sean came through with a pot of tea, knelt down and gave Connie a quick kiss on her cheek. He quickly left the room, giving the small family group some privacy.

After a fairly undisturbed night's sleep, her first in two days, Connie woke early and got out of her bed confused and exhausted. She had very little memory of her journey home from France or of the previous evening spent with her family. Throughout the previous twenty-four hours, she had eaten only a sandwich and was now extremely hungry. She wandered down in her dressing gown to the kitchen where Sean and his colleagues were already preparing the residents' breakfast. Connie nodded to them and they gestured to her before returning to their task of frying eggs and buttering toast.

Connie ladled herself a spoonful of porridge into a bowl, placed a slice of toast and a mug of tea on to her tray and carried it back to her apartment. She sat at the window eating her porridge, but after three mouthfuls she dropped her spoon back into the bowl and stared out at the wide, open space in front of her. What was she going to do? She was really alone now for the first time in many years. Jake had been part of her life and she had always referred to him when she had a problem that needed solving.

"What do you think, Jake?"

"Well, tell me what you think first and then I will tell you if I agree," had always been his reply.

Connie smiled at the memory of their exchanges. Somehow, he always made her feel competent and able. She had gained a great deal of confidence through his continued support. She had never imagined a life without him, but here she was, a widow and, at this moment, she couldn't contemplate her future without him. She felt a panic rising in her chest. Suddenly there was a quiet knock on her door. Connie ignored it at first, but the repeated drum of fingers brought her to her senses. It was Jennie.

"I am sorry to bother you, Connie, but could I have a word?"

Connie beckoned her in, and the two women sat on the sofa facing each other.

"What is it, Jennie? Is there more trouble to deal with?"

"Well, yes, in a way there is. Can you remember the story we told you last night about the death of Mrs Singh?"

Connie was about to nod, but then she confessed, "Actually, Jennie, I am afraid I don't remember much about last night at all. I think I blocked you all out even though I was in the room with you. I felt as though my mind had frozen and it still feels the same this morning. Do you want to tell me again and I will try my best to concentrate."

"You are in a state of shock, Connie. Don't worry. It will take time for you to adjust to the way things are. Look, drink your tea and eat some of this toast and try to listen whilst I go through it again."

The story was recounted and Connie's face registered concern when Jennie got to the point of mentioning that the police had been at Hilltop looking around and asking questions.

"And that is what I wanted to mention to you, Connie. They are coming back this morning to see you. They spoke with Andy previously, but they insist on having a word with you too as you are the owner of Hilltop. Are you up for it, do you think?"

"Well, I don't suppose I have much choice. I had better go and have a shower and get myself ready. They won't want to see me in my night clothes."

Connie arrived at her office to find Beth and Andy busy with the daily running of Hilltop.

"Oh, there you are, my love. Did you manage to sleep well last night?" Andy gave her another hug. He was starting to find it natural to respond in such a way and was actually enjoying his new role.

"Let me get you something. Have you had breakfast?" Beth enquired.

"Yes, thanks. Could we just put our heads together and think about this dreadful incident regarding Mrs Singh."

Connie suddenly found herself in business mode and she was glad of the distraction. She might as well focus on another death rather than Jake's. Mrs Singh's fate might pull her round a bit and help her to reconnect with her family. They talked for over an hour and acknowledged that they had done everything above board and there was nothing that they should be concerned about, but when a policeman and woman were shown into the office Connie felt a wave of anxiety wash over her.

"Mrs Wilkins?"

"Yes, that is me. How can I help you, officer?"

"I am Detective Sergeant Milligan and this is my colleague, Detective Constable Mishra. We have been assigned to investigate the death of Mrs Singh who was a resident here in your care home. Could we ask you a number of questions, please? We appreciate that you have recently suffered the loss of your husband and we offer you our condolences."

"Yes, I hope I am able to think straight, Sergeant. I am tired after my journey home and, as you can appreciate, I am in a state of shock after my husband's very unexpected death."

The two police officers sat down and Constable Mishra began taking notes. Connie furnished them with the records of Mrs Singh's admission and a copy of the death certificate. There was a report from Asha Bitok from Environmental Health and also notes provided by Dr Pollock regarding the norovirus infection that had infected Hilltop. Mary, Mrs Singh's carer, had also obtained a medical certificate to cover the time she had been absent.

"I am not sure what else to show you, Sergeant. We have all the paperwork, as you can see, and her death was very sad, but not entirely unexpected, as Mrs Singh was an old lady and not in the best of health."

"Mrs Singh's family have registered a complaint against Hilltop, Mrs Wilkins. They have accused you of neglecting their mother and not being aware of her death for at least twelve hours. Obviously, as an organisation caring for vulnerable and frail people, you can understand why we must investigate this case in order to protect the other residents."

"Yes, yes, I see the point you are making. All I can say in our defence was that we were caught up in a fast moving and frightening situation that night. My staff worked very hard to try to stop the infection affecting all the residents of Hilltop. There are still seven residents in hospital as we speak, and I intend visiting them as soon as you leave. Mary was the first member of staff to go home sick and then, with such chaos and endless cleaning of rooms and corridors, we forgot to replace her. Mrs Singh's room is tucked away at the end of the main corridor out of sight, so obviously, in all the confusion, other staff forgot about her room. As a result, she was left unchecked for a number of hours."

"We have received medical reports which suggest that Mrs Singh might not have died of natural causes…"

Connie blanched and sat down suddenly. The policeman's voice echoed in her head, his words became indistinct. She felt light-headed and dizzy. Suddenly, she keeled over, her body hitting the ground, her head just missing the edge of the table.

"Oh, my goodness. Look what you have done to her. She has just lost her husband and then you bring this sort of news. Jennie, quickly phone for Dr Pollock and ask him to call around as soon as he can, please," shouted Beth.

The detectives placed Connie in the recovery position whilst Beth ran to get a blanket from her room to keep her sister warm. Connie came around from her faint, but she was pale and pasty. She tried to sit up, but Andy told her to stay where she was until the doctor could join them. Jennie had managed to get through to the doctor's receptionist and she was assured that Dr Pollock would be with them shortly. The surgery was only a few hundred yards from Hilltop. The receptionist had just caught him as he was leaving the surgery to do his rounds and he said he would go directly to Hilltop. Within minutes he was kneeling by Connie's side taking her temperature and monitoring her pulse.

"Well, Connie, it seems that everything is getting on top of you. I think you are in need of some bed rest for a day or so. You have had a huge shock, you are tired after your journey and with all this business regarding the norovirus, I think your body is calling out for some TLC."

"But they think Mrs Singh's death was suspicious." Connie looked at the detectives who had stepped back to let the doctor carry out his examination.

"Suspicious? In what respect?" He addressed his question to the Detective Sergeant. "I attended the body when she was found. I didn't notice anything untoward. Rigor mortis was not at its peak when I examined Mrs Singh. There was no sign of interference with the body."

"We will be asking you for a statement as the doctor attending, so we will arrange a time to visit you at your surgery, doctor."

"Yes, that is fine. If you contact my secretary, she will arrange it."

"We will give you some time to rest, Mrs Wilkins, but I am afraid that we will have to return to continue our investigations." Connie merely nodded then closed her eyes trying to rid herself of this nightmare.

Jennie showed the police out whilst Beth helped Connie back to the flat. She got her undressed and put her in bed. Within minutes, Connie was fast asleep. When she awoke, she remembered the terrible situation in which she found herself. No Jake and the care home under a cloud because of Mrs Singh's death now due to suspicious circumstances. She picked up the phone and rang the police station, asking to speak to Sergeant Milligan, but instead it was Detective Constable Mishra on the line.

"I'm afraid Detective Sergeant Milligan won't be back in the office till tomorrow, Mrs Wilkins."

"I don't understand how there could possibly be suspicious circumstances for Mrs Singh's death," said Connie. "As far as we are concerned, she was very old, not in good health and simply died in her sleep."

"Because Mrs Singh had been dead for some time, we referred the matter to the coroner who asked for a post-mortem examination," said Mishra. "My colleague and I want to interview you tomorrow morning. Could you come down to the police station at 9 am?"

"That's fine. Do I need to prepare myself in any way for the interview?"

"Please bring along your records of drugs administered to Mrs Singh on that day, Mrs Wilkins. There would appear to be a problem in that area, but I'd rather discuss it with you face to face and in the presence of Detective Sergeant Milligan."

The final part of the conversation left Connie perplexed but it was obvious that she needed to do some detective work of her own, so she set off down the corridor to find the nurse, Wahida, the only person at Hilltop who was authorised to administer medication. Maybe she could give some clues as to what the post-mortem had revealed. A few minutes later, Wahida was sitting in Connie's office with the sheet which recorded the dates and times that she had administered drugs to Mrs Singh.

"Looking at the record, it appears that there was nothing abnormal about Mrs Singh's last day. You saw her in the morning and then again at 5.30 to give her an insulin injection. Is that correct?"

"Yes," said Wahida, nervously twisting the hem of her uniform in her fingers, "you may remember that we were encouraging Mrs Singh to use a pump which would automatically provide insulin whenever her blood sugar was low. Unfortunately, she did not like the device because, although it managed her symptoms well, it was uncomfortable, and she just could not accept that it was permanently attached to her body. In the end, we decided, in consultation with her son and daughter to revert to the old system of two injections a day: basal insulin in the morning which kept her stable over a 24-hour period and fast-acting bolus insulin after the evening meal. The bolus insulin is designed to counteract the spike in blood sugar which arises after a large meal."

"So, you gave her the basal insulin in the morning?"

"Yes, at 10.15."

"You haven't recorded the strength of insulin on the sheet, Wahida."

"It was the normal 100-unit strength and that seemed to work well."

"I can see that on other days you gave the bolus insulin at 6.30 after the meal, but on this particular day it was at 5.30 before the meal."

"Yes," said Wahida, her voice trembling and her fingers incessantly fidgeting with a tissue with which she had just blown her nose. "Everything seemed to go wrong that day. Mrs Singh's son and daughter had visited her that afternoon, taking her up to the coffee bar as usual. Apparently, for some reason, she had felt unusually hungry and had eaten several chocolate biscuits.

"Within an hour or so, Mrs Singh's family came looking for me because she felt weak and very tired. They were convinced something was wrong, so I checked her blood sugar levels and found they were very high. I felt that she needed insulin straightaway, so I took the decision to do the injection immediately, at 5.30, as recorded."

"OK," said Connie, calmly, but starting to realise where the problem might lie, "and did you give Mrs Singh the normal dosage?"

"Because I was worried about how badly she had reacted to the chocolate biscuits, I decided to double the dosage of insulin. She was fine when I left her with the Singh family, and because I had so many other patients to deal with, I'm afraid I did not manage to check on her after dinner."

"I'm not a medical expert but giving her a double dose sounds a risky thing to do," said Connie. Wahida's fidgeting increased and the tears started to roll down her cheeks.

"I'm so sorry. I wanted to make sure Mrs Singh was responding well to the injection, but things just got out of control. I needed to be in so many places at the same time. People all over the building were ill with the norovirus and I was trying to make sure that nobody became too dehydrated."

"I fully understand the problem, but could you not have asked somebody else to check on Mrs Singh? Beth or Andy, for example?"

"I suppose so, but I thought she would be in the dining room for the evening meal and that she would be supervised there."

"Do you even know whether she went into the dining room?"

"I assume she did, but I couldn't be sure."

"Wahida, this is a very serious matter. It's more than likely that you will have to answer questions from the police as well. I'm afraid I've got to ask you to go home and stay away from Hilltop until further notice. Let's leave it there for now."

Wahida was sobbing uncontrollably as she left the room. Connie almost felt guilty for not taking her in her arms to comfort her, but the very continued existence of Hilltop was under threat and that had to be her priority. She was now wondering whether Mrs Singh had even arrived in the dining room that evening. Sure enough, none of the staff could remember seeing Mrs Singh in the dining room. More than likely, she had fallen asleep after the injection and nobody had remembered to collect her for the evening meal. The double dose of insulin, allied to the lack of food, would have had a bigger than expected impact, too much for her weak and frail body.

Tomorrow's interview with Milligan and Mishra and the post-mortem report would no doubt confirm her theory but meanwhile the priority was to find a replacement for Wahida, at least in the short term, until a decision on whether she could continue in her present post could be made.

"We have a real problem, Jennie," said Connie on meeting her colleague outside in the garden where she was wheeling one of the residents along the winding concrete pathways to inspect the plants. "Sorry Mr Moore, will you be OK here for a moment while I have a word with Jennie?"

"Don't keep her too long," said Mr Moore, smiling, "spending time with Jennie is very precious to me. She is such a lovely person."

"Don't worry," said Connie reassuringly, "two minutes maximum and she will be back with you." She drew Jennie into a deserted corner of the garden where nobody could hear them. "Jennie, I've had to suspend Wahida for the foreseeable future. We have a problem relating to the way she dealt with Mrs Singh but I don't want to go into any details until I'm absolutely sure of the facts.

"Crucially, this means that we need a qualified person who can deal with the medication for our residents. I know that you are a qualified nurse so I wonder if you'd be prepared to fill the gap, at least on a temporary basis until I can sort out the issue with Wahida or recruit somebody else."

"You know me, Connie, whatever needs to be done. Only in the short term though, as I'm keen to extend my managerial experience."

"I understand that. Thank you so much, Jennie. I think you'd better get back to Mr Moore. He seems to have taken a real shine to you."

"He's an old charmer and I'm very fond of him though. Don't worry about the medication, Connie, I'll start doing the rounds tomorrow."

As Jennie dashed back to find Mr Moore, Connie felt a surge of relief that she had solved the immediate problem. She could not relax for long, however. Dealing with Wahida would be tricky. Unless she offered to resign, Connie would have to build a watertight case for dismissal. A replacement for Wahida would also be hard to find in any case. Not the least of her problems was the interview with Milligan and Mishra the next day. Would she be able to convince them that everybody had acted with the best of intentions? Or would there be criminal charges?

Milligan and Mishra ushered her into the police station's small windowless interview room. Connie had not slept well, her brain overactive with worries about Wahida and what she was about to find out. She almost felt ashamed when she realised with a start that all her professional concerns had overshadowed thoughts about Jake and plans for his funeral. She would find space for that soon enough, but for now she searched the faces of the two detectives for clues about what they were going to say.

There was nothing to either encourage or discourage her: they were so skilled at hiding their emotions, like a pair of poker players, not that Connie knew anything about poker. The surroundings were equally blank and unwelcoming: dull, fading and slightly discoloured white paintwork on the walls, a plain wooden table, three utilitarian chairs that scraped loudly on the hard-tiled floor.

"Thank you for coming here this morning, Mrs Wilkins. Our job is to help the coroner to establish the exact cause of Mrs Singh's death," said Milligan, speaking in a flat monotone that blended well with the room's décor. "Therefore, I hope you don't mind us tape-recording this interview. Have you brought all the paperwork relating to Mrs Singh?"

"Am I being charged with a criminal offence? If so, I need to ask my solicitor to be present," said Connie assertively, though inwardly she felt intimidated by her situation.

"That is your prerogative, Mrs Wilkins, though this is more of an informal chat, just helping us with our investigation," said Mishra. Connie could have been mistaken but sensed a hint of a softening in the hardness of Mishra's expression and she interpreted that as an encouraging sign.

"OK," said Connie confidently. "I want to help all I can, but I cannot understand why you cannot simply accept Dr Pollock's view that Mrs Singh died of natural causes."

"The problem," said Milligan, looking directly at Connie, "is that the post-mortem report tells us that there was an unusual amount of insulin in her blood. How do you explain that, Mrs Wilkins?"

Connie was pleased that she had done her own investigation and was able to explain the circumstances in which Wahida had injected a double dose and Mrs Singh had then missed the evening meal.

"This was an unfortunate combination of circumstances and I have already suspended my nurse until we have completed our own investigation into what exactly happened."

"That does seem to explain the presence of a rather large amount of insulin, Mrs Wilkins. Thank you for being so honest," said Milligan. He was clearly relieved.

"I assume that was the cause of death?"

"No, Mrs Singh had an aortic aneurism. The wall of her aorta was quite thin, apparently. I'm told it's a miracle that she didn't die at a much younger age. Presumably, not long after Wahida left her room, the wall of the aorta burst and killed her instantaneously."

"So, it was nothing to do with the insulin?" asked Connie, incredulously.

"Apparently not, but we needed to find out why the insulin was there for our report to the coroner."

"I fully understand that," said Connie, starting to relax. "I now have to decide whether I feel I can train Wahida to be a better nurse or whether she needs to move on."

"Well, that's a problem for you. We won't need to concern ourselves any further with that. Thank you for your assistance. I hope your care home succeeds by the way. My father-in-law, Fred Moore, is a resident," said Milligan.

"Really," said Connie, moving towards the door, "Mr Moore is a lovely man, always so cheerful." She shook hands with the two detectives, wondering as she left at the stark contrast in the demeanour of charming Mr Moore and the dour Detective Sergeant Milligan.

The rest of her day was spent visiting every resident who was still residing at Hilltop. She hoped to visit those in hospital the following day. She sat with them in their rooms, in the dining room and the residents' lounge and listened to their views on how their home could be improved further. She made notes as they suggested a number of changes, some very small, such as having hand cream and moisturising liquid placed in all the en-suite bathrooms, to a much larger suggestion of staging an art exhibition, primarily for family members, to showcase the creations of the residents.

By early evening, Connie was exhausted. She retired to her room to think through the suggestions she had collected that day and then went to bed. 'I have to keep busy' was her mantra. Being involved in the lives of the residents would help her build her new life without Jake. It was only 7:30 but Connie was glad to stretch out in her bed and within minutes she was fast asleep.

Chapter 13

A sliver of sunlight sliced through the gap in the curtains. The beam bounced on to the opposite wall then disappeared. Connie watched and waited. Once more the sunlight returned and danced around the bedroom. Warm delicate shapes of light flickered across the bland wall turning the mundane surface into a more welcoming space. Her bedroom, once a retreat, now seemed like a prison. She was sentenced to life without Jake.

She stared at the familiar walls and the watercolour paintings of bucolic bliss and suddenly she hated it all. She wanted to rip the pictures down and paint the walls black. This room had once been their private world where they had voiced and made sense of their shared dreams. No one else was encouraged to enter their space without invitation. They had established this rule from day one. Now all she had left was a lonely world. She was a boat adrift from her moorings and she couldn't fathom which direction she should take.

Connie turned her head and stared at the empty space beside her. Her hand caressed the sheet imagining that she would eventually find Jake's slumbering warm body. The space was cold. Empty. She opened her eyes wide and focused on the uncrumpled pillow. So, he wasn't there. She slithered under the duvet letting the weight engulf her and let out a muffled call: "Jake." No reply.

Her body coiled into its embryonic shape and she tried holding her breath. Is this what it feels like to be dead? She gasped as the last trickle of breath left her mouth and innate survival instincts took over. She threw back the duvet and inhaled deeply. Tick, tick, tick. Her heart throbbed its message of concern. Calm down. Don't be frightened. Tick, tick, tick. Settle down. Breathe deeper. Relax. The inconstant sunlight once more flickered into the room like a curious ethereal eye searching the dark corners. Connie watched its progress. She saw the room transforming itself like a chrysalis as the sun changed the ambience. Then it withdrew as quickly as it had arrived.

Time to get up. Connie's limbs felt like overworked plasticine, thin and lifeless. Easy does it. She sat up in bed moving her pillows to support her back, but as she did so, a wave of nausea welled up and she became light-headed. I must have Jake's virus, she thought. She lay down again, but now her bed, crumpled and cooler, was no longer her sanctuary. Connie tried to manoeuvre her legs out of the folds of the duvet, lowered her feet to the ground, then took tentative steps, but the bedroom became a ship in a rough sea. She rocked from side to side as the dizziness toyed with and confused her balance.

She gasped as the sickness gurgled up into her mouth and she lunged for the nearest thing at hand. She was sick into the folds of her green velour jumper. She held it against her mouth as she staggered to the bathroom. Connie knelt down over the toilet rim which was icy to the touch and she emptied her stomach, wave after wave. She gasped like a drowning soul. She coughed to clear her throat of its acidic particles.

Relax. It will pass. Don't be afraid. She sat on the floor waiting for the ghastly moments to pass before she could summon help. The room smelt of her sick and Connie's hair and face were encrusted. She spat out the last of the nauseous liquid and like a shipwreck survivor, she crawled back into her bedroom. She reached the house phone, picked up the receiver and pressed Jennie's coded number.

"Jennie, come quickly. I need your help."

Connie let herself be washed and changed just like she was a child again. Her bed was straightened, the duvet was shaken and then she was returned to its comforting softness.

"I will ask Doctor Pollock to examine you, Connie. It might be another bug so we need to know whether you should stay in your flat until you are better so that you don't pass it on to the residents."

"Oh, my goodness. I saw every one of them yesterday. Dear God, I hope it isn't contagious or that it is the norovirus."

"I will bring you a hot drink to warm you up. You have become really cold sitting on the tiled floor. What would you like? Tea? Coffee?"

"I can't face tea. Coffee will do, thanks, Jenny. Would you mention this to Dad and Beth and ask them to visit me after the doctor has checked me out, please. I don't want to expose them to my germs if I am infectious as they need to be able to carry on managing Hilltop. I think they said that the funeral director was visiting today with a choice of caskets and flowers and that he will want to set the date for the funeral."

"Yes, but he isn't due until after lunch, so meanwhile, rest and try to sleep until the doctor has seen you."

Doctor Pollock examined Connie and he shook his head. "Well, your symptoms suggest a number of things, my dear. It could be the norovirus or another viral strain. I want to do some checks to determine what ails you. I will take some blood whilst I am here and get it checked so we know one way or the other. Just have a light diet at the moment and stay in your flat or bed if you prefer, for a while. One way or the other, you need to get your strength back. You look thin and tired, Connie. By the way, when did you have your last period?"

Connie looked startled and flushed. She had forgotten all about her monthly visitors as the events of the last few months had been all absorbing and distracting. She got out of bed and took out of her dressing table drawer her spiral bound diary. She had always been nagged by Jake about her diary. "Why don't you keep an electronic diary, Connie, then we could keep a track of our engagements?" She had resisted, of course. She loved her paper diary. Each year she had replaced the old one with the same version.

This year the cover was Wedgewood blue with delicate tracings. Her diaries from previous years sat on the bookshelf like works of art. She flicked through the pages. The spiral spine housed the turbulent year's history within. She paused at the days of Jake's illnesses and then continued her search. She always noted her period each month on the day of its arrival. She looked back two, then three months and was surprised to find the last one was nine weeks previously. She had always registered its due date from the age of thirteen and catalogued her fertile progress through womanhood. Funny that something so significant had been easily forgotten.

Doctor Pollock raised his eyebrow and asked her anew about her symptoms. He examined her breasts which Connie had noticed were tender and uncomfortable. She had thought they were symptomatic of the virus. The doctor then carried out an internal examination.

"I will say with caution that it might be possible that your symptoms indicate you are pregnant, Connie. I want to wait for the blood tests results to confirm this and rule out any virus possibilities. You could confirm whether or not you are pregnant yourself, if you want to put your mind at rest, by purchasing a pregnancy test from the pharmacy. When you urinate on the stick you will get an instant diagnosis. You need to buy one today and carry out the test in the morning on first waking.

"If you prefer to have this done by us, then bring a sample to the surgery in the morning and we will carry out the test for you. Your blood test results will be back with us in a couple of days and then we will know for sure what is going on. I have to say though, Connie, with your symptoms, your tender enlarged breasts and the missing periods, I think it is most likely that you are pregnant."

The room emptied of her visitors and Connie stared through her window. The sun had escaped now, leaving grey milky clouds to dominate the sky. Birch trees swayed gently in the breeze. Their thin, delicate branches waved to the tempo of the wind and cascades of dried leaves fluttered like snowflakes to the ground.

She watched as a grey squirrel made its way across the branches pirouetting on to the different levels. She noticed for the first time the dray high up in the far branches. The squirrel made its way home and she waited until it disappeared into its nest. Fat, overblown wood pigeons roosted on the branches looking like old men as they rocked rhythmically on their perches, taking no notice of the more agile tree dwellers. She felt a sense of calm for the first time since Jake's illness. She caressed her stomach and decided she would get dressed and go out to the buy the test. She wanted to know whether the doctor was right. He had suggested that she could even test her urine today if she didn't empty her bladder for several hours so that the concentration of the HCG hormone would be increased. Connie was not naturally patient by nature but the decision to test later that day was made.

She waited uncomfortably for the third hour to pass since she had last urinated and then decided enough was enough. She would administer the test come what may. She sat on the toilet and held the stick under the gushing flow of urine. Her hand became wet with the warm golden liquid which ricocheted off the plastic stick. She sat on the toilet and watched the stick perform its miracle. To be or not to be, that was her question. She saw the result appear in front of her. Her heart kept up its earlier throbbing tempo. Tick, tick, tick.

"Jake, we are going to have a baby," she whispered. The line on the pregnancy indicator was proof positive. She decided she would phone the surgery and leave a message announcing the result. Then she put on her coat and went out into the grounds of Hilltop. She walked through the avenue of birches and picked up a number of leaves left from the autumnal moulting. The delicacy and transparency of each leaf brought a tear to her eye.

How fragile life is. The miracle of nature, the natural course of birth, development and death were hard to comprehend. She was alone in this new venture. Together she and Jake had created a small evolving life and now she would concentrate on trying to keep this tiny growth safe and alive, if fate could just lend her a hand.

Chapter 14

The hearse made its way slowly up the drive to Hilltop and came to a halt in front of the doorway. Connie inspected the coffin, a simple unadorned wicker design to match the unshowy personality of the man within. She then got into the large black limousine that had stopped just behind the hearse. She was accompanied by Beth, her father Andy and Jennie who had become such a good friend as well as colleague.

As if raging against the darkness of the occasion and the weather, the ladies wore brightly coloured dresses, matching hats and high heeled shoes, whilst Andy sported a pale blue suit and yellow tie. They were dressed for a celebration of Jake's life, and in spite of their deeply felt grief, they were determined to give this dearly loved man the send-off he deserved. As they set off for the crematorium, there was a round of applause from a group of residents in support of the family as Jake took his final journey.

"He can't hear you, but thank you anyway," whispered Connie, determined to hold back the tears. She was still emotionally numbed by the shock of Jake's death. In contrast, Beth was sobbing uncontrollably, comforted in vain by Andy and Jennie. Her tears mirrored the raindrops streaming down the windows. The weather underlined the sadness of the occasion: the wind was bending the birch trees that lined the driveway, dark clouds shrouded the sky and the biting cold was winning its battle against the car's heating system.

Arriving in front of the crematorium's chapel, Connie was comforted by the sight of a small crowd of extended family and well-wishers, some of whom were either Hilltop residents or their relatives, and a few of Jake's ex-workmates from the factory that he had abandoned as soon as he had learned of Aunt Agnes' bequest. Heads were bowed as the ushers from the Cooperative Funeral Service eased the coffin from the car and expertly lifted it on to their shoulders carrying it slowly into the chapel, followed by Connie, Beth, Andy and Jennie.

In silence, the rest of the group took their seats behind the mourning family before Connie moved to the lectern. She was determined that the service would be totally secular and conducted entirely without any outside assistance. Andy had recommended the Humanist celebrant who had led the funeral service of a friend, but Connie was not to be persuaded. Nobody but her and her family could possibly be entrusted with this sacred task.

"This is a terribly sad occasion, but I want it to be a celebration of the life of the man I loved. I am deeply honoured that you are here to support us to remember my husband. Thank you so much. Jake was a massive fan of Morecambe and Wise during his childhood and liked nothing better than watching endless repeats of their shows. Reflecting on his life, I am struck by the fact that he was an optimist, even in the darkest hours of his time in hospital, so it seems fitting at this point to listen to 'Bring Me Sunshine'."

As Eric Morecambe and Ernie Wise sang their plea for sunshine and laughter, the atmosphere in the chapel lifted and for a short period, tears were replaced by smiles. The music subsided and then Beth moved forward to the lectern alongside Connie.

"I'm going to read W.H. Auden's poem 'Stop All the Clocks', chosen because I believe that Jake was Connie's 'North, South, East and West'. My sister and Jake were soul mates. How wonderful to have spent a life with the person you love most in the world. I'd better just read the poem before I totally lose control of my emotions."

Her lips quivered, but her reading of the poem was all the more poignant as a result. During the reading, Connie's eyes remained firmly fixed on the coffin. She gave out a long sigh, the only sign of her grief, and hugged Beth before Andy approached the microphone. He spoke of the difficulties he had experienced after the death of his wife, of how much he had come to rely on Connie to help him cope with a young family whilst he was often working away from home. Good fortune had smiled on the family when Jake had appeared in Connie's life, just when it seemed she would never recover from the trauma of her mother's premature death. Their relationship had been launched in that most unlikely of places, a training event for aspiring middle managers.

During the coffee break, they shared their scepticism at the jargon used by the trainers, discovering a shared sense of humour, an ability to laugh at their own inadequacies. Unusually for such a quiet reserved man as Jake, he asked Connie if she'd like to join him for lunch the following day in the supermarket coffee bar. It was an offer she could not refuse. In such unpromising surroundings, their friendship grew, their meetings became more frequent and eventually Connie moved into Jake's house.

"For me, it was such a joy to see the love that Jake and Connie had for each other. Gradually, Jake became my friend too, an integral part of the family. In recent times, as a work colleague at Hilltop, I saw Jake's qualities at close quarters. He cared so much about all those with whom he came into contact. I'm sure I speak for many people when I say that he will be greatly missed."

Connie hugged her father as he returned to his seat. She took her place once more next to the coffin. "Thank you, Dad. It made me smile to be reminded of our first meeting at that training event. The slogan was "Let's get it done," which we found deeply ironic because as far we could see our bosses seemed to get very little done at all. After that, whenever we were faced with a problem, we only had to say "Let's get it done" to collapse into laughter because it just seemed so utterly meaningless.

"On a more serious note, I am so pleased to be able to celebrate Jake publicly because it was easy to underestimate him. He was a great listener, enabling me to moan at length until eventually I felt better and was able to see things in a more positive light. He was not a joke teller, but he often made me smile because he was good at spotting absurdity and puncturing pomposity. He was sensitive to the needs of others, able to establish a rapport with everybody, even with the bank manager who was reluctant to give us our first mortgage. But he has gone now, leaving an enormous hole in my life.

Connie's voice started to falter as the power of her emotions started to overcome her. She paused to steel herself and she turned towards the coffin:

"Thank you for being you. I love you and will love you always." She turned back to face the audience. "It may surprise you to know that not only was Jake a fan of heavy rock but that he loved musicals too. His absolute favourite, unlikely as it may seem, was the *Sound of Music* and he just loved the Von Trapp children singing the farewell song towards the end of the film. It seems particularly appropriate as we say our farewells to Jake:

"So long, farewell, auf Wiedersehen, goodnight
I hate to go and leave this pretty sight
So long, farewell, auf Wiedersehen, adieu
Adieu, adieu, to yieu and yieu and yieu."

As the mellifluous sound of the singing died away, the group filed outside in silence. The rain had now ceased, the clouds had parted, at least for the moment, and a shaft of sunlight illuminated the scene. The mourners came to offer their commiserations to Connie, Andy and Beth before drifting off to the local pub for the wake, a simple buffet meal. Jennie had already returned to Hilltop to make sure all was well there and within half an hour she was phoning Connie to pass on the message that, because of the cancellation of other cases, Mrs Singh's post-mortem had been brought forward and would be taking place tomorrow. Connie simply took the news in her stride.

To Connie's surprise, the coroner was not wearing a wig but was dressed in a smart business suit, dabbing her nose with a tissue as she took her seat. "Please be seated," she said in a sharp but not unfriendly tone of voice, "I do apologise but I'm afraid I have a rather bad cold. Let me introduce myself. I am Gillian Wearing, the Area Coroner, and when not conducting post-mortem inquests, I am a District Judge. Normally the case of Mrs Singh would be conducted by a coroner who is a medical consultant, but my colleague is currently unwell and has asked me to stand in for her." Ms Wearing turned to Detective Sergeant Milligan: "Please explain why we are here, Detective Sergeant."

Milligan, in his usual lifeless monotone, explained the circumstances of Mrs Singh's death, including the fact that, though there was an unusually large amount of insulin in Mrs Singh's blood, her ruptured aorta was the cause of her death. The Judge then asked the representative of the hospital, a rather large lady with short dark hair called Anne Brown, to confirm the cause of death.

"Yes, ma'am, quite clearly the ruptured aorta was the cause of death, but I would like to place on record my concern that Mrs Singh was given her dose of insulin before her evening meal and that it was a double dose when a single dose is normal practice."

The Judge turned to Connie: "You will note that Mrs Singh's son and daughter-in-law are present and I think it would be helpful if you could explain to the court in some detail what happened on the day of Mrs Singh's death, especially as I believe that it was ten or twelve hours before she was discovered in her room."

Connie was amazed at how calm she felt as she gave her account of what happened. Before finishing, she turned to Mr Singh and his wife: "I am so sorry that your mother has died and, though I am now convinced that we did not actually cause her death, I accept that we made mistakes. I have suspended the nurse in question, replaced her with somebody of greater experience and we are currently reviewing our procedures ready for when the next crisis arises. I must emphasise that it really was a crisis during that period, with so many people ill at the same time. Nevertheless, I am determined to uphold the highest standards and I'm confident that such a lapse will not occur again."

"Is there anything that you would like to say, Mr Singh before I make my decision," asked the Judge.

"Obviously, we have been very upset by the loss of our mother. I felt it was our duty, for her sake and for the sake of all the residents, to hold Hilltop to account. I felt that the highest standards were not maintained with regard to the care of my mother on her final day, though it's fair to say that she was very happy at the home and we were pleased with the way the staff cared for her.

"In particular, I would like to praise the work of a carer called Mary: my mother really appreciated the help that she gave her, always so kind and attentive. It was unfortunate that Mary was absent ill on my mother's final day. Whether that would have made a difference, who can tell?" Mr Singh sat down, a look of resignation on his face, avoiding Connie's gaze, wrapped up in memories of his departed mother.

"Thank you, Mr Singh," said Judge Wearing, her tone much gentler than previously. "Having heard all the evidence, I have arrived at my judgement. The finding of this court is that Mrs Singh died of natural causes. I am also stipulating, as a legal requirement, that the practices of Hilltop with regard to the administering of medication are reviewed so that further mistakes are avoided. Do you have any questions, Mrs Wilkins?"

"None at all," said Connie, "the review has already begun. I'd just like to say once again to Mr Singh how sad we are at the loss of Mrs Singh. She was a valuable and much-loved member of our community."

"Thank you, Mrs Wilkins, especially as I know that only yesterday you held your husband's funeral. May I also offer my condolences on behalf of us all."

With no further ado, Judge Wearing walked out of the room, leaving Connie and Mr and Mrs Singh to go their separate ways. Mr Singh had done his duty on behalf of his mother, whereas Connie knew that she and her colleagues had fallen short in the way they had carried out their obligations. Even so, she was relieved that the case was over. The future looked bleak but at least she, in contrast to Jake, had a future and so did her unborn baby.

Chapter 15

The dreary winter months had come to an end. The damp, dark inclement days had seemed interminable as Connie adjusted to life without Jake. She watched her body change in shape as the pregnancy developed. She visualised the new growth within her as a strange alien. She mentally graded its development, first an apple pip, then a small tangerine, then a grapefruit, but now spring was chasing away the tail end of winter she stopped these imaginings and began to dream of a tiny doll-sized human inside her.

She had succumbed to maternity clothes. Her bra size had increased significantly, and her old lace bras no longer served a purpose. Her skirts and jeans were becoming uncomfortably tight around the waistband, so she and Beth had a shopping day purchasing clothes which she knew she would grow into. Her melancholy had now settled into a haze of depression. She sat at her window for long minutes of the day watching raindrops forming momentary patterns before they slid down the pane and disappeared. She traced their course with her finger.

The clock in her room registered the passing moments. Tick tock, tick tock. Her thoughts and energy were supressed by her deep sadness. She was still watchful but couldn't really get involved in the world around her. The Hilltop residents were very kind and patient with her whenever they encountered her on the corridors. Sally, one of Hilltop's oldest, always gave her a warm embrace whenever their paths crossed, and Connie found the strength which came from Sally's thin ancient arms strangely comforting.

"You'll be alright, love. It just takes time. Be kind to yourself and let the tears flow when they need to escape." One widow's advice to another.

Connie had given free rein to Andy, Beth and Jennie since her return from France and she was surprised and proud of how skilled all three of them had become in managing Hilltop. They worked as a team, with no one in particular as the boss. Their collaboration was mutually supportive, encouraging each other to be creative and dynamic in the running of the home. They were determined to ensure a smooth running and safe environment, now that the aftermath of the Mrs Singh episode was settling into history.

Jenny had instigated a daily meeting with all the nursing staff to review the drugs given to each resident. She also made unannounced visits to different residents' rooms at various times of the day to check the medicine cabinets. She scrutinised the medical charts for each resident and counted the number of tablets left in the containers and packets, checking that the appropriate doses had been administered. This routine became an important part of her working day. Connie watched and contemplated the progress of the home and she wondered whether there was actually still a role for her. The systems were in place and there didn't seem to be much that she could offer.

The birch trees outside her window had shimmered silver even in the most bedraggled days, a gift from nature. Rain had fallen incessantly since the funeral with only a few days of thankful respite. On the dry days Connie walked for miles, often tracing the path along the riverbank, where she occasionally paused to watch the variety of waterfowl which paraded along the mudbanks when the tide was low. She marched to the rhythm of music which played through her headphones, her eyes generally averted from the passers-by also enjoying the rare moments of colder drier weather.

When Connie reached the section of the riverbank which was merely a mud track, she picked her way, gingerly jumping over puddles which were forming miniature lakes, taking care not to skid on the slimy surface. At the bend in the river, she left the path and crossed over the road to a new café which attracted walkers and office workers; it was rarely empty. She was glad to enter anonymously into this bustling room and sit without having to make conversation with anyone. After a cup of hot chocolate, she returned along the riverbank and quietly slipped into Hilltop, scurrying upstairs to her apartment before she was seen. No one troubled her. She was left to work her way through her raw grief. The days moved into weeks and, slowly but surely, she began to adjust to her new world.

The miraculous paddle instrument glided over her shining stomach, the gel glistening in the light of the harsh lamp and Connie held her breath. She watched intently the face of the nurse. Stern concentration. Something is wrong…An upturn of the right lip… Oh no. The baby has died. She is going to give me terrible news. She can't find any life. The device slid over her gentle mound. The nurse shook her head and repeated the movement. This is the end. Jake will have disappeared. I am not pregnant after all. Her breathing became shallow. Her palms sweated.

The nurse suddenly frowned, shook the equipment, repositioned it and rocked the paddle back and forth. Connie's stomach was icy cold, wet and rigid. Her startled eyes watched the transducer pirouette over her navel like an ice skater performing some complicated dance. Swish, swirl, swish, swirl. The monitor, stationed near her head, was positioned at an angle to enable her to watch what was happening on the screen, but Connie averted her eyes, too anxious to look.

"Well, my goodness, that is a surprise."

"What is it?" asked Connie. Tick, tick, tick, tick. Her heart suddenly began beating rapidly.

"Take a look at the screen. Tell me what you can see."

Involuntarily, Connie glanced across expecting to see a void, but what was revealed were black and white soundwaves which created an indistinct image. The nurse pointed.

"Look there."

Connie noticed a pulsating sound wave throbbing rhythmically.

"That is the heartbeat."

The nurse pointed to the right side of the central image.

"But look here and you will see another one just slightly behind the first." Connie strained to see the image and as she focused where the nurse's finger rested, she saw the second echoing beat.

"It looks like you are expecting twins, Connie." She paused to let the enormity of the news sink in. A pregnant pause. "Do you have a history of twins in the family?"

Unable to speak, Connie shook her head. Her body began to tremble and shiver. Her legs, in cold shock, became like demented drumsticks beating a complicated rhythm on the bed.

"Just another minute, Connie, then I will clean you up. I think you have had quite an unexpected surprise." The nurse quickly finished her procedure. "Don't worry though. Both heartbeats are strong and your foetuses indicate they are twenty-one weeks."

She smiled at Connie, mindful of the young widow's situation. She tried to keep her tone light.

"I nearly missed the second one as it was hiding behind its twin, but I must have woken it up and it moved just in time for me to see it and now you have a clear image of both of them. You will have a lovely photo to take home with you."

She smiled once more at Connie, quickly wiping away the gel from her stomach with tissues and then she covered her over with the blanket to warm her. The shuddering eventually subsided. Connie opened her mouth and then shut it. She was too overwhelmed to say a word. Tears welled and rolled down her cheeks, the bib of her coarse hospital gown becoming saturated from the intensity of her crying. The nurse held Connie's hand until the crying blew itself out. The women united in this act of intimacy stared at the printed image of the two babies.

"I will need to see you every few weeks for more scans, Connie. We do more monitoring when we know you are expecting twins." The nurse completed her notes. "I would like to see you again in four weeks, please. I will give you an appointment date." She concluded her business on the computer and gave Connie a printed reminder of the appointment. "I suggest when you get home you put your feet up and have a nice cup of tea." Connie shuddered at the suggestion. "Well, whatever you can stomach."

Connie dressed, collected her belongings from the curtained changing area, and made her way to reception. The hospital was a scuttling world, patients and staff constantly on the move. She navigated her way down the endless corridors not noticing the artwork and posters displayed along the long meandering stretch. The cultural façade could not disguise the utilitarian architecture. The walls had absorbed the anxiety of generations and Connie hurried along to make her escape. She treated herself to an awaiting taxi and travelled back to Hilltop. She had become intensely weary and longed for the privacy of her bedroom retreat so that she could think through this further development.

A letter was awaiting her return. Jennie had allocated letter boxes for the family and staff, housed in an attractive unit near reception. Connie lifted the single white envelope from the box and looked at the postmark. London. She went to her room, installed herself by the window and opened the correspondence.

Dear Connie,

I hope I find you well. I wonder whether I could encourage you to meet me in my office one day next week? I have potential developments to discuss with you regarding several of your properties and I think it would be more profitable if we meet for lunch to discuss them.

Kind regards,
Jonathan.

London. Why not? She needed a reason to leave this room. She had noticed that day by day it was getting harder to venture out and she was fearful that if she didn't make a concerted effort to get out more, then she would become imprisoned. Depression was natural, she argued, but now that two lives depended on her she had to force herself back into society. Grief would be part of her from now on, but she had to manage it. She needed to take on responsibility beyond nurturing small developing humans.

Jonathan's letter, short and brief, was sufficiently enigmatic to rouse her curiosity. She emailed his secretary and arranged a lunch engagement in two days' time as her curiosity couldn't cope with a longer wait. She had no restrictions on her as the management team had everything in hand, so she was free to come and go as she pleased.

She announced the next day to Andy, Beth and Jenny at the morning meeting which she had avoided for weeks that she would be going to London and they were all encouraging. They want to see me go, was her thought. I must be becoming an embarrassment to them. What she said next stunned them into silence.

"I had a scan yesterday. All is well, but there is an unexpected twist."

All three registered immediate concern. "Tell us quickly," gasped Beth. "What is wrong?"

"Oh, nothing is wrong, except I am not expecting one baby, but two."

There was an outbreak of joy. They fussed and hugged her. Jennie ran off to tell Sean and returned with four slices of warm cake that he had just been taken out of the oven.

"He sends his congratulations with this celebration cake."

Andy was thankful to watch his daughter's face soften into a smile and then a laugh escaped her lips. He calculated that it must have been three months since he had seen her enjoy a moment.

"Well, love, you certainly know how to make an old man happy. I'll soon have an instant creche of grandchildren to play with. What wonderful news."

The meeting came to an end with everyone thrilled and excited by her announcement.

Connie went about her business of booking a rail ticket for the next day and ordering a taxi. She took down from the shelf the file Jonathan had given her and read through the details of all the properties she owned. She made notes as she read through the information. She had forgotten so much detail about these houses. Over the last few months, they had become forgotten pieces in the jigsaw puzzle of her life. She used the A-Z of London to remind herself where they all were. Did she really want to keep them on? What would they be worth if she got rid of them?

She looked online to get an idea of their value from the websites which offered current estimates. Her eyes swam over the astronomical figures. *But maybe I shouldn't sell them. Weren't they part of Jake? They were his inheritance after all. I can't think straight. Maybe it is my pregnancy which has befuddled my brain. I need some advice. Thank goodness I am seeing Jonathan tomorrow. He will be able to guide me.*

Connie had an early night and that evening slept soundly for the first time in months. She felt that she suddenly had a purpose again. She was uncertain what Jonathan's news might be, but she was interested and that was the first sign she was beginning to pick up her life again.

As the train trundled slowly across the road crossing which signalled its imminent arrival at Manningtree station, Connie gazed across the Stour estuary, the water glistening in the morning sun. Half a dozen ducklings glided behind their mother, following a centuries-old instinct for survival and reminded Connie of her new role as mother-to-be. Jake had been her everything but, though he would live on forever in her memory, she realised that the two babies developing inside her would be his legacy. They were the future upon which she would build her life and help her to move on.

Such reflections, allied to the halo of sunlight shimmering across the water, enabled her despair to be tempered by a new feeling of hope, optimism even, that she could build a new existence without Jake. As the train sped through the countryside south of Colchester, seemingly racing the endless lines of cars on the A12, Connie sensed relief that there was a growing distance from her life in Suffolk and excitement about the possibilities that London offered. She knew that Hilltop was in good hands with Andy, Beth and Jennie and that she had little to offer them or the residents whilst coping with her grief. She needed time to rebuild herself, to be open to whatever life had to offer, perhaps even to return to Hilltop at some future date with renewed vigour and inspiration.

The countryside was replaced by the conurbation of outer London. Towering buildings now dominated the skyline of the city. Connie planned the next stage of her journey as the train slowly entered a tunnel and smoothly glided to a halt in the harsh artificial light of Liverpool Street station. The other passengers hurriedly escaped the train, like prisoners breaking free from prison, but Connie waited till the carriage was deserted before alighting on to the platform. Her meeting with Jonathan was scheduled for 11.00 in the company offices, only a five-minute walk away, so she had a few minutes to spare for a coffee and pastry in the station.

After the meeting she planned to make her way across the capital to Greenwich where she had booked a few nights in a hotel. It provided simple but comfortable accommodation, crucially with modern en-suite bathroom facilities, part of an international chain that prided itself on offering exactly the same facilities regardless of location. For Connie, the hotel had two main advantages. Firstly, it had a wonderful riverside location, close to local shops and restaurants, and secondly it reminded her of happy times spent with Jake on their all too infrequent short holidays in London.

Connie swallowed the last few crumbs of her pastry, drained her cup, brushed herself down and headed for Jonathan Grey's office, the man who had already proved himself a wise counsellor and who would hopefully help her to navigate the future. She soon arrived at the office. She approached the receptionist and said she had an appointment to see Mr Grey.

"He's expecting you. Let me take you through to his office. Can I get you a tea or a coffee?"

"That's kind of you. A white coffee, no sugar, please."

Jonathan rose from behind his desk to greet her: "It's lovely to see you again. How are you?"

"I'm fine at the moment. Have you heard I'm expecting twins?"

"Oh," said Jonathan looking startled.

"Jake's legacy," said Connie with a smile.

"Sorry, you took me by surprise. Congratulations. When are the babies due?"

"In 4 months."

At this point, the receptionist came in with Connie's coffee. "Would you like a coffee too, Mr Grey?"

"No, I'm fine, thanks." As the door closed behind the receptionist, Jonathan continued: "So Connie, will you continue living at Hilltop?"

"I'm looking to make a fresh start. I need to get away from Hilltop, at least in the short term, and I was wondering whether there might be an opportunity here in London."

"It's funny you should say that because one of your properties has just become vacant. The tenants moved out yesterday. They are both young teachers who have managed to obtain posts in Australia and are hoping to build a new life over there."

"Who can blame them? Especially when there is so little funding for state schools."

"They have been working in an independent school in Surrey, but maybe the opportunities there were not so great either. Anyway, you could move into their property if you want."

"Remind me which property it is. If it's the one right in the middle of London, I don't want to raise two young children there."

"No, it's the one just off Lordship Lane in Dulwich. It's quite a large detached house that was refurbished before the last tenants moved in, so it's ready for you to live there straight away if you want."

"Is it a good area to bring up children, do you think?"

"I'm the last person you should ask, never having taken on parental responsibilities," said Jonathan wryly. "There are plenty of green areas round there though. I do think children need space and there's lots nearby, as well as some very good schools. Plenty of independent shops and good transport links too. East Dulwich train station is close by and from there it's a 15-minute journey to London Bridge and central London. The Horniman museum is up the road and the Dulwich Picture Gallery has always been one of my favourites. If you like culture, that is."

"You make it sound ideal. When can I visit?"

"Whenever you like. The house is empty."

"I'll go there when we've finished here, if that's alright with you."

"It's your property, so be my guest, Connie. Shall we have a chat about the other properties though whilst you are here? Do you have time?"

"Good idea," said Connie, though her mind was already on her new home.

Within half an hour, having forced herself to listen to Jonathan's update on the very healthy state of the income from the other properties and her various other investments, Connie was striding across the Millennium Bridge on her way to London Bridge station. Behind her was the traditional majesty of St Paul's Cathedral. In front was the old power station building that was now Tate Modern. Downstream was London Bridge and beyond that she could see HMS Belfast.

Alongside all this history were new buildings like the Shard. There was so much to see and do. Already, this contrast to her old life in sleepy Suffolk was exciting Connie. She wanted to give her new babies the best possible start in life and maybe London would be the ideal place both for them and for her. She needed to look at the house first though: that had to feel right too. She took a train from London Bridge and within a few minutes, she was arriving in East Dulwich.

Connie noticed a large primary school building and reflected how convenient that would be for the twins. She walked up the main street and, wanting to take in the ambiance of this new area that could become her home, entered a coffee shop. For once there was no queue so her favourite cappuccino was served promptly and with a cheery smile.

"Can you tell me the way to Lordship Lane please?" she asked.

"This is Lordship Lane. Turn right when you leave, and it continues for about a mile in that direction. If you go far enough, you'll reach the South Circular Road. Are you driving?"

"No, I'm exploring the area on foot."

"Just as well because that will be quicker. The traffic can be difficult though it's not too bad at the moment. Would you like one of our loyalty cards: after 10 drinks, you'll get one free."

"Well, yes, I'm probably going to move into the area so why not?"

"We love it around here. Lovely people, lots to do, great pubs and restaurants. You don't need to go into central London unless you really want to. The trains run into town every 20 minutes in any case."

"I'm looking forward to it already. Thanks for being so helpful," said Connie.

She sat down by the window, watching the people rushing about their business, stopping to chat or going into the local shops. What a contrast to her own small Suffolk town: the pace of life seemed so different. Maybe this would be the ideal place for the twins to grow up, with lots to stimulate their interest. The coffee was good too.

After a few more minutes of contemplation, she gave the barista a cheery wave and set off along Lordship Lane. She soon spotted the smaller road, Queen's Way, where her house was situated. The traffic noise had diminished by the time she arrived at her potential new home. In fact, she was amazed at how quiet the road was though it was only 300 yards from the noise and pollution that she had just left. Maybe this would be the ideal location to launch her new life.

Chapter 16

Three weeks of telephone calls and conversations with insurance brokers, house cleaners, gardeners and a variety of other trades left Connie exhausted. She was surprised how messy the house had been left. It was in a pitiful condition, not the glowing picture Jonathan had painted. The whole house needed a deep clean and Connie decided she would get a professional firm on the job instead of trying to do it herself. With a growing stomach, she didn't relish trying to scrub walls and floors.

Her old habits were hard to shake off and even though she had a fortune, she still thought paying for services was an extravagance. Nevertheless, she supervised the process and was impressed with the steam cleaning and scouring of every room which was carried out by a local firm based in Dulwich. Once the cleaning was completed, the painters she had previously used moved in. She was amazed at her luck in hiring all the tradespeople and how quickly they were able to begin their work. The Burtons' team worked tirelessly to transform the house, one group dealing with the top floors whilst another painted the lower and basement rooms.

Connie settled for chalk white paint for most rooms and was relieved as the house slowly began to sparkle in the sunshine. The large bay windows let in plenty of light and, once the decorating had been completed, she installed wide slatted colonial blinds to give her some privacy at the front of the house.

Connie was quite unused to home design so she was very fortunate to meet Louise Melton-Jones. She was about thirty years old and had a style which appealed to Connie. I don't want someone who can't dress themselves well never mind a house, she concluded. Louise was an interior designer who was recommended by the owner of the haberdashery store where Connie searched for curtain material.

Connie contacted Louise at home, liked the sound of her and arranged a meeting at the East Dulwich property. She wanted Louise to see for herself the challenge that faced her. After an extensive tour of the house, Louise explained her ideas for colour schemes, fabrics and furnishings. Connie was impressed and before long the two women agreed a price for the redesign of the Queen's Way property.

"Just one thing," Louise said, "I think you are wrong to have one colour throughout. The effect will be cold and clinical. You will soon have babies living here and you probably will be spending quite a lot of your time in the bedroom and nursery throughout the day. I suggest you inject some colour so that you can feel calm and relaxed."

Louise chose tones that were still gentle and restful but gave more character to the rooms. Connie's bedroom was to become a gentle sky blue. Louise told her that a scientific study showed that weightlifters were able to handle heavier weights in the gym when it was painted blue. "Quite a good idea when you will have two babies to carry about with you," laughed Louise. Connie gave a quick glance at her thin arms and then felt the weight of her stomach. She nodded her agreement and became anxious about her fast-changing world.

Louise arrived one day with carpet samples, a file of photos of furniture and her laptop. She had created images of rooms similar to Connie's displaying furniture and where it would sit in the space. She selected the carpet samples for the bedrooms and matched them with the bedding and curtain samples. Connie was overwhelmed at the sight of what these rooms could be like and said yes to every idea.

However, she hadn't prepared herself for Louise's insistence that she must tear out the almost new kitchen and replace it with different carpentry and marble surfaces. She showed images of white central islands and dramatic lighting, but little did she realise that the pantry idea was the thing that swayed Connie. She had always hankered after a pantry, a thing of her childhood when she had played with her dolls in the kitchen when she was about 6 years old. The pantry had been her imaginary shop where she bought her groceries. She would take tin cans, potatoes, and bread from the shelves and place them in her shopping bag then push her dolls into the hallway in their pushchair and wait for the imaginary bus to arrive. She sat on the stairs with her dolls and groceries, seeing in her mind's eye her journey home from town, then she would push the dolls into the kitchen and unload the provisions back into the pantry still pretending it was her own house.

This memory flooded her with nostalgia. The thought of the pantry was all that was needed to make Connie agree to everything. She became intoxicated by the sheer extravagance of it all. She didn't even want to know the cost of the renovations. She would just pay the final bill and enjoy this luxury that she could now afford. Why not? She had to build a new life for her family, and this was her way of realising her dream.

Connie finally moved into the newly furnished home after weeks living in a hotel with only six weeks to spare before the twins were due to arrive. Three suitcases of clothes and photographs were the sum total of what she took with her from Hilltop. Everything else in the London home was new. Andy and Beth were regular visitors to Connie's London home. Jennie and Sean made an excellent team and they loved running the home when Beth and Andy were absent for a few days. Their relationship was now very strong, and they treated Hilltop as their own home which was to the advantage of all the elderly residents. Their collective high standards meant that everyone was happy and enjoyed living there.

Connie insisted that Beth and her father select the bedroom they wanted to stay in whenever they could get to London. They were encouraged to leave clothes and personal items in their rooms when they returned to Suffolk, so they knew that the London home was their bolthole. Andy even installed a television in his room so that he could watch sport whenever he wanted without facing disapproval from his daughters.

Connie still had to return to Hilltop for director meetings and hospital appointments. Beth now insisted that she went with Connie to Ipswich hospital and both women giggled at the grey images of the twins from the scans they were given at each visit. "Morecombe and Wise" became the babies' nicknames. Neither knew the gender of the babies.

"Well, Mum didn't know what we were until we popped out," Connie argued, "so what is good enough for her is good enough for me." Beth bought an album and stuck in the pre-birth photos and she took a whole array of pictures documenting Connie's last stage of pregnancy. A prominent photo of Jake and Connie was displayed on the first page.

"Well, Connie," said the midwife, Sally, who she had gotten to know over the recent months, "it looks good and I think you should be thinking that these two might make an early appearance. They are certainly restless and seem as if they want more space of their own."

"Have you any idea when they will start their move?" Connie asked uncertainly. For the first time she began to feel nervous of the arrival of two babies and having to cope with them both on her own.

"You will need help," Sally said as if she had just read her thoughts. "There are agencies which offer the services of 'baby nurses'. London naturally has quite a number to choose from. They are experienced maternity nurses and they can live in your home and be with you from the moment you give birth and will stay up to six months or even longer so that you can get into a routine and also catch up on some sleep each day." Sally laughed at Connie's face which registered horror at the prospect of being even more sleep-deprived than she was. "You will find out soon enough," she said and winked at Beth who also looked anxious at what was ahead of her sister in just a few short weeks.

"I want to see you again in two weeks, please, Connie. We might know the intentions of these two by then, hopefully."

The journey back to London was pleasant and both sisters shared memories of their childhood which made them laugh and occasionally cry. Back at Queen's Way Connie and Beth made a quick lunch of soup and bread in the utility room which acted as the replacement kitchen whilst the new cabinets and surfaces were being installed in the main kitchen. Connie was comfortable with the kitchen fitters, cousins of the Burton family, Tom and Joe, who jollied her along and made her feel almost like an old friend. They had been in the property for two weeks working from 8 in the morning until 6 each evening without stopping for lunch.

Every little change to the original plan that Connie suggested, as she watched her kitchen take shape, was carried out without fuss and she rewarded their efforts with endless drinks and biscuits throughout the day. The oak cupboard doors that had been in the room were discarded and as soon as they were replaced with white cabinets and glass fronted display units the whole kitchen came alive. The marble worktops arrived, ironically from Martlesham in Suffolk, whilst Connie and Beth were at the hospital and as the fitters manoeuvred the heavy tops into position the kitchen was transformed into a beautiful and luxurious room.

The white cabinets, with white mildly veined marble tops and chrome handles, transformed the place. Joe was going to fit the long suspended pendant lights above the island in the next couple of days and Ron, the painter who had supervised the painting of the whole house, was returning to give the room its final coat of paint the next day. Boxes of new kitchen equipment, pots, pans and other paraphernalia were stored in the dining room waiting to be placed in their new home. Connie peeped into the boxes most evenings after Joe and Tom had gone home. She picked out forks and spoons, admiring their beautiful style and craftsmanship.

Louise had taken her to a kitchen specialist in the West End and they had spent a day picking out what was needed. They fingered every item, feeling the weight and shape of the cutlery, turning them one way then the other to admire their crafted design. Connie was like a child peeping inside the torn corners of her wrapped Christmas presents, fully aware of what they were, but longing to see them unwrapped and in use. The endless distractions of decision making and looking at mood boards, but particularly the daily company of the tradesmen, eased her into her new life in London.

Connie felt like a grotesque whale and she regularly needed to lie down and catch up on her sleep. Morecombe and Wise were now most active at night and they pressed on her organs, giving her heartburn. Seemingly every moment she nodded off, one of them would give her a kick which awakened her, and she had to scuttle off to the bathroom to relieve her full bladder.

"Oh, give it a rest, you two. Just think about your poor old Mum and let her get some sleep."

She turned on Spotify. The music had a magical effect on the twins who settled into a more comfortable position and let Connie sleep.

Chapter 17

Back at Hilltop, in the heart of rural Suffolk, the building was shrouded in a cool damp mist that seemed to deaden the sound of a group of cars appearing through the trees. It was the day shift of care workers arriving to relieve their colleagues who had been on duty through the night.

"Morning Andy. In a bit of a rush this morning?"

"Slept in," muttered Andy.

"Why is one sock black and the other red?" enquired Sophie, one of the newer recruits.

"That's what happens when you get dressed in the dark."

"I thought you lived at Hilltop anyway?"

"I do, but I didn't last night," said Andy, forcing a smile. "You're very inquisitive. Have you considered a job in the secret service?" By this time, they were at the entrance to the building. "Let me test you now, Sophie. Can you remember the security code?"

Sophie confidently tapped in the 6 digits, releasing the lock on the door which swung open. A blast of warm air met them, immediately creating condensation on Andy's glasses. Rather than stopping to clean them, he stepped blindly forward right into the pathway of Mrs Rose's mobility scooter.

"Good morning, Andy," she said in her beautifully correct voice. Amazingly, she spoke better English than most people even though her native language was Dutch. "I nearly ran you over there, sorry."

"My fault, Mrs Rose, no need to apologise. I'm in a bit of a rush this morning."

"Ask him why he's wearing odd socks, Mrs Rose," said Sophie, enjoying making Andy feel ill at ease before disappearing up the corridor to change into her uniform.

"Are you sure you're wearing enough clothing, Mrs Rose?" asked Andy, keen to change the subject. "It's cold out there and a bit damp."

"I'm only going outside for five minutes, just to get some fresh air and a change of scene. I'll be fine. But what about you? Have you looked in the mirror this morning?"

"Why? What's the problem?"

"You have what looks like blood on the side of your face. On the left."

"It's probably from shaving. I thought I might have nicked myself with the razor, but I was in a rush and didn't stop to check. I'd better go and clean up," said Andy ruefully. "Now remember, Mrs Rose, it's very cold out there so don't be too long."

She negotiated the doorway with ease and disappeared into the mist, heading down the driveway. Andy moved back into the warmth, reflecting that sooner or later they needed to introduce an electronically operating door that would be more wheelchair-friendly.

"Hello Dad, I've been looking all over for you."

"Sorry I'm a bit late, Beth. I met up with some old friends in Diss last night. It was a very good evening and I lost track of the time. I had a few drinks so obviously I couldn't drive back."

"Thank goodness you didn't. So, where did you stay?"

"I was just about to phone for a taxi when Geoff said I could sleep on his floor. You remember him, don't you?"

"Vaguely, is he the one who played cricket with you?"

"Yes, we've been mates for a long time. He's divorced now and so had to move into a flat, three doors from the pub where we spent the evening. I must admit we had a couple of whiskies as we caught up on old times."

"So, you spent the evening in the pub, continued boozing at Geoff's place and then you've driven to work this morning?" Beth's tone was accusatory.

"Yes, well what's wrong with that?" said Andy defensively.

"What's wrong with that is that you are probably still intoxicated. If the police had stopped and breathalysed you, you would probably still have been over the limit." Beth was now warming to her theme. "Do you want to lose your driving licence? Especially now, when you'll be wanting to visit your grandchildren in London."

"OK, OK, I take your point," said Andy, starting to look a bit sheepish.

"Had you considered the negative publicity for Hilltop? Headline in the local papers: 'Care home boss banned for drink-driving'. What is that going to do for our reputation? You know perfectly well that we need every room to be full to make this business work and which family is going to choose us if people think you are a drunkard?"

"Drunkard?" At this point Andy looked startled. "Drunkard? One night out with friends and suddenly you're calling me a drunkard."

"Well, don't drive the morning after you've had a lot to drink the night before. I can't believe you could be so reckless." By now Beth's anger was visible. Her cheeks were flushed red with the blood that was pumping through her veins. "Are you even fit to work? I suggest you go and lie down for a few hours so that the residents can't smell the alcohol on you. Then have a shower. You just don't look clean. We'll have to cope without you for the rest of the morning."

With that Beth stormed off down the corridor. Andy watched her disappear, admiring the way she transformed herself into her normal calm and smiling demeanour as she came across residents and colleagues. She's talking rubbish, of course, he thought to himself, but I love the way she's developed into a responsible, caring adult. I must have done a good job, he reflected, as he made his way to his room and slumped fully clothed on to the bed. Within seconds, he was fast asleep, the effects of the alcohol rendering him unconscious for the next few hours.

He awoke with a start, uncertain for a few seconds where he was. He fumbled in his pocket to check the time on his phone. 2.30: why was he waking up in mid-afternoon? Then he remembered that Beth had told him that he was unfit for work. He felt a sense of shame that he had let himself down. His absence during the day would have increased the workload of his colleagues. It wasn't fair on them and he would have to make sure that it didn't happen again. He couldn't resist a smile at the memory of the previous evening though. It had been great fun. What harm could a few pints do?

Then he remembered the whiskies that had followed at Geoff's place. How much had he drunk? It must have been a fair amount because they had bought a bottle at the pub and, before leaving, he'd noticed that only a small amount remained. Goodness. No wonder he'd felt so rough this morning. Not surprising that he'd slept for five and a half hours during the day. These "sessions", as Geoff called them, had become a bit of a regular event in recent months after the relationship with Maria had broken down. Not every day, but certainly two or three times a week.

It was the first time that he'd been found out, however. He'd been surprised how angry Beth had been. Next time he'd need to be much more careful. And make sure that he didn't drink so much. The phone rang and Geoff's name was on the screen.

"Ah, good, you got back OK. How are you, Andy? I thought you were never going to stop drinking that whisky."

"Hi Geoff. Why did we even start drinking the whisky? We'd already had a few pints before we left the pub."

"Don't blame me. You insisted on buying the bottle to take back to my flat. Once you started, you just kept on drinking. In fact, you carried on until you passed out."

"I passed out?"

"Yes, you stopped talking mid-sentence and seemed to go to sleep. I left you in the chair and went to bed. When I got up this morning, you'd gone."

"How much of that bottle did you drink, Geoff? Please tell me that I didn't drink all of it."

"I'm afraid you did. I don't like whisky, so I just had a couple of beers."

"So, I drank most of the bottle, as well as several pints beforehand. That's ridiculous. Mind you, we had a really good time, didn't we?"

"That's why I'm phoning, Andy. Some of the lads are getting together on Sunday night. Same pub. You can stay over again if you want, as long as that armchair is good enough for you."

"Great, I'll be there. The armchair will have to do, though I don't remember much about it. Whatever happens, don't let me buy any more whisky."

On Monday morning Andy returned to Hilltop in a taxi. He looked around furtively, relieved to see that he'd arrived early enough to avoid the other day shift workers. With a big effort of concentration, he steadied himself sufficiently to enter the 6-digit security code on the front door and crept past the door to the main office. He thought he was in the clear till a voice behind him called: "Morning Andy. Do you have a minute?" Jennie had spotted him.

"Of course. Is there a problem?"

"Yes, there is really, and I wanted to ask your advice. You know Mrs Douglas who arrived a couple of months ago?"

"Oh yes, I remember. The Scottish lady who was very proud of her son. Kept reminding us how important he was."

"Yes, and how wealthy he is too. Well, ironically, we've had no payments from either Mrs Douglas or her family since she arrived."

Andy looked pensive. "If I remember correctly, she was hoping to be fully funded by the local authority. Her savings were quite small, meaning that she could be eligible for the local authority to pay the fees."

"Yes, but she had been living in a little cottage and we were trying to find out who owned it."

"Because if she owned it, she'd have to sell it in order to be able to cover the fees."

"And she was moaning that if she lived in Scotland, she wouldn't have to pay at all. Anyway, whatever the truth of the matter, we have not been paid a penny and she's already been here 9 weeks. What should I do?"

"Have you been in touch with Social Services?"

"I tried to phone them on Friday. They said somebody would phone back, but typically nobody has." Jennie looked at Andy curiously. "Are you OK? You look tired."

"Oh, I'm fine. I had a night out with Geoff and the lads. Spent the night on Geoff's floor so didn't have the best night's sleep. It's great to keep in touch with old friends but I'm not as young as I used to be."

"Who is?" quipped Jennie. "There's nothing I like better than a night at home in front of the television these days.

"Me too, but it's good to keep in touch too. I just wish I had a bit more energy. Anyway, I must get on." With that Andy slipped away to his room, breathing a sigh of relief that she hadn't noticed the full extent of how awful he felt.

That morning Andy kept a low profile and spent quite a number of hours locked away in his office. He looked startled whenever anyone entered the room and bent his head low over his papers to avoid making conversation. He was particularly pale and his clothes, although clean, looked crumpled and neglected. He was noticeably starting to look unfit and Beth had commented recently on the way he now seemed to shuffle along the corridors. It was only four or five months previously that he had been playing badminton twice a week and walking about Hilltop with a straight back and his head held high.

Beth was sorry to see such a change in her father. She wondered whether Connie's pregnancy and depression were having an effect on him. She kept her counsel though. It didn't seem right to be gossiping about her father to Jenny and she certainly couldn't tell Connie about the change in him. She had had far too much to cope with and she had made such a lot of progress recently that Beth didn't want her to start sliding back into her dark days. She busied herself with her own jobs and left Andy to work quietly in his office. At least he is not out with the boys when I can see him here, she consoled herself.

Having finished her morning round, Jennie went to speak with Sean in the kitchen. Moments later she was standing outside Andy's office. She tapped on his door.

"Do you want lunch, Andy? Sean is wanting to clear up in the kitchen, but he isn't sure whether you have eaten today."

"No, thanks, I'm fine. I think I have got a bit of tummy upset so I don't want to eat anything at the moment. Tell him to clear away and not to save me anything, thanks."

Jenny paused and was about to say something to him but thought better of it. She closed the door and went about her business. She had a frenetic week ahead of her as she wanted to check every resident's medication, but she didn't want to make it obvious that she was monitoring the daily routines of the carers. If word got around, all the nursing staff would make sure that they had done everything according to the book. Funny, thought Jennie, I want things done properly but not just because I am carrying out an inspection.

She started on the top floor, moving along the corridor, room after room, chatting to the residents. So far, so good. The day continued apace. Jennie was delighted that all the medicine checks tallied with the charts and the quantity of tablets left in the bottles. She locked up every medicine chest after the inspection, then she went through her questionnaire with each resident asking the same questions to ascertain whether they felt they were being well looked after.

She certainly expected some negative replies, particularly from Gladys who lived on the ground floor. She always had something to get off her chest: it was too hot, too cold, too noisy, too quiet. Gladys was one of life's discontented and probably always had been. Old age had possibly intensified her contrariness, but Jenny had to remind herself that Gladys was alone in the world. She had one grown up daughter who never came to see her. She never had visitors and Jenny would sometimes glimpse her in the bistro watching other residents having tea and cakes with their grown-up children and grandchildren. Her face didn't give away any emotion as she occasionally looked up from reading her newspaper and then quickly lowered her eyes back to the page, but Jennie noticed that the same page was never turned. She was probably trying to listen to the exchanges between the families and imagining herself in that world.

The week passed quickly for the staff who had particular routines and responsibilities but, for some residents, seven days were interminable. Gladys entertained herself throughout the week noticing what was going on in the home. She was always the first to know when the undertakers had been to remove a deceased resident. She would pass this information on to the others mentioning the drama in a conspiratorial manner. She kept an eye on the number of visitors who arrived and whether they brought gifts for their loved ones.

She had recently started to worry about Samuel Jones in the first room along the corridor. He had had no visitors for four weeks now and she noticed that he had begun to withdraw from any social contact. Samuel had always been the first to visit the bistro in the mornings. By 10 am he was installed in his wing chair by the window hogging *The Times* and trying hard to complete the quick crossword before anyone else could have a go. Now, since his visitors no longer put in an appearance, he stayed in his room and whenever Gladys went past and his door was slightly ajar, she noticed the same scene: him sitting in his chair looking out into the garden unaware of anyone else. He will be the next one who will be having a visit from the men in black, she told herself, and she moved along the corridor a bit more quickly for fear of contaminating herself through association.

Whilst Jennie checked the medicines, Gladys remained quiet and bided her time. As soon as the counting of the tablets was completed, she launched into her topic.

"I have noticed a great change in Andy recently, haven't you?"

Jenny looked surprised. "Well, no, not really."

"Oh, you must have done. Haven't you seen the state of him? He used to be so particular about his appearance. I used to think that was rather nice. He was making an effort for us. But now, well you must have seen a difference in him?"

Jennie shuffled her questionnaire forms and was about to say something innocuous when Gladys dropped her bombshell.

"I think something is up with him. He looks really troubled when he walks down the corridors. He's always on his phone, haven't you noticed? All times of the day and night he is either reading or writing things on his little phone. It pings, he then reads something and his face crumples up. I've noticed that he looks really upset after he has read the message. He mutters under his breath, but

I can't hear what he says. I don't think it must be very polite if his face is anything to go by. He then writes a reply, but within seconds there is something else on his phone that he reads and frowns over. I don't know what it is, but he certainly isn't the happy person he once was. I am sure that is why he is staying out late."

"What do you mean by that?" asked Jennie who couldn't contain her curiosity.

"You know how I like to keep up with what is happening in Hilltop." Jennie nodded. "Well, Andy has been troubling me lately. I've seen him many a night coming back into Hilltop when everyone is asleep. I have my curtains open so I can see the stars. You know that I don't sleep very well at night, so I watch through the window at all the happenings outside. You would be amazed at the number of foxes that wander past my window and the other night I could have sworn I saw a badger cross the path there and disappear into the wood. It's amazing what you can see when you train yourself to look in the dark.

Gladys paused and checked Jenny's face to see her reaction. "I've seen Andy driving up the drive on several occasions recently," continued Gladys warming to her subject and enjoying the chance to have an interested listener to her gossip. "Sometimes it is about 2 or 3 in the morning, but he leaves his car in the lower carpark. He then walks the rest of the way up the drive and lets himself in. I know it is Andy as I can see him clearly when he passes under the lamppost on the drive. He never used to do any of these things when Connie and Jake were living here."

"I expect it is all to do with the running of this place," said Jennie defensively, "as there is so much that needs to be done to ensure everything runs smoothly." She decided that she had better make a hasty retreat, before the conversation became even more difficult, and report back to Beth. Once Gladys has a theory, Jennie reasoned, she spreads it around Hilltop like a dose of measles.

"Right, I'll be off now, Gladys. Don't forget your hair appointment is in half an hour. They will be expecting you."

With that Jennie scuttled out of the room and went straight to Beth's office, but as she passed, she glimpsed through the glass door of Andy's office and, sure enough he was tapping a message into his mobile phone. She watched him remove his glasses, wipe his brow and then scrutinise his messages once more. Oh heck, she muttered, there certainly is something wrong here.

167

The stillness of the following night was broken by the loud cursing of Andy as he frantically tapped every number on the security pad. He fumbled in his pocket for his keys but only pulled out old receipts and crumpled tissues. He hiccupped, looked at his right hand as though it was an alien force then tried to batter the pad in the hope that the door would magically open. He began to titter, stretched himself to his full height and shouted out "Open sesame." Suddenly, the front door opened. Sean stood there dressed in pyjamas and dressing gown, his hair dishevelled and his face registering thunder.

"What on earth do you think you are doing, Andy? It is four o clock in the morning, and we have precisely 90 minutes before we start work. Where have you been and, for goodness' sake, how much have you drunk? You smell like a brewery."

Andy began to chortle, which made Sean even angrier. "Oh, for goodness' sake, let me get you up to your room before any of the residents and staff see you. They will be horrified at the state you are in and you won't do the reputation of Hilltop any good if they see you like this."

Sean almost lifted Andy off his feet, half carrying and half dragging him up the stairs to his flat. Beth's door, next to her father's, opened just as Sean unlocked Andy's front door.

"Oh Dad, not again. How could you?"

"Now then, my darling, have you not been to bed yet?" Andy giggled at what he thought was a splendid joke. Ignoring Beth's enraged face. He laughed even louder and began singing.

"O my darling, o my darling, my darling, Clementine. Why should anyone want to call his sweetheart an orange?" He giggled at his own joke and was oblivious to the fact that Sean was manhandling him into his room. He was almost catapulted onto his bed and Beth yanked off his shoes and threw his duvet cover over him.

"Just stay in bed until you have slept all this alcohol out of your system, Dad."

She turned away from her already snoring father, patted Sean's arm, mouthed silent thanks to him and the two of them retreated to their own flats. Within two hours, Sean was in the kitchen preparing breakfast for the residents and Beth, who had been unable to sleep any more that night, was in the office going through the accounts looking for something, she didn't know what.

Jennie tapped on her door and walked in. She looked concerned as well as frustrated at the recent turn of events. She had known what was happening outside the flat she now shared with Sean a mere two hours ago, but she had decided it was more diplomatic to stay out of sight and leave any talking about Andy's drunkenness until the morning. She was relieved to be able to share with Beth this growing problem, now that it was out in the open. They had to have a proper conversation about Andy's changed behaviour. She began by telling Beth what Gladys had said the previous day.

"I wanted to tell you, but you were with Connie at the hospital and you looked far too tired when you got back here so I was leaving it for today."

"Oh, goodness," was all that Beth could reply as she tried to process what she had been told.

"Well, what do we do about all this, Beth?" Jennie asked. "Should we confront him or get the doctor involved? He has gone downhill pretty rapidly with his drinking, which now seems nightly. He is going to ruin the reputation of Hilltop unless we do something radical. What do you think?"

"We have an even bigger problem than that, I'm afraid," said Beth, a look of grave concern on her face. "I've been checking the accounts. You know that to save money by employing a bursar we decided to let Dad manage the Hilltop finances. Dad argued that, having owned more properties than us, he was more experienced with money." Beth's face was now registering disbelief and anger. "These bank statements from the last six months show that huge sums of money have been withdrawn. The sums are taken as cash or transferred into Dad's personal account. Look here, you can see his account number. There is more money going out than coming in. What on earth is he doing with all this money?" Beth looked hopefully at Jennie as though she could offer some explanation.

"We had better not do anything too quickly," Jennie advised. "We need to take our time and look into this. He won't tell us anything if we confront him when he is in this state. We need to find out what is going on and where all the money is going. We'll have to wait until we know he is sober before we challenge him. We also need a plan to keep him in Hilltop in the evenings rather than disappearing over to Diss."

Beth and Jennie decided to meet up again later in the afternoon to decide how to handle things. Left alone in her office, Beth wondered how she could find out more information about what was happening with her dad. Who could she talk to? What about Geoff? Maybe he would be able to shed some light on the situation. After all, he and Dad seemed to be spending a lot of time together these days.

Beth wandered along to Andy's room. He was still slumped on his bed, snoring loudly. Beth scanned the room, noticing his jacket strewn on the floor. She felt in his pockets and found his mobile phone. What would his password be? She tried Andy's date of birth. Wow, how easy was that? She searched in the contact list for Geoff's name and noted down the number. She was sorely tempted to check his emails too. Why not? After all, Andy had already overstepped the mark with the money that he had been siphoning from the accounts. Beth returned the mobile to Andy's jacket. As she left the room, she noted that he was still in a deep sleep, so now would be a good time to phone Geoff.

"Hello, is that Geoff?"

"Speaking." Geoff sounded business-like, so Beth guessed that he was at work. He had a small building company and was constantly taking calls from people who wanted quotations or from suppliers who could not source materials that he had ordered.

"Sorry to bother you, Geoff. I'm Andy's daughter, Beth. I wondered if you had noticed anything unusual about him recently."

"Well, he's certainly developed a strong liking for whisky."

"Yes, we have noticed. Can you remember when this started?"

"I suppose it would be round about the same time he started working at your care home. He talks about people there a lot. He's a bit of a worrier because basically he wants to do the best for them, although I don't know if that's the reason that he's drinking a lot."

"Have you noticed him constantly looking at his mobile phone?"

"Now you mention it, I suppose I have."

"Has he got a girlfriend?"

"If he has, he's never mentioned it. We spend a lot of time trying to solve the problems of the world, so to speak, but his main interest seems to be Hilltop. The rest of us love arguing about our favourite football teams but Andy would rather talk about work. If you need a longer chat, Beth, call me later. Somebody is trying to ring me, so I'll have to go."

"Many thanks for your time, Geoff. Much appreciated."

No clues there then, she surmised. I will just have to wait and see what Andy has to say for himself. Outside her office, she bumped into Gladys.

"Good morning, Beth. You look worried."

"Why do you say that? I'm fine," said Beth, with a quick and unconvincing smile.

"I expect you're concerned about your dad."

"What do you mean?" asked Beth hesitantly. She knew it was not a good idea to talk to residents about staff members but Gladys was right because she really was worried.

"He doesn't look like his normal self anymore. Always head down, fiddling with his phone, out late at night, smelling of alcohol."

"Smelling of alcohol?"

"Oh, yes, quite a few times in the mornings after I've seen him coming back late. My ex son-in-law was like that. He became a nightmare for my daughter. She thought he was having a few drinks with his mates in the pub, but it turned out that one of the group was a young lady who took a fancy to him. Then he took a fancy to her. Eventually, my daughter cottoned on to his carryings-on and, after a massive row, she told him to leave. So that was the end of that marriage. I don't know why these young people get married at all if they are not going to stay together.

Whilst Gladys paused for breath, she noticed tears forming in Beth's eyes. "Oh, don't worry, my dear, Andy is one of the good guys. Maybe he's just having a mid-life crisis." She patted Beth's arm reassuringly.

"A bit late for that, don't you think, Gladys? Unless 63 is still mid-life these days." Beth wiped her eyes. "Well, I had better go. I've got a number of things to deal with urgently, so I must get a move on."

Beth went back into her office, closing the door behind her so that Gladys would not overhear, and phoned Jenny.

"Hi, can we both make ourselves free to meet in Andy's room at 4 o'clock, whether he's awake or not. We need to talk to him."

Andy's door was locked so Beth knocked and then used her master key to enter, followed by Jenny. Rather nervously they tiptoed across the lounge area towards the bedroom. The door was open, and they could see that Andy was fast asleep. Beth was about to shake him awake but froze when she spotted that there was another form now in the bed alongside him. The two women quickly made their way out of his flat. Back in Beth's office they both looked shocked.

"He's got somebody in bed with him!" said Beth incredulously.

"Did you see who it was?" asked Jenny.

"No, I really didn't want to look too closely. He's supposed to be working but there he is, still in bed at 4 o'clock in the afternoon, and into the bargain he has got somebody in there with him. Who on earth is it? He can't just bring anybody in. There are safeguarding issues for our residents after all. We can't keep pussyfooting around. He'll either have to sort himself out or he'll have to leave."

"We're not at that point yet, Beth," cautioned Jennie. "We need to handle this in a professional manner. I know he is your dad, but he is a work colleague and he needs an opportunity to explain himself. I suggest that you type out a formal letter which we can both sign asking him to report to a meeting with us at 9'o'clock tomorrow morning. Just slip it under his door. That will give him a shock and he'll know that something is afoot."

"He needs a shock. You're right, we'll do this formally and keep a record of what he has to say. I'll do the letter now while you are here and then we can agree the exact wording."

During the evening, both Beth and Jennie stayed well away from the vicinity of Andy's room, not wanting to meet him or his friend. Neither slept well, dreading the day ahead, and they were relieved to chat beforehand and to plan the interview. Things didn't turn out quite as expected though. For a start, Andy did not turn up at 9 o'clock. By 9.30 Beth and Jenny were drinking their second cup of coffee and eating their third biscuit, nervously awaiting a knock on the door which would signal the start of the interview. At 9.35 Sean appeared. "I'm a bit concerned because I've just seen Andy wandering around the garden with a bottle of whisky in his hand and a strange lost look on his face. Before I could talk to him, he'd made his way around to the carpark, got into his car and driven off. I doubt if he is in a fit state to be driving."

"Oh no," exclaimed Jenny. "He's supposed to be in a meeting with us now. Do you have any idea where he has gone?"

"No idea, though he turned right to head towards Diss."

"I bet he's gone to the Four Horseshoes, hoping to see his mates," said Beth, "I'm really worried about him. I need to try to find him before he does any more damage either to himself or somebody else."

"Shall I come with you?" asked Sean. "You might need a hand."

"It's fine, I'll manage. We're short-staffed here in any case. I'll phone for assistance if necessary."

With that, Beth grabbed her bag, and within 15 minutes she was pulling into the carpark of the Four Horseshoes in the centre of Diss. Sure enough, Andy's car was there in the far corner. She was about to go into the pub when she spotted somebody in the car, bending down behind the steering wheel. What on earth is he doing? She walked over to the car, opened the passenger door and sat next to her dad. Beth had never seen him in such a state: pale, bedraggled and stinking of whisky.

"They won't allow me in the pub, Beth," he said by way of explanation.

"Why not?"

"They said I'd already had enough to drink."

"You do realise that you were supposed to be meeting Jenny and me this morning?"

"I couldn't face it, Beth. Things are very complicated. I'm in a mess and I don't know how I'm going to get out of it." Andy's voice was shaky, and his face was contorted.

"The drinking is certainly not going to help, is it, Dad. How long has it been going on?"

"I've always enjoyed a drink, but I seem to be drinking more and more. I can't see a way forward and the whisky takes the edge off things."

"I thought you were enjoying working at Hilltop, so I don't understand why you have been letting yourself down so badly in the last couple of months. You keep coming home very late, your drinking has been an embarrassment and you've become very unreliable. We used to love working with you but at the moment your behaviour has become impossible."

"I know, I know, you're absolutely right. I'm letting everybody down. I'm ashamed of myself, that's the truth. I can't go on like this and I know that I need help. I wanted to explain things to you and Connie, but I could never quite get round to it. Connie has got enough problems of her own and you are always so busy. I am just totally exhausted."

"Look Dad, come back to Hilltop with me now, have a good sleep and then we'll have a proper talk later over a cup of coffee."

"What about my car?"

"I'll drive you in my car. I'll ask the landlord to keep an eye on yours until we can collect it later. Come on, let's go." Beth supported her dad as they stumbled over to the other car. Having installed him safely in the passenger seat, she went into the pub to check that the publican did not mind having an extra car

173

in the car park and then drove back to Hilltop, thoughts whirring around her head to the sound of Andy's snoring.

He looked defeated and lost as Beth glanced across at him in the passenger seat. Her anger dissipated and she started to feel sorry for him. This was no time for any kind of formal meeting, so she took him back to his flat, seated him in a comfortable chair and made them both a brew of strong black coffee.

"Do you want to tell me what's going on, Dad. I've never seen you in this state before."

"This is so difficult for me. I'm your father and I should be the one offering you advice. I've certainly been drinking far too much. I'm not sure whether I'm an alcoholic but it seems the only way I can forget my problems at the moment." Andy was hesitant struggling to maintain eye contact with Beth: "Do you really want to know the full story?"

"Yes, of course I do." Beth's phone rang but she quickly switched it off. "I don't want any disturbances till I've heard what you have to say."

"I suppose things started to go wrong during the period when your mother was very ill and then died. Afterwards, I was totally numb and, although I tried to keep things as normal as possible for you and Connie, I know I did not do a very good job, not least because I was away from home working. I'm afraid I was the absent father when you both most needed my support."

Beth watched Andy's face intently but refrained from making any comment.

"Yes, when I was at home, I did my best, but the truth is that I became totally dependent on Connie to run the home and look after the two of you. At least I was earning the money to pay the bills but that was all. As you know my work involved a lot of travelling and I stayed in hotels all around the country. It was a soul-destroying experience, separated from my family, and I was struggling to cope with my grief. It was at that time I started spending time in pubs to while away the evenings and one time, whilst I was staying in Blackpool, I spent the evening with a guy and we became quite pally.

"Every time I went to Blackpool, I would meet up with him. Harry was his name. One night after we'd had a few drinks, Harry said, 'Come on, let's go to the Lido Club.' I'd never seen anything quite like it: so dark it was difficult to see anything, loud disco music, strobe lighting, packed with people on the dance floor. We ordered more drinks and I gradually realised that all the dancers were men, some of them snogging each other. I realised that we were in a gay bar.

"At first, I was quite shocked. I'd never been anywhere like it before, but we'd had a lot to drink and Harry dragged me on to the dance floor. The atmosphere was intoxicating, and it wasn't just the alcohol. A man that I'd never seen before bumped into me and instead of apologising he pushed his tongue down my throat. Ever since that moment, I've realised that I'm attracted to men as well as women and, over the years since then I've had many one-night stands.

Beth stared at her father. "I've really struggled to come to terms with who I really am. I guess I am bisexual, and I suppose that may be part of the reason that my relationship with my last girlfriend fell apart. I think she sensed that I was up to no good when I was travelling away, though she never knew the truth. Since Jake died and I've been working with you at Hilltop, the fact that I've been concealing the 'real' me has been eating away at me and that's when my drinking started again."

"So, the person in bed with you the other day was a man then, was it?" interjected Beth.

"How did you know about that?"

"Jennie and I let ourselves into your room. We had things to discuss, but when we saw you weren't alone, we thought it better to meet you at another time."

"Yes, it was a man."

"Is it anybody we know?"

"Adrian, Sean's assistant in the kitchen."

"But he's only just arrived from Romania with a temporary visa for 3 months. He will only be able to extend the permit if we can continue to employ him. What on earth are you doing having a relationship with a member of staff? Didn't you think someone was going to notice?"

"I don't know. I didn't intend to get involved with him, but we started on a bottle of whisky in my room one night and one thing led to another. I told him a while back that I was finishing it as I knew Connie would be mad if she found out. He didn't like it and started to get unpleasant. That is why I stayed out late over the last few weeks. I was trying to avoid seeing him. I couldn't exactly sack him, could I?

"And Sean thinks he works well in the kitchen, so I had a problem and I didn't know how to deal with the situation. I was OK if I stayed out of Hilltop in the evenings when he was off duty and he is too busy to trouble me during the day. I never go near the kitchen, but he has been leaving me messages on my phone which have started to get ugly. He must have come to my room last night as he had a key which I forgot to get back from him, but I can't really remember much about it. Anyway, he wasn't there when I woke up. I suppose you are appalled with everything I've told you."

"Well, at least I'm starting to understand where you're coming from. What a mess."

"Look Beth, what I've told you so far is only part of the story. If you don't mind, I've just got to get some sleep. Can we talk more in a couple of hours?"

Andy lay down on his bed. Beth left him to it, wondering what else she was about to discover about this man that she had known all her life. A man that, clearly, she had not really known at all.

Chapter 18

Connie had a restless night. She couldn't get comfortable no matter how hard she tried. Her stomach felt like a gigantic mountain: the twins had been moving around for hours and it felt as if they were fighting. She decided that she could no longer stay in bed and got up to get herself a hot drink. She sat in her almost completed kitchen leafing through the local paper which had been delivered the night before and she jumped as Joe, the builder, walked in. His usual starting time was 8 o clock, but he arrived half an hour early.

"Morning. Sorry I made you jump. I wanted to make an early start to get this job finished so that you could have the house to yourself before the grand arrival day."

"Morning Joe. That is kind of you. It looks like a nice day out there. I might go for a walk a bit later. I will make you a drink first then I will go and have a shower. I am exhausted because I must have had about two hours sleep last night. I suppose this is nature's way of preparing me for sleepless nights in the future."

She grinned but her eyes betrayed a look of fear. She was becoming quite fretful about giving birth, not once, but twice. How she missed Jake at these moments. He would have been supportive and dispersed her dark thoughts. She missed his hugs and cuddles. She felt starved of affection and her whole body ached for human contact. She filled the kettle and suddenly felt a surge of pain and discomfort.

"Oh, ouch. That is a new feeling."

Joe stopped emptying his toolbox and looked across at her. They both watched as a pool of liquid cascaded to the ground and settled between Connie's feet.

"Oh, no. Is it…it can't be. There are four more weeks to go." She winced at the pain that shot through her.

"I think we had better get you to the hospital. They say twins come early and I think your pair are no exception. Where are your things? Have you got a case packed?"

"But I haven't had a shower and I am in my dressing gown. I need to get changed…" She moaned with the pain which once more electrified her body.

"I don't think you have time for that. I'll get your case and I'll grab whatever is handy upstairs whilst you put on your shoes and coat."

With that he ran upstairs, found the room with the ruffled bed and grabbed toothbrush, paste, hairbrush, in fact anything that was lying on the surface in the bathroom. He stuffed everything into the weekend case Connie had left by the bed and ran downstairs. He found her doubled over in pain moaning and blowing through her mouth as she had rehearsed at the antenatal classes.

"Right, let us just think. You need a bit of money and one credit card, but don't take any more than that. Anything else you need I will bring tonight."

"Oh, Joe, I'm sorry I have spoilt your work plans…" She let out a muffled scream as the next contraction felt as if it was ripping her body apart. Joe instinctively put his arm around her whilst she travelled through the pain. Connie lent against his chest and panted heavily as the next wave tore at her body.

"I'm no expert, but I think those two are keen to make an appearance. Let's get you into the van and hope that the rush hour is still as light as it was on my journey here."

Connie could hardly bear the seatbelt across her and moaned at each new spasm. Joe drove quickly and rather erratically across town taking shortcuts to the hospital whenever he saw a queue ahead. He kept looking across at her and during the journey he offered soothing words of reassurance. Mercifully, the roads were still quieter than normal.

"School summer holidays, that is why it is not hell on earth," he blurted.

Joe pulled up at the front of the hospital doors and got Connie out of the van. He ran into the entrance and came back with a wheelchair and helped her into it. He loaded her case on to her lap. "Just sit here a minute whilst I move the van into that parking bay. It will save time later and I won't need to come out of the hospital to move it." He ran across, paid for a parking ticket, moved his van and then jogged back to Connie who had watched his every move. She had started to laugh.

"I bet you didn't think, when you set off this morning, that you were going to get this much exercise today."

He smiled and then pushed her into the hospital. She was fast-tracked through to a ward in the maternity wing and pushed into a single room at the side of the ward. Her contractions were coming every few minutes and Connie looked distressed by the unexpected intensity of pain. Joe pulled up a chair beside her and she gripped his arm.

"Don't leave me, Joe, please. I'm really scared. I don't think I can do this on my own." Her hair was dampened by sweat and she looked exhausted.

"No problem. This is my first birth…" he grinned at her.

"Mine too." They both laughed and another wave of pain exploded through her. A nurse came over and examined Connie.

"My goodness. You only just got here on time. You are already dilated and soon we will be able to see the crown. Try to keep her calm, if that is possible," she addressed Joe, supposing that he was the father of the babies about to be born.

"Yes, I'll do my best." He soothed Connie's forehead, gently caressing it and then wiping her face with the dampened cloth he had collected from the bathroom. Connie instinctively relaxed under his touch. Strength from his hands radiated through her.

A loud cry exploded through the mouth of the first-born. A little girl. Connie smiled as the nurse tilted her so she could get a glimpse of her small but perfect daughter. Not long after, her brother was competing to make the loudest noise in the room. Connie lay back on the pillow, her face a mixture of pleasure and exhaustion.

"Well done, Connie. You did it and in record time too. I could even go and make a start on your kitchen…" Joe smiled at her and then went back to the twins who had been weighed, cleaned and dressed in little all-in-ones. "I can't decide which one is which now they are dressed," he laughed.

Connie raised herself up, looked across at the cribs and pointed to one.

"That is Isabelle and that one is Jacob. Am I right?"

He quickly checked and nodded. "It must be a mother's instinct. They both look the same to me."

She tutted and smiled at her two offspring who were now catching up on their lost sleep from the night before.

"I'll let you get some rest like these two are doing. Do you want me to come back later? I've not got anything planned and I would like to see how they are settling in."

Connie was surprised how readily she agreed to this. She didn't really want him to leave, even though he said he would be back later that day and she felt as though they had formed a closer bond after the adventure that had just unfolded. He had been at her house each day now for several months, at first working with his small group of workmen and then on his own. He explained that he took the responsibility of finishing off the jobs and checking that everything had been done correctly.

When he was working alone, Connie had spent time sitting in the kitchen chatting away to him as he worked. She found him easy to talk to and surprisingly entertaining. As time passed, they shared their life stories with each other. Joe had had a number of failed relationships. He had been engaged once but they both parted after agreeing that they weren't totally compatible. He devoted his time to work and his hobbies. He spent long hours on each job so really had little leisure time, but eventually, he confessed that he was filling in the day as he didn't enjoy returning to his empty flat that much.

At first Connie felt guilty for laughing and chatting with him. She felt disloyal to Jake, but as the weeks rolled by the two of them formed an easy relationship and she found herself looking forward to his arrival. She even dreaded that the renovations would soon be complete and that he would move on to some new project.

"Right, you three, I will be back for visiting time. Have a good sleep. Do you want anything bringing from the house?"

"I can't think of anything at the moment, but I bet the minute you have gone, I will remember something."

"Well, just ring me if you think of anything. I will probably work at your house until it is visiting time. I'll try to get the kitchen finished before the three of you come home. The last thing you will want is me in your way when you are trying to start a new routine with your family."

She reached across to him.

"Thanks, Joe. I can't thank you enough. Thank God you arrived early as I am not sure what I would have done without you."

He gave her a swift kiss on her forehead and left the room, tiptoeing in an exaggerated manner past the two sleeping babies. Connie suddenly felt alone and tearful. The nurse came into the room as soon as Joe had departed and reassured Connie that most mothers cried after giving birth so she should let her emotions take their course. She checked on her and then went to order her a light meal.

She hadn't eaten since the evening before and when the soup and sandwiches arrived, she ate them with relish.

The nurse made regular visits to the room over the next couple of hours to check on mother and babies. All was well. Connie began to feel calmer and enjoyed her phone conversation with Beth explaining that she was now an auntie and Andy a grandfather. They would be visiting her as soon as they could get away. She watched her two little babies sleeping peacefully at the foot of her bed and the gentle rhythm of their breathing eventually lulled her to sleep.

Chapter 19

"Twins. Isabelle and Jacob. That's fantastic, Connie. Congratulations. I love the names too." There was a couple of minutes silence as Beth listened to Connie updating her on the day's events: "I'll tell everybody your great news. Nothing to worry about here. All fine. The nurse has arrived? OK, I'll ring you again later. Bye for now. Love you."

Dammit. This should have been a moment for celebration. If only there was nothing to worry about, thought Beth. She considered taking Jennie with her to see Andy but, on reflection, she thought he'd probably be more open if it was just her. She poured a coffee from the machine in her office, stirred in a couple of sugars and walked down the corridor to his room. Gladys's door was open, but she moved past as quickly as possible. The last thing she needed at the moment was a conversation with Gladys. Andy was still asleep, so she shook him gently to return him to consciousness:

"A strong coffee for you, Dad, 2 sugars, to bring you back to life. Did you sleep well?"

"I suppose so, Beth. I do feel groggy though."

"I'm not surprised with all that alcohol in your system. Anyway, I have some very good news. Connie has had twins, a girl Isabelle and a boy Jacob."

"Are they all OK? I didn't realise it was happening so soon."

"It was a bit earlier than expected but Connie and the babies are fine."

"I'd better go to see them." Andy started to stir.

"All in good time," replied Beth quickly. "There are a few things we need to sort out here first."

Andy's brow furrowed, suddenly remembering his problems. "You're right. We need to talk." He sat up, held his face in his hands as if to wash away the sleep and took a sip of the coffee. "That's perfect, thank you. You always know how to make a good cup of coffee."

"Right, so far you've told me that you have discovered that you are bisexual and that you have had relationships with men as well as women. What is the situation with Adrian?"

"Well, it's complicated. I thought he was lonely when he first arrived. I actually felt sorry for him, so I invited him for a drink and when we came back to Hilltop, he stayed the night with me. We fell into a routine of socialising in the pub and ending up in my room for the night. One day he asked me for some money. He said that the reason he was working in the UK was to earn money to send back to his family in Romania.

"The coal mine near his hometown had closed down, meaning his father had lost his job there and could not find work. His mother was looking after two young children, one of whom was severely disabled and needed lots of cash. Naturally, I was sympathetic. After all, we had gradually built up a relationship, even though he is obviously a lot younger than me. I know this will all sound completely ridiculous to you, but I became very fond of him, so I gave him £50."

"OK, I follow the story so far, but it didn't stop there, did it?" said Beth, starting to see how the saga might be unfolding.

"No, it didn't, and I really regret that I was ever involved with him. The requests for money became more frequent. I was told that the disabled brother had been having treatment from the free Romanian public healthcare system but apparently his needs had become more severe. The story was that the only treatment available in Romania was at a private clinic and this was expensive. Up to that point, I'd been happily lending Adrian money at about £50 a time, thinking it was all in a good cause, but suddenly, he was asking for a couple of thousand pounds."

"So, what did you do?"

"Well, naturally, I put my foot down, saying that I just could not afford that sort of money. But he turned around and said that I was a member of a wealthy family who owned the care home. He knows that Connie owns properties in London too, so he said I just had to find the money somehow to help his brother. When I explained that I could manage £50 every so often but that was all, he started screaming and shouting. He went into a terrible tantrum that finished in floods of tears. Finally, he owned up to the fact that he had been filming us having sex and that he would post the footage online if I didn't find a way to give him the money."

"Are you sure that Adrian really did have this film?" asked Beth who had become disturbed by Andy's story.

"Oh, yes, he showed it to me. We had a terrible row. At the end I told him to get lost. I said we'd sack him. He said that if he was sacked, he would send copies of the film to the local paper. What's more, he gave me 3 days to find the money. It was blackmail."

"Why did you not go to the police?"

"What would they do? After all, I'd been voluntarily giving him money. We'd been having a consensual relationship. How could I prove that I was being blackmailed, even if the police had the resources to investigate?"

"Well, why did you not at least say something to me or Connie?"

"I was so ashamed that I'd gotten myself into this situation. All I wanted to do was to cover up the problem and I kidded myself that I could handle things on my own. After all, Connie has enough to deal with and you are so busy running Hilltop. I just felt I had to sort out my own problems."

"So, did you pay him the £2,000?" asked Beth.

"Yes, I drew out some of my savings, saying that would be the end of the matter. But, of course, it wasn't. The scenario was repeated to the point where I had no savings left."

"And all this time, your relationship with Adrian continued, did it?"

"You'll find this difficult to understand but, in some kind of strange way, I seemed to find him even more attractive. We were having fun whilst at the same time he was blackmailing me, so bizarrely the relationship continued as before. Later, I discovered that he was using drugs."

"Where was he getting the drugs from?"

"It's a complicated story. Apparently, he started getting his supply from a friend, also Romanian, who works in another care home. Of course, before long, his need to find drugs grew and he was buying extra supplies to sell on to youngsters in Diss. When I realised what was happening, I said it would have to stop. It was at this stage that I developed an understanding of how these drug gangs operate.

"The drugs come over from Romania, hidden amongst imported goods in the back of vans. There appears to be a big boss based in Felixstowe who hides behind the façade of a respectable jewellery business. This guy has a team of subordinates who impose harsh discipline on anybody who steps out of line. The story goes that somebody started supplying information to the police. Not long afterwards he was killed in an unexplained car accident. His car ran off the road and into a tree in the middle of nowhere. Adrian said he was terrified of losing his supply of drugs and above all of displeasing anybody in the gang. He thinks his life is at risk."

"So are you using drugs as well, Dad?"

"No, I've never been interested, apart from alcohol, of course. But I was now needing to bail out Adrian to help his family in Romania. Except that I soon realised that the disabled brother in Romania did not even exist. It was all a ploy to extort money from me as part of the drug dealing enterprise."

"You've already said that you've used up all your savings, so how did you manage to keep giving him money?"

"It started out as a loan. You didn't need to know about it because I was eventually going to pay everything back, but I think I've now gone past the point of no return so you might as well know the full story."

"I think so. I don't believe I can be any more shocked than I am already."

"I'm not sure about that. Do you remember Mrs Douglas arriving a few months ago?"

"She's somebody I don't know very well because Jennie often deals with her. Anyway, I think you dealt with all the paperwork when she arrived."

"Exactly. I'm afraid Mrs Douglas provided a simple solution in the short term for the urgent need for cash."

"What do you mean?"

"Well, Mrs Douglas and her family visited Hilltop and I confirmed that she could have one of our rooms. I went through the payment details with them but made one slight alteration to the paperwork. I'm afraid that I changed the Hilltop bank account details to my own so that her monthly payment has been coming into my account."

"So that's why Mrs Douglas had seemingly defaulted in her payments. All along she's been paying the money into the wrong account. We thought it was very odd, because her son is apparently quite well off. You do realise that you've committed a criminal offence against the owner of Hilltop, your own daughter." Beth looked exasperated and crestfallen at the same time.

"I know only too well and I'm deeply ashamed of what I've done. But look at it from my point of view. Either I found the money or Adrian was going to be given a very severe beating, or possibly worse. Or the sex film would be all over social media. Just imagine: Father of care home owner involved in sex scandal.

What would that do for the business? To say nothing of the shame it would bring to me and my family. I got deeper and deeper into this situation with Adrian. I was drinking far too much, probably to hide away from the horrific situation I was now in, and I just could not think clearly. I know you'll be totally shocked at what I've just told you, but I can't tell you what a relief it is to finally be able be honest with you." He paused. "So, are you going to turn me in to the police?"

"You're my dad and it's the last thing I want to do. But, on the other hand, you've basically stolen thousands of pounds of Hilltop's money. You know perfectly well how hard it is to keep the business on an even keel whilst providing the best possible care for our residents. You also know that Connie and Jake did not set up this care home to make money. They wanted to create new high standards of care for needy old people. They wanted to demonstrate exactly what could be achieved with the right approach. They wanted to treat old people with the respect they deserved. They wanted them to be valued in the same way that children are valued rather than being looked upon as a nuisance and hoping that they will die sooner rather than later.

"We are now running at a loss because of the money that you have been filtering away. And all for what? To support Adrian's drug habit? To pay for the gang leader's yacht in Monte Carlo? You've jeopardised the whole business and it makes me sick to think about what you have done. How could you do this to us? How could you do this to Connie when she is finally achieving some happiness and recovering from losing Jake? And all of this nonsense coming to light at the same time as your first grandchildren are being born."

By now, Beth's fury was exploding over him. Her eyes were wild, her face flushed with anger and she moved to strike him with a clenched fist but restrained herself at the last moment.

"I wouldn't blame you if you did hit me," said Andy quietly, his head bowed. "What are you going to do?"

"I don't know what I'm going to do," shouted Beth. "Except that I need to go and see Connie in London. This is not something I can discuss over the phone. While I'm away, please stay right away from Adrian and don't you dare touch a drop of whisky. Maybe you could start thinking about how you are going to repay us all the money you've stolen." With that, Beth stormed out of the room, slamming the door behind her.

Chapter 20

Connie said her farewells to the maternity staff and Joe helped her carry the two bundles down to his van which was parked outside the main entrance. Isabelle and Jacob breathed in the unfamiliar fresh air and blinked in the sunlight as they were transported home. Joe quickly unlocked the door, stepped aside as Connie, cradling Isabelle, entered. The hallway was festooned with bunting welcoming the new arrivals and two vases of beautiful flowers filled the air with perfume.

"I hope you don't mind, Connie. I just wanted to make your arrival home special."

"Oh, Joe, such a lovely gesture. How good you are to me. To us, I mean. You have been a huge support, and this is just amazing."

"Come through and look at your finished kitchen."

Joe had somehow managed to lock his van, then carry Connie's case and Jacob safely into the house. He had spent every evening of the last week, after visiting Connie and the twins, finishing off the jobs in the house. The kitchen sparkled with newness and, even though the pots and pans still needed to be rehoused, Connie could see how much work he had done to get everything sorted.

"You must have spent hours working here after seeing me every day at the hospital. It must have really set you back with your schedule, so let me pay you some extra to thank you for all you have done for us."

"No need. I did it because I wanted to and, after all, it was the job I was being employed to do. All the other rooms are now finished so you won't have the smell of paint lingering and upsetting these two. I am a bit behind with my plans, but I have already contacted my next clients and told them I am starting soon. Fortunately, they were fine about the delay. It is another big job so a few days over the next nine months won't make that much difference to them."

He grinned, pleased that she seemed happy with the finishing touches to the extensive renovation jobs. "I hope you don't feel that I am making a nuisance of myself, Connie. I don't usually have this sort of relationship with a client and if you are bothered about it let me know and I will leave you in peace. I have just enjoyed this time with you so much over the last few months and now that the twins are here, I am having a great time getting to know them too. I haven't had close contact with babies since I was a kid and I just love it. But you must let me know if you feel stifled or threatened by my presence. I would understand and just get on with my own life."

Connie settled Isabelle in one of the wicker cots which were now in the corner of the huge kitchen. She had decided that this was the room they would spend most time in as it combined the lounge area, kitchen and dining room in one generous space and had a lovely view through the wall of windows looking down the rear garden. An impressive old oak and some rowan trees screened off any sign of the neighbouring houses.

Joe cradled Jacob who stirred in his sleep and let out a small cry before going back into his dream, rocked back into peacefulness. Connie filled the kettle and found a couple of mugs on the surface. Joe had also put out a jar of coffee and teabags so she could find them easily. Such small touches were noticed by Connie even though she didn't say anything. She prepared them a drink whilst Joe gently swayed Jacob in his arms.

"Come and sit down, Joe. I think we do need to talk about this and probably now is as good a time as ever."

They sat together, Jacob still sound asleep, and they talked through their feelings. Connie explained how she had at first felt totally disloyal to Jake harbouring any thoughts about another man.

"It was if I was cheating on him. I know he has been dead for nearly a year now and I thought he was the only person for me. But life is strange. Who would have thought that I would ever have lived in a house like this? I never imagined just a few years ago that I would have no financial worries. I've been thinking through my life whilst I have been in the hospital. It is almost like looking at clips of an old movie. The Connie of ten years ago was constantly tired, each day worried about which bills would drop through the letterbox and she saw no real future other than staying in the same job and living in that tiny house with the man she loved. How fate has changed my prospects."

Jacob started to cry loudly. Joe placed him in the cot next to Isabelle. He seemed to sense her presence and, after a short while of being gently rocked, became quiet and fell back to sleep.

"You know, I have almost got to the point where I feel that I have had two bereavements. I've lost Jake, but also, I have now lost the old Connie. She was my other self, my younger life. She will always be part of who I am. A few months ago, when I was at Hilltop I wanted to die. I saw no point in living without Jake. It is funny how things change though. Since these two arrived I feel different. I am alive and must live my life for the sake of my babies."

She reached across, moved aside the blanket and stroked Jacob's face gently and smiled at this tiny life.

"And I have to say that you are the person who has helped me move on, Joe, and I am grateful to you for that. You have given me confidence and, you know something, I do actually miss you when you go home in the evening and I look forward to you arriving in the morning. I know that would be true of any company arriving into this big house, but I feel that we have a connection, just like Jake and I had all those years ago. It is as though I have known you for a long time." She paused and looked at his face. He smiled at her and nodded acknowledging what she was saying.

"I am waiting for a but…"

"Yes, there is a but coming. I don't want to rush into anything. There is too much going on at the moment. I have these two to consider now and I need to get to know them and learn how to look after them. I can't commit to a relationship just now as I am probably just a hormonal mess and need time to settle down. It doesn't mean that I am rejecting you, Joe, or to use your words, sending you away. I want time to get to know you better. I don't really know that much about you other than you are a kind and decent bloke who has helped me out at one of the most difficult times of my life."

Joe patted her hand and smiled at her. "Don't worry, Connie. I think there is some good news hidden in what you have just said. I will hold on to that hope. Do you mind if I still come to see you three as a friend for the time being?"

"I would be very upset if you didn't," she replied.

"Right; well, I will let you get on. You have my number so when you fancy some company just give me a call or send me a message. You know my work routines." Connie leaned across and gave him a peck on his cheek in much the same way as she had done with Jacob a few minutes earlier.

"Keep my house key, Joe. I want you to know you will always be welcome here and that you are part of this family. After all, where would we have been without you when my waters broke in this very room? Not many men would have been able to stay so calm with that little drama to cope with."

He had been gone for just an hour and Connie had tried to catnap on the sofa whilst the twins slept. The doorbell rang. She glanced at the twins to check that they hadn't been disturbed and hurriedly opened the door to find Beth standing there, clutching gifts. She beckoned her in and put her finger to her lips to show that they needed to talk quietly so they didn't waken the two sleepers. Beth was ecstatic as she looked from one to the other.

"Oh, Connie, they are beautiful and so tiny. How many weeks early were they?"

"Only four, but they have put a bit of weight on since they were born and they both certainly enjoy their feed."

"I wish I could have come sooner, but we were coping with a bit of a crisis at Hilltop and I couldn't really get away."

She looked sheepishly at Connie to see what effect the words had on her, but Connie was distracted by her babies and only made a slight sound of interest. Her attention though was brought fully back into the conversation when Beth began her saga.

"Yes, it centres on Dad, who sends his love, by the way. We didn't want to say anything to you whilst you were in hospital, but it is important that I now bring you up to date about what has been going on over the last weeks whilst you have been living here." She paused hoping Connie was really listening to her. "He has been living quite a secret life whilst he has been at Hilltop."

Connie was suddenly attentive and began to twist the ends of her cardigan preparing herself for the bad news. When they were small Beth used to love giving her bad news and she now wore the same serious face Connie remembered from all those years back.

"Yes, you see, Dad has formed a relationship with Adrian, you know, the young chap who works in the kitchen with Sean. Do you remember him?" Connie nodded and looked quite alarmed at the unexpected news and Beth hurriedly continued her tale. "Well, it turns out that Dad is bisexual." She paused to let the information sink in. Connie sat down quickly on the sofa, unsure of what might come next. "Dad was giving him money and, as you might imagine, the money was used to buy drugs.

All Connie could respond was "Oh, no" and Beth motored on with her prepared speech which she had rehearsed endless times on the train to London.

"Yes, and then Dad was blackmailed and threatened by Adrian who wanted more money. We are talking thousands here, Connie, not just a few pounds. And of course, Dad was dipping his finger in the till and paying over the sums to avoid exposure to the newspapers.

Connie had closed her eyes, trying to shut out the invading stress which Beth's fast flowing words were creating. "And then he, Dad that is, began to drink heavily. He has been doing it for weeks, coming back in the early hours of the morning as drunk as a lord and, of course, the staff and some of the residents have been aware of this as he has looked a real mess." She paused, checked the effect on Connie who had looked up hoping this was the end of the nightmare, and then she finished with a flourish. "And so, we, that is, Jennie and me, have read Dad and Adrian the riot act as we are keen not to involve the police.

"I hope you agree. Adrian has promised to leave at the end of the month and then stop seeing Dad, but Dad says he wants to continue the relationship. Can you imagine after all that? He has been ordered by us to stop drinking, so we have him almost under house arrest in Hilltop trying to get him sober."

Without saying a word, Connie got up and put on the kettle, she rocked the cradles as the twins had started to stir and then she spoke, sounding like a headmistress addressing her senior team. "Right, we have this huge problem which needs sorting out so we need to think our way through it. How exactly has Dad been dipping his fingers in the till?"

"When he did the paperwork for Mrs Douglas, he gave her family the account number for his personal account, so essentially, we have had no payment from her for some time."

"How long has this been going on?"

"I was checking that before I came to see you and it's been 10 weeks."

"OK, so Dad owes Hilltop £10,000. I'm going to insist that he makes arrangements to repay all of it. I'll discuss the details when I see him. Do you think he is capable of returning to work and doing a proper job for us? Or do you think we should just ask him to leave too?"

"If we can keep him off the booze, I'd like him to continue but I think it would be better if you made that judgement when you see him."

"What about Adrian? Is he still threatening to blackmail Dad if he doesn't receive his money?"

"Jennie and I met him on his own and we simply told him that we were asking him to leave. He begged us to allow him to stay till the end of month so that he had time to look for another job. We agreed but said that we would need to check that you agree with that. Other than that, he didn't say very much."

"So, we don't know whether he is still asking Dad for money, or what he is doing with the film footage? Or whether he is going to create problems for us with the media. In an ideal world both Adrian and Dad should be sacked immediately but we have to be pragmatic and try to limit the damaging fallout from this dreadful business. I need to go and speak to them face to face. Not exactly convenient, but it needs to be done."

Although Beth reassured Connie that she and Jennie could manage for a few days without any extra help, Connie felt that she needed to see the situation at first hand and to talk directly to her dad and Adrian. She had a suspicion that the problems were not going to be resolved quite as easily as Beth had intimated. Beth busied herself in organising a hire car for a couple of weeks. Connie had sold her car on leaving Suffolk, preferring to use public transport in London but travelling on public transport with two babies and all the accompanying paraphernalia was just not worth the hassle. Within a couple of hours, Beth arrived with a large people carrier. Bags and babies loaded, they headed for the Dartford bridge and by the end of the afternoon, Connie was confronting Adrian in her office.

"Adrian, while you have been with us, you have done a very good job, but I want you to understand the seriousness of the situation you have created for yourself, for Andy and for Hilltop Care Home. I am totally determined to protect the interests of the people who live here, but your actions have put their futures at risk. Do you understand what I am saying?"

Adrian nodded and said nothing. It was difficult to tell whether he was sorry, so Connie continued, "I want you to be totally honest with me and if I think that you are trying to mislead me, I will have no sympathy for you." Adrian watched her intently, wondering what she was going to say. "How serious is your relationship with my father? Do you love him?"

Adrian laughed and spoke for the first time. "Love? No, no, love is too strong. Like yes, but love no. We have fun together, we like drinking. Lots of fun." He communicated well, though with a strong accent.

"But you have used my father. You have been blackmailing him, haven't you?"

"He is a nice man. He likes to help me with money for my family in Romania. They are very poor."

"It's more complicated than that, isn't it? You've been blackmailing my father. Do you realise that blackmail is a crime? You could go to prison." As Connie spoke, she was assessing Adrian. Was he somebody who could be helped? Or was he somebody that she had to be rid of, regardless of the consequences? "Prison could be the least of your problems too, if what I'm hearing about the gang boss is correct. Why have you been filming my father in bed with you?"

Adrian thought carefully, trying to analyse how Connie was going to react.

"It's difficult for me to explain. I met up with some Romanian people who are living in the area. We have the chance to speak in our own language and we have some fun. But we are very poor, and we need money. We started getting drugs. It's quite easy in this area, as it arrives in Felixstowe on the boats and the boss has a jewellery shop there. He is a big man.

"At first, we thought he was our friend but if we say we want to stop selling drugs he threatens us. He lets us keep some of the money from drug selling but most of it goes back to the big man. One day he asked to see me alone. He had heard that I worked at Hilltop with Andy and he had heard from the others that we had begun a relationship."

"How did he know that? Did you tell him? Was it your idea to blackmail Andy?"

"No, no. Please believe me. It was his idea. He told me that if I didn't do it, he would kill me. I was terrified because I know how powerful he is. I said Andy has no money, but the big man knew that you had inherited lots of money, so he insisted I film us having sex. Then I had to ask Andy for more money."

"Who has this film? Does the big man have a copy?"

"No, he wasn't bothered as long as he got his money."

"So, it's on your phone and nowhere else?"

"Yes, that's right."

"You realise that if I report you to the police, you will probably lose your visa. Also, if I sack you, you will be deported because you don't have a job. If I am asked to give a reference, I will have to explain why I sacked you. Do you understand all of that?"

"Beth has already told me that I must leave at the end of the month. Is there any way you could give me a second chance? I so desperately wanted to build a new life here. I can earn better money and the people are so friendly. I wanted to get married, have children, buy a house and build a future for my kids. I know I haven't got kids yet but, when I do, I want them to have better opportunities than I had in Romania."

"Adrian," said Connie sternly, "blackmailing people is not the way to build a better future. You have to work hard and earn money legally. I've been asking people about your work here and I've had some good reports, but do you want me to help you?"

"Yes, yes, yes. But what can you do? I need to escape from the big boss. He knows where I am and if I stop giving him money, he will come looking for me." Adrian looked despairingly at Connie.

"If I help, I want you to hand over the recording that you are using to blackmail my father?"

"Yes, I will, but what can you do?"

"You need to get away from here. You need to cut all your connections with your friends in this area, including my father, and you need a job which will enable you to extend the time limit on your visa. I think I can arrange all that for you, but firstly you need to destroy the recording. Will you do that?"

"Yes, yes. No problem. Look." With that Adrian moved alongside Connie. He opened the file which immediately began to play. Connie recognised Andy's room and saw enough of the film to be sure that Adrian and Andy were indeed the stars of the show.

"Stop, stop. That's more than enough, thank you, Adrian. Now please delete the file."

Adrian closed the file and deleted it.

"How do I know that you haven't got a copy?"

"I promise on the life of my future children that there are no copies."

"OK, I believe you, but if a copy suddenly appears, you'll be going back to Romania quicker than a jet plane. Here is my plan for you. I have a contact in the building trade in London. Painting, decorating, plumbing, generally repairing things. I will see whether you could work with him. In the time you have been at Hilltop, you have shown that you have the skills and I'd rather see you doing that than waste your life selling drugs and blackmailing people. This is a really big opportunity for you, but you must not let me down. One false move and that will be the end. You will have to earn my trust."

"But where will I live?"

"I will arrange all that for you. I'm not going to tell you yet because neither the big man nor any of your friends must know where you are. You have to disappear otherwise you will be in danger. You will have to trust me on this. Be prepared to go to London either later tonight or tomorrow morning. One other thing: stay away from Andy from now on. You don't try to see him tonight and you don't contact him in any way. Is that clear?"

"Yes, I understand. Please tell Andy I'm sorry for causing so much trouble. I like Andy but I have been very unkind to him, so please apologise for me."

"OK, I'm going to see him now. Go to your room, gather your things together, stay there and wait for me to collect you."

Connie ushered Adrian out of the room, breathing a big sigh of relief as she closed the door behind him. She knew she was taking a big gamble, but if her plan worked, she would be able to keep the whole tawdry business out of the public domain. Now all she had to do was come to an arrangement with her father. She wondered how on earth she had arrived at this point. Usually the father bailed out the daughter, not the other way around.

"Come in, Dad," she said on hearing a knock on the door. They embraced and after exchanging pleasantries about the grandchildren, Connie decided she needed to confront him head on.

"Are you in love with Adrian?"

"Wow, you don't mess about, do you, Connie? In love is a bit strong. I suppose the truth is that I've been infatuated with him. Flattered too because he's so much younger than me."

"Dad, this relationship has got to stop, for everybody's sake. Adrian is going away from here and you must have no further contact with him. The bribery will stop, the recording of your exploits with Adrian have been destroyed and there will be no more demands for money."

"How have you managed that?" Andy looked at his daughter in amazement.

"Never mind. You will just have to trust me. Under no circumstances must you get in touch with Adrian otherwise you may be endangering him and yourself. Secondly, you can forget about any ideas you may have had about going into retirement. You have taken many thousands of pounds out of this business and you are going to pay it all back, which means continuing to work here, probably for quite a long time until the debt is repaid.

Andy looked sheepish and continued listening to his daughter. He had to admit she was impressive, even though she was giving him the biggest rollicking of his life. "The drinking has to stop too. You have disgraced yourself in front of the residents here and that is totally unacceptable. If it ever happens again, you will leave Hilltop for ever, and without a job you will struggle to repay the debt which I am determined to recover from you. I don't want to hear any excuses, nor do I want to hear any more about your private life. Your sexuality is no business of mine, but I would advise you to be more careful in the future.

"Within a few short months you have become almost an alcoholic, a thief and involved in drugs. I am giving you a chance to sort your life out and to make amends. I do love you, in spite of everything, but it's now up to you to decide whether you can respond positively to this final chance I'm giving you. Now, I suggest you get yourself ready to go on duty because I have a lot to do." With that, Connie ushered him out, internally praying that she was taking the right course of action.

Connie phoned Joe shortly after she had sent Andy on his way armed with a list of jobs he had to complete before the day was through. She had two priorities: firstly to tell Sean he needed to find a replacement for Adrian and then to sort out Adrian's new life. Joe listened to the story Connie related over the phone and he agreed to give Adrian a job working on his new project which was to begin on Monday. He would meet him at Liverpool Street station later that day and drive him to his flat where he would stay for the time being.

Connie arranged to pay Joe a generous rent for the use of his flat by Adrian, who would also be charged for his accommodation. She didn't feel much loyalty to someone who had nearly ruined her father's life and her business, but she wanted to make sure Joe was rewarded for his ready agreement to help resolve this family mess. After listening to her sorry story, Joe agreed to move out of his flat and stay in her London home for the time being. He was totally familiar with that property after having worked on it for months so it wouldn't be that much of a hardship for him.

The timescale for this arrangement however was left vague. Connie was determined to stay at Hilltop with the twins until she was convinced that everything was getting back to normal. She wanted her presence to be felt by Andy and she thought it was a good idea to check on the general running of the place. She argued to herself that if Andy could have gotten away with this deception since she departed then there could be other problems to uncover and she wanted to be sure that Hilltop was protected.

Connie bought a one-way train ticket for Adrian. She went to his room only to find that he had already packed his bags and was sitting looking out of the window. He stood up as she entered. He could remember a moment like this when he was sent to the Headmistress's study when he was thirteen and was given a severe dressing down for bullying another boy in his class. "Right, good, you are ready to leave."

She repeated her warnings to him and told him that a taxi would be arriving to take him to the station at 5pm. She explained the plans she had made for him to disappear and he listened, his face registering no emotion. She showed Adrian a photograph of Joe, taken two days before as he held both twins in his arms, so that he would recognise his new boss when he arrived in London.

"Don't let me down, Adrian. If I hear from Joe of any problem you have caused for him or his clients, I will go straight to the police and have you arrested for blackmail. Remember, you are starting a new life and you are to make no contact with Dad or anyone in this area again. I am informing my solicitor and recording this arrangement with him. In this envelope is a statement written by Dad, a summary of everything you have done with him. I also have copies of bank statements showing the amounts of money that have been stolen.

"I will be asking my solicitor to store this in case we need to produce the evidence against you in the future. He has connections with powerful people in London and I will not hesitate to set the ball rolling for your arrest and deportation, so I hope we understand each other. One more thing. I want you to hand over your phone. Joe will get you a replacement when you get to London, but I am lodging your phone with my solicitor. I am not as trusting as my father, Adrian. What you have done to this family is why I am not prepared to take your word at face value. Don't think we are all as gullible as my father."

Adrian looked at her open hand and, after a long pause, he eventually dropped his mobile on to her palm.

"The only numbers you need are for your immediate family and I am sure you know their contact details which you can put into your new address book when you get your phone…if they actually exist, that is." Connie's eyes were glaring at him as she spoke. She could see that he was getting fearful of her, the very effect she was seeking. "Right, I will arrange some food to eat here before you leave so that you won't need a meal when you arrive in London."

She handed him an envelope. "This contains one week's wages in cash, to enable you to buy provisions for the next few days before you receive your first wage packet from Joe. Spend it wisely and not on drugs." With that, she turned and left him alone so that he could mull over her words. No one saw him off when the taxi collected him. Connie watched him disappear from the window of her apartment, hoping that she had done enough to protect Hilltop.

Chapter 21

The residents of Hilltop were thrilled to have two tiny infants to coo over. They were a fantastic distraction from their daily lives. Within days, a routine was established for several of the more agile residents to wheel the prams around the grounds and visit the chicken run. The twins were constantly stimulated by adoring 'grandparents', a dozen or more who took it in turns to nurse, change and rock them to sleep when they cried.

If Connie had wondered how she was going to manage two small babies, she now worried whether they would ever recover from so much attention. Gladys, in particular, had monopolised looking after Isabelle. She adored her. She had started knitting cardigans for the twins and was a surprisingly skilled craftswoman. She could knit complicated patterns without ever having to watch her needles. She would accompany the rhythm of knitting with gentle songs which soothed the twins when they needed to sleep.

Gladys blossomed with her new role. She became kinder, less watchful of others and when she was in the bistro, she had endless conversations about the twins with visitors. She called them 'my little minxes' and she proudly chatted about how much weight they had gained and how bright they appeared to be, even at this young age.

This set the management team thinking. If two babies had had such a positive effect on a large number of the residents, then perhaps they needed to encourage more visits from the local children. Instead of being a home exclusively for the elderly, it could be a multigeneration establishment, a family environment. There were several rooms underused and Jennie suggested that they could establish a creche, offering parents a chance for their children to enjoy the added attention of the residents who would act as grandparents, helping with the day care of these children.

Nursery staff would run the group, but any resident who wanted to be involved could go along during the day and play or read stories with the children.

Two carers who had small children struggled to pay for childcare. Jennie suggested that they could bring them to Hilltop, leave them free of charge in the creche whilst they worked, and this perk would encourage them to stay on rather than looking for another better paid job. Isabelle and Jacob had had such a positive effect on the morale of the residents that Connie decided to explore Jennie's idea of developing a creche. Andy had always loved little children so why not use his talent to build a unique facility for the local community? Would this not be an ideal opportunity for him to re-establish himself not only with Beth, Jennie and colleagues but also with the residents?

Connie broached the idea with Andy first of all, couching it in such a way that it was an offer that he could not refuse. Even so, she was pleased at his positive reaction. He was delighted that he should be given such a key role, especially after recent events which had not exactly portrayed him in the best possible light. Beth also thought a creche was a great idea, so Connie called a meeting of all the care staff at the beginning of the day just before the night staff went home and the day staff took over.

She explained how she had noticed that her twins had brought lots of smiles to the faces of the residents. Her thinking was that the elderly residents had one main asset that was in very short supply with everybody else: time. Little children needed lots of attention so bringing the children and adults together seemed like a good idea. Obviously, the residents would act as surrogate grandparents, helping with the day care of these children, but there would need to be regular staff to take overall responsibility. Connie hoped that staff would be supportive of the idea in order to give it every chance of success.

One or two carers said they were concerned about potential health and safety issues. What about little children as hazards that residents might fall over, for example?

"Let's just try it," replied Connie, "we'll learn as we go." Overall, there was an enthusiastic response. One carer asked if her two-year old could join the group. "Of course," said Connie, "and we won't charge you for the privilege. Think of it as a perk of the job. For you, it will be free. We'll make our money by charging a reasonable fee to local people. I've spoken with several other employees who said they would bring their children to the creche as soon as they could see it was operational."

Buoyed by the positive response of the staff, Connie asked the carers to round up as many residents as possible to meet in the dining room just before lunch time. Everybody agreed that this was a good time as most of the residents ate in the dining room in any case. Just before 12.30 the dining room came alive with curious chatter as people wondered why they were being called together in this most unusual way. Sherry was provided and the residents gossiped with each other, almost in party mood.

"This has never happened before while I've been here," said Mrs Douglas. "Connie must have something important to say."

"Maybe we're all going to be sacked," said one elderly chap, thinking back to his days in the mining industry when the pits were being closed down.

"How can we be sacked?" asked his neighbour. "We don't work here, do we?"

"Oh, I suppose not. Well, perhaps Hilltop is closing down and we'll need to find somewhere else to live."

"You're such a pessimist. Maybe there will be some good news."

"You're joking. When did we last get some good news? Bring back the good old days."

The pessimist was still grumbling away, despite lots of eye-rolling from his neighbour, when Connie banged a spoon on the table to call the meeting to order.

"Before I start, I want to say what a pleasure it is to see you all together like this. As you know, I've been in London for a few months and I've really missed your company. I want to thank you for the love you have shown to me especially over the last year. It helped me more than I can say. I've missed Jake a lot and I know you have too. However, Jake left me with two very special gifts, Isabelle and Jacob." She pointed to the two baskets where the twins slept soundly. "Aren't they absolutely gorgeous?"

A spontaneous round of applause broke out around the room, accompanied by shouts of "Well done, Connie". Tears rolling down her face, Connie thanked them and went on.

"I've noticed that a number of you have really enjoyed spending time with the twins. My impression is that it's been a good experience for you. Am I right?" There was a general chorus of assent. "Well, it's given me an idea. I am thinking of setting up a small creche, run by qualified nursery assistants, which you can help with if you want. For example, you could go along at any time during the day to play with the children or read stories to them. What do you think?"

"I'd love that," said Mrs Douglas, and a few others smiled and nodded.

"What about the noise?" asked the pessimist Bert. "I like my peace and quiet and I don't want little kids racing about making a racket." A few usual suspects, mainly men, grumbled in support of Bert.

"I absolutely understand that, Bert. That's why I'm planning to run the creche in the west wing where there is a larger room and a couple of smaller rooms. They are quite a distance from where you live, so I don't think you'll be able to hear anything."

"That's all very well, Connie, but when they arrive, they will have to come past our rooms. They will make a noise when they leave as well. I'm not happy about this at all."

"Look, this is a suggestion. I think it is probably a good idea for many of you. I know that one or two other care homes around the world have experimented with it and the results have been encouraging in terms of raising morale and giving people something to look forward to. However, I do genuinely want to know what you think."

"We know you are trying to do the best for us, Connie, and we trust you."

Everybody looked around to see who was speaking. A very old lady was sitting at the back in a wheelchair. It was Mrs Atkins, a recent arrival at Hilltop. Her words were delivered surprisingly powerfully for somebody who looked so frail. Her skin was almost translucent, the veins on her forehead clearly visible, but her voice was strong and clear.

"I think it's a wonderful idea and I for one will come along to read to the youngsters or to help out in any way I can, for as long as I can. I know it will not be everybody's cup of tea, but I've always felt rejuvenated when my grandchildren and great grandchildren come to visit." When Mrs Atkins had finished speaking, a murmur of approval spread around the room and a number of others voiced their support. Bert remained silent, realising that the consensus of opinion was against him.

"Thank you all for letting me know what you think. We have to sort out all the details before we open the creche, especially the health and safety issues but also making sure there will not be too much disruption for those who like their peace and quiet." Connie looked across at Bert as she spoke and was relieved to see him complaining about something else, the issue of the creche already forgotten. "Enjoy your lunch everybody."

Back in her office, Connie let out an extended sigh of relief as she poured herself a cup of coffee. Beth and Jennie had plenty to do with looking after

Hilltop without bothering about the creche so it was essential that she could trust Andy to take the lead in organising everything. She knew that he had the ability, but she had to be sure that he would be reliable and committed. She could not risk damaging Hilltop's reputation again. She phoned through to Andy, asking him to pop into her office.

"Am I in trouble again?" he asked on arrival.

"Not at the moment," she said, "but I want to check that you are prepared to organise the creche."

"I'm very interested but I want you to explain exactly what you expect from me."

"I'm not talking about you running it completely on your own. Obviously, you'll need to recruit a couple of nursery assistants, depending on how many children arrive, but I want to be able to trust you to work completely independently. This is a big risk for me because you've let me down badly with the money that you have stolen. On the other hand, this is your chance to make amends, to pay back what you owe to Hilltop and to launch what I feel could be a really exciting venture. I also think you could be really good at this because you've always been great with children.

"I need you to tell me that you want to do this and that you are totally committed. If you are not keen, I'd rather you tell me now." Connie looked carefully at him trying to gauge whether or not she was making a mistake. He had at least smartened himself, being well dressed and groomed, and crucially there was no smell of alcohol.

"Well, my love, I am so pleased that you are giving me this opportunity. I am already excited about it. When can I get started?"

"You can begin drawing up a job description for the nursery assistants now. Have a look at the rooms in the west wing to see whether they need any refurbishment or redecoration. Find out what resources you need too. Chat with Jennie about funding because the budget is really tight at the moment but I'm hoping that in the end the creche will be self-financing. I want you to focus on this job so that Beth and Jennie can concentrate on what they have to do."

"OK, great, but there's something I've been meaning to mention to you, and this seems as good a time as any."

"What is it? Already you're making me worried."

"Somebody came to reception earlier today asking to see me."

"Is that a problem?"

"In the end, I didn't meet the chap because, as I came down the corridor, I overheard him speaking to the receptionist in an accent very similar to that of Adrian. I quickly made myself scarce and he left saying he'd call back."

Immediately, Connie tensed: "So you think he's trying to find out where Adrian is?"

"That's my guess."

"I think you're probably right. Fortunately, you don't know where he is, do you?"

"No, but these are dangerous people who won't give up easily. I'm telling you so that you can be prepared. What do you want me to do?"

"You've done the right thing so far by avoiding him. What does this fellow look like?"

"I only caught a brief glimpse, but he was dark-haired, going slightly bald at the back. He was wearing jeans and a leather jacket. I'd say he was in his 40s, certainly younger than me, overweight. He had a deep voice and sounded quite intimidating, although that may have been because of his accent."

"This is tricky because we really don't want to involve the police. I was hoping we could avoid any negative publicity, especially when we're trying to embark on our new venture with the creche."

"Well, forewarned is forearmed as they say. I'll certainly be trying to keep well out of their way because Adrian has told me how dangerous they can be."

At that moment the phone rang. It was the receptionist, informing Connie that a man wanted to see her. Looking resolute, she headed off down the corridor.

"Yes, how can I help you?"

The man sized her up and down. "I am looking for the boss."

"Well, you have found her. What can I do for you?" Connie was determined to be professionally cool and she didn't change the stern look on her face. She settled into her authoritarian pose and held in front of her the papers she had quickly picked up from her office to indicate she was busy, but also to create a physical barrier between them.

"My name is Stefan Popescu. I am the cousin of Adrian who worked here. I am looking for him to tell him some family news."

"How did you know that Adrian worked here?"

"He kept in touch with me, but I haven't heard from him now for several weeks. I can't get through to his mobile."

"And what is the news you want to give him?"

"Well, that is…what you say…privé."

"You mean private."

"Private."

"Well, I am sorry to tell you that we have no idea where he is. He left one day and never returned. He left no forwarding address and took all his things with him."

"Why did he leave?"

"I really should not be discussing my employees with a stranger, but, as you say you are his cousin, I will tell you that Adrian stole from us. I informed the police who were going to question him, but before they arrived, Adrian disappeared. The police are still looking for him, I believe. If and when they find him, he will be deported."

Stefan looked at her shiftily and was about to say something more when Sean walked across the hallway and stood with his arms folded, staring at him. Connie had never really noticed how large and intimidating Sean could be, and his dramatic stance suggested that of a nightclub bouncer. His quiet presence was all that was needed to silence Stefan.

"Right," Connie took strength from Sean's presence, "I will ask you to leave now, Mr Popescu. Your cousin will clearly not be returning to us and as we have no idea of his whereabouts, we don't expect to see you again. We hope the family news you suggested you wanted to relay isn't too serious. I am sure this gentleman," she pointed towards Sean, "will see you off our premises. Good day to you."

With that Connie returned to her office and moved quickly to the window to watch him depart. She was shaking and Andy, who had listened to it all with his ear against the door, came over and hugged her. Sean knocked on the door and entered the room.

"I was just coming over to discuss next week's menu choices with you. I hope you didn't mind my little bit of playacting, Connie."

"Oh, Sean, you have no idea how glad I was that you appeared at that moment. He horrified me. There is no way on this earth that he is Adrian's cousin. He will be part of that gang and he will have been sent to find out why their boy hasn't been paying his dues recently. I am sure of it."

"Why did you lie about the police?" Andy naively asked.

"Why do you think? I wanted to show that we weren't going to continue this ridiculous transfer of funds into their hands. If they believe the police are in the know, they will probably leave us alone, but who knows?"

She scowled at Andy. He had caused this problem and all her happiness over the future plans of the creche disappeared. She walked up and down the room trying to calm herself down.

"Right, this is my plan. I am going to the police station to explain what's happened and give a description of this Stefan. Don't worry, Dad," she added when she saw the alarmed look on Andy's face, "I am not pressing charges, but if we need the help of the police in the future, at least they will have a record of what has recently happened. I might as well give some credibility to what I have just told Stefan and if he is watching Hilltop then it won't do any harm if he follows me to the police headquarters and sees me go inside." Before any further conversation could take place, she picked her car keys off her desk and hurried to the headquarters just a quarter of a mile away.

Connie was away for more than two hours. When she returned, Andy, like a frightened child, returned to her office and asked what had happened. Connie had recounted the arrival of Stefan, given a description and had also supplied information regarding the jewellery boss in Felixstowe; information, she said, which had been passed on by a former employee, a Romanian national who had now disappeared. What she kept secret were the whereabouts of Adrian.

She had watched too many crime thrillers to be totally trusting of the police. She wouldn't make contact with Joe for a while, as she speculated that less communication with him at the moment would ensure the safety of both men. She decided against furnishing the police with the whole story fearful of adverse publicity and she wanted to keep the family name out of any investigations. However, for her own peace of mind she was relieved to have told them just a portion of the story and, in any case, she was happy to let Andy sweat it out. She didn't expect any follow up as the policeman who interviewed her had an air of disinterest in what she had to say.

"So, you see, Dad, you are off the hook for the time being, but this means you now have an even greater obligation to me. I have protected your reputation, so you are not going to gossip about this with anyone, I mean no one, and you are going to work doubly hard to make this creche work and pay back your debts. You do understand me, don't you?"

He nodded his head and went away sheepishly. As soon as she was alone, Connie set about documenting everything that had happened. She was intent on sending the details in a sealed envelope to Jonathan Grey, exactly as she had told Adrian she would do. That was her afternoon chore. When she had completed what she wanted to include, she took the envelope to the post office and registered it. The following afternoon, she called Jonathan's office.

"Well, Connie, this is a nice surprise. I was thinking of you only yesterday wondering how you were getting on. Does motherhood suit you? Are you still in London?"

"Oh, I almost forgot that you are not up to date with everything that has been going on. Somehow, I feel the world knows my business, silly I know, but I do need to confide in you, if you don't mind, Jonathan."

She brought him up to date with what had happened to her over the last few months: the early arrival of the twins, Hilltop, her father, Adrian and his new life, Joe and today's visit to the police. She explained that a sealed account was on the way to his office and she wanted it stored alongside her house deeds.

"But I am not sure why you didn't tell the police the whole story."

Connie discussed with Jonathan why she hadn't exposed Andy to the police and that she had felt rather threatened by Stefan. "The fewer people who know where Adrian is living, the safer for all concerned."

"OK, normally, as your solicitor, I would advise you to tell the police everything, Connie, but at the moment you have a domestic problem involving a member of your family which you are managing. It is up to you whether you want to press charges and I can see and perhaps understand why this isn't your intention. Let us hope your new venture with the creche will encourage your father to face up to his responsibilities and ensure he makes a success of this scheme."

"I have asked Jennie to contact local builders to give us some quotes for a new entrance on the other side of the building with an extension to the driveway so the young children, parents and nursery staff will avoid coming through our front door. To be perfectly honest, I hadn't thought through the logistics of how they would get to the rooms where the nursery will be based until Bert, one of our residents, mentioned it at our meeting."

"You have checked your insurance details cover the building extension, haven't you, Connie? Also, any resident who volunteers to help with the creche will need DBS clearance, don't forget."

"Ah yes, that was one thing I had thought about, so that is being built into the plan which is now several pages long."

For the first time in days she managed to smile. Jonathan always had this effect on her. His professional approach made her feel safe and secure in what she was doing. He also made their relationship, solicitor and client, seem special. He had become a friend, a confidant and, over the last year he had listened to many of her stories regarding Jake, her family and the business. She pictured him sitting in his office and his secretary arriving to give him his afternoon tea, just like in an old English movie, and she had to shake herself to attention when he said:

"I am hoping to pay a visit to Hilltop in the next few days, Connie, if that is all right with you. I want to know exactly what this business is like. Obviously, I have a good working knowledge of your London properties, but the Suffolk venture remains a bit of a mystery to me. Do you mind if I came to Hilltop soon…let me see…" Connie could hear the pages of his diary being turned, "actually tomorrow is empty and that looks like the only day free for the next two weeks."

"Oh, my goodness," she was quite shocked at his proposal, "yes, that is fine. What time should we expect you? I'm suddenly quite nervous. It sounds like an Ofsted visit…"

They both laughed and he reassured her that he was mainly being nosey, but he also wanted to acquaint himself with Hilltop in preparation for when planning permission for the building work was sought.

"I am also curious to see your children, Connie. I know Jake's great aunt would have loved to have met them. She always regretted not having children and that was why she wanted Jake to be her sole heir."

He was due to arrive at 11 the next morning, so Connie dispatched orders to make sure the place was looking its best for when he arrived. She had no idea why she was anxious to impress, but this was her business, not some house which had been handed to her which effortlessly generated an income. She and Jake had worked hard to make Hilltop successful and she wanted Jonathan to be impressed with what they and now she had achieved.

She suddenly realised that he was the link between Jake's aunt and herself and she felt a responsibility to prove that this windfall was being used wisely. Beth and Andy were less impressed with Jonathan's imminent arrival and wondered why Connie was treating it like a royal visit. They grumbled together about the added pressure when there was so much to be done with all the new plans.

Andy no longer felt able to express his dissatisfaction to Connie, but he was less inhibited with Beth. He was mid-sentence when suddenly, she turned on him and said: "Just remember why we are in this situation, Dad. We wouldn't have had some intimidating Romanian at reception threatening Connie, so I think you had better just grin and bear it."

Beth's patience with Andy was running thin, so she stormed off to check on the evening meal which was nearly ready to be served in the dining room. Over half of the more mobile residents liked to eat together, but there were still a good many who had to have their meals brought to their rooms. Even in these difficult times it was important to maintain the daily routine of the residents, so Beth kept an eye on who wasn't eating much and who needed to have a visit from the doctor.

She made sure she spoke with each of the carers towards the end of the day shift. She noted what they had to say which, in addition to the daily morning meeting, provided a clear picture of the residents and their progress. This information was passed over to the night shift as soon as they arrived on the premises. During all the turmoil that was taking place, the normality of dealing with the day-to-day routines of Hilltop was a comfort for Beth.

Jonathan Grey was punctilious in everything he did, so Connie was surprised to see him alighting from a taxi at the front door at 2 minutes past 11.

"I'm so sorry," he said to Connie, shaking her hand, "I said I'd be here at 11 o'clock and it's two minutes past. Unforgivable. Couldn't be helped, I'm afraid. The train was late leaving Liverpool Street."

He spoke in the polished public-school tones of an earlier bygone age and his voice was deep and reassuring, just what Connie needed in these uncertain times.

"I'm so pleased to see you again," said Connie smiling. "Would you like a coffee?"

"Normally, I'd say yes but I had one at Liverpool Street and another on the train so I'm fine for the moment thanks. Let me say straightaway, Connie, how impressed I am with the building and the setting. That long sweeping driveway through the gardens creates a calming atmosphere which I'm sure you are creating inside too."

"I'm pleased that we have impressed you, Jonathan. Would you like to look round and meet some of the lovely people who live and work here?"

"I'd love to. Let's do just that."

Connie took Jonathan along each corridor, pointing out the various lounge areas, the dining room and some of the private rooms before arriving at the west wing where there was to be a new entrance and the conversion of some rooms to create a creche.

"What gave you the idea of creating a creche in a care home? It seems so counter-intuitive to be looking after both the very young and the very old in the same place."

"Yes, I know, but it's been tried successfully in parts of Scandinavia and the United States. I noticed too how positively the residents reacted to Isabelle and Jacob, so I thought why not give it a try? It's an experiment. Even if it fails, we won't lose anything because, if necessary, we can reconvert the space into something useful for the residents. The other advantage is that it will help with the childcare for the carers.

"As you know it's difficult enough to recruit and retain them so offering them free childcare will be very attractive. The staff are so vital to everything we do, and I'd love to be able to pay them more but, just at the moment it's not feasible if we are to build a sustainable business."

"Maybe that's something we can discuss later," said Jonathan thoughtfully. "After all, I presume that with a higher salary, you could recruit better qualified people?"

"Probably, though to what extent such people are available is another matter. Although our work is fulfilling, many other jobs are less demanding and better paid. As you say, once we have resolved our current problems, we should give it some attention. After all, we all get old, many of us will need care and why should we not have the best support possible?"

"I totally agree. I think we should look for additional sources of funding?"

"Great idea, Jonathan, but where from?"

"I don't know at the moment. I'll think about it. Out of interest, may I ask you a question, Connie?"

"Of course."

"When I've visited other care homes, drawing up wills and so on for residents, the care staff seem to be so busy and always on the move. In the lounge here, I was very struck by the way that the some of the carers were seated alongside the residents. I don't know why I noticed that in particular, but I did."

"Good, I'm glad you noticed. You are very observant. Let me try to explain my thinking. I want people here to feel valued and one way of doing that is to hold proper conversations with them. In order to do that, I encourage the care staff to sit down and talk to people properly. Not just a quick 'How are you?' and then rushing off to the next task. I want these conversations to be an integral part of the daily routine for everybody, as far as possible. So far it seems to be working well. I've had good feedback from both staff and residents.

"The carers like being encouraged to build a proper relationship and the residents like being treated with respect. I'm trying to facilitate good social contact amongst the residents too, but that's difficult for some. At least they all have at least one decent conversation a day. The residents tell me that it makes a difference. For them, the days can be very long, so anything we can do to keep them alert, engaged and entertained is so important."

"And can you manage to do all the other jobs as well? The washing, feeding, medication-giving and so on?"

"Occasionally, we have crises when we don't achieve everything that we want but on the whole spending a few minutes talking to each resident does not seem to hamper the running of Hilltop. Jonathan, I'm happy to talk all day with you but I'm stopping you from meeting Beth, Jennie, Andy, Sean and the rest."

"Don't worry, Connie. You're the one that I've come to visit. I can see that generally all is well here at Hilltop and that you are dealing with the problems that you outlined in your letter. Could I have a coffee now, please? I'd like to chat with you for a while."

Connie poured each of them a coffee. "This jug was brewed a while ago so let me know if you want some fresh."

"It's fine," said Jonathan, unwrapping one of the biscuits which were next to the coffee machine. "I wish you'd hide away these biscuits though. They are too much of a temptation for weaker souls like me." He was in no hurry to begin the next part of the conversation. "I really could do with losing some weight."

"Something seems to be bothering you. What's on your mind, Jonathan?" Connie could see that he was prevaricating. What on earth was he going to say? It must be something serious.

"This is not easy for me, Connie. I've been weighing up the pros and cons for some time but, like you with the Andy and Stefan issue, I've decided that it's better that you find out directly from me. Since we've known each other, I feel that we have built a relationship of mutual trust and I cannot possibly jeopardise that by concealing from you some information that has just come to light."

"Oh, you are troubling me. You know I've been very grateful for your support and advice, particularly since Jake died. In fact, you are now the person that I trust the most in the world, especially since my dad has been such a disappointment."

"Well, I'm afraid that I've let you down rather, Connie, because I have not carried out faithfully some instructions given to me by Jake." Connie looked startled. "When he first discovered that he was the beneficiary of all Aunt Agnes' wealth, he gave me a sealed envelope which I was to keep in the company safe, only to be opened in the event of his death. The envelope was addressed to me."

"What do you mean that you failed Jake?"

"I failed him because I've only just found the envelope. I have no excuse really, but the fact of the matter is that when Jake died so unexpectedly young, my main focus was to ensure that his wishes were carried out. By that I mean transferring the money and properties into your name, Connie. It was a big estate and there were a number of inheritance tax issues that had to be sorted with the Probate Office. To cut a long story short, this envelope was so small and in the middle of lots of large files it was simply overlooked. It was only when I was placing your account of the problems you've had with Andy and Stefan in the safe that I spotted it. I recognised Jake's handwriting immediately. As you know, he had a very distinctive style, all the letters leaning to the left."

"Have you opened the envelope?"

"I have indeed."

"Well, now you have gone so far in the story, you might as well tell me the rest. I hope this is not another bad news story," said Connie, trying to read the signs on Jonathan's normally inscrutable features. He looked distinctly uneasy.

"It turns out that Jake had, or should I say has, a son."

"A son!" exclaimed Connie. "A son! He can't have. We tried for years to have children with no luck, until the twins happened like a miracle. How can he have a son?"

Even as she spoke, a flash of understanding made her suspect that perhaps she was the one who couldn't conceive in those earlier times. All these years, she had thought that Jake's sperm might be faulty. What an irony, given that he seemingly now had three children.

"Hang on a moment. I'm trying to process the information. You're telling me that he has a son. Are you also telling me that the man I loved had an affair?"

"Yes, obviously, he must have had some sort of relationship, but I'm not sure you'd call it an affair. It would appear that for a few weeks he was dating a girl that he'd met on a night out at a pub. He was only about 19 or 20 at the time. After a while, they went their separate ways. Maybe that was when he met you, Connie?"

"I first met Jake at his 24th birthday party in a pub that a few of us used to go to. We got talking over a few drinks and we were almost inseparable after that. The thing is we used to tell each other everything and I knew he'd had girlfriends but nothing very serious. Jake never even hinted that he might have had a child."

"That's probably because he didn't even know himself."

Connie pulled her hair back from her face. "How can he possibly not have known. I'm finding all of this very difficult to believe."

"Apparently, according to his account, what happened was that after a few drinks, Jake agreed to drive the girl home. The fact that he was driving after spending the evening in the pub tells you that things were out of control. I don't want to go into the details but, as they were both still living with parents, they pulled off the road into a field who knows where, and um, one thing led to another. I'll leave the rest to your imagination.

"Afterwards as they drove to the girl's house, Jake asked her if she was on the pill. When she said no, he was furious, saying that he assumed that she was. The girl then blamed him for not using protection and they had a furious row. By the time they arrived at the girl's house, they both said they never wanted to see each other again. Jake's story is that they never met again and had no further contact, no phone calls, no emails, no texts, nothing at all. Although Jake kept going to the same pub, the girl never reappeared. It was as if she had completely disappeared."

"Who was this girl?" asked Connie.

"That's the thing, Connie. He does not give her name."

"Well, how do we know that he had a son?"

"The girl, after giving birth, eventually moved on to another relationship and before long she and the new man were living together. The child was brought up as the son of the couple. Life continued its normal course until her son went to university. For the first time in his life, the son was asked to prove his identity with a birth certificate and this was when he discovered that the man identified as his father on this official document was none other than Jacob Wilkins. His mother had kept the matter secret all these years, allowing him to think that her partner was his father.

"When the boy found out, he rejected his father and blamed him for the secrecy about his natural father. This revelation tore the family apart. The relationships of all three disintegrated and they have not communicated with each other for some time." Jonathan paused to allow the information to sink in as Connie sat totally still, drained of all energy, struggling to make sense of how her life history was being changed.

"So how did Jake find out about all this?"

"Apparently, the son did a bit of online research. He eventually found the correct Jacob Wilkins and wrote to him. I think I am right that you worked late into the night, so the post would have arrived before you woke up in the morning. The letter informed Jake that he had a son and he was asking to meet up. Maybe he was waiting for a good time to tell you. As we know, that time unfortunately never arrived."

"Did they actually meet, Jake and his son?"

"In his letter, Jake says that he was afraid to meet up and had no intention of doing so. He was worried that it would damage his relationship with you. I can't be sure, but as far as I know they never did meet. If you are in agreement, I will forward you Jake's letter when I return to the office. It's entirely up to you, but it should be possible also to find out the identity of the son, but I'll let you reflect on that."

Connie had been frozen to the spot whilst this news swept over her. She couldn't process what was being said and her inner voice kept repeating "Listen, pay attention, it's important." Once Jonathan had finished talking, she pulled herself together. He was surprised that she made no comment about this story. "I want you to meet my children before you go, Jonathan. They are getting bigger by the day and they should be just waking up now. Beth has been looking after them whilst you were here, so let's go up to my apartment and see them."

She never said a word about this bombshell as they made their way upstairs. She opened the door and both Andy and Beth were cuddling a baby and there was a lot of jiggling around with the twins gently swaying in their arms. Both Isabelle and Jacob smiled with pleasure at the attention. Introductions were swiftly followed by a photo session with Jonathan balancing both babies in his arms trying to look casual and experienced, yet only achieving a fish out of water look. He was relieved to hand the twins back to Beth and Andy. Connie sensed his need to escape and she phoned for a taxi to return him to the station.

"You have quite a lot to think about, Connie, so I will send you the letter and any information we find out about Jake's son. I want you to phone me when you have got used to the idea and then you can discuss anything that you think should happen. On the other hand, you might want to do nothing and just let sleeping dogs lie. It is entirely up to you."

Once Jonathan had left Hilltop, Connie scuttled back to the apartment. The twins had been taken down to the residents' lounge for the afternoon. This was their daily routine. The lounge filled rapidly after every lunchtime and the residents seemed to have an agreement amongst themselves about how long they could play with the twins. Animated conversation now flowed amongst the group. They talked about the progress of the twins, who had noticed what in their development, and they compared their growth to that of their own grandchildren. Babies' toys were piled in the corner of the lounge and Hilltop was changing day by day, much to the satisfaction of all the residents.

Safely alone, Connie burst into tears the minute she shut the door. She felt betrayed, jealous, confused and guilty. One side of her brain argued that she was being unreasonable. Jake hadn't betrayed her as this all happened long before they had met. She realised that what hurt the most was the fact that he had kept this information from her, and he had thought a letter was the safest way for her to find out about his son through a third party. Why did he think she couldn't have been told face to face? Was he scared of her reaction? Yes, just look how she was responding now.

If Jake had been here, what would she have done? Screamed at him? Connie's mind continued this two-way conversation, reason versus emotion. Eventually, she calmed down, her tears spent. Suddenly, reason became the victor as she realised that they were even. Jake would never know that he had twins, another son and daughter to go alongside his older son. She might never have known that he was already a father. Connie felt comforted by this thought even though she had daily been torn apart at the notion that he would never get to know his two offspring. She looked at the garden which spread out before her.

She was the survivor of this relationship, so she needed to take action. She would wait for Jonathan's letter to arrive and then she would begin her own investigations. But suddenly she realised that she didn't need to wait. She knew where the story began for this son. She was a member of Ancestry, the genealogy research site, and she could start her own investigations. Her first job was to search the births section. She knew Jake's name was on the birth certificate, the year the birth was possibly registered and the location. She would surely be able to discover the name of the mother with this information.

Where she went from there was a bit of a mystery, but she then realised she could also search the marriage section with the mother's maiden name and that would expose her married surname, presumably the one used by her son. She would have his Christian name and surname and then she had the identity of someone to google. Suddenly, she was energised. She felt empowered and she set about solving this mystery. In a sense, she wanted to resolve the matter before Jonathan did.

Connie got to work straight away. She opened the search site and typed in the details. The son had been born about twenty-two years previously and his father's name was Jacob Wilkins living in Suffolk. Immediately, the site threw up possible details. There were only two fathers called Jacob Wilkins during this period, one living in Bradford and the other in Suffolk. The birth registration also showed that the mother's name was Hannah Robinson and the son was called James. "Right, got you. You are the mother, Hannah, so now we need your married surname to find out more about James."

She moved to the marriage and divorce section of the site and typed in Hannah Robinson, left the spouse's name blank, but indicated that they had married in Suffolk. She guessed they had married not long after James had been born so this narrowed down her search. Again, without a pause, the details were presented to her. Hannah Robinson had married John Arden in Diss. "Hence," she summed up, "James became James Arden, I suppose through deed poll. I had better check that area too so that I am completely sure." She also went through the death registrations just to make sure that she wasn't on a wild goose chase, but there were no deaths registered under the names she had in front of her, so she was happy to believe that they were all alive.

After quite a bit of further research, she also discovered the deed poll details which showed that James Wilkins had become James Arden when he was eight months old. She sat back and smiled with satisfaction. Connie forgot that she had been shocked by the news only a short time earlier. She saw the tracking down of James as her new mission. The creche project had already been delegated to the team so she could devote her time looking for James. She had no idea what would happen when she found him, and she was in no doubt that she would find him, but she could think about all that at a later stage.

For now, she was just keen to trace him, so she decided to get started immediately. However, apart from confiding in Jonathan, she kept this news secret until she had found and met James. Should she also find Hannah? Well perhaps not. Instead she would channel her focus on James, the half-brother of her twins, Isabelle and Jacob.

The trouble was that, try as she might, Connie could find no trace of James Arden. She spent hours searching but all in vain. It appeared that James had no on-line presence at all, or if he had, he kept it well hidden. Connie's desire to find this person who was directly descended from her deceased husband grew stronger and stronger, almost to the point of obsession. Was he related to her too? Yes, through marriage, that would make him her stepson, she supposed. Having spent many years of her adult life with no children, and seemingly no prospect of having children, Connie liked the way her family was suddenly growing.

Maybe if I find his mother, Hannah Arden, I'll be able to trace him through her, she mused. How would she feel about meeting the woman with whom Jake had a fling all those years ago? Connie set aside her doubts and typed Hannah Arden and Suffolk into the search engine. The first page gave her several people with the correct name, but none based in Suffolk. It wasn't until she had searched through several pages that she spotted an advert for "Hannah's Hairdressing Salon".

She clicked on the website showing customer reviews: "friendly staff, great service"; "lovely atmosphere and free coffee"; and "I always see Hannah, she's fantastic at her job." There was also a photograph of a woman that Connie presumed was Hannah. It was difficult to be sure, but she could well be in the correct 40's age bracket. There was a contact telephone number and email address, but Connie suddenly became hesitant, nervous at the very real prospect of meeting this woman.

"Hi Connie, everything all right with you?" Beth popped her head around the door.

"Fine thanks, Beth. Is it OK if I leave the twins with you and the residents for a couple of hours? I just want to pop out for some fresh air."

"Absolutely, those twins are doing everybody a power of good. At least until they start crying. They are being very good today though."

"Thanks Beth. I won't be long."

Connie drove down to Framlingham, past the High School and the newly built houses and arrived in the town centre. There was nowhere obvious to park, but she found a space on a side street, glad to be able to walk and clear her mind in the fresh air. The hairdressing salon was near the Railway Inn, on the main road south towards Ipswich. It's in a good location, thought Connie as she wandered slowly past the window. A woman very like the one in the photograph was cutting a man's hair but he was the only customer, so Connie plucked up her courage and went in.

"Hello," said the woman cheerily, "can I help?"

"Is there any chance of a haircut?" asked Connie. "I haven't got an appointment. Can you fit me in?"

"I'm just finishing up here. If you'd like to take a seat, I've probably only got time for a dry cut because I have another appointment in twenty minutes. Is that OK?"

"That suits me fine. Thank you so much." Connie sat down, picked up a magazine but listened intently to the conversation between Hannah and her customer and watched her every movement. She could see straightaway how Jake would have found her attractive. Although starting to thicken around the waist, she had a good figure, a friendly face and fizzed with energy as she talked non-stop.

"Would you like to come over?" asked Hannah, once the man had left. "I haven't seen you before. Do you live locally?"

"Not too far away. I work at Hilltop Care Home near Diss."

"Are you happy for me just to trim around and tidy up?" Hannah asked and when Connie nodded, she continued, "My mother lives there. Do you know her?"

"What is she called?"

"She's now called Mrs Douglas, but when I was growing up, she was Mrs Robinson. She remarried a few years ago after my dad died. Unfortunately, Mr Douglas died too, leaving her all alone and not very well. I couldn't look after her as well as run this business. That's why she's now with you at Hilltop."

"Does she like it there?"

"She took some time to settle in, but she seems to be enjoying herself a lot more at the moment. Apparently, the owner has got twins living there and she loves seeing them every day. It's given her a new lease of life. Every time I see her, that's all she talks about. Apparently, the boy is very quiet and calm, and the girl is always smiling. I can't remember their names."

"Isabelle and Jacob. Yes, they are my children. I can already see that they have different personalities."

"How old are they?"

"Just coming up to five months old. Unfortunately, they don't have a father. Well, obviously, they do have a father, my darling Jake, but he died before they were born."

"I'm really sorry to hear that."

"I'm starting to get used to the idea that he is no longer here. The twins are a big help because, although they are a handful, they give me so much joy. They fill the huge hole in my life that Jake left behind. On the other hand, I feel so sad when I think that he will never see them. I bitterly regret that the twins will grow up not knowing him. He would have been a wonderful father. I certainly won't be able to forget him because already I can see Jake's features in their faces."

"How did you cope with everything after your husband died?"

"Keeping busy has been a massive help. I've tried to fill every minute of my day. It's not been difficult because running Hilltop is a really big job."

"Oh, I didn't realise you were the manager."

"Well, I'm actually the owner but I have a team that help me to run the home. When we started the business, Jake and I had a vision of trying to create a care home that acted as a sort of family for the residents, a place where they actually enjoyed living. We didn't just want it to be a soulless place where people went to die."

"That's certainly worked for my Mum because she loves being there," said Hannah. "Hang on, things are just starting to slot together in my mind. Would it be you that we wrote to a while ago? We had a letter from Hilltop saying that they had not received the monthly fees from my mother and yet, when we checked, the money had been transferred in the normal way."

"You probably wrote to my father Andy or possibly my sister Beth. I'm glad we have been able to resolve all that."

"So am I," said Hannah anxiously. "I was really worried that so much money had gone astray. The amount of money I am paying each month is frightening. I only hope I am going to be able to afford it as long as Mum is alive."

"I agree," said Connie, "the costs are astronomical. It would be nice to have more help from the government. I don't want to get political, but we don't seem to care for old people in the way that we care for children."

"Maybe things will change in the future. Mind you, there never seems to be enough money for anything. Right, I think I'm about finished Mrs…Sorry, I've already forgotten your name?"

"Wilkins. I'm Connie Wilkins. I used to be Connie Abbott till I married Jake. Did you know the Wilkins family? They used to live around here."

Hannah was holding up a mirror so that Connie could give her approval for the cut. Connie noticed Hannah's face suddenly taking on a reddish tinge as she looked away, discomfited by something.

"Actually, yes, I did know the Wilkins family. In fact, I went out with Jake for a while. Meeting his wife after all these years, how amazing is that?"

At that moment, the door opened, indicating the arrival of the next client. As she took payment from Connie, she spoke hesitantly, "After this customer, I'm free for a while. Is there any chance we could meet for a coffee and a chat?"

"I'd love to. How about The Dancing Goat Café in half an hour?"

Connie spent the next 30 minutes wandering up to the castle and around the town before ending up at the café just as Hannah was arriving.

"I'll get these," said Connie. "What would you like?"

"Thank you. Just a filter coffee for me please."

Connie ordered two filter coffees and a couple of cookies. "Our little treat," she said. "I'm trying to keep my weight down, but I can't resist these."

"You're a bad influence but, you're right, we deserve a treat every so often," said Hannah mischievously.

The two women sat in a quiet corner by the window, chattering away about nothing important. Connie was again struck by Hannah's attractiveness. She couldn't stop herself thinking wryly that Jake had good taste. She forced herself to concentrate on the conversation, remembering that she was on a mission.

"So how well did you know Jake then, Hannah?"

"We met in a pub with a group of friends. Jake was always so easy to talk to and we went out for a while. We were both very young and we had a lot of fun, but it all ended badly. As much my fault as Jake's, I suppose. One night we had a lot to drink. Stupidly, I asked Jake to drive me home. Not a good idea, because he'd drunk several pints. There's no getting away from the fact that we both found each other attractive so we stopped in a quiet layby, not far from my house, for a kiss and a cuddle. We just got carried away. I didn't intend to have sex, but it happened."

"Afterwards we had a massive row about the fact that we'd had unprotected sex. He blamed me and I blamed him. He dropped me off at home, both of us saying we never wanted to see each other again. That was it, we never did see each other again. I deliberately stayed away from the pub where we had met, desperately trying to get my life back to normal."

Connie could see the distress in Hannah's face as she recalled this difficult time in her life, listening intently as Hannah continued, "I don't know why I am telling you all this, but somehow I need to confide in you as you are the only link I have with Jake. I missed my next period and then the one after that. I bought a pregnancy test and, sure enough, it was positive. I was terrified. What would my parents think? In the end I had to confront them with the news, and they were furious. They were as mad as hell for days before they calmed down enough to have a proper conversation with me. Who was the father? Was I going to have an abortion?"

"They would have preferred me to make the problem disappear, but I just couldn't do it. I'd always gotten on well with my aunt who lived in the south so I asked if I could go and live with her until the baby was born. She was so loving and understanding, but after the birth, I had to try to pick up the pieces of my life. I came back to Suffolk and with a child, it was much easier to get a flat.

"Once Mum and Dad met the baby, they doted on him. In fact, they helped me to choose his name, James. They insisted on looking after him whilst I went out to work in a salon in Ipswich. That's how I met John Arden. He came in to get his hair trimmed one day and we hit it off straightaway. To cut a long story short, we got married very quickly and John adopted James as his own son." Hannah's words had poured out in a torrent, the coffee standing untouched alongside her on the table.

"Did you never get in touch with Jake?" asked Connie quietly.

"No, I've felt guilty about it ever since. I just wanted a return to normality after such a traumatic time. Once I met John, I tried very hard to forget about Jake altogether. I'd married another man and he was now James' father. Everything was fine. Why did I want to spoil things by raking over the past?"

"So, did you tell James who his real father was?"

Hannah looked shame-faced. "No, I kept meaning to get around to it, but I just couldn't face it. James got on so well with John and I didn't want to damage the relationship."

"So, John never knew who the father was either?"

"No, and he never will now. It didn't bother him that he wasn't the real father. He couldn't have had more love for James if he had been the real father."

"You realise that this means that Isabelle and Jake have a half-brother?" said Connie.

"Yes, and James has a half-brother and sister."

"What are we going to do about that?"

"I don't know, Connie. What are we going to do?"

Chapter 22

Connie was surprised by how much she liked Hannah. They had known each other for two months and met for coffee whenever Hannah could get over to visit her mother at Hilltop. They talked about Jake, their childhoods growing up in Suffolk, their businesses and naturally enough, James. Hannah gave Connie a photograph of James taken two years previously when he graduated from university. He had taken a business degree and, once he left Suffolk, he didn't really make much of an effort to return.

At first, after graduating, he set himself up in a flat in Leeds and joined an established family firm. He competed against five other graduates who were on the same university course and James was astonished that he landed the job. The management team were impressed with him, aware that he had a common-sense approach to the problems they posed at the interview and not a purely theoretical way of seeing their world.

As the business had been established forty years previously, they employed engineers and production staff who had worked at the factory most of their lives. The staff kept pace with the changing world, adapting well to new equipment and the automation of fine component parts, but the next generation of owners hoped to make the company even more efficient. They wanted James to familiarise himself with the entire workings of their company. His task over a three-month period was to become acquainted with every aspect of their factory which specialised in making medical equipment and his brief was to quality assure the running of the company.

James began by working for two weeks at each area of the operation. As he worked alongside the employees and watched the jobs they did, he formed an opinion about how the company was wasting resources and not using its personnel effectively. He began to understand how the company could become more profitable by reducing waste. Two years later, James was promoted. His bosses suggested that in the future he could be in a position to join the management team. Many of his innovations were implemented and the company showed a healthy growth in sales.

Connie felt that she was beginning to understand James. His photograph at first shocked her. He was a younger version of Jake, but instead of brown hair like his father, he was blond like Hannah. He had, she said, been a happy boy, studious and serious. His mother was full of pride as she furnished Connie with a series of anecdotes about his early life. But Connie was waiting for the moment when Hannah would reveal the state of their relationship now.

It took Hannah fully two months before she was able to discuss her estrangement with James and her husband John. They were sitting together in Connie's apartment whilst the twins were having their afternoon nap. Hannah always made a point of playing with Isabelle and Jacob during her visits and she talked about them as James's brother and sister. This particular visit was very different. Connie felt Hannah's nervousness from the minute she had arrived.

"I haven't told you everything about James, Connie, and I want you to know something."

"Oh, my goodness, what is it?" Connie watched her anxiously as Hannah's face became distorted with emotion.

"I am not sure I will ever see him again. When James discovered that John wasn't his father, he became aggressive. He needed a copy of his birth certificate for some reason and that was when he found out about Jake. This is a boy who was gentle and placid most of the time. He shouted at me, called John a whole variety of awful names. I tried to reason with him, explaining that life was different twenty odd years ago compared to now.

"I tried to make him see that in small market towns attitudes were still Victorian compared to life in the bigger cities but he wouldn't have any of it. He accused us of ruining his life. He said he had been living a lie. He also accused John of deliberately misleading him and that he wanted to know who his real father was. I was helpless, you see, Connie. I had no idea where Jake was. I hadn't seen or heard from him since before James was born and I never tried to find him. Why should I? It all worked out just fine and John was a good father to James. He never once encouraged me to tell James the truth about his birth father.

"John devoted his life to James and gave him everything he needed. Why rock the boat when we were a happy family? But when James discovered the truth, everything changed. He had been deceived and that was that." Hannah paused. Her voice had become more agitated as the dysfunction of her family life was laid bare in front of Connie. "He packed his bags that night and the next morning he returned to Leeds. He had just started an MBA in Business at the university and we were so proud of him, but when he left that day, he almost totally cut me out of his life apart from the occasional email.

"I was in touch with Jeremy, James's university friend, and he updated me with details, such as the job interview and getting promotion. But now even Jeremy no longer answers my emails, so I am not sure how he is getting on." Hannah blew her nose and wiped away her tears. She looked at Connie and shrugged. "You think you are being fair to your children and doing the right thing, but really, you never know."

Connie waited for Hannah to settle then she hugged her. She realised how alone Hannah was feeling. She no longer had John to turn to because he walked out on her after the argument with James over the birth certificate. He returned once James left for Leeds but the arguments between the two of them intensified. Twelve months after the revelation of James's natural father, they separated for good and filed for divorce.

John had had a healthy income and now Hannah was feeling the financial pressure. John's aggrieved view was that as he wasn't James's birth father, and he had devoted time and money to his upbringing, then he didn't owe Hannah anything. He refused to pay maintenance, insisting that they sell their family home and split the money two ways. The stubbornness of both men left Hannah dizzy. Eight months later, the house sale was completed and divorce proceedings were well under way. Neither of them contested the divorce. John pocketed his money from the house sale and, much to Hannah's surprise and hurt, he moved to Australia with the intention of becoming a permanent resident. The last she heard of him through her solicitor was that he was working in Sydney.

Hannah was left alone, without husband or son and with a business to run. When the family home was initially put on the market, she began looking around the town for a cheaper property to buy. To make matters worse, her father died and her mother, who had shown obvious signs of dementia over the last few years, moved into Hilltop. They were able to manage the costs at first whilst John was still at home. Once he left, she found the financing of the fees much more difficult. Hannah accepted the responsibility, as an only child, to stay in the area so she could visit her mother and hopefully rebuild her life. It would only add to her stress to move to another area. She decided to put all her energy into making her salon effective, so she began advertising in the local free newspapers and on the Internet.

"You see, Connie, when you are trying to make a business flourish in a small market town, you need to attract customers from the surrounding towns. I wanted to make people aware of my name and so I spent quite a lot of money designing a website to advertise my business. On the whole, it has worked well so far. I've now got regular customers travelling from Norwich, Ipswich and one woman even comes to me every two weeks from Cambridge."

Hannah needed a roof over her head once her house was sold, so she rented a two-bedroom flat just on the edge of the town. She remained ever hopeful that James would come to visit her. She settled into the more confined space and devoted any leisure time to making her business more efficient. After 6 months, she heard from her landlord that he was putting the flat on the market. Hannah was overwhelmed by this news. She couldn't face another eviction and so she offered the landlord the full asking price and the flat became hers.

Even though her business was becoming more stable, she felt that her emotional life was on a downward spiral and the day Connie entered her salon she had reached rock bottom. Under normal circumstances she would never have revealed the truth to this stranger who that day had watched her attentively in the mirror as she cut her hair. The revealing of her secret had a cathartic effect on her. The pressure that she had constantly felt in her chest lifted and she began to breathe more easily. On her way home that evening, she bought herself a bunch of flowers, a half bottle of wine, curled up on her sofa and watched two episodes of her favourite boxset.

A deep friendship developed between the two women. Jake was their common link and they became sisters in crisis. They felt able to confess their hurt and shock centred around James without being judged. Hannah was the rejected mother and Connie still harboured a sense of betrayal by Jake, no matter how often she presented the facts to herself that the conception of James happened long before she had arrived on the scene. What she focused on was the fact that Jake hadn't trusted her with the information when he had been contacted by James. Their unhappiness united them and as the months ticked by they discovered they had quite a lot in common.

One day, Connie surprised Hannah. "Right, I have made a decision. Your unhappiness will never end until you have made peace with your son. I have an idea." Hannah shook her head. In her view, nothing would change James's opinion of her, but Connie continued: "This is what I have planned. Next week I am going to Leeds to meet James and I am taking Isabelle and Jacob with me. I am going to introduce him to his extended family.

Hannah gasped and was about to object but Connie carried on without a pause, "I want you to come with me, but I warn you, I want to meet him without you whilst I talk to him. You have never been to Leeds before so we will treat it like a little holiday and stay overnight. I have already done some research. There is an amazing hotel which has belonged to the same family for centuries. I read a fascinating article about it. Amazingly, this house was turned into a maternity home for several years after the war. It then became a hotel. I've been researching the place and it looks a fabulous building.

"It is called Hazlewood Castle and it will be my treat, Hannah. We both need cheering up and I have the money to give us this well-needed break in beautiful surroundings. I suggest you look at your appointments, decide which day is the quietest in your salon then tell your assistant, Tess, to manage on her own for one day. What do you say?"

Hannah turned pale. The thought of James rejecting her once more when she got to Leeds dominated her thoughts. However, her optimistic side argued that nothing ventured, nothing gained. "Yes, let's do it. If all fails, at least we will have had a short holiday and I really could do with a change of scene at the moment."

They arranged to travel to Leeds the next Tuesday, just three days away. In the meantime, Connie booked the accommodation, a family room for her and the twins and a separate room for Hannah. She then desperately searched the internet for any reference to James Arden. Meeting him was after all the main point of the trip, but after a couple of fruitless hours she had to abandon her efforts in order to help Beth and her colleagues in the home, and the twins preoccupied her for the rest of the day. Tired and becoming increasingly dispirited, Connie was about to go to bed when her mobile rang. It was Hannah.

"Sorry to be ringing you so late, Connie, but I thought that you would want to know that I've made some progress. I haven't yet found James, but I've had a response from his friend Jeremy for the first time in a couple of years. I used to get on well with him till he stopped answering my messages. Anyway, I told him that we urgently needed to get in touch with James. He's emailed back that he too has lost touch with James recently but will see what he can find out from their circle of friends. I know that doesn't sound like very much, Connie, but actually that's the best news I've had for a while."

"OK, let's keep our fingers crossed. That's lifted my spirits, so well done and thank you. I'm glad we have something to go on. I am now going to try to get some sleep before the twins wake up."

The following day Hannah and Connie continued their independent attempts to track James, in between work commitments, but without success. The whole day passed with no communication from Jeremy either, until midway through the evening Hannah finally received a text. Apparently, James was sharing a house with a group of friends in the Headingley area of Leeds.

"Connie, some good news. Jeremy says that James is house-sharing on Bentley Lane, Headingley and he's given me the exact address."

"Great, that's real progress. Is there a phone number or an email address so we can contact him?"

"No, that's all the information he has been able to find out."

"Well, hopefully we can manage with that. OK, so tomorrow I'd like to make an early start as it will probably take about 4 hours to drive to Leeds, given all the roadworks. Could you drive over here ready to set off by 7.30? There is plenty of space in the car park for your car."

"That's fine. I'm getting quite excited now."

"So am I. See you soon."

Tuesday morning dawned cold and fine. When Hannah arrived, Connie had already been up for a couple of hours feeding the twins, having a shower and finishing off some administration. Early mornings were no problem at all to her.

"I've been thinking about our plans for today, Hannah. Originally, I was thinking of taking the twins with me, but I wanted to ask if you'd mind looking after them whilst I search for James?"

"No problem at all Connie. I'll enjoy spending time with them. Will you drop me somewhere in the middle of Leeds?"

"I could do. Or we could try to book in early at Hazlewood Castle so that you have all the facilities there whilst I go to Headingley. There's a swimming pool and extensive parkland around the hotel so there's plenty of scope for fresh air and walking."

"I think I'd prefer to be left at the hotel. It will also be easier for you to meet up with me afterwards."

Having negotiated the complexities of choosing the correct exit from the motorway, Connie found herself heading towards Tadcaster before realising she needed to make a U-turn in order to find the almost hidden driveway leading to the hotel. They marvelled at the trees that lined the narrow driveway which eventually opened out into a wider parking area in front of the castle.

"Is this where we are staying, Connie?"

"Yes, what do you think?"

"It's like a fairy tale castle. I love the solidity of the pale stonework. How old is it?"

"You'll find out when you go in but I think it dates from the twelfth century. The gardens are lovely too, aren't they? Hannah, do you mind if I leave you with the twins to check in? I want to head off straightaway so that I have as much time as possible to track down James."

They unloaded their considerable piles of luggage, harnessed the twins into their double buggy and wheeled everything to the main entrance. Connie gave Hannah a quick embrace and hurried away, hoping the twins wouldn't notice her departure. As she got in the car, she could hear the upsetting distressed howls of her children who had clearly awoken and spotted the absence of their mother. She drove off confident that Hannah would enjoy being with them and look after them really well.

It wasn't long before Connie was arriving on the edge of the city of Leeds. She pulled into the carpark of a big supermarket and headed for the café area. She ordered a cappuccino and sat down to reflect on her plan of action for the day. She felt a little jaded after the long drive, but the coffee and cookie revived her. She realised that actually there was no plan other than to turn up at the house. She had no means of contacting James beforehand so she would just have to arrive there and see how things panned out. Once her thinking had crystallised, her anxiety subsided. *What will be, will be*, she thought.

Although the last part of the journey was only a few miles, it took the best part of an hour to arrive outside 65 Bentley Lane. Somebody had fortunately left a parking space directly outside so Connie was able to take stock of her surroundings. The house was part of a terrace of similar houses, all built in the same pale but pollution-tarnished stone typical of the area and built probably a hundred years ago. The front door and the four windows were all of different colours, indicating that the landlord had repaired them at the lowest cost but was not too concerned about the aesthetic value.

It was clearly a rented house which did not match the story Hannah had told her about James' successful career. Connie approached the front door and rang the bell. There was no response but on the second ring she heard somebody coming down the stairs. A fresh-faced lad who looked about 12 but was probably in his early 20s opened the door cautiously:

"Hello. I'm not buying anything, thank you," said the lad, about to close the door again.

"I'm not selling anything, don't worry. Does James Arden live here?"

The lad thought for a moment and then shouted upstairs: "Does James still live here, Sam?"

A tousle haired half-dressed girl appeared.

"Who is it?"

"I'm a relative of James but we've lost touch and we're trying to find him," said Connie.

"Is he in trouble?"

"Not at all. It's just that we're worried about him."

"Come in out of the cold," said the lad, closing the door behind Connie. The floor was bare and the paint was peeling off the walls.

"Make the lady a cup of coffee while I look for his address," shouted the girl from above. Connie could hear her rummaging about whilst the lad led her into the kitchen.

"Don't trouble yourself," said Connie, noting the piles of dirty crockery in the sink. "I've just had a coffee so I'm fine. So, James did live here then?"

"Yes, I believe he left recently. I'm not sure whether the landlord evicted him or whether he found a better place. As you can see, we don't live in the lap of luxury."

Connie nodded. "It needs a coat of paint, that's for sure. I suppose it's cheap though."

"Actually, no, especially when you're living off a student loan like we are."

The girl arrived, holding out a scrap of paper on which was scrawled an address. "We said we'd try to stay in touch, so he left us this. Whether he's actually there or not, I couldn't be sure."

"That's something for me to work on. That's really helpful. I'll head straight there. If I can't find him, do you mind if I call back?"

"No problem," said the girl, "here's my mobile number too, just in case you need it."

Connie put the postcode into the Sat-nav and headed off directly into the low sun which was now peeping through the clouds. She followed signs for Huddersfield, eventually ending in a small town called Heckmondwike. I've heard that strange name before, she mused, something to do with carpets. She circled the green in the middle of this small nondescript town and fairly soon found herself on Jeremy Lane.

She searched for somewhere to park and then walked back down the road until she found the right house. It was also a terraced house but much smaller than the one in Headingley and in better condition. Connie was staring up at the windows, trying to see if anybody was at home, when she was taken aback by the person who came out of the front door. It was as if she was seeing a young Jake being reborn in front of her eyes.

"You must be James," she said.

"Hello," said the lad cheerily, "that's me alright. Are you trying to sell me something?" He looked her up and down, totally unconcerned one way or the other. "If you want to talk to me, for whatever reason, you'll have to walk with me because I have to be at the bank for an appointment within the next 15 minutes. I'm hoping they'll lend me some money."

"Is that OK with you?" asked Connie, already a little out of breath. He was definitely a fast walker but at least they were going downhill.

"Sure. Who are you anyway? I know I'm good-looking but it's not every day that I'm accosted by a strange woman."

"I'm your step-mum."

"Oh my God, you can't be serious." He stopped and looked at her. "First, I find out I have 2 fathers. Now I'm discovering I have 2 mothers as well. That's crazy. How can you possibly be my step-mum?"

"Well, I'm not really."

"You either are or you aren't. This is confusing. One minute you say you are my stepmother and the next you say you're not. My life is messed up enough without this nonsense. Look I have to go. Sorry I don't mean to be rude but…" He began to walk away from her. Connie called after him.

"Hang on, James, what I mean is that your birth father was my husband."

James stopped and turned to face her. "You're the wife of Jacob Wilkins? Are you serious?" Connie nodded. "So where is he and why is he not here? It's a bit late in the day to meet my real father but better late than never. Or has he done a runner again?"

231

"He died a while ago, I'm afraid, and I think he would have loved to meet you. You look very like him. Even if you never want to see me again, it's wonderful for me to meet you, though you think I'm a nuisance."

"You seem a very nice lady but what is the point of all this now that he has died. Would it not have been better to try to contact me when he was still alive?"

"That would have been better, but believe it or not, I've only just found out about you."

"This is too much for me to take in. Look, as I mentioned, I have an appointment and I can't afford to be late. I'm not totally sure whether I actually want to see you again but here's my suggestion. Find Café 54 on Market Square in town. Go inside and treat yourself to a drink. If I decide I want to talk to you, I'll join you in half an hour after my bank appointment. If I don't, I simply won't turn up and, in that case, I'd be glad if you'll leave me alone. That's the deal." With that, James strode off at top speed, leaving Connie to reflect on this very strange first meeting.

Connie waited for over an hour at the café. She was just about to collect her things together to leave when the door opened and in walked James. She waved at him and he came over to her table, looking furious.

"Right, sit down and let me get you a drink," said Connie. "Tea or coffee?"

"Coffee, please, no milk."

Connie brought over the two drinks and two cookies on one plate. She sat down and watched as James stirred sugar into his drink. She noticed he had Jake's hands, long and powerful. "It looks like it didn't go so well at the bank," she ventured.

"Yeah, well, they can get stuffed. When your luck runs out, everyone wants to kick you in the teeth," he growled. "Anyway, that is my business. Who exactly are you anyway?"

"My name is Connie Wilkins. I live in Suffolk and was married to Jake, your father, for twenty years. He died almost a year ago and I only found out about your existence three months ago. Your father, Jake that is, only recently discovered you existed because you contacted him. He never mentioned this to me but wrote a letter explaining your existence which was sent to my solicitor's office in London. It was filed away and given to me just a matter of weeks ago and since then I have been trying to find you."

"Oh, yeah, why would you want to do that if my Dad is dead?"

"Because I have quite a lot to discuss with you. I have gotten to know your Mum." She was interrupted by James's growl at the mention of her name. "We have been looking for you everywhere." James was starting to get edgy. "Look, I want to show you some photos."

She took out of her bag a series of photographs of Jake and her at their wedding, Jake in his thirties and then just after his attack. The photograph showed him in hospital bruised and wired up. She also showed him Hilltop where his grandmother was living, and then photographs of Isabelle and Jacob. "These two little mites are your brother and sister, James. This photograph explains why I wanted to find you. They were born after Jake died and he never knew they had been conceived as I was early in my pregnancy when he died. Even I didn't know I was pregnant.

"So, history repeats itself, James. Jake didn't know about you until you contacted him and by then he was too ill to meet you. This photo shows you the state he was in when you sent the letter. He was very ill after the attack and spent most of the short time he had left in a wheelchair." She paused to let the story sink in. James took a bite of the cookie then picked up the photos. He looked closely at Isabelle and Jacob. "You actually look very much like your father. I could see the resemblance the minute I met you today."

"So, you say they are my half-brother and half-sister?"

"Yes, and I want them to grow up knowing that you exist, James. I think we both understand that secrets can be very hurtful when the truth is revealed years later." Connie drank her second cup of coffee and watched his face. It softened as he scrutinised the photos of Jake and the twins.

"It's funny, I don't think I even imagined what he would have looked like. I was only making contact as a way of getting my own back on my Mum. I don't know what I would have done if he had agreed to meet me."

"I can understand that. You have had a great shock. Everything you have taken for granted has been turned on its head. The man who brought you up wasn't your birth father, but I'm sure he did the best for you, nevertheless. He had to cope with your discovery the best he could, but it ended badly for your parents so why don't we try to rescue something good for the future? I would like you to meet the twins, James."

"Why, where are they? Have you brought them with you?"

"Yes, they are resting after their long journey in a lovely hotel near Tadcaster. Your Mum is looking after them for me."

Connie waited to see his response and then she judged that she might just have time to tell him about Hannah before his patience ran out.

"Have you got any commitments here now?" He shook his head. Connie got him another cup of coffee and cookie, giving time for the news to settle into his brain. He ate the second cookie ravenously. She imagined he hadn't eaten much that day and she hoped a bit of nourishment might help him adjust to the story she was about to unfold. She decided to rush through the account before James decided to get up and disappear. She told the story of Hannah's life since he left home and explained the divorce and desertion of his stepfather.

"At first when I found out about you, I was cross too, James. I thought Jake had cheated on me even though we hadn't even met when you were conceived. Funny, isn't it? We grab hold of a resentment and let it fester and grow. However, what you must understand is that times were different then. Although it appeared that we were a liberated generation, there were big local differences and attitudes. Growing up in sleepy Suffolk wasn't the same as growing up in London."

She watched his face as he listened to her and he drained his coffee cup, but thankfully stayed at the table. *Good*, thought Connie, *at least he is interested to hear more and isn't going to flee.* "Your mother actually did you a favour, James. She went through with her pregnancy at a time when many young women were having abortions. She then found a partner who raised you as his own son and she worked hard to give you security." She paused for dramatic effect. "Did you ever go without anything, James?"

"Well no…"

"Did you believe your parents loved you?"

"Yeah, well of course, they did."

"And did you think your mother's love stopped because you were hurt and upset and walked away from her?"

"Well, I didn't even think about that. I was more bothered that she had kept the truth from me."

"Of course, that's understandable. It is the most natural thing in the world to be shocked by news like this. But remember that she had no idea where Jake was. Where would she start to look for him? She went down south for her pregnancy and when she returned, which you have to admit was a very brave thing to do, how was she going to find him? There was limited internet and finding a missing person was even more difficult then.

"Believe me, as a mother of young babies, I wouldn't have the energy to start to look for someone I barely knew. It is so important that you remember that she had no further contact with Jake after the night you were conceived. She also had the anger of her parents to deal with, as well as carrying this secret with her for the rest of her life. Did she ever seem resentful of you, James?"

"Resentful?" He sounded shocked. "No. Why should she? She loved me and…" It was dawning on James just how loving Hannah had been throughout his life. He hadn't even tried to see the problem from her point of view and now he was beginning to regret being so unpleasant and hateful towards his Mum. She had supported him through thick and thin. His finger squashed the remaining crumbs on the table.

Connie could see that something else was troubling him. "Right, now tell me about your job and the bank rejection this afternoon."

James found Connie easy to talk to and half an hour later he had told her about losing his job at the factory. He had made several suggestions how they might expand their business and these ideas proved a costly mistake. He was asked to leave and after that experience James lost confidence in his own judgement. He moved from a rented house to rooms over the last few months and he had simply run out of money. "I'm glad you are buying this drink and biscuit because I don't have any money on me. I think the bank assistant said I had the grand total of £7 in my account. What a surprise!

"They won't lend me money as I have no job security. And I have no job because I made the wrong call. I thought I was helping to modernise the firm. They had asked me to evaluate the business but, in the end, I think they were happy to carry on as they had been doing for years. I began to feel that I was doing the wrong job in the last few months. Maybe I am not suited to the cut and thrust of the commercial world." He shifted his weight in the chair and then looked at her closely. "You know, it is really tough to be penniless. It knocks all the stuffing out of you. You lose confidence and you think you will never work again."

Connie timed her next suggestion perfectly. "Well, as you have nothing to lose, let's go to your lodgings and collect your things, James. I think it is time for you to have a short holiday with your Mum and the twins and then we can consider what you might do in the future. The hotel is grand, and we can have a slap-up meal tonight and talk about your future. You need to have time to chat with your Mum and clear the air. We were going back to Suffolk tomorrow, but

I think we need another night at the hotel to let you two talk things through in neutral territory. What do you say, James?"

"Well, the choice is another night in that damp revolting rented room or a plush hotel. Which should I choose?" He smiled and once again Jake's cheeky expression was written across his face.

Connie's heart beat quickly at the flash of recognition. He was so like Jake. "I also want you to know that your Dad inherited some money, James. We invested quite a lot of it in Hilltop where your grandmother is now living. I would like you to come and visit her and then you can see what your Dad and I have built up. He would have wanted me to help you, so before you have time to reject my offer, let's get going and see whether we can turn your life around."

Connie phoned Hannah to say they were beginning their journey to Hazlewood Castle. She also asked her to go to reception to book a room for James and reserve a table for them for an evening meal. Connie explained that they would all need another night at the hotel so that they could have a bit of a holiday. Could Hannah ask Tess, her assistant, to stay in charge of the salon just another day? Hannah sounded giddy with happiness. She would gladly sort out the practicalities in the salon. "Right, James, let's get going. Your carriage awaits!"

"So, you're not the wicked stepmother then," he smirked. "I hope you have a magic wand."

He couldn't believe that an hour ago he was waiting outside the café weighing up whether or not to go in and meet this stranger. He actually tossed a coin in the end. Heads meant that he had to open the door and step inside, tails meant walking away and thinking about how he would pay his rent for the next month. Heads won.

When they drove up the drive to the castle, James gasped at the imposing building. Connie parked in the side carpark and they went through the main entrance following the black and white chequered floor which led to the reception.

"I believe you have a room booked for two nights for James Arden."

"Yes, it is room 302. I'll just get you the key."

"And could you tell us the room numbers for me, Connie Wilkins and Hannah Arden, who has already checked in, please."

James and Connie made their way up the imposing ornately carved staircase and looked at the portraits which lined their route. They discovered that their three rooms were on the same floor and when Connie knocked on her own door it was immediately flung open by Hannah. She was nursing Jacob in her arms and when she saw James, she flushed with excitement. James noticed that she had the tell-tale blush on her neck that always appeared when she was nervous.

"Oh James, how wonderful!"

"Hi Mum," was his reply and he moved forward and gave her a kiss on her cheek. "Well, who is this little one?" James let his finger be grabbed and Jacob's tiny hand curled around and clenched his finger. The baby gurgled at him.

"This is your brother, Jacob. Here, let me pass him to you and then you can meet Isabelle too." Hannah buzzed around like a demented fly. She was overwhelmed at having her son back in the same room as her.

Connie took Hannah aside and spoke quietly, "Calm down a bit, Hannah. Don't rush things. Let James settle in and get to know these two first and then we can take it from there. Why don't you make us all a cup of tea and then we can relax a little after the journey? We hit the rush hour coming out of the city, so we could do with winding down before the evening meal. What time did you book us in?"

"Oh, the first slot available was for 6.30. They are only using the small restaurant which has been built in what seems to be a crypt. It has a vaulted ceiling and exposed brick. It looks quite intimate, so I hope the twins don't get fractious and disturb other diners."

"If they do, I will ask for my meal to be taken to my room and then you and James can have a quiet talk together. Right, what about that drink?"

In the restaurant the twins were at the centre of everybody's attention, including the other diners. James in particular focused on Isabelle and Jacob, not least because it helped him avoid having too much conversation with Hannah. The atmosphere between mother and son was noticeably tense though Connie thought she detected a gradual thawing during the meal. She was a bit disappointed when at the end he asked if he could help put the twins to bed, but maybe, she thought, it would help him to readjust to his new family situation. There was no point rushing things and Hannah helped Connie's decision-making when she said she wanted an early night to prepare for the next day.

The following morning, Connie asked Hannah and James how they would like to spend the day. She was delighted when they both said they'd like to go to York because she'd never been there before. "I've always wanted to visit York Minster," she said. "How about this for a plan? We drive to the Park and Ride, take a bus into the city, visit the Minster, have a bite to eat somewhere and then finish up at the Designer Outlet which is next to where we'll be parking the car. How does that sound?"

York Minster shimmered in the morning sunlight and clear blue sky. At the doorway people had already begun to queue to buy entrance tickets.

"I didn't realise you had to pay to go into a church," said Hannah, "it's expensive too. I'll stay outside with the children. They won't be interested anyway. We'll go for a walk around the city walls."

"Are you sure, Hannah? I don't mind paying," said Connie.

"I'm absolutely sure. We can admire its beauty from the outside and anyway I fancy a walk with the children. I'll enjoy getting some exercise."

"Alright, if that's what you prefer. Will you come in with me, James?" When James nodded, she continued: "Let's meet for lunch at Café Concerto. It's in High Petergate near here and it's supposed to be very good. Try to be there just before 12, Hannah, before it becomes too crowded, so we'll have space for the buggy."

Inside the Minster, James and Connie wandered round together, admiring the magnificent stained-glass windows in particular. After a few minutes, Connie said, "I'm sorry, James. Do you mind if we sit down for a couple of minutes? I feel a bit faint." They found a pew in a quiet corner of the church away from the crowds.

"Are you OK, Connie?"

"I'll be fine. I'm probably just tired. I've had a lot to deal with recently."

"Tell me about Jake. I'm curious now I've met you."

Connie told James everything about their life together: how it had been quite mundane and normal; how it had been transformed by the inheritance from Aunt Agnes; how tragedy had struck when Jake was nearly killed in a violent assault; how magnificently he had coped with his resulting disability; the massive impact he had made in developing a wonderful care home; his premature death.

James listened intently. "Do you think I would have liked him?"

Connie showed him a photograph of Jake on her phone. "I'm sure you would, but he's gone, and we have to move on. We have to live in the present. I've learned that over the time since Jake died. Having the twins has been a big help, though it's exhausting. Just sitting here talking to you feels a bit like talking to Jake. I've really missed that. Like him, you're a good listener, James. This is the first time I've been able to talk to somebody properly since Jake died."

By now the pair had been lost in conversation for a lengthy period, unaware of the growing crowds who were milling around nearby and keeping a respectful distance, somehow sensing their conversation was important. "I've told you my story, James. I want to know more about you."

"Really? Once I start, I'll probably be moaning because things have not gone well in the last couple of years."

"You've listened to me. Now it's your turn, and actually I'm fascinated by your story because of your connection with Jake."

"OK, I grew up with my parents and had a fairly normal childhood in a little village near Diss. It was safe and boring. I quite liked school, I made lots of friends and I got on well with my parents even during the supposedly difficult teenage years. I didn't work particularly hard on my studies because everything came easily to me and my grades were always good. I had no idea what I wanted to do beyond school, so I went to university without any particular goal in mind. It just seemed the natural thing to do. Money was tight at home, even though both my parents were working. I went to the University of Suffolk in Ipswich so I could continue to live at home. Like a lot of people, I thought doing a Business Studies degree would be a passport to wealth and happiness but so far it hasn't quite worked out that way."

"How did you like living at home whilst you were doing your degree?"

"There were advantages. It was cheaper in that I didn't have to pay for accommodation, and I could eat at home too. Even so I had to have a student loan and my debts started to add up. But then I decided I needed a further degree as so many people now have first degrees and I needed to be one step ahead of my competitors if I wanted a good job. As you can imagine my debts rose hugely. Things started badly too because I had to present my birth certificate to prove my identity when I was enrolling at Leeds and that's when I discovered John wasn't my real Dad.

"I had a massive row with Mum and our relationship started to sour. It was such a shock and even now I'm struggling to come to terms with finding out that my childhood was built on a lie. Maybe if I find out more about my birth father, I'll be better able to adjust." James paused. The brash, self-confident young man had become uncertain and dispirited.

"It's bound to take time, James. You'll be stronger for coming through the difficulties. Well at least, that's what Jake always used to tell me. There's no question that it's hard though."

"Things have seemed to go from bad to worse. For the last 3 years I feel as though I've been in a long dark tunnel and, even now, I don't know if I can see any light. During the row with Mum, John wanted to know what was going on and I blurted out that he wasn't my father. Probably, not the most sensible thing I've ever done, but I was so angry with both of them though John had done nothing wrong. He had always been my father as far as I was concerned, but he couldn't handle my reaction and walked out on Mum. I haven't seen him for a long time, and I've lost touch with him completely. At the moment, weirdly, it's feeling like I've lost two fathers. Very strange."

By now, as Connie listened, she could see that he was reliving these sad episodes in his mind and didn't feel she could interrupt him.

"Whilst at university I started a relationship with a girl from Leeds. I supposed I was desperate for love to numb the pain of my domestic problems. The last thing I wanted was for her to meet Mum when everything had gone so badly wrong. I think she struggled to understand me, probably because I was unable to talk to her in the way that I'm talking to you now." Connie was now holding his hand to reassure him. She could see that his eyes were filled with tears and that he was desperately trying to conceal his emotion.

"Anyway, after university, she got a job in Leeds and for a time she lived at home. When I got a job in the city as well, we decided that we'd try living together. Emotionally, I was still a wreck and financially it was tough too. The rent was high, even in a shared house where we basically only had a room and shared a bathroom and kitchen, and our starting salaries were low."

"So, did your relationship improve once you were living together?"

"Strangely, we became more distant. She was working full-time, and my new job meant long hours so that, when we were together, we were exhausted. I should have made more of an effort but allowed myself to be drawn into taking more and more responsibility in designing new products for the firm. Unfortunately, the job went wrong too. I had what I thought was a world-beating idea for a device that would revolutionise the treatment of diabetes. There was a key component that was available only in the United States.

"It was very expensive, so I scoured the world for an alternative without success. One of the things I've learned about myself, Connie, is that I can be extremely determined, and I just would not let the idea drop, even though my boss told me to forget it. I'm afraid I overstepped the limits of my authority by ordering a large consignment of the component at a substantial cost. When the boss found out, she sacked me there and then on the grounds that I had broken the company's code of conduct and could not be trusted.

"I appealed to an employment tribunal, but the termination of my contract was confirmed, and I was left without a job. The irony is that though my purchase was extremely risky, it appears that the company is now going into production with this piece of kit, most of which was designed by me, and I reckon it will be a big seller. At least diabetics will benefit, but I won't see a penny of the profits."

"How long have you been out of work then, James?"

"About 6 months. It's tough obviously to find a new job, especially when companies wonder why I'm not using my previous employer as a referee." He paused: "I think it's nearly time to meet up with the others but let me just finish my story because it's such a relief to tell somebody about my problems."

"We can arrive a bit late if necessary. Hannah will have reserved a table for us so take your time," said Connie kindly.

"Being out of work," continued James, "was hard. I felt a failure and that was reinforced by the rejection letters I kept receiving. I know I was miserable, in fact I think I became a bit depressed, and my girlfriend found me impossible. In the end, she just got so fed up with me that she wanted to finish the relationship. I asked at least to have enough time to find somewhere else to live. For a while she agreed but then finally she'd had enough and asked me to leave. I had nowhere to live and all my money had gone. That's when I met you, on the way to the bank to ask for a loan."

"So, are you renting that house in Heckmondwike?"

"Crikey, you must be joking. I can't afford that. I'm on Universal Credit and believe me, that's not much. No, I met this guy at the Citizens Advice Bureau when I was checking whether the way I'd been sacked was legal. He must have felt sorry for me and said I could sleep on his floor while I got myself sorted out."

"You've really been having a tough time, James," said Connie, giving him a hug. "I'll have to see if there's anything I can do to help you, but for now let's go and have lunch."

During the evening meal back at the hotel, they talked about their futures. Hannah was keen to make her hairdressing salon a success, primarily to afford the fees for her mother's care at Hilltop. Connie wanted to make Hilltop a highly respected care home and had a catalogue of ideas to improve it further which she shared with her dining companions. James talked about himself.

"I think I have discovered that I am quite a loner really. I didn't enjoy working in a team at the factory. I don't want others telling me what to do and what targets to meet. I want to monitor my own performance, not be assessed the minute I walk through the door of the business."

Hannah and Connie looked at each other and waited for James to continue. His eyes were focused on his food and he ate and talked at the same time. His hunger was still evident.

"I am not sure I particularly like city life either. I prefer a bit of peace and quiet. I used to get out into the dales every weekend and walk for miles on my own. I chose routes which were less popular with other walkers so that I could spend time thinking. When I got back to the city after a day in the countryside, I felt stifled and even the air tasted different." James paused from his eating and had a gulp of his red wine.

Connie had treated them to an expensive bottle and all three of them were starting to relax as the wine took its effect. James even managed to smile at Hannah occasionally and Connie saw the nervous blush reappear on her neck. *How important this is for her*, she thought. *She is scared of making any wrong moves in case James flies off like a startled bird.*

"So, what do you think you want to do then, James?" asked Hannah.

"Well, that is the million-dollar question, Mum. One major problem is that I have no funds, so I might have to get a temporary job somewhere just to bring in some money."

"OK," said Connie, "you are right about needing to build your finances, but, put that to one side for the moment, and let your imagination have free rein. What would you really like to try your hand at, James?"

He looked at both women and tested whether they might laugh at his idea, but he judged that they were keen to encourage rather than censor him.

"I actually would like to do something practical. I have spent months working on a small coffee table which I decided to make for myself as the house didn't have one and I thought we could all use it in the lounge which we shared. The only problem was that I had to try to build it in the back garden and I only had a few tools such as a hammer, saw and nails, so it wasn't the most beautiful piece of furniture, but all the time I was working on it I felt happy. I was using my hands and building something of practical use." He paused. Hannah and Connie were smiling at him. "So, what's funny about that?" he asked defensively.

"Nothing, James. I am just delighted with what you have said, that is why I am smiling."

"Me too, James," Hannah added.

They completed their desserts and on cue, Isabelle and Jacob woke up and began to demand attention. Connie quickly scooped up one baby basket and Hannah lifted the other. The fellow diners had turned their attention towards the small family group, so Connie mouthed her apologies, remembering how irritated she used to be when she and Jake dined out and their evening was spoilt by howling children.

"I will have to wish you both a good night as they won't settle for a while yet."

"Don't worry, Connie, I think we are all finished here. Thanks for this delicious meal and a really great day. I feel much better just being with you four and I think an early night will give me a chance to think through everything we have been talking about. Goodnight, Mum, sleep well."

"Night, love, see you at breakfast."

All three of them vacated their table and once in their own rooms, they contemplated what had happened over the last fourteen hours.

Chapter 23

The table was laden with bacon and eggs, cereal, toast and jam. Hannah and James had already started their breakfast. Connie's porridge now arrived steaming hot and as she waited for it to cool, she laid her plans before them. She poured herself a cup of tea and held the drink in her hands as she spoke.

"I have spent the night thinking through what you both discussed last night during the meal. I think I have two ideas to put to you both. First of all, you, Hannah." Hannah was biting into her piece of toast and suddenly stopped and shifted her weight on the chair. She wore her usual worried look that Connie had gotten to know over the last few months. "No don't worry, my suggestion can be rejected by you and I won't be upset. Let me just talk it through then you can tell me what you think."

Hannah nodded and listened intently to Connie.

"You said your intention with the salon was to make it successful so you can afford your mother's fees. At first, I was shocked by this and I thought back to the time when Jake and I struggled financially and spent every hour working just to pay the bills. We were so tired by the time we got home that we hardly had conversation with each other. Life was just drab and without hope. I don't want that for you, Hannah. I was much younger when I had to work like crazy, but you are middle-aged, and you have got to build your future. What I propose is this."

James fed Isabelle whilst Jacob slept in his basket. He watched his mother and waited for Connie to reveal her plan. Connie had three spoonsful of her porridge then continued.

"I have gotten to know you over these many months, Hannah, and with our shared interest in James, you as his birth mother and me his stepmother, I consider you my sister. I want to be able to help you because good fortune provided me with the means to do this. Mollie, my hairdresser at Hilltop, is five months pregnant. She told me last week that she thinks she will have to give up the salon at our care home as she already has two other children under six years old and she knows she won't be able to work with so much going on at home. She currently has the salon open Monday to Friday.

"What I propose is that you take over the running of this salon when Mollie finishes in two months' time. You can decide which days you want to open for our residents, or you might want to offer a weekend if you think it will interfere too much with your own business. However, this is just an idea, you could get Tess to run your salon during the two days when you are at Hilltop as it would be good experience for her as she seems to be managing fine, according to your phone conversations with her whilst we are here in Yorkshire."

Connie paused and quickly spooned more porridge into her mouth. She glanced at James who was expertly feeding Isabelle and his face was relaxed, entranced by his little sister. "However, Hannah, what I suggest is that instead of receiving wages from Hilltop, you run the salon and in return your Mum will receive free care."

Both James and Hannah looked at each other. Connie could see them doing mental calculations to work out whether it was a good deal or not. They both came to the conclusion that Connie was making a very favourable offer.

"Don't say anything yet," Connie interrupted their thoughts. "I want you now to hear what I propose for James. But first, eat up before the food gets cold and then we can carry on talking whilst we drink our tea." Isabelle, satiated, had now gone back to sleep. Jacob slept on so James wolfed his food down and then poured his drink. The plates and dishes were cleared away by the waiter who had kept an eye on them from a discreet distance. Another fresh pot of tea was brought to their table.

"Right then, James. I heard what you said about wanting to work with your hands and become independent. I also picked up that you are no longer thrilled by city life." He nodded and waited. "Well, I have been thinking about Hilltop. My father, Andy, has many talents but the thing he excels in is craft work. He made most of the furniture in our house as we were growing up and the quality of what he produced was comparable to anything you could buy in the shops.

"Mum always boasted about our stuff to neighbours. He made dolls' cribs and all sorts of toys when Beth and I were young. Anyway, I haven't discussed this with him yet, but I think he could teach you how to become a skilled and creative woodworker." James looked interested, drained his cup and poured himself another.

"I have an old cottage in the grounds at Hilltop. It used to be the home of the caretaker apparently. I haven't checked it out recently, but it has a bedroom, a very small lounge, kitchen and bathroom. At the moment it is very basic, but it could look fantastic with some care and attention. It even has its own private garden. This could be your home, James, whilst you are apprenticed to Andy." James's mouth opened but Connie continued, "In return, I would expect you, like your Mum, to work either in the home or in the garden. That would be your choice.

"You would have free accommodation in the cottage with your meals provided at Hilltop if you want, but I would like to see you eating most of the time with your grandmother who would enjoy your company. Whilst working at Hilltop, you would be trained up by Andy." James let out a whistle. He was already imagining himself living there. "I suggest this arrangement is for six months and if you think this is what you wanted to do in the future, I will help to set you up in a small business."

"Would I then be expected to leave the cottage at that stage?"

"You could continue to live in the cottage, but that would be your choice." She paused and assessed James's reaction. He frowned for a minute or two whilst he processed what Connie had proposed. Training, mentoring, a bit of outdoor work, free food and accommodation.

"Why would you want to do this for me, Connie?"

"Because you are my husband's son and I will look after your interests in the same way as I hope to help these two." She pointed to the sleeping twins. "You will notice it isn't all a handout and I have set certain obligations. I think this is very important for both of you. The last thing you want is to feel beholden to me and I don't want to feel that I am supporting people who might start to take me for granted and think that I am just a money tree.

"You would soon become resentful when things started to go wrong which is always a possibility. It's only natural. I have experienced problems with both Beth and Andy. However, if you know you are working on your own behalf then you will feel that your fate is in your own hands."

The dining room had emptied of clients and even the waiter had long disappeared into the preparation area where he filled the pots of tea. Connie, now that she had said her piece, sat back and looked at the fluted stone arches in the ceiling. She became aware of everything around her.

For the first time that morning, she suddenly heard the low distant sound of classical music piped into the room. She had been so distracted by her ideas that she hadn't even noticed her surroundings when she started her breakfast. She waited for a reply and noticed the shared look between mother and son. "Well, what do you both think about my ideas?"

Chapter 24

Connie was enjoying a few moments of solitude watching a pair of blue tits playing in the hawthorn bush outside her office window. These tiny birds were almost weightless, yet their singing was robust and could fill the space of a concert hall. Are they eating the leaves or are there tiny insects that I can't see, she pondered? She reflected that life was beginning to settle into a more predictable pattern after months, years even, of turmoil.

She had spent quite a bit of time on the margins letting others get on with the business of running Hilltop whilst she learned the art of being a mother to two entertaining but demanding babies. The twins were spending a few hours each day in the creche along with youngsters of other staff members. Their individual personalities were becoming clear, and they remained a fascination for the residents of Hilltop. The new building, a timber-framed extension, had proved a godsend to her colleagues, enabling them to carry on with their work without having to worry about childcare commitments.

Aren't we lucky to be able to enjoy having young children alongside a career, she thought. She remembered her grandmothers and great grandmothers, all of whom had had large numbers of children to rear whilst coping with mundane household tasks which had to be completed without modern machines that made life so much easier today. In contrast she was so lucky. Yes, she had been widowed and there was no question that it had a left a gap that would never be filled. However, her female ancestors also had husbands who died prematurely: some had been killed in industrial accidents or wars. A number of children died in childbirth or succumbed to childhood diseases. One of her great, great grandmother's sisters died from measles at the age of 5. What a waste of a life, she reflected, but with no vaccine at the time survival was a matter of chance. Yes, I'm very fortunate indeed. At that moment, Beth popped her head around the door.

"Sitting there daydreaming? Have you no work to do, Connie?"

"Morning, Beth. Come in. Let's have a chat. I was just thinking that things seemed to have calmed down recently. Probably foolish of me to tempt fate."

"Let's cross all our fingers and toes then."

"Can I ask you for an update on Andy's repayment of Mrs Douglas' fees that found their way into his bank account?"

"Everything is going to plan as we agreed. £300 is automatically deducted from his salary every month. The arrangement is working well. I know it's going to take a long time to clear the debt but at least he is back on track. As far as we know he has stopped drinking altogether. He tells me that he's frightened that having one drink will lead to several more, so it's easier to remain alcohol-free. Another piece of good news is that he is getting on well with James."

"I was going to ask you about that, Beth."

"It's still early days but they already seem like old mates. For the first couple of weeks, James followed Andy everywhere as he carried out repair and maintenance jobs. Now he knows how everything works and recently, he's been able to fix things independently."

"So, he's a quick learner, is he?"

"That's what Andy says. At the moment the two of them are building a gazebo with the wood that was left over when the creche was built. It's going to look really nice, especially when we have trained some clematis to grow over it. It will create a lovely shaded seating area for the residents during the summer."

"Yes, I've seen what they have been doing. We know that Andy is talented in that area and it looks as if James is too. Do you agree?"

"I certainly do. I can see from the look on your face that you're up to something, Connie. You've got that glint in your eye that I know only too well."

"Mmm, yes, you do know me too well, Beth." Connie turned to face her sister to judge her reaction when she told her the plan. "I was wondering whether we could support Andy and James in setting up a little furniture-making business?"

"Or even a furniture repair business, Connie. That TV programme on repairing things has become really popular, and if we were to do some advertising people might be encouraged to bring things in that would otherwise be thrown away." Beth suddenly was animated by the idea. "Since James has arrived to help Andy, there are certainly times when they are looking for things to do," said Beth pensively.

"I'm wondering whether, in the longer term, a business like this could be the future for James. He's a young man, with lots of skills and ideas. He needs a project that he can develop in an area that really interests him. What do you think, Beth? I feel a bit of a responsibility to help him and I think it would be good to make a start whilst Andy is still here to act as a mentor."

"Would you be prepared to give them some funding so that they can get started, Connie?"

"Yes, I would. Not too much though, because I don't want James to think that money grows on trees, but enough to help him get established. I know you're busy, but have you got a minute to tell me how Hannah is getting on. I've been so busy that I haven't seen much of her since she started running the hair salon."

"I'm glad you asked because things have not been as smooth as I expected. The residents like her but one day she came to see me because she was upset."

"Oh, I didn't know about that. What was the problem?" asked Connie frowning.

"She'd had a problem with Mrs Biggins who, I must admit, can be a bit awkward. Hannah has introduced a booking system. Molly, of course, operated a more casual drop-in arrangement. On the whole, having specific times for residents has been a benefit, not least in terms of saving the time of the staff who have to wheel residents to the salon. Anyway, on this particular day, Mrs Biggins turned up at the wrong time. Hannah asked her very politely to return at the correct hour."

"Let me guess, she then exploded? It doesn't take much for Mrs Biggins to go off at the deep end," interjected Connie.

"Since she had her stroke, she's become much more aggressive, as you know. Hannah finished up in tears in my office, saying she'd never been spoken to like that before by a customer and that she'd had enough."

"Do you think it's just Mrs Biggins? Or are there other problems?"

"Hannah said that working here is very different to her salon in Diss. She likes the characters that we have here and truthfully she gets on well with them, but she says they are just so old and doddery. Everything is slow motion and sometimes the residents can be awkward and even rude."

"What do you think then, Beth? Is she not suited to working in a care home? Or is there something else that's bothering her?"

"Well, have you noticed that her relationship with James is still rather cool? I wasn't brave enough to ask her about that but my feeling is that all is not well."

"It's going to take time but eventually the relationship will repair, I hope. James has a lot of forgiving to do and he's maybe not quite ready yet. From our point of view, it's important that Hannah makes up her mind that she wants to work here. I know that some of our residents are not perfect, but I don't want her working with them if she's not happy. Do you think you could you have a discreet chat with her to find out about the situation. I mean, after all, one possibility would be for Hannah to swap with Tess, the girl who's running the salon in Diss."

"Oh, that is a good idea. Yes, that's fine, Connie, I will have a word. My hunch is that she will want to stay near James, but we'll see."

Several times during the conversation, Connie's mobile had lit up and buzzed but she had deliberately ignored it because ensuring that all was well with Hannah and James was her key priority. They were connected with Jake and so were part of her family now. As Beth left, a quick glance at the phone told her that Joe had been trying to ring her. She suddenly became worried because he only got in touch if there was a problem.

She dialled his number. "Hi Joe, Connie here. How are you?"

"Thank goodness you've answered. I've been trying to contact you for the last couple of hours."

"I'm well, Joe, thanks for asking."

"Oh, I'm sorry for being rude, Connie. It's just that I've had the morning from hell. I'm in the middle of an important job for a customer whose heating boiler has broken down and obviously he wants it functioning as quickly as possible. I was hoping to finish today but instead, I've been wasting time searching for Adrian."

"Go on, Joe. I don't like the sound of this," said Connie with a sigh.

"As you know, Adrian has been living in my flat and I've stayed in your house. This morning, as usual, I parked the van outside the flat and waited for Adrian to appear. Normally, he's waiting on the pavement, all set to go, but today there was no sign of him. Thinking he may have slept in, I phoned him but there was no reply. Obviously, I've still got a key, it's my flat after all, so I went inside.

"There was no sign of him anywhere. Even worse, he's totally cleared everything out of the flat: TV, washing machine, dishwasher, furniture, literally everything. I can't believe he's done this to me after everything I've done for him. He was in a real mess when he first came to London and this is how he repays me for all the help I've given him."

"Oh, bother. Joe, I'm so sorry. I feel guilty for landing you in this situation. I asked you to take Adrian on as a favour and this is what happens. I can't believe he's let us both down so badly."

"Well, he has. Don't blame yourself too much, though, Connie, because we were getting on so well and, like you, I thought he was basically a nice lad. I can't understand it. Do you think his Romanian friends have been putting pressure on him?"

"Maybe. In fact, that's probably the case. Why steal all your belongings though? That doesn't really make sense to me. I mean, second-hand goods don't fetch big prices, do they?"

"I can't understand it either, but what really bothers me is that I store some valuable tools in the flat that are vital to my work."

"Don't tell me they have gone too?"

"Yes, like I said, everything has gone."

"Does this mean you haven't got the tools to finish the boiler job? Because if that's the case, don't hesitate to go and buy whatever you need so that you can carry on working. Can you explain to the customer what has happened and that you need to spend the rest of the day replacing your equipment?"

"Believe me, they won't be pleased."

"They will have to understand that it's one of those things. In any case, with luck, you'll be able to finish the job tomorrow, won't you?"

"Hopefully, yes."

"Joe, just make sure you pay for everything on your credit card and then tell me how much you've spent. I will transfer the money directly into your account, so don't worry in the least about expense. It's the least of our problems. By the way, did you tell the police?"

"I tried to but all I got was the answer machine. I'll try again later when I've sorted out some new tools."

"Let me think about that, Joe. You concentrate on buying your equipment and I'll call you this evening to discuss what we do about contacting the police." Connie put the phone down thoughtfully. Was it a good idea to involve the police? Would there be repercussions from the Romanian gang? What should she do?

Connie phoned ahead to check whether she could see Jonathan. He was free at the end of the afternoon explained his secretary, so by mid-afternoon Connie was on the train to London. She needed an unbiased response to this new problem. She waited in the small reception area and, after twenty minutes, was shown into Jonathan's office.

"Hello, Jonathan, many thanks for fitting me in so quickly."

"It's good to see you again, Connie. I take it that there is some problem or other that needs sorting." He gave a fatherly smile and she felt about ten years old.

"Yes, the bad penny has turned up again, I'm afraid."

"I wouldn't say that, Connie. I always enjoy seeing you. Anyway, do sit down and we'll have some tea. Then we can discuss what is troubling you."

They chatted casually about Hilltop and the twins until the tea was delivered and then Connie told him about Adrian's flit and the clearing out of Joe's flat. Jonathan listened intently and made notes whilst she talked. She got agitated the more she talked.

"Well, you have two choices as far as I can see. You could report it to the police and then you will have to divulge the history you have with Adrian or you could stand the cost and hope he has gone out of all your lives completely." He popped another biscuit into his mouth and crunched away, his eyes focused on Connie to see her reactions to the choice he had laid before her.

"Yes, but the point is that I really don't know what to do and that is why I have come to you. I weighed up the pros and cons of each of the two options whilst I was on the train. If I go to the police, I have to expose Andy which would be a problem because he is doing pretty well now. He isn't drinking and he has taken James under his wing and seems really fond of him. I don't want to create any problems for James as he has had a tough few years.

"On the other hand, I don't like the idea of Adrian and his lot getting away with another crime against us. They must think we are absolutely stupid. Wealthy English people with more money than sense and therefore easy pickings. They probably feel it is their right to rebalance the injustice of their lives compared to ours." She paused. She was conscious of sounding like a spoilt child who was about to say: "It's not fair", and so she too reached for a biscuit and broke it into bits as a way of distracting herself.

Jonathan got up and walked across to the window. "Right, so which of those two options do you think is the better one for you and your family?"

"I can't bear the thought that we'd have to go through all that nightmare again. I tempted fate earlier by thinking at last it was over. I certainly don't want Andy to be questioned by police about his sexuality or his theft of our money.

He knows that he was irresponsible and stupid and if I set up a situation where he has to confess his previous dealings with Adrian, I won't forgive myself.

"Especially if, as a result, he turns to drink again. That could ruin him and us too. Just imagine if the papers got hold of the story. It has taken months of hard work to keep him focused and James has been a godsend really because Dad is totally involved teaching him how to become a really good craftsman." She stopped speaking. She realised she had answered her own question. She smiled at Jonathan who had a knowing look on his face.

"So, that is what you must do. You will just have to pay for all of Joe's goods to be replaced. I think it is important that you don't tell too many people about this new incident. If Andy hears about Adrian, he might get angry and try to find him. Or he could become very nervous and worried that Adrian will try to contact him again. Worry leads to drink. Do you see the problem you would have, Connie?"

"I do, but you have just given me an idea."

"And what is that?"

"I remember that Adrian had a Romanian friend who lived in Diss. They were quite close, and Adrian always referred to him when we chatted. He thought of him as a brother. It is a long shot, but I could see whether he has been in contact with Adrian recently. It was only yesterday when Adrian disappeared, but you never know, if I could track down this friend then I might be able to find out what is actually going on."

Jonathan looked alarmed. "Don't you think you might be putting yourself in danger, Connie?"

"Mm, maybe, but if I don't try to find him, I will be watching the driveway of Hilltop every hour of the day to see who is arriving to cause us more harm." On the train back from London, Connie devised a plan. She would first find the address of Florin, Adrian's friend, and pay him a visit.

The small terraced house was similar to the one she and Jake had lived in when they were first married. The narrow frontage had no garden to screen the windows from passers-by. The downstairs curtains were drawn back in a slovenly manner and the bedroom curtains were still closed. Everything about the house looked neglected. A refuse bin, with the lid half open, had been placed outside the door ready for collection and blocked part of the narrow pavement.

Connie knocked on the door and within minutes a young man stood there looking as if he had just got out of bed even though it was nearly lunchtime.

Connie first asked whether he was Florin and he nodded but looked wary. Connie introduced herself as a friend of Adrian's. Florin suddenly was less defensive as he now knew who she was. He'd had endless conversations with Adrian about his workplace. Without hesitation, Florin invited her in. The small dingy hallway housed two bikes, books, an assortment of clothes and bags strewn across the floor. Connie picked her way gingerly into the sitting room.

"I am hoping you can help me, Florin. I am looking for Adrian. He worked for me months ago and he mentioned that you were friends. I only managed to track you down through talking to people at the pub where you used to meet him." Connie soon realised Florin's English wasn't as proficient as Adrian's, so she spoke slowly. "The reason I want to find him is that I haven't paid him for the last two weeks he worked for us. He left very suddenly so we owe him some money," she paused. "I wonder whether you know where he is so that I can pay what I owe him? I would make it financially worth your while if you could give me any clue where Adrian is so that I can contact him."

Florin looked closely at this smartly dressed woman standing before him. He had heard of her from Adrian who had said that she was a decent boss, even for a woman! Well, he thought, let's see how fair she is. His English was less fluent than Adrian's, but he had no difficulty in making his intentions known. He asked how much he would receive for any information about his friend. She said she would pay £50 now and give him another twenty if she found Adrian.

He clearly wasn't earning a lot of money at the moment, so she assumed her offer would be a welcome bonus. Florin weighed up his options. After all, he knew where Adrian was as he had heard from him only yesterday and had managed to get an address out of him. There were others who wanted to know where he was living. Well, both Adrian and he would benefit financially from this woman. Why shouldn't he get a reward for a bit of harmless information. What was it to him, anyway? He quite liked Adrian, but he had grown tired of him and his stories of the care home.

Florin's work consisted of temporary shifts at different factories. Recently, he had worked in a gang picking cauliflowers on a farm somewhere in Suffolk. It was back-breaking work and long hours. He had no idea where the farm was as he and the rest of the immigrant team every morning at the break of dawn were picked up by minibus and driven through endless country lanes to a farm. The gang master was ferocious. He snapped orders at them at the start of the day indicating where they should begin cutting the crop and any time one of the pickers stopped to stretch his back he was shouted at and the master noted down in his book how long he had avoided work. Time lost meant wages reduced.

Florin was unsure how much longer he could stomach this work, so a wad of notes for an address would give him time to look for alternative employment. Connie and he exchanged money for a scrap of paper bearing an address. She arranged to return with the rest of the money if she found Adrian. Well, thought Florin, if he isn't there at least he had got fifty pounds for not a lot of effort.

Back at Hilltop, Connie was busy deciding which train to book for her trip back to London the following day when there was a knock at the door. Not more problems, she thought.

"Hello Connie. Sorry to disturb you. I just wanted a quick word. I'm Mrs Biggins' son, Frank." He was a ruddy-faced, burly chap, well over 6 feet tall.

"No problem at all. I've seen you somewhere before, but I didn't realise you were Mrs Biggins' son. I remember now who you are. You used to work in the gardens."

"That's right. I had to pack in a few months ago. I have a bad back and gardening was making it worse."

"I'm sorry about that, Frank. I'm sure we could have fixed you up with some less strenuous work."

"The timing was quite good actually, because my wife had just reached retirement age and we decided we wanted to do some travelling. I've got a good police pension so we can afford it."

"You don't look old enough to be retired, Frank."

"I'm older than I look. Anyway, we're about to go off on a world cruise so we'll be away for 3 months and I wanted to ask you to let me know immediately if there is any problem with Mum."

"Of course, we will. Let me check we have your number and email address on file. Yes, there it is," said Connie, quickly scanning the database on her laptop.

"I know Mum can be a bit awkward at times but she's not malicious. When she gets confused, she thinks that people are being unfair with her and then she can become a bit aggressive."

"Don't worry, Frank, she's fine. I know she can be a bit impatient if she can't have her hair done at any time of the day or night, but we're used to her and know how to handle her. Did you say you used to be a policeman?"

"Yes, I retired 5 years ago. I was ready to finish after 25 years, believe me. I enjoyed it though. I had spells all over Suffolk, finishing up in Diss."

"Do you keep in touch with your pals in the police force?"

"I still meet up with a few of them at the Social Club every so often. Why do you ask?"

"Have you ever heard rumours of a mafia-style Romanian gang operating in this area?"

Frank smiled and shook his head. "That would be exciting for my old mates. No, the only Romanian gangs I know about are the ones who come every year to work on the farms. Why do you ask?"

"It's just something I heard."

"This is sleepy Suffolk, not New York or Miami."

"What about that jeweller's in Felixstowe? I think he is called Joe."

Frank laughed loudly: "You're not suggesting old Joe is a mafia boss? I think he would quite like people to think he was a gangster the way he always wears dark glasses. No, maybe he fiddles the taxman from time to time but he's a gentle soul. I've known him for a long time. He's a mason in the same lodge as me."

"So, you think all of that is rubbish then?"

"I couldn't be more certain." He smiled at her. "I think you've been watching too many movies."

"Maybe. Nevertheless, you have been more helpful than you realise."

"Always glad to help." Frank's smile became more genuine compared to the patronising look of a minute earlier. "Thanks for everything you do for Mum and remember, if there's any problem, please let me know straightaway."

"I promise. Have a lovely holiday, Frank."

With that he lumbered off down the corridor to see his Mum, still amused at the thought of mafia gangs in Suffolk and old Joe as the big boss.

Having arranged with Beth to look after the twins again during her absence, Connie headed back to London. Adrian's address was an apartment block in Bermondsey, south of the Thames, so she enjoyed the walk from the station over the Millennium Bridge and along the South Bank. On the way she reflected on how she would handle the conversation with him. How would he respond to her? Was there any chance that he would be prepared to hand back the property stolen from Joe?

Connie was not optimistic, but she felt she had to try to gain some redress for the way he had treated Joe. She was puzzled as she found herself in an area of new apartment blocks, not the old high-rise ones that she had been expecting. He's doing well for himself if he lives in one of these, she thought. Right next to the Thames as well. Sure enough, a brand-new building matched the address she had been given. She pressed the intercom next to the flat number she had been given and immediately somebody responded:

"Hello, can I help?" It was not Adrian's voice, more that of a city banker. His public school accent was confusingly welcoming and intimidating.

"I'm looking for Adrian. Does he live here?"

"Yes, but he's not here at the moment."

"Can you tell me when he'll be back?"

"Any time now, more than likely. You're welcome to come up and wait for him though."

With that, there was a buzz and the outer door unlocked. Arriving on the third floor, Connie was surprised at the stillness in the building. Not a sound from anywhere. What a difference thick carpet makes to sound insulation. There was a choice of four doors on the corridor in front of her and number 34 was the one at the end. She rang the bell, wondered if anybody would answer as she heard no movement and then suddenly in front of her stood the archetypal city gent.

"Come in, my dear, I'm Lawrence. Do take a seat. Adrian will be back soon." He had a deep baritone voice, hoarse from many years of smoking, she presumed. She struggled to comprehend the connection between Adrian and this bald, overweight gentleman in his mid-50s with his pin-stripe suit and riverside apartment overlooking the Thames. Why should it be a surprise? After all, her own Dad was over 60. "I hope you don't mind…"

"Connie," she interjected.

"Yes, I hope you don't mind, Constance, I really must close this deal before I rush off to the office." He tapped away furiously on his laptop whilst Connie gazed around the spacious open plan area, transfixed by the large plate glass window that showcased the boats gliding up and down the river with St Paul's Cathedral sitting to her left. Outside was a large terrace decorated with ornate pots filled with shrubs. Presumably access was from the bedroom, unless the plate glass somehow slid magically into the ceiling though she couldn't see how that was feasible. The American kitchen was cluttered with unwashed crockery waiting to be loaded into the dishwasher. An aroma of coffee and stale cigarette odour pervaded the place.

"Right, I'm off, Constance. He won't be long, I'm sure. Make yourself at home." With that, he was gone.

How can he be so trusting, she thought? He's never seen me before and yet he's left me unattended in his home. It must have been easy for Adrian to wheedle his way into his affections. And yet, how wonderful to be so carefree. Maybe I ought to take lessons. On the other hand, maybe he's never had to worry about money whereas being wealthy is a new experience for me.

She wandered over to the coffee machine, still switched on, and, taking the last clean cup from the cupboard, tentatively poured herself a half measure. It was strong and had been stewing too long. She wrinkled her nose but swigged it down, moving to a door at the far end which led to a large bedroom with adjoining bathroom. Only one bed, she noted, so they were living à deux, no question. Yes, the door to the patio was here. Her hand was on the handle when Adrian appeared silently behind her.

"What are you doing here, Connie?" he said, seemingly unperturbed by her presence.

"I need to talk to you. Do you mind if we sit outside?" Without waiting, she slid the unlocked patio door to one side and sat on one of the well cushioned wicker chairs. She motioned for Adrian to join her. "What a wonderful view you have here," she said, as he settled himself alongside her. "You seem to have done well for yourself. How do you manage it, Adrian?"

He smirked. "Maybe it's my charm."

"You've certainly moved upmarket a notch or two since sharing a room with my Dad at Hilltop. How long will it last though, I wonder?"

"We'll see. I don't usually hang around very long but our arrangement here is working well enough at the moment. Why are you here though?"

"You know perfectly well why I'm here. Let me remind you how helpful we've been with you. You stole thousands from us through deceiving my father, but I created a new life for you in London, a flat, a job."

"A job. That's not the kind of job that I want. It's hard work digging foundations, lifting heavy goods, crawling under cupboards. No, not for me. And Joe was very tough. He gave me all the difficult tasks."

"So, you're complaining! I don't believe it. You're a crook and a thief. You're a liar too. We helped you escape to London, well away from a gang of thugs. But the gang doesn't exist, does it, Adrian?" She looked at him angrily, before continuing, "Why did you steal all Joe's belongings, after all the help he has given you?"

"He deserved it. I was fed up with being bossed around and bullied."

"You had a better offer, moving in here, that's the truth, isn't it? I don't blame you for that but why steal all Joe's things. He didn't deserve that, did he."

"He did deserve it. He kept calling me names, saying I was idle, making comments about people from my country. I needed to teach him a lesson."

"Where is all the stuff then? It's obviously not here. Have you got a big warehouse where you store all your stolen goods?"

"I'm not telling you. What I can tell you is that it has gone. I couldn't return it to you if I wanted. And I don't want to. It's only what Joe deserved."

There was no point continuing with the conversation. Connie now knew quite clearly the sort of person Adrian really was. She had misjudged him. They had all thought he was a decent human being, but they had been wrong.

"Thank your friend for the coffee and hospitality, Adrian. He seems a decent man. Maybe you could learn something from him."

With that, she left the flat and made her way to the walkway by the river. As she continued towards Tower Bridge, she took out her phone and searched through her contact lists for the number of the Border Force Officer that Mr Biggins had given her the previous day. Apparently, he was an ex-colleague of Mr Biggins who said that, following Brexit, there was a major new initiative to round up all illegal immigrants. To her surprise, the number worked and her call went straight through.

"How did you know my number?" a voice queried. Connie explained the care home connection with Mr Biggins before asking if the officer would like a tip-off about an immigrant whose visa had expired. "Definitely, especially if he's up to no good, as you say. If you give me the address, we'll go there straightaway."

Job done, thought Connie, with a sigh of satisfaction. *That will put an end to his tricks. In this country at least.*

Connie called at the local supermarket to collect a sandwich and some milk for her lunch. Her short walk to her London house was very pleasant. The sun shone and the trees were in leaf. The house was remarkably in fine shape when she explored the rooms to see how Joe had left them. It was, in fact, immaculate. Sign of a good workman who cleans up after himself, she smiled.

She had been thinking long and hard over the last few weeks about selling this house, but now she was back she decided against it. Although she had only lived here a matter of weeks, it was now part of her history. It had been her retreat from Hilltop, the birth of her twins had begun in this kitchen and the house was

Jacob's and Isabelle's first home. She realised that they hadn't actually lived here for more than a few hours, but it still felt a place of significance. After all, she mused, they can't really grow up in a care home. They will be in need of more lively stimulation in the future. She was sure that this house would be a perfect base for them as they get older. After all, London could offer young people much more than sleepy Suffolk.

She brewed herself a cup of coffee and ate her sandwich looking out of the window. The lawn and flower borders will need attention during the coming months. She had better employ a gardener to keep it tidy. She put the job on her list of things to do. She then phoned Joe at work and invited him out for a meal that evening before she caught the late train back to Hilltop. He sounded pleased to hear her voice and was delighted at the prospect of a meal out. He said he could get to a restaurant by six o clock. They chose a pizza place not far from Joe's flat.

Connie was glad. She wasn't in the mood for an ostentatious, overly expensive restaurant during this fleeting visit when she just wanted to update Joe on her conversation with Adrian. She drained her cup and pecked at the crumbs left on her plate. She reached for the chocolate bar which she had secreted in her bag before she left Hilltop. London always made her hungry for something sweet and indulgent, so she was well prepared. She viewed it as her emergency kit.

Her next phone call was to Jonathan's office. She felt the need to keep him informed and up to date about her life. She now understood how Jake's aunt had formed a special relationship with him. Jonathan was old fashioned in many respects, but he was compelling company. She had no explanation why this was. He was an excellent listener and a wise counsellor. She had found herself telling him much more than the details about her businesses. As such, the confessional quality of their relationship had created strong bonds between them. She knew almost nothing of his private life, however, but that didn't matter. He had become her friend and mentor.

After the call with Jonathan, she checked the timings of her return train and then she made another cup of coffee with the fresh milk she had bought. She thought about Hilltop and the twins. Jacob and Isabelle had been the stimulus for the creche and, credit where credit is due, Andy had worked wonders. She smiled at the memory of the party he and James had organised for the third birthday of Sandra's daughter.

Sandra had worked at Hilltop for six years and was one of their most reliable carers. She treated every resident as if they were her own grandparent and they all loved her for this. Connie mused on the fact that now parents of many of the young children who attended the creche came back at weekends to visit the residents. A number of them had 'adopted' the elderly residents, often arriving for Sunday lunch with them as family members of the residents were encouraged to do, sharing stories about the toddlers at the creche.

Connie was amazed how quickly these relationships had formed. The older generation were excited and stimulated by the presence of the younger ones. A number of them regularly arrived at the creche early so they could be there to greet the toddlers arriving for the day. They kissed and cuddled them, helped remove hats and coats and within minutes, one of them, with the blessing of the creche assistants, would begin the first reading of the day. The youngsters sat on their cushions in a semi-circle in front of the storyteller: it might be Alice or Mary or Frank, in fact, it was exciting for them to discover who would be the day's first storyteller.

Connie was convinced it was one of the reasons why the creche was successful. Everyone had a challenge and there was little predictability about the day with so many eager people to share the creche assistants' role.

Her mind drifted to Hannah and James. What a pity that they were still not so close, she thought. Hannah was a curious mix. She gave the impression of being outwardly confident and ambitious. She now realised, however, that behind the façade was a nervous and timid individual. Hannah had found it hard to adjust to working at Hilltop. Whenever she had a customer in front of her, her attention seemed to be elsewhere. Her clients began to complain that she wasn't a good listener and they felt that she wasn't interested in anything they had to say. Eventually, Connie met up with Hannah to discuss the complaints.

"Yes, I know, the residents are right," said Hannah. "I wouldn't dream of being like this in my own salon back in Diss. I always give my customers my undivided attention and we have really good conversations. It is just that I am always conscious of James being around here somewhere. I never know what he is doing and because I am so close physically, I feel tempted to go and find him. It just isn't working as I thought it would."

"Why don't we try the option we discussed months ago?" Connie ventured. For some time, she had wanted to suggest a change, but she hadn't wanted to hurt Hannah's feelings. However, she was very concerned about the needs of the residents: they had to be her main priority. This session at the hairdresser's was their weekly treat. Many of them looked forward to it with excitement. They didn't have many appointments to look forward to. It was like an outing for them. They liked the individual attention that was vital to their sense of well-being. Their nails were cut, filed and polished; their hair was washed, cut and styled. So often they left the salon rejuvenated and more relaxed. It wasn't right that this major pleasure was being undermined by Hannah's distraction and inattention.

"OK, Hannah, I think it is time to do what we discussed. Let us give Tess a try. You go back to the salon in Diss and Tess can take charge of the salon here at Hilltop. She was keen enough when we discussed it with her, so we can see whether she fits in and gets on with her new clients."

And that was what they did. Tess thankfully took to the new salon like a duck to water. She loved the old men and women who arrived for their treatment. She lapped up their gratitude, their endless stories of when they were young and enjoyed getting to know them as characters. She was as surprised as anyone that she enjoyed these clients more than those in Diss. Tess had found the different generations at the salon in town sometimes difficult to please, but at Hilltop, the old folk were so grateful that she did her best to make their appointment special. They loved her and Connie received very positive feedback about the salon's new manager.

The arrangement became permanent and Tess became a valued member of the team. Hannah meanwhile adapted to her life back in Diss. Connie and she chatted weekly and Connie always gave an update on James's progress. Both mother and son eventually started to meet for Sunday lunch back in Diss. Hannah was overjoyed and she put a great deal of care into the meals she prepared. James admitted that he had felt stifled by Hannah's presence at Hilltop, so much so that he tried everything to avoid going near the salon. Once she left, James curiously missed her, so he was the one who suggested they spent part of Sundays together. After a while they became more relaxed in each other's company. The sore was beginning to heal.

Suddenly, the doorbell rang and broke into her thoughts. Her taxi had arrived to take her across London to the restaurant. She quickly rinsed her cup, grabbed her coat and bag and opened the door to the taxi driver. She had used the same driver for many of her journeys. He had eventually given her his personal number to call him rather than going through the firm's switchboard and she greeted him like an old friend. Her meal with Joe was enjoyable, just two friends enjoying a quick catchup. Connie thanked him profusely for looking after Adrian. He was rightly angry when she recounted her meeting with him just a few hours before.

"Well, the selfish, spoilt brat," was all Joe could say. When she got to the part about her phone call to the immigration officials, he laughed.

"I doubt if we'll see any more of him then. There was something about him that I didn't like, you know. I'm not sure why, especially as I normally get on well with people. He was someone who made me wary and watchful. A bit ironic, isn't it? I was watchful, but not watchful enough when he was clearing my flat of all my possessions."

He drained his wine glass and poured them both another one. They clinked glasses and spent the rest of the meal in pleasant conviviality. Another taxi had been booked to ferry Connie across to Liverpool Street and before she left, she pecked Joe on the cheek, thanking him once again for all his help. She gave him a generous cheque to cover his expenses for the stolen furniture and tools.

"I will call on your services again, Joe. I hope that will be alright. Or will you be too cautious to get involved in the future?" They both laughed. She felt, as they departed, that one chapter of her life was closing. She looked ahead to her future with her family. Hilltop was home for the moment, but London would always play a part in their lives.

Two hours later, when she let herself into her flat back in Suffolk, she smiled. *It's really good to be back home again*, she thought. After looking in on the twins who were sleeping in Beth's flat, she sat down in front of the television. A few minutes of mindless entertainment before going to bed. A time to relax.

When the news began, the main item was about a virus. It was sweeping through a city in China and lots of people had died. Coronavirus. *Thank goodness it's on the other side of the world*, she thought, switching off the TV and heading gratefully for her bed.